Raves for

RICK RIORDAN

"Riordan has a knack for showing readers a crazy good time." —*The New York Times Book Review*

"In Rick Riordan's case, believe the hype, he really is that good." —Dennis Lehane

"Riordan writes so well about the people and topography of his Texas hometown that he quickly marks the territory as his own." —*Chicago Tribune*

"There's a reason why this guy keeps winning awards....Rick Riordan is a master stylist. I can't wait for his next." —Harlan Coben

COLD SPRINGS
Named one of the year's best crime novels (2003) by the ALA

"[An] unorthodox suspense novel...Chadwick...is a complex and interesting character, and the pressures on him are believable and absorbing.... Knife-throwing, wild shooting and hairbreadth escapes up the ante...but Riordan is so good at moving his story along—and showing how fragile children's lives can be—that most readers will forgive him his excesses." — *Publishers Weekly*

THE DEVIL WENT DOWN TO AUSTIN

"Rick Riordan is on a roll….If you like the writing of Dennis Lehane…you'll enjoy getting acquainted with Rick Riordan." —*BookPage*

"Funny and tough…Riordan kneads plots like lovingly baked bread, and they are almost as tasty." —*New York Daily News*

"Powerful…A fast-paced tale, expertly told." —*The Denver Post*

"A dang fine Texas writer and fun to read. He actually can write a good mystery." —*San Jose Mercury News*

"Loaded with suspense and sizzling with emotional power." —*Abilene Reporter-News*

"Terrific…just about everything you could want from an action adventure." —*Houston Chronicle*

"Sarcastic humor, memorable characters, and spectacular acting scenes round out a spellbinding adventure." —*Library Journal*

THE LAST KING OF TEXAS

"Tres's taste for excess is as ferocious as his addiction to fiery food, and the fearless joy he takes in his roughneck adventures gives a real kick to this colorful series." —*The New York Times Book Review*

"A winner…perfect pacing, expert switching between subplots and an unusually strong cast of supporting players." —*The Washington Post*

a vivid setting, multidimensional characters—this series has it all." —*Booklist*

"Like a good bowl of chili, the mystery is filled with flavor and just enough spice to keep you wanting more."
—*The Baton Rouge Advocate*

"Wry and low-key, Riordan writes the Tex-Mex voice and local topography well."
—*Booknews* from The Poisoned Pen

"A furiously paced story with authentic Tex-Mex detail. The dialogue is razor sharp....Sure to be a nominee for all the best mystery of the year awards."
—*The Tennessean*

"A well-crafted private eye novel of the classic mold."
—*The Drood Review of Mystery*

"Riordan's character descriptions shine like soapy water on the cheek. This is '30s noir yanked past the fin de siècle. The action scenes sped by like they were being driven on a closed track with professional drivers. Read this book!" —*San Jose Mercury News*

"Riordan hits every note perfectly in this appealing story of long-ago treachery and contemporary revenge."
—*The Dallas Morning News*

"Near pitch perfect in its pacing. And like a good carnival ride, just when you think all the surprises have been played out, Riordan pulls out that last little snap, that surprise curve, just so you don't forget what a satisfying ride this has been."
—*Fort Lauderdale Sun-Sentinel*

COLD SPRINGS

RICK RIORDAN

BANTAM BOOKS

New York Toronto London Sydney Auckland

COLD SPRINGS
A Bantam Book

PUBLISHING HISTORY
Bantam hardcover edition published May 2003
Bantam mass market edition / March 2003

Published by
Bantam Dell
A Division of Random House, Inc.
New York, New York

Library of Congress Catalog Card Number: 200304365

ISBN 0-553-57997-5

Manufactured in the United States of America
Published simultaneously in Canada

OPM   10 9 8 7 6 5 4 3 2 1

To Kate Miciak
Every so often, one gets to work with
a master teacher

ACKNOWLEDGMENTS

Many thanks to Sergeant Derwin Longmire, Oakland Police Department Homicide Section; James Doebbler, CPA; Scott McMillian, Redstone Consulting; Brian Kaestner, science teacher and naturalist; Dr. Pepi Klecka, DVM; Dr. John C. Klahn, MD; Dr. Michael Belisle, GS-09, Lackland Air Force Base; Kate Miciak and Gina Maccoby for their guidance and support; and Becky, Haley and Patrick, without whom none of it would be possible.

PART I

1993

1

Chadwick struggled with his bow tie.

He was thinking about what he would say, how he would break the news that would end his marriage, when Norma came up behind him and told him about the heroin in their daughter's underwear drawer.

He turned, the bow tie unraveling in his fingers.

Norma wore only her slip, her bare arms as smooth and perfectly muscled as they'd been when she was nineteen. Her eyes glowed with that black heat she saved for lovemaking and really huge arguments, and he was pretty sure which she was planning for.

"Heroin," he said.

"In a Ziploc, yeah. Looked like brown sugar."

"What'd you do with it?"

"I smoked it. What do you think? I flushed it down the toilet."

"You flushed it down the toilet. Jesus, Norma."

"It wasn't hers. She was keeping it for a friend."

"You believed that?"

"She's my daughter. Yes, I believed her."

Chadwick stared out the window, down at Mission Street, where the Christmas lights popped and sparked under the sudden weight of ice.

He'd lived in this house almost all of his thirty-seven years, and he couldn't remember a November night this cold. The glass storefront of the corner *taquería* was greasy with steam. Lowriders cruised the boulevard billowing smoke from their exhaust pipes. Twenty-fourth Street station was swept clean of the homeless—all gone to shelters, leaving behind piles of summer clothes like insect husks. Next door, the Romos had turned up their music the way other people turn up the heater—the sorrowful heartbeat of *narcocorrido* pulsing through the townhouse's wallpaper.

Chadwick wanted to turn to steam and disperse against the glass. He wanted to escape from what he had to do, what he had to say. And now this—Katherine.

"The Zedmans will be here in a few minutes," he told Norma. "I've been home since yesterday."

She tilted her head to put on an earring. "What? I should've told you earlier? Last week I needed your help, you ran off to Texas. Maybe I should've told you at the airport, huh? Let you get right back on the plane?"

Chadwick felt his throat constricting. His Air Force buddy Hunter used to tease him about marrying Norma Reyes. Hunter said he wasn't getting a wife, he was getting a Cuban Missile Crisis.

He wanted to tell her why he'd really run.

He wanted to tell her that out there in the woods of Texas—for a few days—he had remembered why he'd fallen in love with her. He'd remembered a time when he'd been excited to have a woman half his size take him on so fearlessly, grab his hand like a toddler's grip on a shiny new toy and pull him onto the dance floor with a look that said, *Yeah, I want to marry an Air Force man. You got a problem with that?*

He had decided Norma deserved the truth, even if it destroyed them. But that had been at a distance of two thousand miles. Now, getting too close, the feeling was like a computer photo. Expand it too much, and it turned into pixels of random color.

He shucked his tuxedo coat, walked down the hallway to Katherine's room, Norma calling from behind, "I've already grounded her, Chadwick. Don't make it worse."

Katherine was on her bed, her back to the wall, her knees up to her chin—prepared for the assault. The Guatemalan fabric had fallen off her headboard, revealing the decorations

Chadwick had painted when Katherine was two—rainbows and stars, a baby-blue cow jumping over a beaming moon. Kurt Cobain's picture sagged off the wall above, where Babar the Elephant used to be.

Sadness twisted into Chadwick's chest like a corkscrew. How the hell had Katherine turned sixteen? What happened to six? What happened to ten?

He tried to see something of himself in her, but Norma had dominated their daughter's genes completely. Katherine had her mother's fiery eyes, her defiant pout. She had the coffee skin, the lush black hair, the build that was both petite and combat-sturdy. As a child, Katherine would clench her fists and lock her knees and she'd be impossible to pick up—as if she were molded from stone.

"Heroin," Chadwick said.

She rubbed her silver necklace back and forth over her lips, like a zipper. "I told Mom. It wasn't mine."

"You went back." Chadwick tried to keep his voice even. "After everything we talked about."

"Daddy, look, a friend asked me to keep the stuff. A friend from school."

"Who?"

"It doesn't matter. It's over. Okay? I didn't want to piss him off. I was going to throw the stuff away, give it back, whatever. I didn't have time. Happy?"

Chadwick needed to believe her. He needed to so badly her words gained substance the more he thought about them, began to harden into a viable foundation. But goddamn it. After last Saturday . . .

He wanted to grab Katherine by the shoulders. He wanted to wrap his arms around her and hold her until she went back to being his little girl. He wanted to take her away from here, whether Norma liked it or not, put her on a plane to Texas, bring her to Asa Hunter's woods, teach her how to live all over again, from scratch.

It had seemed so simple when he talked to Hunter. Hunter saw things the way a gun did—narrow, precise, certain. Hunter had coached him, prepared him on what to say to

Norma. He'd let Chadwick imagine Katherine walking those woods, free from drugs and self-destructive friends and pictures of asshole rock stars on her wall. He'd even offered Chadwick a job as an escort, picking up troubled kids from around the country and bringing them to the ranch.

This school I'm starting— It is the future, man. Get your family out of that poison city.

"Katherine," Chadwick said, "I want to help you."

"How, Daddy?" Her voice was tight with anger. "How do you want to do that?"

Chadwick caught his own face in Katherine's mirror. He looked haggard and nervous, a hungry transient pulled from some underpass and stuffed into a tux shirt.

He sat next to her on the bed, put his hand next to hers. He didn't touch her. He hadn't given his daughter a hug or a kiss in . . . weeks, anyway. He didn't remember. The distance you have to develop between a father and a daughter as she grew into a woman—he understood it, but it killed him sometimes.

"I want you to go to Texas," Chadwick said. "The boarding school."

"You want to get rid of me."

"This isn't working for you, Katherine. School, home, nothing."

"You're giving me a choice? If you're giving me a choice, I say no."

"I want you to agree. It would be easier."

"Mom won't go for it otherwise," she translated.

Chadwick's face burned. He hated that he and Norma couldn't speak with one voice, that they played these games, maneuvering for Katherine's cooperation the way a divorced couple would.

Katherine kept rubbing the necklace against her lips. It seemed like yesterday he'd given it to her—her thirteenth birthday.

"You can't baby-sit tonight," he decided. "We'll tell the Zedmans we can't go."

"Daddy, I'm fine. It's just Mallory. I've watched her a million times. Go to the auction."

Chadwick hesitated, knowing that he had no choice. He'd been gone from work the entire week. He couldn't very well miss the auction, too. "Give me your car keys."

"Come on, Daddy."

He held out his hand.

Katherine fished her Toyota key out of her pocket, dropped it into his palm.

"Where's your key chain?" he asked.

"What?"

"Your Disneyland key chain."

"I got tired of it," she said. "Gave it away."

"Last week you gave away your jacket. A hundred-dollar jacket."

"Daddy, I hated that jacket."

"You aren't a charity, Katherine. Don't give away your things."

She looked at him the way she used to when she was small—as if she wanted to touch her fingertips to his chin, his nose, his eyebrows, memorize his face. Chadwick felt like he was melting inside.

Down in the stairwell, the doorbell rang. John Zedman called up, "Candygram."

"This isn't over, Katherine," Chadwick said. "I want to talk about this when I get home."

She brushed a tear off her cheek.

"Katherine. Understood?"

"Yeah, Daddy. Understood."

She made the last word small and hot, instantly igniting Chadwick's guilt. He wanted to explain. He wanted to tell her he really had tried to make things work out. He really did love her.

"Chadwick?" Norma said behind him, her tone a warning. "The Zedmans are here."

Little Mallory made her usual entrance—a blur of blond hair and oversized T-shirt making a flying leap onto Katherine's bed.

"Kaferine!"

And Katherine transformed into that other girl—the one

who could attract younger kids like an ice cream wagon song; the natural baby-sitter who always smiled and was oh so responsible and made other parents tell Chadwick with a touch of envy, "You are so lucky!" Chadwick saw that side of Katherine less and less.

She tousled Mallory's hair. "Hey, Peewee. Ready to have some fun?"

"Yesss!"

"I got Candyland. I got Equestrian Barbie. We are set to *party.*"

Mallory gave her a high five.

Ann and John stood in the living room, cologne and perfume a gentle aura around them.

"Well," John said, registering at once that Chadwick wasn't even half ready to go. "Grizzly Adams, back from the wild."

"The carnivores say hello," Chadwick told him. "They want you to write home more often."

"Ouch," John said, his smile a little too brilliant. "I'll get you for that."

Ann wouldn't make eye contact with him. She gave Norma a hug—Norma having dressed in record time, looking dangerous in a red and yellow silk dress, like a size-four nuclear explosion.

Chadwick excused himself to finish getting ready. He listened to Norma and Ann talk about the school auction, John flipping through Chadwick's music collection, shouting innocuous questions to him about Yo-Yo Ma and Brahms, Mallory setting off all the clocks on the mantel—her ritual reintroduction to the house.

When Chadwick came out again, Katherine sat crosslegged by the fireplace—his beautiful girl, all grown up, drowning in flannel grunge and uncombed hair. Mallory sat on her lap, winding the hands of an old clock, trying to get it to chime.

Chadwick locked eyes with his daughter. He felt a tug in his chest, warning him not to go.

"Don't worry, Dad," she said. "We'll be fine."

Those words would be burned into Chadwick's forehead. They would live there, laser-hot, for the rest of his life.

When the front door shut, Katherine felt herself deflating, the little knots in her joints coming loose.

She took Candyland down from the shelf. She joked with Mallory and smiled as they drew color cards, but inside she felt the black sadness that was always just underneath her fingernails and behind her eyes, ready to break through.

Katherine wanted a fix. She knew it would only make her depression worse—buoy her up for a little while, then make the blackness wider, the edges of the chasm harder to keep her feet on. Her therapist had warned her. Ann Zedman had warned her. Her father had warned her. They were all part of the educational team, all looking out for her best interests.

We're here to help you be successful again, Katherine.

Fuck that.

If there was anything worse than having a dad who was a teacher, it was having your dad at the same school as you. And not just for a couple of years. A K–12 school. A *small* K–12 school, so you had thirteen years of absolute hell, no breathing space, no room to be yourself. And if that wasn't bad enough, have your dad be best friends with the headmistress for a gajillion years—Ann Zedman always over at your house, peeking into your life.

That was why Katherine loved the East Bay. It was *hers*.

At least, it had been until last week—the stupid cops separating her out, scolding her, asking what the hell she was doing with *those* people. She remembered the ride home from the Oakland police station, her wrists raw from the handcuffs, her anger building as her father glanced in the rearview mirror, insisting that she *not* tell her mother what she'd been doing at the party because it would break her mother's heart. Katherine had snapped. She'd told her dad everything—to hurt him, to prove it was even worse than he thought. She did have a life of her own. Friends of her own.

Oh, Daddy.

She hated herself even more than she hated him. She'd told him. She'd ruined everything. Now he would send her away to goddamn Texas.

Mallory tugged at her sleeve. "Come on, Kaferine. You got a double red."

Katherine looked across the game board.

Mallory had been her dress-up doll, her pretend child, her toy self she could slip into whenever real life sucked too bad. But now that Mallory had started kindergarten at Laurel Heights, Katherine felt sad every time she looked at her. She never wanted to see them ruin this little girl, the way they'd ruined her. She never wanted to see Mallory grow up.

She forced a smile, moved her double red.

Mallory drew Queen Frostine and squealed with delight.

It was an easy skip from Queen Frostine to King Kandy. Mallory won the game while Katherine was still back in the Molasses Swamp.

"What can we play now?" Mallory asked. "Horses?"

"I have a better idea."

"No," Mallory said immediately. "I don't like that."

"Come on. It's our little secret."

"It's scary."

"Nah. For a brave kid like you?"

Katherine went to the secret panel in the wainscoting, the storage closet that her grandfather had constructed when the bottom level of the townhouse had been his shop. He was a clockmaker, her grandfather. He loved gears and springs, mechanical tricks.

The door was impossible to see from the outside. You had to press in just the right spot for the pressure latch to release. Inside, the space was big enough for a child to crawl into, or maybe an adult, if you scrunched. The back was still crammed with clock parts—copper coils, weights and chains, star-and-moon clock faces.

She remembered her grandfather telling her, "Never wind a clock backwards, Katie. Never." He had always called her Katie, never Katherine. Her father said it was because he couldn't bear to think of his wife, whose smoker's lungs had shut down while she was waiting for her namesake to be born. "Winding backwards will ruin the clock. Always go forward. Even if you only want to go back an hour, always go forward eleven."

She wondered if her dad had been made out of clock parts, like the latch on the cabinet. She wished she could wind him backwards one week, to see if something would break.

She reached into the closet, to the little rusty hook only she knew about, and pulled out a copy of her Toyota key.

Ground me, Daddy. Go ahead.

She turned to Mallory, who was balancing Equestrian Barbie's plastic pony on her knee.

Poor little Mallory—the headmistress's daughter. She would have an even worse school experience than Katherine did. So what if she liked kindergarten? It was only a matter of time before she felt the walls closing in on her, that chasm opening at her feet. It sliced into Katherine's heart whenever she passed the lower school windows, saw Mallory wave a sticky hello to her, fingers covered in primary-colored gloop.

No, Katherine never wanted to see her baby doll grow up.

She smiled to cover the blackness. "Come on, Peewee. Let's go for a ride."

Laurel Heights School blazed with light. Luminarias lined the sidewalk. Arcs of paper lanterns glowed red and blue over the playground, transforming the basketball court into a dance floor nobody could use, thanks to the weather.

Inside, the two-story building was buttery warm with jazz music and candlelight, waiters bustling about with trays of champagne and canapés, parents laughing too loud, drinking too freely, enjoying their big night away from the children.

For an outside party brought inside at the last minute, Ann had to admit the staff and the caterers had done a great job. Cloths had been draped over the teachers' supply cabinets. Banquet tables had replaced school desks. A hundred tiny articles of lost-and-found clothing had been taken off the coat hooks and stashed in closets, broken crayons and Montessori rods swept off the floor. Fresh-cut flowers decorated the music teacher's piano. The kindergarten teacher's desk had been converted to a cash bar.

The school was too small for so many people, but the cramped quarters just proved Ann's point, the purpose for the auction—the school needed to grow. They weren't the neighborhood school they'd started out as in the 1920s, with fifteen kids from Pacific Heights. They were busting at the seams with 152 students from all over the Bay Area. They needed to buy the mansion next door, do a major renovation, double the size of the campus. What better way to kick off the capital campaign than cram all the parents together, let them see how their children spent each day?

Despite that, despite how well the evening seemed to be going, Ann was a mess. The two glasses of wine she'd had to steady her nerves were bubbling to vinegar in her stomach.

She should have been schmoozing, but instead she was sitting in the corner of the only empty classroom, knees-to-knees with Norma Reyes on tiny first-grade chairs, telling Norma that marriage counseling was a great idea. Really. It was nothing to be ashamed about.

Hypocrite.

She prayed Chadwick would forget about their agreement—just forget it.

At the same time, she hoped like hell he had more guts than she did.

Norma kept crying, calling Chadwick names.

Parents streamed by the open doorway. They would start to greet Ann, then see Norma's tears and turn away like they'd been hit by a wind tunnel fan.

"I want to kill the *pendejo*," Norma said.

Ann laced her fingers in her friend's. She promised that Chadwick was trying his best, that Katherine would be okay. Her therapist was sharp. There were good programs for drug intervention.

"Bullshit," Norma said. "You love this. You've been warning me for years."

Ann said nothing. She'd had lots of practice, diplomatically saying nothing.

For years, she had been the mediator between the family and the faculty, who would ask her—no disrespect to their colleague Chadwick—but why wasn't Katherine on probation? Why wasn't she taking her medication? When do they decide that they just can't serve her at this school? Ann endured the insinuations that if Chadwick hadn't been her friend for so long, if she didn't know the family socially, she would've jumped on Katherine's problems sooner and harder.

On the other hand, there was Norma, who had never seen the problem, not since seventh grade, when Ann had first pushed for psychological testing. Norma only saw the good in her daughter. Laurel Heights was overreacting. She'd never forgiven Chadwick for supporting Ann's recommendations for testing and therapy.

"You know what he's planning, don't you?" Norma asked.

Ann's heart did a half-beat syncopation. "What do you mean?"

"Come on. Me, he keeps in the dark. You, never. Asa Hunter. The school in Texas."

Ann's shoulders relaxed. "He mentioned it."

She didn't say that Chadwick had obsessed on it at length, been impervious to her reservations. A boot camp? Wilderness therapy? What was she supposed to say—yes, lock your kid up with drill sergeants for a year? Turn your back on everything Laurel Heights stands for—the child-centered philosophy, the nurturing environment—and give Katherine a buzz cut? The whole idea only underscored how desperate Chadwick was to be out of a failing marriage.

But she'd agreed to let him take time off for his trip to Texas, despite how hard it was to get a substitute around Thanksgiving, despite the fact that the eighth-graders hated it when Chadwick—their favorite teacher—was gone. It was in Ann's interest to let Chadwick get his thoughts in order—about Katherine, about everything.

What bothered her most was that she had been tempted to

endorse the idea of sending Katherine away. In a selfish, dishonorable way, wouldn't it make things easier?

"We both know," she told Norma. "He only wants what's best for Katherine."

"He wants to use her as a fucking guinea pig." Norma ripped another tissue out of her purse. "Christ, I must look like shit."

Oh, please, Ann thought.

As if Norma ever looked like shit. She had that petite figure Ann had grown up hating. She wished, just once, she could look like Norma. She wished she could cry in public and call her husband a dickhead and not give a second thought how it would affect her public image.

Okay. She was jealous. She hated herself for it, spent hours at night thinking, *That's not the reason. That's not the reason.*

John appeared at the door, a margarita in either hand. He surveyed the situation, smiled straight through Norma's tears.

"You'll never guess," he said. "The mayor thinks Mallory's panel is the best one on the kindergarten quilt. We're going to have lunch next week, go over some ideas for the Presidio."

Ann fought down a surge of irritation. She hated the way John skated across other people's emotions—so completely incapable of sympathy that he made it his personal mission to pretend bad feelings didn't exist. You could always count on John to be the first to tell a joke at any funeral.

"Lunch with Frank Jordan," Ann said. "Big prize, John."

He raised his eyebrows at Norma. "I get a piece of the biggest development deal in the city's history—you'd think that would please my wife. Lots of money. Lots of publicity. But what do I know? Maybe it's nothing special."

"Hey," Norma said, dabbing her tissue under her eyes. "Tonight is supposed to be fun. Remember?"

John handed her a margarita. "Your husband got stuck with that pretty blond Mrs. Passmore—had a question about her daughter's history project. Can't take him anywhere, huh?"

Ann wanted to slap him.

"We're about to start, honey," she said instead. "Why don't you go check with the cashiers?"

"Done, honey. Spreadsheet. Printer. Cash box. Don't worry about it."

He gave her a smug smile that confirmed what she already knew—letting John chair the capital campaign was the biggest mistake of her life. It was a pro bono thing for him, a good tax write-off, and since the school could hardly afford a full-time development director, Ann truly needed the help. But as she had been slow to figure out, the charity work made John feel superior, affirming his belief that Ann's career was nothing more than a hobby. Raising her $30 million would be his equivalent to helping her power-till a tomato patch or driving her to yoga lessons. *My wife, the headmistress. Isn't she cute?*

"I'll take Norma upstairs," he told her. "You go ahead. The faculty is probably paralyzed up there, waiting for your orders."

Ann contained her fury. She gave Norma's hand one last squeeze, then went off to join the party.

Upstairs, the removable wall between the two middle school classrooms had been taken down, making space for a main banquet room with an auction stage. Ann made her way toward the head table, past parents and student volunteers, waiters with trays of salads. Chadwick was talking to one of her sophomore workers, David Kraft, who sported a brand-new crop of zits. Poor kid. He'd been one of Katherine's friends until last summer, when Katherine gave up friends.

"Excuse us, David." Ann smiled. "Duty calls."

"Sure, Mrs. Z."

"You going to spot those high bidders for us?"

David held up his red signaling cloth. "Yes, ma'am."

"That's my boy."

She maneuvered Chadwick toward the faculty table.

"How's Norma?" he asked.

"She's right, you know. Your idea stinks. Boot camp school? It absolutely stinks."

"Thanks for the open mind."

"Things aren't complicated enough right now?"

They locked eyes, and they both knew that Katherine was not the foremost question on either of their minds. God help them, but she wasn't.

Ann wanted to be responsible. She wanted to think about the welfare of Katherine and Mallory. She wanted to think about her school and do the professional thing, the calm and steady thing.

But part of her wanted to rebel against that. Despite her wonderful little girl, her successful husband, her ambitious plans for Laurel Heights, part of her wanted to shake off the accumulated infrastructure of her life, the way she suspected Norma would, if their roles were reversed. Norma, who had become as much her friend as Chadwick was. Norma, the woman Ann probably admired more than anyone else.

Ann was thinking, *Don't say anything tonight, Chadwick. Please.*

And at the same time, she couldn't wait for the auction to end, for all four of them to get somewhere they could talk.

Ann felt like two different people, slowly separating, as if the Ann on the surface were a tectonic plate, sliding precariously over something hot and molten.

And right now, the Ann underneath wanted an earthquake.

Even blocks away in the dark, Katherine could see the trees—four huge palms, much too tall for Oakland.

They made her think of Los Angeles—trips to visit the Reyes side of the family every other Christmas, her father always looking for excuses not to go, her mother tossing dishes and slamming pots around the kitchen until he agreed.

Katherine used to think a lot about L.A., about escaping, moving in with her cousins. Her cousins knew how to have fun. They knew the best Spanish cuss words and where to score dope. Their fathers weren't goddamn teachers.

But running away wasn't a fantasy she believed in anymore.

Katherine curbed the Toyota in front of the house. She stared up at the night sky, a few stars peeking through the mist and the palm fronds. The palm trees would die tonight. As huge as they were, they weren't designed to withstand this kind of cold. The freeze would turn their insides to mush. It made Katherine sad to know this with such certainty.

When she was eight, she and her dad had planted morning glories in the backyard, her dad telling her not to get her hopes up, the San Francisco climate was really too cold for them. But over the course of the summer, the vines had overgrown their cheap metal trellis and bloomed with a vengeance—red, purple and blue flowers like a mass of alien eyes. Every day they'd crumple, every night they'd reopen.

"Don't they ever die?" Katherine had asked.

Her dad smiled, cupped his fingers gently around her ear. "I don't know, sweetheart. I thought they were ephemeral. I guess they're not."

Katherine hadn't known what *ephemeral* meant. Her dad never explained words, never watered down his vocabulary. But she liked the sound of it.

Eventually, the weight of the flowers made the trellis collapse. Her father had moved the beautiful, broken heap of metal and plants to the side of the toolshed, and still the flowers kept blooming for weeks, without their roots, not realizing they were dead.

"Kaferine?"

She'd completely forgotten Mallory. They must have been sitting in front of the house for minutes, Katherine staring up the sidewalk at the dark windows, the open front door. She must be freaking the poor kid out.

"Yeah, Peewee. Sorry."

"It's scary."

"What's scary?"

"The animals. The faces."

"They're just decorations, Peewee. You've seen them before."

But Katherine looked up at the house and thought— *Mallory's right. The place is kind of creepy at night.*

It would've been a normal West Oakland house—a little two-bedroom with yellow siding and a shingled roof—except a former man-of-the-house, an amateur sculptor, had encased the outside in swirls of weird metalwork. Instead of burglar bars, the windows were smothered under fancy iron vines. Cut metal silhouettes covered the walls—wild animals, African-style masks, big-butt women scolding little porkpie hat men. A steel-pipe Santa Claus sleigh with reindeers permanently decorated the roof.

Katherine had loved the metalwork since the first time she'd come here with her boyfriend—God, let's be accurate about that, *ex*-boyfriend. How he'd found the place, Katherine didn't know. It was much too cool for him. The sculptures reminded Katherine of the clock parts in her grandfather's closet, as if the wheels and gears had been taken out and planted and allowed to grow wild.

"Kaferine?" Mallory said. "Let's go home. Okay?"

Katherine was shivering, her teeth going like a telegraph machine.

She fingered her necklace—her old birthday gift from Daddy. She hated that it was such a talisman for her—so important for calming her nerves, but it had been, ever since he gave it to her, as if it held some of his strength—the silent determination of a giant.

She was crying now. No control over the tears. She had to get inside before she broke down completely.

"I'll be back in a minute," she told Mallory. "You want to listen to the radio?"

"No thank you."

"Sure. Listen. Good song."

She left on the music, and got out of the car. She imagined her dad's voice, *This isn't over, Katherine. I want to talk about this when I get home.*

And Katherine felt that frantic, just-before-the-darkness smile tugging at her lips. *Ephemeral, Daddy. It means dying too soon.*

The cold turned her breath to steam as she hurried up the porch steps.

John Zedman fucking loved it.

Just walking through the locker area, the housing commissioner, the supervisor from District 1 and the head of the biggest construction company in town had gone out of their way to shake his hand.

Last year? Same auction. Same John Zedman. But would they talk to him? No way.

It'd been as if the smell of burning ferry engines—the aura of grease and fried pistons that came home on John's father every day from the Embarcadero wharf—still lingered on John's tuxedo, an unwanted odor that came from his pores, straight through the $500 cologne, announcing, *I am not a member of your club. I do not have your cell phone number. My wife does not lunch with yours—she only teaches your kids.*

That last part was what John hated the most. Because these people—the hell what John thought—to them, there was absolutely no difference between a teacher and a maid. Consuela from Guatemala. Ann Zedman from Laurel Heights. Whatever. You work with my kids, hold their future in your hands? So does my housekeeper.

No matter how John tried, the other parents had always looked at him through the lens of his wife's job, not his. To even see him, they had to make a conscious effort. Saying hello to him was not something that occurred to them, the way he had to think to say hello to the school custodian.

But not tonight. Tonight the richest guests were introducing themselves, telling him that they were remiss in scheduling that lunch. Surely they'd talked about it—when was it, last month?

And John smiled, knowing they were full of shit, but loving it.

Three months since John Zedman made his first million-dollar commission, and he'd been on a roll ever since. He would wake up at night, go to the bathroom, stare at the new Buddy Rhodes concrete counters, the gold sink fixtures, and he would tell himself, "You're a millionaire. You're a goddamn millionaire, John Boy."

This week, with a $1.2 billion redevelopment deal in the bag, well, John Zedman had arrived. He was never going backwards. His daughter would never know the smell of grease and burning axle rods.

He walked through the banquet room, and every step was on air.

He thought about his old neighborhood, the south side of Potrero Hill. Most of the smarter guys, the ones who lived past eighteen, had all joined the Army or the mob. John had come close to choosing between those paths himself. Even getting where he was today—he'd done some rough things. He'd taken care of problems, some of them recently.

He wondered what the mayor would say if he knew John was carrying right now—the weight of a .22 tugging at his tuxedo coat like a child's hand, nagging for attention.

John had to smile.

Fuck it if he'd made some mistakes. Made some enemies.

He'd been talking to some of his friends at the polo club—they said you could buy a bodyguard, ex–Mexican military, for a couple hundred a month. A friend of a friend had this number. And damn it, but John was liking the idea of a guy behind him, a little muscle to make people sweat. Hell, everybody had bodyguards these days. The Baptist preacher downtown, the local radio talk show host.

It wasn't about being nervous. Not at all. It was about showing your influence. Making a statement.

Twenty feet out, John saw the dilemma coming—Chadwick standing alone by the cash bar, and beyond him, chatting with the city comptroller, was Hays MacColl, biggest developer on the Peninsula, one of the movers and shakers behind the China Basin waterfront.

John needed to walk past Chadwick, give him a smile and a punch on the shoulder maybe, and go talk to MacColl. Test the new power.

Chadwick was looking forlorn. Goddamn, but put a powdered wig on the guy, and he could be George Washington—that same square jaw, that look of sad dignity. John figured it was some kind of genetic karma that the guy taught American history—like people evolving to look like their dogs. Chadwick was the right height, too—six foot eight. John had never thought of himself as short, until he became friends with Chadwick. Then, by comparison, people had started to call him "the shorter guy." Soon, he was a little man.

He should walk past.

The Chadwicks had been their friends...well shit, Ann and Chadwick since high school. All of them, socially, since Ann hired Chadwick, back in what—'82? The same year Katherine had started kindergarten downstairs.

The friendship had been nothing but trouble ever since. Like business and friends, education and friends didn't mix. You teach their kids, you see how they raise them—it changes your perspective. Like, Katherine. Christ. John hated himself that he'd let Mallory stay at their house, even though it would've hurt Chadwick's and Norma's feelings if he hadn't, sent the message that he didn't trust his daughter with theirs.

So? It was true. Katherine was trouble. John dreaded letting her baby-sit. What he dreaded more, his little Mallory following in her footsteps—being at the same school with Ann, having Chadwick as her teacher someday. That couldn't be healthy. Laurel Heights had good prestige, sure. But it wasn't the only show in town. If he could just get Ann to quit, he could put Mallory in Burke, or Hamlin—someplace safe, ordinary.

It wasn't as if John hadn't done his best to be Chadwick's friend. How many guys would do as much as he had? But Chadwick and Norma were bad for them. And what the hell was that carnivore crack earlier? Shit.

He was primed to walk past Chadwick—fuck the consequences. What had he been thinking, getting sentimental? It had been his idea that they go out together after the auction tonight, have some drinks, get the old friendship back on track. He hated that maudlin streak in himself. It was a weakness he always had to suppress.

Then Chadwick locked eyes with him, gave him that forlorn smile, that weary but affectionate look John's dad used to give him coming home from the Embarcadero every night, and it was like a window into a world that John had spent his whole life trying to escape. Despite himself, John stopped, leaned against the bar.

"Here's the man," he said.

"Lost our wives, again."

"Nah," John said. "Can't lose mine. She's always on stage."

Sure enough, there Ann was, applauding and smiling as the auctioneer drove up a bidding war between two families over the beautiful third-grade ceramic whatever-the-fuck-that-was their kids had made.

Hays MacColl drifted off through the crowd with a young lady in tow, and the moment of opportunity passed.

"Norma?" John asked Chadwick.

"Around somewhere." Chadwick shook his head. "Thought I could make some sense out of things, John. I thought a few days away . . ."

"Hey, man," John said. "I'm sorry."

And he was sorry. Honestly. God knows, he and Ann had their differences. They were as mismatched as Chadwick and Norma. But if John was constant about one thing—it was marriage. He'd seen what divorce did to a man, what it did to his dad when his mom had left them. No. Not for John Zedman. His kid would not grow up like that. It was another kind of mirror John saw in Chadwick—and he didn't like it.

Chadwick passed him the auction program. Three more items—the trip to Barbados, a weekend in Aspen and the kindergarten quilt. John had to be there for that, of course. Mallory had made one of the panels—a picture of a horse, naturally. Always a horse. He had to join the frenzy of bidding to turn a week of kindergarten finger-painting into hard cash.

"You still want to go for drinks after?" Chadwick asked. "Little cold out there."

John realized he'd been scanning the crowd, probably looking like a dog on a leash in the park, ready to bolt. Chadwick gave him the sad eyes, telling him it was okay to leave. Go ahead. But John saw the apprehension there, too, and he knew that Chadwick—the tall one, the one who could wrap a grown man around a pole—needed him.

Whatever else he was, John was a man of action. He did not spend his time vacillating over what to do. If he made a mistake, he didn't waste time grieving over it.

Without him, Chadwick was a mass of indecision, whether it was about his wife, or his daughter, or their plans tonight to relive their first outing as a foursome, so many years ago, when they'd gotten drunk on Veuve Clicquot and wandered through Pacific Heights, singing "When I'm Sixty-Four" in the dark until the old ladies in the mansions started yelling at them, using words old ladies in mansions weren't supposed to know.

John Zedman wasn't afraid of living.

He imagined taking out his .22, right here in the middle school area, making Chadwick pale with fear.

There's nothing to be afraid of, he would tell Chadwick. *Johnny will take care of everything.*

The idea made him smile.

He said, "Why wait? This round's on me."

Twice, Mallory had dreamed about the house. Each time the metal vines on the walls started moving like hair, and the dark doorway opened like a mouth. It would start to inhale, pulling Mallory toward it, trying to bring her inside.

Mallory shivered. She breathed into her hands and tried to capture the warmth, but that just made her palms sticky.

A song was playing on the car radio—men with funny voices, singing that they were going to come back home from five hundred miles away.

Mallory didn't like the song, but she didn't want to touch Katherine's radio. She was afraid she'd make the music even louder.

When Katherine finally came out of the house, talking to somebody on the porch, Mallory started bouncing in her seat, willing her to hurry.

She liked being with Katherine, the way she liked the spinning teacup on the carousel or her daddy dipping her upside down. But Mallory didn't have bad dreams about the spinning teacup. She had bad dreams about the yellow house with the dark door and the metal vines.

Katherine slid in the driver's seat. She smelled like smoke. She had a brown lunch bag, and Mallory asked what was in it, because she was hungry.

"Medicine," Katherine told her.

"Are you sick?"

Katherine smiled. "Let's get back home, Peewee."

"Why do you like coming here, Kaferine? I don't like it."

Katherine laid her hands on the steering wheel. She seemed to be feeling it for a special vibration. "I had to say goodbye to somebody, sweetie. I had to tell them something. I don't expect you to understand, okay?"

"We won't come here anymore?" Mallory asked hopefully.

"No," Katherine said. "Our little secret. Okay?"

Katherine squeezed Mallory's knee, her fingers biting like ice. Mallory felt so relieved tears welled up in her eyes. The house seemed to be looking at her, waiting for her to promise.

"Secret," Mallory said.

She promised she would never tell anyone about the house. Never in a million million years.

Norma Reyes was worried about the girls.

She wanted to call Katherine, make sure everything was all right. She wanted to pull her daughter straight through the phone line—kiss her forehead, pinch her cheeks, tell her, *M'hijita, I am on your side. I am not mad anymore.*

But she couldn't be the first to suggest calling. That would prove something to Chadwick—a lack of trust in Katherine, an admission that things were as bad as he believed they were.

He never approved of how she dealt with crises, and the crises always happened on her watch, because everything was Norma's watch. Twenty-four hours a day.

Norma had learned to be defensive—to play down Katherine's problems, because if she didn't, Chadwick would fly off the handle. Not emotionally. Never emotionally. But he'd get worked up with some crazy idea—like the therapy. Like medication. Like sending Katherine to *pinche* Texas. He would bring home educational manuals and the flavor-of-the-week child psychology book and make up a game plan to fix their daughter like she was some broken carburetor.

Qué cacada.

And he wondered why she hadn't been anxious to tell him about the heroin.

Now here they were, on the school playground, freezing their asses off, she and Ann sitting at the base of the play structure, watching their husbands teach each other karate like a couple of drunk idiots. John was laughing, the kindergarten quilt he'd paid $7,500 for draped over his shoulders so he looked like an Indian chief of the Crayola tribe.

Everyone else had left except the cleaning crew and a few staff members, who were putting their classrooms back together inside.

The wood plank under Norma's butt felt like an ice block. The paper lanterns above them dripped icicles. Inside, the night custodian Juan Carlos was blaring Frank Sinatra Christmas carols while he ran the vacuum cleaner, sucking up the booze and pâté crackers the parents had trampled into the classroom carpeting.

This was not fucking quality time. They would have to leave soon or freeze to death, but who was going to be the first to admit this idea was a failure? Who was going to break down and confess that they were nervous and unhappy and just wanted to go home?

Somewhere along the line, Norma's life—her marriage, her friendship, even the way she raised her daughter—had become a game of chicken. She and Chadwick were barreling along at top speed, pretending they weren't on a collision course, trying to be the last to flinch.

"You sure there's nothing I can do?" Ann asked.

What Norma heard: *You need help because you're a failure.*

Maybe that wasn't Ann's fault. She had the same tone of voice Chadwick did—steady and calm, bleached of emotion so you had to guess her feelings.

Norma was raised in a family where if somebody was mad, if somebody had a problem with you—you knew it. It would come flying at your head as a Bible, a tortilla press, a hand towel—something. Then you'd yell a little, and it was over. The way Chadwick and Ann expressed themselves— Norma had learned to be suspicious of every comment, because they weren't obvious. Their criticisms were like Chinese water torture. Norma guessed it must be a teacher thing.

John clunked his champagne bottle on the ground, tripped on the edge of the kindergarten quilt. "All right. Look. They have this thing they do with their elbow, right?"

"Give me that before you ruin it," Ann said. "I'm freezing."

John tossed her the quilt, and Ann spread it over her knees and Norma's—sharing automatically, moving in closer. The smell of acrylic paint wafted up from the fabric.

John did an elbow strike at Chadwick.

Chadwick shook his head sadly. "That would never work."

"No? The Japanese should know, man."

"John, karate's not Japanese. It's Okinawan."

"What the fuck ever. Look, you're an Air Force guy. Come on, throw me a punch. Pretend I'm the Vietcong or whatever. I'll show you."

They went at it, Chadwick halfheartedly playing the game, John laughing, trying to egg him on.

Ann mumbled, "Pathetic."

John kept swinging. "Look, Chadwick. All I'm saying is, it's not all about muscle. You could—"

"Granted. It's about knowing when to get the hell away."

"You could have a little more training than I've got, and one elbow strike could take you down."

Norma smiled, despite herself. It was so ridiculous—her enormous husband who could never hurt a fly. If Chadwick had half of John Zedman's bravado, he could take over the world. The guy had been security police in the military, for God's sake, but in seventeen years of marriage, not a harsh word. Not a fist through the wall. Nothing. It drove Norma crazy.

She'd married him because he was handsome and intelligent and had been in the Air Force—all of which reminded her of her father. She'd thought that she would eventually get inside his silence. She knew there was something there—a spirit that came out the few times she saw him teach his classes. Or the nights when Katherine was little, when Norma would creep close to Katherine's bedroom and listen to Chadwick's stories, the way he would bring everything alive for her. But for Norma? She tried to think of a time he'd been truly on fire for her, and she had to convince herself there had been a honeymoon period like that. More and more, she wondered if it was just her imagination.

She thought it would've been acceptable consolation if he'd just applied himself to making some money, taken a career that would get them out of that inherited dump of his in the Mission. After all, hadn't Norma given up her own plans for him, dropped out of college to raise their child? Couldn't he make some sacrifices?

Apparently, he couldn't. He still looked at her with guilt, sometimes. Sorry he'd followed his dream and become a teacher. Sorry they couldn't pay the goddamn credit card bills this month. But he'd been meant for the classroom.

The last year or so, he'd been giving her the same kind of guilty look, every time he'd come back from his camp-outs with Hunter, broaching again and again the idea that perhaps, just perhaps, Katherine was beyond their help.

She'd be damned if Chadwick would take her baby away.

She shivered, her right knee trembling against Ann's under the quilt.

"Okay, enough," Chadwick told John, holding his hands flat.

"Yeah, but the kick is the best—"

"Come on, John. All right?"

"Oh, scared. The big man is scared now."

Ann murmured, "I'm convinced eighth grade is just about the limit."

"What?" Norma said. "The limit for what?"

"Men growing up."

Ann smiled conspiratorially, and Norma wondered, *Are you going to tell me? Is that what we're here for?*

Something told her Ann would come clean with her tonight. She hoped so. In the end, the only thing Norma couldn't forgive would be disrespect—the disrespect of Chadwick and Ann believing she was stupid.

Surely Ann didn't think Norma had failed to notice the smell of her perfume on Chadwick's shirt that one time, back in October, the subtle change in the way Chadwick said her name, starting a few months ago. During the summer—their faculty retreat. A week in that big sprawling house on Stinson Beach, just the teachers and Ann. Plenty of time to sneak away, Norma guessed.

Norma's marriage was an eggshell, held in shape by Scotch tape. She knew that. She knew she had pushed Chadwick to be something he couldn't—pushed so hard for so many years that he'd cracked, and whatever was inside had seeped out, slowly, until he was hollow to her. But still, Norma needed to believe he would respect her enough to come clean. That was one reason, in itself, to hang on to the dying marriage—that and Katherine.

She could forgive Ann. She loved Ann. She loved her calmness, which Norma could never possess, and the way Ann really listened. When Norma had gone through breast cancer, it was Ann who helped her. No pity, no platitudes, no false sympathy—she was there from the second doctor's appointment on. She'd helped Norma accept the mastectomy, accept the fact that Katherine would now be an only child forever because the chemo had poisoned Norma's womb.

And of course Chadwick would be drawn to her for comfort. Ann was his oldest friend. Always platonic, he'd sworn—*Ann knows me too well to fall for me,* he'd told Norma years ago. But hell, things had changed.

Maybe Norma was crazy—still wanting Ann's friendship. But love and forgiveness had nothing to do with logic.

Tonight, despite the heroin problem, Ann had given Mallory over to Katherine without a hesitation. "I'm sure it will be fine."

Norma had wanted to hug Ann. It was a vote of confidence not just for Katherine, but for Norma, too. It was somebody saying, "Yes, I understand you gave up your entire life to be a mother, and I do not think you failed."

Norma waited for Ann to say something.

The hands of her watch glowed half past midnight. They really should have been home by now.

"Oh, I give up," John said. "This guy is too tough."

He punched Chadwick in the gut, and came over to the play structure, grinning. "Spread that quilt, girls. Let's picnic."

"Not a chance, *hijo,*" Norma told him. "It's warm. It's also seventy-five hundred dollars worth of artwork."

"Tax deductible," John said.

"You're not putting your butt on it, John Zedman."

He laughed, scooped up his champagne bottle.

Chadwick stood off to one side, looking up at the murky orange soup of the sky.

Norma suddenly longed for L.A. She wanted warm nights—shorts and T-shirts, a dry Santa Ana wind. She had lived here too long, allowed her child to be raised here. It wasn't healthy. Time had passed too quickly.

She should have been a money manager by now—a banker, an accountant.

Everybody at her public school had known Norma Reyes would make it. She could breathe numbers the way most people breathed air. The first girl ever to complete AP calculus. She would go far. It was the bitterest irony that she had ended up a full-time mother in a working-class barrio, just like her mother.

But Norma was still young. Only two years, and Katherine would be off to college. Katherine would overcome her problems—Norma was confident of that. Norma took fierce pride that her daughter had inherited her talent at math. Katherine could go to MIT. Or Columbia. She could get a scholarship.

Then Norma could have her own career. She could let her marriage with Chadwick crumble, if it had to. Or perhaps, who knew? What kind of couple might they be without Katherine? They had never had the chance to find out. Maybe they would work things out after all.

"Hey, Chadwick," John said. "What—you lose something up there?"

And when Chadwick looked down, straight at her, Norma knew it was coming. She knew him well enough to know he was planning a confession.

Well, all right, she thought. We need a good fight. For once, maybe—a true knock-down-drag-out. Maybe the game of chicken ends here.

And then the door at the top of the stairs burst open, and Gladys, Ann's secretary, came running down from the office, her dress shoes clacking against wooden steps, her breath smoking.

"There's a call," she gasped, stopping halfway down, shouting to them. "Oh, God. The police are asking for you."

At ten-thirty, Katherine put Mallory in front of the television, settled her into her father's recliner. Mallory was so small she looked like a stuffed animal in the midst of all the black leather. Katherine rummaged for a good video—something from the war chest of her childhood—and settled on *The Little Mermaid*. It was a bootleg video, something her dad had taped for her, knowing that the official VHS version wouldn't be out for years. She'd loved the movie when it first came out, even though she'd been twelve going on thirteen—a little too old to admit she liked cartoons. Her dad had told her the story many times when she was young, but she liked the Disney version even better, because it had a happy ending. She figured that's why her dad had gone to such trouble to get her a copy—it was the last thing she'd ever enjoyed as a kid, the last happy ending that had ever appealed to her.

She put it in the machine, waited for the intro music to start.

"I don't like that one," Mallory complained.

"This is a good one, sweetie. I love this one."

"Could we play a game? I like it when we play games."

"Maybe later." Katherine tried to keep the smile in place. It's paint, she told herself. Spread it a little thicker, hold it in place, give it time to dry. "I'm going to lie down for a little bit. Okay?"

"You're getting sicker?"

"Just a little tired. I'll be fine."

"Can I come, too?"

The plea tightened across Katherine's chest like a seatbelt. She felt the urge she'd been feeling for several weeks now—to shed her possessions, to let Mallory know she loved her.

"Here, sweetie." She unclasped her birthday necklace, poured the chain into Mallory's hands. "This is a present, okay?"

"That's yours. It's your favorite."

"Hold it for me. I want you to, Mal. I love you."

"I love you too, Kaferine."

"That's good. Now watch television for a while."

Katherine closed her bedroom door, then went into her bathroom. She opened the brown paper bag. She took out the spoon, the rubber tube, the lighter, the needle. She was surprised by the color of the heroin—almost white this time, like baby powder. Her fingers were cold as she worked, but she knew how. She'd been taught by an expert—deft hands, without fear, taking her wrist, tapping the inside of her forearm for a vein. Just like a nurse. Better than a nurse. Oh God, Samuel. She would miss him.

Katherine shot up and immediately shuddered. This was better. This let her feel the sadness and the happiness at the same time. Her dad was never coming home. They wouldn't have any more arguments. Her mom would never yell again.

Katherine stared at the mirror, smiling at the girl there. She looked like her mom, only younger, without the frustrations of raising some stupid kid.

Katherine wished her mother had gone back to college. Goddamn it, but Katherine would have preferred that. She'd rather have her father at home, away from Laurel Heights, and her mother out making the money. Hadn't they thought of that? Didn't it occur to them it would make them all happier?

The pleasing sensation of floating off the ground wasn't working as well as Katherine had hoped. She could hear Sebastian the Crab singing in the living room. Should she check on Mallory? No. She'd be fine.

Katherine tried to remember—had she shot up yet? It didn't feel like it. Her friend had warned her, *You may not get the right high off this batch. You may need to try a little more.*

That's what it is, Katherine decided. Weak drugs. Weak, like everything else.

She went through the process again—holding the lighter under the spoon, jerking back her thumb when she realized she'd been holding it too close to the flame without even feeling it. The tip looked like she'd dipped it in charcoal. She put it in her mouth and started to giggle. *Don't suck your thumb, m'hijita.*

Finally, she shot up . . . was it for the second time?

She felt better now, like she was encased in cotton. She stood up from the toilet and her feet sank several inches into the floor. She made her way to the bed, dropped onto the sheets. She tried to touch her face, but she wasn't sure whether she was stroking a pillow or her own cheek.

Above her, upside down, were the pictures on the headboard—the cow and the moon and the stars that had kept her company since she was little. Where had they come from? Hadn't she covered them up?

She could hear her own breathing, felt the breath being reflected back on her face, as if she were against a window.

She remembered crawling into her parents' bed when she

was small, her head next to Daddy's, listening to him while he slept. She tried to align her breathing to his, but his breaths were too deep. She couldn't hold that much air in her lungs without bursting. She couldn't go that long between breaths without suffocating. She had felt a failure, not being able to match her father's rhythm. So she had stayed up, unable to sleep, studying his closed eyes, the small freckle on his right eyelid, the blond lashes you never noticed when he was awake.

The Little Mermaid was playing, somewhere far away. Her mother and father needed her to stay in bed a little longer. It was too early to get up—too early even for cartoons.

Katherine closed her eyes. She felt her breath slowing, aligning itself at last to her father's.

Mallory got up once during the video and went into Katherine's bedroom. Katherine was asleep on the bed. The air smelled funny—like a toaster.

There was a spoon on the floor, and when Mallory picked it up, it was warm. She dropped it.

"Katherine?" she called, trying very hard to say the *th* right. Her teacher had been coaching her on that sound. They played a game with flashcards. *Math. Bath. Katherine.*

Mallory pressed on Katherine's shoulder, called her name again. But Katherine kept sleeping.

She didn't want Katherine to be mad at her.

She went back into the living room. She curled up in the big black chair and rubbed Katherine's necklace between her fingers. There was a silver rectangle on the necklace, with words on the back, but Mallory couldn't read many words yet. She was in kindergarten.

She watched more of the video.

Maybe her parents would come back soon. If Katherine was asleep, it must be time for bed.

But they didn't come back.

The video ended. There was fuzz on the screen.

Mallory tiptoed back into the bedroom. There was something funny about Katherine's face now. It was as if Katherine were taking a nap in a swimming pool, at the bottom of the shallow end. Her skin looked that color.

Mallory tried to wake her up, but she couldn't. Katherine's hand was really cold.

Mallory's stomach felt like she'd eaten too much candy.

She was scared Katherine would wake up and get mad, and her eyes and her mouth would be like that dark house. Mallory tried to think how to call her parents. She knew her own number at home. She had memorized it. But her parents wouldn't be at home. They were at the school party. They'd said.

There was one other number her mother had taught her for emergencies. Mallory was scared to get in trouble for calling it, but she was more scared to be alone with Katherine sleeping, her face the wrong color.

She stood on a kitchen stool so she could reach the phone. She dialed—wrong at first, 119, and nothing happened. Then she remembered the nine went first, and she dialed again.

The woman on the other end of the line asked Mallory a question she didn't understand, but Mallory told her what the problem was, anyway. Carefully, she said, "Katherine won't wake up."

The woman asked her some more questions. She told Mallory not to hang up, but Mallory was scared by her tone—hard and not friendly, just like a robot's. Mallory hung up. She went back into the living room, and turned the big black chair around, facing the bedroom doorway. The phone rang, but she didn't answer it. She knew it was the woman with the hard voice—and she didn't know what else to say to her. *Just hurry. Tell my parents to hurry.*

She held Katherine's necklace in her hand, wrapping and unwrapping it around her wrist. The silver smelled like vinegar.

Mallory wasn't sure what she was waiting for. Katherine to wake up and answer the phone. Her parents to come home and answer it. Someone. Anyone.

Years later, Mallory would wonder if she'd ever stopped waiting, if she'd ever left that black chair, staring at Katherine's doorway, waiting for someone who would never come back.

PART II

2002

1

Talia Montrose was an hour away from a whole new life.

She had twenty grand in a leather satchel in the trunk of her LeBaron, a receipt in her pocket for two hundred thirty thousand more, just deposited in a brand new BofA account.

Her old checking account was closed, her meager savings liquidated. She'd quit her job at Pay-Rite, told her general manager, Caleb, to go fuck himself for once instead of the teenage cashiers.

Talia had three sets of winter clothes, a photo album, a box of Tampax and a down ski jacket, all folded tightly into a single paisley suitcase.

Her palm was still warm from the rich man's handshake—her fingers cramped from signing and initialing the contracts. She could still smell his cologne—alien and spicy, like a Middle Eastern drink. She could still see the cold eyes of the Mexican who stood behind him.

After making sure she understood the deal, making sure she had signed in all the right places, the rich man had smiled, and given her the satchel, and said, "Off you go."

Too easy. She was still in shock.

Eight A.M., Vincent would be waiting for her at the Pancake & Chicken House on Broadway. Vincent had a gun. He could protect her, and the cash. They would turn the LeBaron toward Tahoe, and they would never look back.

So why was she going back to the house—the place she had been so anxious to be rid of?

She turned on Poplar, drove through the neighborhood

she knew too well—the grave-sized yards, the pastel siding, the aluminum-foiled windows and cement flower planters that looked like Easter baskets. Brand-new cars and satellite dishes marked the drug dealers' houses. Old Mr. Benjamin was out in his white tank top and his U.S. Navy cap, watering his grass.

Wasn't a bad-looking neighborhood. People heard West Oakland on the news, they heard about the homicide rate and drugs and gangs, they thought about a war zone—fires in trash cans and burned-out buildings and evil-looking kids with machine guns.

Truth was scarier than that. Truth was West Oakland looked like a normal place. Clean, tidy, most of the residents hardworking, decent people. You had to look close to spot the bullet holes in the doorjambs and the windowsills. You had to be unlucky, or just plain stupid, to catch a drive-by. And the kids—you couldn't tell the dangerous ones by looking at them. Talia knew that firsthand.

She took a left on Jefferson, past the homes of childhood friends—more and more of them dead, the older she got. She passed places where she'd grown up, raised her children, met her men.

Six houses down on the left, the great brown stumps that used to be her palm trees years ago rose up in the front yard like a leper's fingers. The house's siding, once bright yellow, had faded to the color of stained underwear, tattooed with rust from the years it had spent under a ton of Johnny Jay's ornate metalwork. The roof sagged. Half the windows were webbed with cracks.

Place wasn't worth a quarter million, even if the rich man's bullshit was true about a redevelopment project. No, this wasn't going to be the next Emeryville. They weren't going to put up any fucking artist lofts here. He'd just paid her off, plain and simple—paid her to go away. And she'd jumped at the chance.

She backed the car up the driveway, took her satchel out of the trunk. No way she was gonna leave that much money unattended.

The autumn air felt like satin.

A pumpkin was smashed on her porch. Somebody had put a paper black cat on the door, too. Not her, she hadn't been home in four days. Been planning with Vincent, doing his coke, dreaming of fifties and hundreds. They wouldn't have gotten any trick-or-treaters here anyway. Never did.

She put the key in the lock and found the door was open. Damn. She hoped the kids hadn't trashed the place. She figured the deal was final with the house, but she didn't know—hadn't understood half the stuff she signed. She didn't want anything going wrong.

She stood in the living room and wondered why she felt guilty. Wasn't a thing here except hardwood floors, the old green sofa, the particleboard table. Morning sun was soaking through the windows, filling the old gray curtains with light.

She had lived her whole miserable adult life in this house, failed over and over with her children, her relationships. Her first husband, Johnny Jay, the metalworker, spent years caging up the house in decoration, as if it could make up for the fact that he couldn't keep Talia home with his manhood. Her second husband, Elbridge, gave her four more children and a world of hurt before getting himself shot to death. A dozen other men—Bill, the night manager at the Pay-Rite, who supplied her kids with prescription drugs; Ali, the Nation of Islam bodyguard with his friggin' bow tie, who thought Johnny Jay's metalwork was satanic and worked every weekend to tear it down, painted Talia's bedroom for her and paid the utilities and turned out to like little girls better than he liked her. And those were only the highlights. All of them had left marks on Talia, and her kids, and this house.

So why was she back here?

She thought about Vincent—with his gun, his silver tooth and his brilliant smile. Doorman at the Royale Club, he had some fine manners. He'd been nice to her—even nicer since she'd told him about the money.

Maybe her luck would change. Maybe Vincent would be the right one.

But Talia knew her optimism was a disease. She had been suckered by men again and again and again, allowed herself to keep trying because hope was all she had to feed on. She had children for the same reason. She couldn't afford them, couldn't commit to them, couldn't support them. And yet she had them. In the end, they hung around her neck and weighed her down.

Could she leave her children behind? The answer came easy—she already had. One dead. Two in jail. Another dropped out of school and moved away. The one who did make it through school—well, the less said the better. All of them dealing drugs, gang-banging at one time or another. Even her baby, Race—she just didn't know what to do for him. Mostly he took care of himself now—staying with friends, or at Crazy Nana's place, or sometimes here. The money in her satchel told her she'd better go along with the plan, take Race with her, get him away from that rich man's daughter. But Vincent wouldn't like it. Race wouldn't give up the girl. Even after getting kicked out of that school of hers, Race had gotten closer to her than ever. He would never agree to leave, and he was too big to force.

Besides, this house had bought Talia a ticket out of West Oakland. Selling it was the only thing she'd ever done right. She'd scraped to buy it in the first place. She'd saved, she'd done honest work. Now she was getting a good payoff—four times what she put in. It was the first fair thing, the first good break she'd ever gotten. Who could blame her if she took off by herself—started fresh? She wasn't doing her kids any good anyhow, and everybody knew it.

She went into her bedroom and found it messed up—two sleeping bags on the floor in front of the old TV. Race and his girlfriend been staying here. There were her clothes, her purse, that little necklace. No sign of the kids. Last night being Halloween and all, they probably stayed out causing trouble, left in a hurry to catch a ride, left their things behind. The girl was just like Race that way; she'd leave her prissy ass behind, it wasn't attached. Still, they'd been here, maybe every night Talia had been gone. Taking advantage.

Fifteen years old and sleeping together. They said they weren't. Swore up and down. But Talia had been about that age when she met Johnny Jay, yeah, and it pained her to remember.

Out of habit, Talia knelt down and looked through the girl's purse. Nine dollars. She put it in her pocket, thinking to herself it was funny, with a goddamn briefcase full of cash, she was still trained to lift what she could from the girl's wallet. Every dollar counted. And wasn't the girl staying in her house? Why should Talia feel guilty?

She lifted the girl's necklace, read the inscription on the back of the silver charm, *For Katherine Elise Chadwick, on her thirteenth.*

Girl had some nerve, bringing that name back into this house. But what did Talia expect? Sending Race to that school wasn't no accident. Wasn't about giving him no education, neither. Sending him there was payback, and it wouldn't stop with those kids messing around together, especially now that Race got himself kicked out of the school. The last nine years, Talia had been riding the edge of a thunderstorm—hair prickling up on her arms, the air smelling like hot metal—just waiting for the violence to start. And she knew when things were about to turn violent. Lord yes, she'd had experience with that. She couldn't hold it off much longer.

Was the rich man so wrong, wanting their children apart?

"Gone," he had said. "I want you completely, totally gone. You and your son. That is the deal."

The Mexican dude had stood behind him, making it clear—silent, but clear—what the other alternative was.

Talia felt angry, all of a sudden, and she wasn't sure at who.

She stuffed the girl's necklace in her pocket.

Seven thirty-five now.

Talia should get going, get downtown to meet Vincent. He was a decent man, but she was still nervous. She probably shouldn't have told him about the money, but she needed a man the way she needed the photo album or the clothes or the Tampax. It was just one of those traveling essentials.

She wished Race were here. She didn't want to go without

him. He was her last baby. If it was too late for the others, maybe she could still make things right for him.

, She would break the news to him. Maybe he would see the logic. He'd gotten himself in trouble at that school anyway. Now was a good time to leave. He shouldn't be there, shouldn't be with that white girl, anyway. It had been a mistake, taking that partial scholarship. Like Talia going into the Starbucks this morning—a place she'd never stepped into, never wanted to. What were those people thinking? How much for coffee? Shit.

Race didn't belong at that school any more than Talia did at Starbucks. She'd take Race away to Tahoe. The boy had never seen snow. She'd fix that.

Talia felt better the minute she made her decision. Lighter. She would take Race with her, be a good mother. He would get her complete attention, the way it should be. And if Vincent didn't like it, Vincent could get the fuck out.

Then Talia looked out the window, saw the black Honda Civic sliding into the driveway, blocking her in, and she felt the new world she'd been painting for herself start closing up like a night flower.

Samuel hadn't planned it. He didn't mean to go over the edge.

He was the kind of guy who had turned his life around. He'd had his share of bad breaks as a kid. Now he worked with children. He helped people. He got up on time, went to work, did a good job.

But see, he'd been hearing these stories. Race had been kicked out of school. Race was getting in trouble on account of that girl, following a path Samuel knew too well. And Samuel was paying the bills for that school. Race had better goddamn be there.

At first, he hadn't minded Race hanging out with that girl. Wasn't something Samuel could've planned on, but he'd gotten some twisted satisfaction out of it. Race wanted to mess around with her, drive her parents crazy, remind them of the past—that was cool, as long as he didn't get himself in too much trouble. Three more years. Race would graduate from that school—the school Katherine never finished. He would go on to college. That would be justice—a future gained for a future lost. Then Samuel would close the books, call it even. He promised himself that would be it—no more revenge. He would make something good come out of the past.

But if Race started compromising his chances at graduation, if he got kicked out of school, especially if it was the girl's fault— No, that wasn't part of the plan.

Samuel had never shown himself to the girl. He'd taken care to stay out of the picture. But he would, if he had to.

He expected to catch Race at the house this time of morning, maybe the girl, too, but instead there was Talia's car, and Talia herself looking out the living room window.

What the hell was she up to?

This was way too early for her. She should have been off with her latest boyfriend—whatever the hell his name was. Samuel couldn't keep track. He'd lived through so many of them over the years. He never got mad. The memories just settled on him like sediment, hardening to rock, until his gentlest touch could smash through a wall.

He waited behind the wheel, trying to steady his nerves. Swear to God, he had worked at forgiving that woman. He had helped her with money, time, whatever she needed. He'd spent years telling himself she wasn't guilty of anything except being born poor and stupid about men.

Samuel walked up the steps of the house. He kicked a piece of smashed pumpkin into the weeds, ripped the paper black cat off the door. He hated that shit—Halloween. The whole idea of children in costumes.

First thing he saw when he came into the living room was the leather satchel at Talia's feet. Wasn't right—wasn't something she'd be carrying. She was dressed in her Friday night clothes—skintight red jeans, leopard-skin sweater. Her hair was the color of crusted sap.

"Stylin'," he said. "You going somewhere?"

"I had to." Her voice leaked guilt, like it always did, even when she hadn't done anything.

Samuel could smell her—the cheap watery magnolia perfume. He wondered if that's what men were attracted to. He didn't know. He couldn't imagine it.

What was Talia planning—weekend in Vegas? No, Tahoe. Closer. That would be more within her scope. No doubt the latest boyfriend was waiting for her.

But there was more to it than that.

Samuel slipped his fingers in his pocket, tapped against the hard rectangle of wood and metal there—the six-inch knife he always carried, ever since the old days, before he turned around. He never planned on using it—certainly not this morning, hoping to talk sense into Race. But the knife sat on the dresser every morning, and it made his fingers itch until he picked it up, slipped it into the pocket where it belonged. Otherwise Samuel felt dizzy—ten ounces off balance.

He tried for a smile. "What you up to, Talia?"

"Was I supposed to say no?" she asked. "He give me a lot of money."

Samuel could swear she was accusing him—turning her guilt on him.

Then she added like an afterthought, "Race be okay."

"Oh—yeah," Samuel agreed. "He's always better without you."

Talia let a tear escape, and Samuel thought, *That's good. Now you cry.*

She started to leave, but the anger in Samuel was building. He hated this woman. She was always leaving—like a cockroach. Every time you turned on a light, there was Talia, scurrying away.

He knocked the satchel out of her hand. It split open, spilling bricks of cash.

They stood close enough to dance, the cash scattered around their feet. Talia's perfume burned his nose. She was staring down at her wrist, squeezing it.

"Look here," Samuel said. "Goddamn."

"I was gonna leave some for you," Talia said.

"What you done?"

"Some for Race, too. Y'all both got a share. He can stay at the house a few more days. After that, I figure Nana take him."

Then Samuel understood—the whole thing clicked into place. "What's your end of the deal?"

"Just disappear."

"Just disappear," he repeated. "With Race."

She stared at the rug.

Samuel's throat felt dry. "Well, then. You'd better do it."

She started to push past him, leaving the money behind, but he said, "You forgetting something?"

She turned, glanced down at the cash. She looked nervous and hungry, like an animal, waiting for permission to grab some food.

"You got to disappear," Samuel said.

"Yeah. Vincent waiting for me—"

"That's his name. Vincent."

"He's a good man."

"Oh, yeah. All of them, good men. So checking, savings, real estate. You got it all into cash, huh?"

"Yeah."

"Liquidated," Samuel said. "Everything about you gone—squeezed into dollar signs. Like you never existed—not to me, not to your boys, not to nobody. That the way you want it?"

Talia's eyes were Christmas-ornament fragile, the way they always looked when a man started to turn angry on her, got ready to knot his hands into fists. Samuel had seen that look too many times, and it made the bones in his fingers turn to acid.

"I'll leave you the cash," Talia said. "Let me take Race."

"Oh, now you're taking Race."

"He's my son. Just take the money. I owe you."

"You owe me what?"

She wouldn't say.

"You owe me what?"

"Please."

"Look at me. Say my name."

"I got to—it's eight o'clock—Vincent, he—"

"Look at me, girl."

The knife was in his hand now, melting into his palm, becoming an extension of his fingers.

"Samuel," she murmured.

"You're not gone yet," Samuel said. "Not totally. You need to disappear, girl."

Talia stepped back, sensing that moment on the edge of the railing, when you are still sure you can recover, before you tumble and realize the void is void. That you don't get second chances.

Samuel's knife slashed up, splitting leopard-pattern cloth like the leather satchel, spilling everything like the cash, everything she'd kept inside all those years—her softness, her warmth. He and Talia sank to the floor together like lovers, her fingers hooked into the flesh of his shoulders, her magnolia perfume and her sap-crust hair and the little sounds she was making, whimpering as he made heavy, desperate thrusts—so much like making love—a warm wet spray on his face, dampening his shirt, sticking his sleeves to his arms.

He stopped only when the handle of the knife slipped from his grip, the blade biting his index finger, tangling in a fold of what used to be Talia's sweater. Samuel stayed on his knees, straddling her, his breath shuddering. He sucked at the salty cut on his finger joint. He was wet all over, but it was already starting to dry, starting to cool.

After a long time, he stood, flexed his fingers to keep them from sticking together. He stared at a twenty-dollar bill, floating in a wet red halo. Talia's shoe, twisted at an unnatural angle.

He walked to the bathroom, turned on the shower. He stripped and stood under the warm water, naked, until the needles of heat stopped causing any sensation in his back. He watched swirls of pink curly clouds in the water, tracing the outlines of his toes.

Samuel forgot where he was. He forgot who he was. He felt like someone had gone carefully under his skin with a hot filament, separating the skin from the muscle, so that his face floated on top of someone else's—some other person he didn't like, someone who hadn't turned his life around, who carried a knife and spent every dark hour of the evening, for the past nine years, studying a reflection in the blade, seeing Talia's eyes, Talia's mouth, Talia's cheekbones.

He stepped out of the shower, the house too quiet without the noise of water.

What would he do if Race walked in with his girl right now?

He stood naked in the bedroom doorway, looking down at Talia in her sticky nest of money, her eyes soft and dewy and staring at the ceiling, looking straight through to Jesus.

Something glinted at her hip. Samuel knelt beside her, hooked his pinky around a loop of silver chain, and pulled the necklace out of her pocket. He laid it across his palm, read the inscription. His eyes began to burn. He remembered a warm brown throat, slender fingers lifting the chain, rubbing it nervously across full red lips.

Samuel looked at the flattened leather satchel at Talia's feet. He imagined the phone call, the offer to buy the house. He understood the deal better than Talia ever had—the rich man trying to get around him, trying to take control of the situation, get his daughter free of the Montrose family.

Samuel had tried to be restrained. He had tried to forgive. And now the girl's father had broken the rules, stepped over the boundary.

He wanted a final settlement? He wanted to pay the big price?

Samuel could arrange that.

He wiped the necklace clean, then dropped it into the blood next to Talia's left breast.

2

The call haunted Chadwick all week.

Monday, he and his trainee Olsen escorted a student from Cold Springs to Hunter's Playa Verde campus in Belize. The whole flight down, the 737 angling into the sun, making hammered gold out of the Gulf of Mexico, Chadwick thought of Ann Zedman.

"It's Mallory," she had said, her voice so thick with worry that Chadwick hardly recognized it. "I don't know who else to turn to."

Chadwick had wanted to ask a thousand questions, but each was a jump across a nine-year chasm. He knew he couldn't make it.

Tuesday, he and Olsen flew back to the States for an escort job in Los Angeles—a Korean girl named Soo-yun who had neon-blue contact lenses, a severe case of bulimia, and the keys to her father's gun cabinet. She locked herself in the bathroom at her parents' produce market on Western Avenue. Chadwick tried to talk her out, but when that didn't work he called her bluff, busting down the door and pulling the gun out of her hands. The gun turned out to be unloaded. Soo-yun's dazed but relieved parents gave him a basket of papayas to take on the plane. That night, on the red-eye flight east, his clothes smelling of ripe fruit, Chadwick thought of Ann Zedman.

"We don't have to accept the girl," Hunter had told him. "If it bothers you—"

"It doesn't bother me," Chadwick answered. And the two

of them had let the lie hang between them like a piñata, waiting for a stick.

Wednesday, Chadwick and Olsen dropped Soo-yun at the Bowl Ranch facility in Utah, which was equipped to deal with eating disorders, then flew west, arriving in the Bay Area after midnight.

It wasn't the first time Chadwick had been home. He'd made dozens of Bay Area pickups for Asa Hunter since he started escort work in '94, but each time Chadwick returned, he feared the familiarity of the hills, the eucalyptus smell in the air, the shadows in the canyons between downtown skyscrapers and the mist shrouding Sutro Hill. He feared the sadness that seeped into his limbs like anesthesia whenever he saw anything that reminded him of Katherine.

He and Olsen spent Thursday tracking Mallory Zedman, scouting all the locations her friends said she might be, looking for a boy she liked to hang out with, a young dealer by the name of Race Montrose. The boy's last name bothered Chadwick. He was bothered even more when one of Mallory's friends told him Race was a student at Laurel Heights. Ann hadn't mentioned either piece of information on the phone, and Chadwick tried very hard to believe he'd heard the last name wrong, or that it was simply a coincidence.

"You okay?" Olsen asked him.

He realized his hand was clenched in a fist.

"Yeah. Just praying for no more papayas."

"You know this family, right?"

"A long time ago."

"And?"

Chadwick folded his paperwork. He slipped a recent photo of Mallory Zedman out of his briefcase. "Take Shattuck south. There're three or four more places."

They spotted Mallory at a sidewalk café on College and Ocean View, just south of the Berkeley city limits. She was sitting across from a tall African-American boy in a camouflage jacket.

Chadwick parked across the avenue. He and Olsen watched for twenty minutes until the boy in the camouflage got up to take his empty espresso cup into the café, leaving Mallory alone at the table.

Chadwick said, "Now."

Olsen stuck her pepper spray canister into her denim jacket. Her hands were trembling.

"You'll do fine," Chadwick told her.

"This is the one who attacked her mother with a hammer, right?"

Olsen was a big Swedish girl, a former college basketball player with a drill sergeant's haircut and a master's degree in child psych, but at the moment she didn't look much older or tougher than the girl they were picking up.

Chadwick said, "Don't worry."

"Don't worry. Yeah. Okay. Her friend is a dealer. You think he'll be armed?"

"That's why we've waited. We don't want to have to hurt anyone."

"You're kidding."

Chadwick opened his car door, looked at her expectantly.

"You're not kidding," she decided.

They got out of their rental car, stepped into the cross-walk.

The evening fog was snapping down over the East Bay like a Tupperware lid, muting the sound of the BART trains at Rockridge station, the hum of traffic on Highway 24. The air smelled of roasting coffee and fresh-cut freesia.

Chadwick was glad for the commuters on College—the moms with strollers, the black-clad students on their way to the bookstore or the burrito shop. When you're six-foot-eight you welcome all the help you can get covering your approach.

At the café table, Mallory Zedman was studying a chess-board, her middle finger resting on the head of a white pawn.

She was fifteen now. Her blond hair had been dyed a com-bination of orange and black, thin braided strands of it looping above her ears like racing stripes. Her face had filled in, mak-ing her look more like her mother, but she still had the sharp nose and intense eyes of her father—eyes that could go from humor to anger in a millisecond. Her biker jacket was too big for her, her tattered jeans rolled up several times at the ankles. The skin under her eyes was pneumonia blue, and the way she shivered, Chadwick figured she was hungry for her next fix.

He tried to imagine her as a small bundle of energy in an oversized T-shirt, shouting with glee as she flew onto Katherine's bed. But that little girl was gone.

"Mallory," he said.

She looked up.

No recognition—just fear. She glanced inside the café window, saw her friend Race with his back turned, talking to the guy at the espresso machine.

"That's not my name," Mallory said.

Then she looked at him more closely, and her wariness eroded into bewilderment. "Chadwick?"

"Long time, sweetheart. This is my colleague, Ms. Olsen."

"What are you—" The color drained from her face. "Don't hurt Race. He didn't do anything. My father's lying to you."

"Easy, sweetheart."

Mallory started to get up.

Olsen made the mistake of coming around the table, taking Mallory's arm. Mallory yanked away, overturning the plastic chair.

"We're not going to hurt anybody," Chadwick assured her. "Your mother hired us. We're escorting you to a boarding school—Cold Springs Academy."

"A boarding...you're fucking crazy. You're shitting me."

Inside the café, Mallory's friend in camouflage hadn't turned around yet, but it was only a matter of seconds.

"Your mother's made the decision, sweetheart," Chadwick said. "Cold Springs is a good place to turn your life around."

"I don't need turning around."

"You're living on the street with a drug dealer," he reminded her. "Is that where you want to be?"

Mallory glared down at the chessboard—a lopsided game in progress, her white pieces sweeping the board.

"He's not a dealer," she said. "He's my friend."

Chadwick heard no conviction in her voice. She was a little girl, trying to explain a nightmare.

"Let's talk in the car," he said.

"His mother was killed. She fucking died, Chadwick."

"Okay, honey."

"I can't leave him. He's in trouble. It's my fucking fault."

"Okay, honey. Okay."

A few people at the inside tables were now watching them through the glass. Olsen kept a nervous eye on the guy in camouflage.

Chadwick willed the young dealer to keep chatting up the espresso guy. He willed Olsen to stay put—*don't press the girl. Don't ruin it.*

"Mallory," he said, "we can work it all out. I wouldn't be here if I didn't believe this was the best thing for you. Come with us."

Chadwick could feel the situation teetering. Mallory was about to crumble, to let herself be a kid again and cry, probably for the first time since she'd run away from her mother.

Then the camouflage boy, Race, turned and saw them.

Olsen made a small noise in her throat like a bedspring snapping loose.

"Get in the car," she told Mallory. "Now."

She grabbed Mallory's arm, but underestimated the strength of a desperate kid.

With all ninety pounds of her body weight, Mallory shoved Olsen away, into the table, which collapsed under her. Chess pieces clattered down the sidewalk and Mallory took off up Ocean View.

Chadwick saw things unfold in slow motion—Race coming out the door, reaching into his jacket; Olsen scrambling up, not ready to defend herself; Mallory Zedman ducking into the alley behind the café dumpster.

Chadwick cursed, but he had to let Mallory run.

Race came around the corner.

Chadwick registered the boy's features with the instant clarity you get when looking at a person who is trying to kill you—nappy rust hair, jawline like a lightning bolt, Arabic nose and eyes as hard and bright as amber.

Race's face transfixed him, resonating with an old, dark memory even as the gun came out of the boy's coat, the muzzle rising toward his head.

Chadwick only unfroze when Olsen screamed his name.

His right fist caught Race in the nose, his left coming from underneath, hitting the kid's gut hard enough to slam him backwards onto the sidewalk, where he curled into a combat-colored heap, the gun clattering into the street.

Olsen looked at Chadwick, her eyes blank.

"Come on," he told her, then he ran.

Chadwick had lost precious time, but his stride carried him well. He saw Mallory at the opposite end of the alley. She crashed into a sidewalk flower seller, knocked over a bucket of yellow roses, dashed into the street and barely missed getting run over by an SUV.

Chadwick started closing the distance. When he came out of the alley, Mallory was pounding up the steps of the BART station sandwiched between lanes of traffic on the Highway 24 overpass.

An eastbound train was pulling into the platform. Mallory could easily be on board before he got there.

Chadwick ran, kicked up a cloud of pigeons, took the stairs four at a time. He got into the terminal in time to hear the station manager yell, "Hey!" and see Mallory hurdle the turnstile.

Chadwick yelled, "She's mine!" and jumped the gate.

The BART manager yelled, "HEY!" with more outrage.

The escalators to the platform were all moving the wrong way. This was the evening commute—everybody coming back to Rockridge, not going out. Chadwick got up top, did a quick visual sweep. The wind and the cold were intense, the view stunning—hills streaked with fog, lights of houses like fairy glow; the Oakland-Berkeley flatlands spread out to the west, trickling to a point at the red and silver lights of the Bay Bridge; the Bay itself, an expanse of liquid aluminum.

Then he spotted Mallory—thirty yards down the platform,

pounding on the closed doors of the train, trying to get in. She pried at the rubber seal with her fingers. The train slid away, pulling Mallory with it for a few feet before she stumbled backwards, cursing.

Chadwick closed in, pushing against the wave of exit-bound commuters. Mallory stared at him like a cornered possum.

Another train was coming from the hills—its yellow headlights just now visible in the east. Chadwick would have Mallory in hand before it reached the station.

Mallory moved back, to the very end of the platform, then glanced across the rail pit—at the chain link fence that separated the station from the highway.

Don't be crazy, Chadwick thought.

Mallory jumped.

She hit the fence, but failed to hold on to it and tumbled back into the rail pit, her back slamming into the metal, money spilling out of her coat pocket—a brick of cash. Her foot was inches from the electric third rail.

The train was coming fast—only a quarter mile away now. Chadwick could see the lights of the operator's car, hear the electric blare of his horn.

"Give me your hand!" Chadwick yelled.

Mallory wasn't getting up. The look in her eyes told Chadwick her paralysis was more than physical—she had decided she wasn't going anywhere.

Chadwick jumped into the pit, picked her up like a sack of apples and heaved her onto the platform, another stack of currency tumbling out of her coat. Chadwick turned, saw the train bearing down on him—saw the eyes on the driver's face, white with terror—not even considering the possibility of so sudden a stop, and Chadwick pulled himself out of the pit.

The wind of the train ripped at his clothes. A funnel cloud of money spun into the air.

Chadwick lay unhurt, on top of Mallory Zedman, who made a poor pillow.

He sat up as the train's doors sucked open, and found himself face-to-knees with a cluster of passengers who hesitated, stared at the money falling from the sky, then parted around Chadwick as if he were a rock in the current. Nothing can surprise a Bay Area commuter for long.

Chadwick looked toward the station, saw a dour-faced BART policeman running up, the station manager, Olsen behind them, limping.

Underneath him, Mallory Zedman wept, as fives and tens fluttered around them, snagging on the shoes of commuters and the doors of the westbound train as it pulled away.

3

"Mr. Z, the police are here."

John stood on his deck, reading the latest letter.

He closed his eyes, found that the words still burned in front of him, white in the dark. A reverse image, like every other fucking thing in his life.

"Boss?"

Emilio Pérez was squinting at him through the red glare of the sun, the shoulders of his leather jacket glistening like butchered meat.

"Which police?" John asked.

"The one from Oakland again, Damarodas. One of ours, Prost, holding his leash."

John stared down the side of the hill toward the Pacific. There'd been a time when this view meant something to him—the acres of blue and green ice plants, the jagged profile of the Marin headlands, the cold churn of the surf two hundred feet below. He crumpled the paper into a tight ball, tossed it into the sunset.

"What'd it say?" Pérez asked.

John wondered why he'd ever let Pérez into his confidences. How low had he sunk, that he needed consolation from his hired help?

"You want to read it," he said, "go get it."

Pérez's neck muscles tightened. "All I'm saying, you been taking that shit too long. You let me deal with it—"

"Emilio."

Pérez stared down at the ocean, his razor-thin mustache

and goatee too delicate for his face, like lipstick on a bull. "They're in the living room, Boss."

Then he stood aside, his right hand flexing as if closing around a metal pipe.

Sergeant Damarodas of Oakland Homicide was an unimpressive man. He had unruly brown hair and a clearance-rack suit of no particular color and a doughy face that was forgettable except for the eyes. All his charisma had drained into his eyes, which were atmospheric blue and dangerously intelligent.

He stood by the white linen sofa, drinking coffee Pérez must've offered him, examining the glass-framed quilt that hung next to the fireplace. The Marin County detective Prost hovered behind him, watching Damarodas' hands as if to make sure he didn't steal anything.

John tried to remember if he'd met Prost before. John gave generously to the department's retirement fund. He remembered them at Christmas, played golf with the sheriff. After a while, all the deputies had become facets of the same entity to him—a huge, friendly guard dog nuzzling his hand.

"I'm sorry, Mr. Z," Prost said. "I tried telling the sergeant—"

"Quite all right, Detective. Sergeant Damarodas, tell me some good news. You've arrested the Montrose boy."

Damarodas gestured toward the quilt on the wall. "Local artist, sir?"

"My daughter's kindergarten class."

Damarodas' eyes sparkled. "That's a relief. Here I was thinking, this looks like it was done by a six-year-old. And it was. So much of the art these days, you can't tell."

Damarodas smiled into the silence he'd created.

"Sergeant," John said, "was there something you wanted to discuss?"

Damarodas set down his coffee cup, turned the handle so it pointed toward John. "Actually, sir, I wanted to ask you a real estate question."

"You're in the high-end market for a home, Sergeant?"

"No, sir. We found out where the money came from."

"The money."

"In Talia Montrose's account." Damarodas raised his eyebrows. "I'm sorry to bother you with all these details. You do remember Talia Montrose. She's the woman who was knifed to death."

"Yes, Sergeant," John said. "I remember."

"Maybe I mentioned somebody opened a new checking account for her—deposited two hundred and thirty grand in it. We think she probably had the rest with her, in cash, when she was murdered."

"The rest."

"Mrs. Montrose acquired the money by selling her house. Title was processed this week. Some development corporation bought the place—paper corporation, we're still trying to find the real owners. They immediately sold it at a loss to a Realtor in Berkeley. Would you say the Montrose house was worth a quarter of a million?"

"I'd have to see the house."

"Never picked your daughter up there? Never visited?"

"No."

"Your—uh—driver, Mr. Pérez, ever pick her up there?"

"No."

"Your daughter was friends with her son for how long—about six, seven years?"

"Sergeant," Prost intervened. "Mr. Zedman said no. Twice."

"My apologies," Damarodas said. "Mr. Zedman, one Realtor I spoke to told me the Montrose place wouldn't sell for more than a hundred grand, tops."

"Why are you telling me this, Sergeant?"

"Thought you could help me understand how Mrs. Montrose got such a good deal."

"Ask her family."

A tick started in the corner of Damarodas' eye. "Love to. You wouldn't happen to know where they are?"

"No idea."

"Funny. I get that answer a lot. Neighbors can't even tell

me how many kids she had. Talia Montrose's mother—you ever had the pleasure?"

"No."

"She supposedly took care of the grandkids from time to time—turns out she's an unmedicated schizophrenic. Morning I talked to her she was busy swatting pink cockroaches out of her dress, couldn't really answer my questions. That leaves us with Race, who hasn't been seen since the murder. A boyfriend, Vincent, seems to have left town. And of course, your daughter."

"My daughter has nothing to do with this."

"Probably not. Probably we could clear this up if we could ask her a few questions, seeing as Race was her best friend..."

"Classmates." John said the word with distaste. "Not best friends."

"Okay," Damarodas agreed. "Classmates who were staying together for several nights. Her personal effects were found at the crime scene. Her voice was on the 911 tape reporting the murder. She and Race disappeared before the patrol officers arrived—"

"Sergeant," Detective Prost broke in again.

Damarodas paused from ticking off the items on his fingers, his index finger hooked on his pinky. "You haven't heard from your daughter, Mr. Zedman?"

John hated that his lips were quivering. He hated that this insignificant man could make him nervous. "I told you, Sergeant. Mallory only comes here every other weekend. Her mother has full custody."

Damarodas nodded, looking disappointed. "My mistake, then. I came out here thinking perhaps you'd heard from Mallory today. I thought she would be here."

"And why would you think that?"

"We had a lead on your daughter," Damarodas said. "A possible sighting."

"A sighting."

"We're still piecing things together. This just happened about an hour ago."

John resisted the urge to ask. Damarodas wanted him to ask—wanted that little bit of power—but John wasn't going to give him the satisfaction.

"The BART police," Damarodas said at last. "A supervisor I know, he called me, reported a girl matching your daughter's description at Rockridge station. Apparently she made an impression with the officer on duty. Jumped a turnstile, spilled cash all over the platform, threw herself into the rail pit. She was pulled out by a large man—white guy, like six-six, six-seven, blond buzz cut, beige overcoat. Said he was picking the girl up for her parents, had paperwork to prove it. They let him go. Supervisor heard about it, made the connection, called me. I figured the girl would be back here by now."

Zedman's throat was closing up. He couldn't breathe. Damarodas' eyes were like the air at thirty thousand feet—clear and thin and inhospitably bright. He wanted to put them out with a poker.

"Sir?" Damarodas said. "You know this guy?"

"I hired no one to pick up my daughter."

"Your ex-wife, then?"

John had a sudden, vivid memory of holding Mallory the day she was born, stroking his thumb over the warm velvet of her forehead, the blond fuzz of her scalp, understanding what it was like to love somebody so much you would take a bullet for her.

He remembered the night Katherine had died—rushing back to the Mission, scooping up Mallory and holding her in that big black leather chair while she trembled, so small and cold, John knowing even then that something inside her had broken. In the next room, Chadwick had been sobbing, his fingers curled in the fabric of Katherine's empty bed, and John had vowed—*Nothing else will ever happen to my girl. I will never again let Mallory out of my sight.*

He swallowed his bitterness, the coppery taste of failure. He thought about the demands in the latest letter. He thought about Chadwick, coming back into his life, taking his daughter.

"I know the man you're describing, Sergeant. My ex-wife must've hired him."

John told him about Chadwick, what he knew about Chadwick's job in Texas, which wasn't much—bits and pieces of gossip from Norma, rumors of his pathetic self-imposed exile that they shook their heads over when they had lunch in the city.

He should've seen this coming—Ann's revenge for him challenging the custody arrangement again. While he was busy trying to save their daughter, all Ann could think about was hurting him.

"Chadwick." Damarodas wrote the name in his notepad, stared down at it. "Well, damn."

"Sergeant?"

Damarodas closed his notepad. "Unfortunate timing, your wife sending your daughter out of state. You knew nothing about this?"

"That's another question Mr. Zedman has already answered," Detective Prost said. "I think it's time we left."

Damarodas picked up his coffee, took a sip, then set it carefully back on the table. "I appreciate your openness, sir. I'll be in touch."

The two cops walked through the entry hall, Damarodas scanning the art prints with a look of mild consternation, as if wondering which of them were done by professional artists, which by six-year-olds. John realized the sergeant's unimpressive demeanor was a weapon—he came into your house and infected it, made everything there seem as meaningless as his smile or the color of his cheap suit.

Damarodas gave him one more appraising look from the porch, then tapped his fingers against the golden oak door frame, as if wondering if the wood were real.

It wasn't the first time Pérez had watched his boss go crazy.

Zedman cursed the hills. He shattered the coffee cup the policeman had been drinking from. He threw a $300 piece of pottery at his quilt and cracked the glass.

Then he started weeping. He touched the broken glass,

like he wanted to caress the quilt panels—the fading stick figures, the peeling scraps of felt.

Pérez didn't know what to do for him.

He imagined writing to his estranged wife back home in Monterrey—*Dear Rosa, These americanos are locos.* He never actually wrote her, but thinking about it made him feel better.

He had been with Mr. Zedman for five years, since just before the Boss got divorced. The pay was good, the work easy. He'd never fired his gun, never protected Mr. Z from anything worse than panhandlers.

Then a month ago, out of the blue, Mr. Z told him about the letters.

He wouldn't say how long they'd been coming, or what the demands were, or what leverage the blackmailer had, but Pérez understood it had been going on a long time, it was ugly enough to ruin Mr. Z, and Mr. Z, for some reason, was convinced the Montroses were behind it.

That was why no matter how much he hated that kid Race, or how close Race got to Mallory, Mr. Z wouldn't let Pérez touch him. The Boss put up with them messing around together. He endured the bad stories Ms. Reyes would bring him from his ex-wife's school. And the more Mallory flaunted her punk boyfriend in her father's face, the more Mr. Z drank, yelled at Pérez, bit his nails and slammed things around in the middle of the night. Finally, after Mallory's visit three weeks ago, Mr. Z had found a hypodermic needle in her bedroom. That sent him ape-shit over-the-top crazy. He sat down with Pérez and explained a game plan—not the one Pérez wanted, the simple, violent kind, but a plan to end the blackmail "peacefully, to everybody's satisfaction, once and for all."

The whole idea had pained Pérez. A quarter of a million dollars. For what—silence? Peace of mind?

A bullet cost seventy-five cents.

He remembered Talia Montrose in the Starbucks—that piece-of-shit whore, could barely keep from drooling at the satchel full of money. Pérez had told the Boss it was a bad idea. You didn't make people like Talia go away with money.

Pérez hadn't been convinced she was even the blackmailer. She didn't have the look.

And now—Mr. Z had fucked up. He'd paid off the wrong person. Another letter had come, and just from Mr. Z's attitude, Pérez could tell the stakes had shot up. The police were asking about Talia Montrose's murder. Mallory had gotten herself abducted. Shit, if John Zedman was a number, he'd be a big red thirteen.

But maybe it was all a blessing in disguise. Maybe the Boss would finally get smart.

Pérez came up behind Mr. Z, waited for him to cry himself out. Mr. Z had cut his finger on the broken glass of the quilt frame, and was pressing it into the tail of his dress shirt.

"Let me help, Boss," Pérez said.

Mr. Z stared at him, his eyes glassy. "My daughter's been taken away, Emilio. Do you know what that means? Do you know what the police will think?"

"We'll get her back," Pérez said.

"It wasn't supposed to get out of hand. I just want my daughter safe, Emilio. That's all I've ever wanted."

"I know that. So what are you paying me for—driving?"

The Boss wiped his face. He took a long few minutes putting himself back together. "What do you suggest?"

Pérez watched a thin line of Mr. Z's blood trickling down the glass, streaking the face of a kindergarten stick figure.

He felt like that quilt—something useful stuck in a display case, gathering dust. What was a little blood if it meant breaking the glass once and for all?

"For starters," Pérez said. "Who the fuck is Chadwick?"

4

"Where are you going?" Olsen asked. "The airport was that way."

She leaned forward from the back seat, her fingers gripping the top of the headrest like she wanted to rip a chunk out of it.

Chadwick took the Ninth Street exit, drove west into downtown. "I need to talk to her mom."

"Our flight."

"We have time."

"This is against policy, isn't it? You told me that, didn't you?"

Chadwick zigzagged across the intersection at Market. The streets glowed with fog and neon, the crosswalks swarming with Friday night crowds—commuters and prostitutes, transients and tourists, like schools of hungry fish mixing together.

"Hey!" Mallory shouted, pounding on the window, kicking the back of Chadwick's seat with her bound feet. "Hey, *hey!*"

Chadwick couldn't see what she was doing—probably showing off her handcuffs to somebody on the street. Someone she recognized. Or a policeman. There were few escape tactics Chadwick hadn't seen in his years as an escort.

Olsen was right. He shouldn't be doing this. They had all the papers signed. The plane left in two hours. There was no reason to torture himself, or Mallory, by visiting the school, seeing Ann in person. The whole idea of escorting was to remove the child from her environment as quickly and cleanly as possible. No detours. No stops on Memory Lane.

But Race Montrose's face stayed with him—that rust-colored hair, the lightning bolt jaw, the amber eyes. The more he envisioned that face, the more he wanted to punch it again.

He took Divisadero north, then California west, into the quieter streets of Pacific Heights. The night closed around them, making a deep purple aurora along the tops of the eucalyptus trees. Chadwick turned on Walnut and pulled in front of Laurel Heights School.

He had expected the place to look different, thanks to Ann's construction plans, but the outside was unchanged—redwood walls covered in ivy, peeling green trim, mossy stone chimney. From the roof of the school hung a long yellow banner—OUR CHILDREN'S DREAMS——MAKE THEM HAPPEN! A thermometer showed $30 million as the top temperature, the mercury painted red up to $27 million. Apparently, fund-raising had gone a little slower than expected.

Chadwick cut the engine. He turned to Mallory. "Tell me about Race."

"Screw yourself," Mallory said, but her heart wasn't in it. She had worn herself out screaming and kicking all the way across the Bay Bridge.

"He was your classmate," Chadwick told her. "Your mother allowed him to go here."

"You sound like my fucking father. Race made better grades than I did, Chadwick. Get over it."

"You understand why I'm asking?"

Braids of her black-dyed hair had fallen in her face, so she seemed to glare at him through a cage of licorice. "Stop messing with me, okay? I know why you're here. This is some kind of chickenshit revenge for Katherine."

"I'm here to help you."

"Bullshit."

Chadwick felt Olsen's eyes on him.

He stared up at the schoolhouse, butcher paper paintings hung along the fence to dry—a chain of smiling people in every skin color, including purple and green. "Mallory, why'd you run away?"

"My mom's a bitch. She found a gun in Race's locker."

"Same gun he pointed at me today?"

"Fuck, no. They confiscated the one in his locker. Today was a different gun."

"I see," Chadwick said. "Another from his collection."

Mallory shrugged, like that should be obvious. "My mom expelled him. Told me I couldn't see him anymore."

"And you thought that was what—too harsh?"

"She had no right to look in his locker in the first place, or punish him, or anything. Race needs a gun."

"Why?"

She was shivering now. Heroin withdrawal pains, probably getting worse.

"Look, just let me go in and talk to her, okay?" She moderated her tone—going for the calm approach. Adults are idiots—speak to them softly. "I guess I got a little crazy on her. I'll apologize."

"You attacked her with a hammer. You ran away to Race's house."

"I didn't hurt anybody, okay? Neither did Race. I'm not going to a school for mental cases."

"What happened to Race's mom?"

Her eyes slid away from his. "We— We didn't do shit. We were out all night, came back in the morning, and we just opened the door . . . And . . ."

Her voice broke. She brought her palms up into the light, as if looking for a reminder she might've written on her skin.

"Don't protect him," Chadwick said. "Race is a drug dealer. His whole family is toxic."

"He's not a goddamn dealer."

Chadwick fanned the stack of money that had spilled from Mallory's coat pocket—$630 in crisp new bills. "Where'd you get the cash, Mallory?"

She twisted her wrists against the plastic cuffs. "Just keep it. All right, Chadwick? Keep it and let me go. Nobody has to know."

He looked at Olsen. With her blond buzz cut and her denim, the tight set of her mouth, she could've passed for Mallory's peer. But there was fear in her eyes—a bright emptiness that had blossomed the moment Race Montrose pointed his gun at Chadwick's chest.

"I'll make this brief," he promised.

"Hey," she murmured. "Wait—"

He got out of the car, Olsen leaning across the roof, protesting. "Chadwick, what the hell . . ."

"Just a few minutes."

"Mallory . . ."

"She'll be all right."

"So what am I supposed to do?"

Chadwick heard the edge of panic in her voice. He wanted to reassure her. He wanted to warn her that Mallory could smell her nervousness like a piranha smells blood. But he couldn't say any of that—not with Mallory there.

"She's cuffed," he said. "Just lock the doors, wait for me."

"Who the hell is Katherine?"

He left her staring over the top of the car, her fingers splayed across the black metal, grasping at the reflection of the street lamp.

On the playground, half a dozen kids were still waiting for their parents to pick them up. Two little girls spun on the tire swing. A trio of middle school boys played basketball; the yellow floodlight above them swirled with moths. A sleepy-looking after-school attendant sat on a throne of milk crates, reading a college textbook. She didn't look up as Chadwick walked in.

Once inside, he was immediately disoriented. The doors weren't where they were supposed to be. The walls were too white, the linoleum floors too shiny. Even the smell was different. The old odors—decades of peanut butter apples, dried Play-Doh, burnt popcorn and peeled crayons—had been replaced by the industrial lemon scent of an office building.

The first phase of Ann's expansion plan, Chadwick remembered—to remodel the interior of the existing building to maximize space.

The basketball dribbled outside.

In a way, Chadwick was relieved to look around and see almost nothing he remembered. On the other hand, the changes in the school seemed uncomfortably like his own changes—shuffling interior walls, laying down new carpet to conceal old floors, making everything look as different as possible. Yet the underlying structure was the same. You couldn't change the size and shape of the foundation.

He was still trying to get his bearings when a young man came down the stairwell. He was in his mid-twenties, short blond hair, navy business suit. A kindergarten parent, Chadwick assumed.

"Mr. Chadwick?"

It took a moment for his features to resolve themselves in Chadwick's mind—for Chadwick to see the boy he had been, an awkward zit-faced kid, waving a red handkerchief to spot the high bidders.

"David Kraft?"

David grinned. "This is awesome. What are you doing here?"

Chadwick shook his hand, tried not to look like a man on his way to the rack. "Don't tell me you have a child . . ."

"God, no. I mean, no, sir. Ann—Mrs. Zedman—hired me to help in the office. I'm assisting with the capital campaign drive."

"You're out of college."

"Yes, sir. Working here part-time. Working on my MBA."

Chadwick felt like he had needles in his eyes. Of course David was out of college. He would be twenty-four now. An adult. He had been in Katherine's class.

He tried to swallow the dryness out of his throat. "Congratulations, David. That's wonderful."

David blushed, just as he had in eighth grade, trying to recite the Declaration of Independence in front of the class. And in high school, when he'd taken the BART train all the way from his house in Berkeley and shown up at Chadwick's doorstep, asking to see Katherine—advising Chadwick in a heartbreakingly awkward, gallantly honest way that he was here to—you know, *see* her. Not just like a friend, anymore. Was that okay with him?

David looked down, pinching at his silk tie. "Listen, Mr. Chadwick, I never got to tell you . . . I mean, after the funeral . . . I wanted to write, or something."

"It's all right, David."

"No, I mean . . . You were the best teacher I ever had. This place wasn't the same after you left. I just wanted to tell you that."

Chadwick felt as if he were standing in the loop of a snare. If David said one more thing, if he spoke Katherine's name . . .

"Thanks, David," he managed. "Listen, I really should get upstairs."

"Oh. Right." David pointed behind him. "You know Ann is meeting—um—about the campaign, right? With Ms. Reyes?"

"I'll try not to keep them long," Chadwick replied. "Good to see you again, David."

He left David Kraft's waning smile—the look of a pupil who'd just gotten a B+ on a project he'd put his heart into.

Upstairs, Chadwick's classroom had vanished, the space it had occupied filled with a computer lab and a faculty lounge. The doorway, where he and John had stood talking at the auction so long ago, was a blank wall.

The old student cubbies, which Katherine had so despised, had been replaced with a row of red metal lockers. Chadwick wondered which was Race Montrose's. He tried to imagine Ann opening that locker, finding a gun—at Laurel Heights, where the kids weren't even allowed to play with water pistols. The kindergarteners downstairs, singing "Itsy Bitsy Spider." The rainbow parachute being spread on the playground for PE.

Ann's office was right where it had been, still dominated by a giant window, the same Japanese curtain hanging over the doorway. Ann's byword: Openness. No closed door between her and her school.

She was standing behind her desk, Norma leaning across

it, showing her something on a laptop screen. Baguette sandwiches on wax paper and bottles of water were spread out between them.

Chadwick parted the curtain.

Norma sensed his presence first. She turned, and her face shifted through several phases, like a projector seeking the correct slide.

She touched Ann on the arm. "You've got a visitor..."

If anything, Ann seemed younger since Chadwick last saw her—thinner, her caramel hair longer, her eyes with a new, hungrier light. Chadwick's memories had been of a plump gentle girl who had comforted him when he most needed it in high school, counseled him and mentored him since they were teens together, but this Ann looked as if she'd been pared down to just the essentials. She reminded Chadwick, disconcertingly, of the kids who had been through Cold Springs.

"Where's Mallory?" she asked, without greeting him.

He glanced at Norma.

"It's all right," Ann told him. "She knows."

"Doesn't mean I approve," Norma inserted. "Did you find her?"

"She's in the car," Chadwick said.

"Safe?" Ann asked.

"Yes."

"Alone?" Norma asked.

"My partner is with her. Mallory got confrontational. We had to handcuff her."

Ann pressed her fingertips to the desk, as if gathering strength from the wood. "Chadwick, thank you. I knew you'd find her."

"Handcuffs," Norma said. "He puts your daughter in handcuffs, and you're thanking him."

Norma wore a black dress, as if she'd never changed from the funeral. She looked cold, beautiful in a stark way, like a black and white picture of herself. Friends and former colleagues had kept Chadwick updated about her new life, even when he didn't want to be. He knew about her degree in accounting, the connections John Zedman had made for her, the multimillion-dollar funds she now managed. He knew she'd taken John's place as development director for the school after the Zedmans' divorce, and kept up her friendship with both of them.

Chadwick tried to believe that he'd ever touched this woman, ever been close to her, raised a child, shared a life. The whole idea now seemed alien. A bomb had been dropped on that existence—a holocaust of grief so powerful that it sucked all the air out of the old house on Mission—love, anger, memories—creating a vacuum where nothing could live, even hate, without becoming irradiated.

"Norma," Ann said softly. "Let's finish business later."

"She has no money." Norma's eyes blazed at him. "I want you to know that, Chadwick. She's been to court three times to keep custody of Mallory. She's mortgaged her house."

"Norma—" Ann tried.

"The woman is busting her ass raising thirty million dollars for her school, trying to help kids. Meanwhile, she's scraping to pay her PG&E bill. Now you've sold her on this fucking wilderness school, and she has no money to pay for it. I hope that makes you feel good."

"Ann called me," Chadwick said.

Norma slapped the laptop closed. "I tried to talk her out of it. I tried to convince her what I knew a long time ago, Chadwick—the only good thing you ever did was leave."

"I'm here to help Mallory," he said. "Not argue with you."

She slashed out, raking her fingernails across his face. *"Cabrón."*

Ann tried to take her arm, but Norma jerked away, knocking over a bottle of water.

"You don't help children, Chadwick," she said. "You steal them. You're a goddamn child-stealer."

She pushed past him on her way out. If there'd been an office door, Chadwick was sure she would've slammed it.

Chadwick felt the warmth of blood making its way along his jawline. He took a tissue out of his pocket, dabbed it against his cheek.

"I'm sorry," Ann said. "I didn't know you were coming."

Chadwick's legs were shaking. All week long, chasing children, talking them out of suicide, dragging them screaming through airports—that he could handle. But a few minutes with Norma, and he was a basket case.

His eyes strayed to the sleeping bag rolled up in the corner, the carryall tucked between the wall and the fax machine. "You camping out here?"

He meant the comment to express concern.

But when Ann looked at him, an uninvited memory flashed between them—an August night a decade ago, at Stinson Beach, two sleeping bags spread out on the sand dunes. They had stayed up all night at the faculty retreat, watching the Big Dipper rise over the Pacific. They had talked of a life that might've happened, had they been wiser when they were younger—a life that was impossible now that they both had families. And yet they'd pretended otherwise, that night.

"I'm not living on the street, yet," Ann said, "if that's what you mean. I stay here overnight sometimes to get my work done."

"Cold Springs costs two thousand a month."

"I know that."

"The average stay is one year."

"Why are you discouraging me?" Her voice was getting smaller. "Do you have any idea how hard it was for me to call you—to admit I need help with my own daughter?"

"I think I might have some insight."

Her ears tinged with red. "No, Chadwick. No. I *hate* what you do for a living. I *hate* Asa Hunter's approach. It goes against everything I stand for as an educator. As a mother, though..."

She spread her hands, helplessly.

Out the open window, night fog was swirling in from the Pacific, tufts of white drifting like ghosts through the dark eucalyptus branches. Downstairs, a parent called good night to the attendant, then footsteps clopped down the front stairs, the age-old conversation between mother and son fading into the evening quiet of Walnut Street: "What did you do today?"——"Nothing."—— "Nothing? I can't believe you did nothing."

Chadwick checked the tissue against his cheek. The blood had made a row of fuzzy red dots on the paper, like Orion's belt. "Why Cold Springs, Ann? Why now?"

"I told you—"

"The truth, this time. The friend Mallory was staying with—his name is Race Montrose."

"Yes."

"You admitted him as a student here."

"What would you have me do—punish him for his older brother?"

Chadwick had been trying to convince himself there was no connection. The fact that there was, and Ann obviously knew about it, sparked a string of firecrackers in his stomach.

"Samuel Montrose was Katherine's dealer," he said tightly. "He supplied the drugs that killed her. Your own daughter identified the house they went to that night."

"Yes. And the spring after you left, Mrs. Montrose applied for Race to come here. It was no accident. She knew about the school because of Katherine. She desperately wanted her youngest son to have a good education."

All Chadwick could do was stare at her—waiting for something. An apology? An explanation? Something.

Ann came around the desk. She sat on the edge, in front of him. Her hair, he saw, was frosted with the slightest tinge of gray. A fine web of wrinkles spread from the corners of her eyes. She smelled like a holiday kitchen—cider and nutmeg.

"Would you have advised me to turn him away?" she asked. "Race has three older brothers, all criminals. Samuel left town years ago. The other two—nineteen-year-old twins—they're in jail for a convenience store robbery. He has a sixteen-year-old sister who's pregnant and living in L.A. with a boyfriend. He has a schizophrenic grandmother, and a mom who's attracted to abusive men. Why do you think Talia Montrose brought her youngest son to me, Chadwick?"

"Spite."

"You know it wasn't. She wanted the best for her son. She

wanted one of her children, her baby, to escape. She knew he was special, and she didn't know where else to go. And he is brilliant, Chadwick. I could tell he was gifted even in first grade. Was I going to turn him away because someone in his family had done something evil? Look into that seven-year-old's eyes and say, 'I'm sorry, you can't come here. I have to assume you're going to grow up to be a bad person'?"

"You're rationalizing."

"Am I?"

"Because now you're paying the price. Race became best friends with your daughter. You wish it had never happened."

"You're talking like John. That's why he wants custody so badly. He'll tell you Mallory is an innocent victim and I'm not worthy to be her mother, because I didn't protect her from bad influences. But you know better than that, Chadwick. Mallory is who she is. No one corrupted her. No one *made* her a troubled child. Not Race. Not Katherine." Ann's eyes were the color of a waterfall. "Not even you and me."

Chadwick tried hard to be angry with her. He resented that she knew his guilt so well. He resented that she would even consider giving Race Montrose a chance.

But that was Ann—what he'd always loved and always feared about her. Her infinite, infuriating capacity for faith. She had believed in Chadwick in high school—urged him to go ahead into the Air Force for the education benefits, told him not to settle for a blue-collar job. She had sold him on the dream that someday, they would be teachers together, help kids more than they had been helped. She had believed in her vision of rebuilding Laurel Heights, ignoring the indisputable reality that $30 million was too big a goal for such a small school. And she had forgiven Chadwick after Katherine's death, immediately and unconditionally. She had insisted he wasn't to blame, insisted they could still be together. That had been the real reason Chadwick left Laurel Heights—not Norma's condemnation, not even the memories of Katherine or the pain of watching her class progress without her. Chadwick couldn't bear to be forgiven. He couldn't allow himself to be near Ann, for fear he would begin to believe her.

His trip tonight across the Bay Bridge had been so much like that other trip long ago, from the Oakland Police Department, when Katherine confided what she'd been doing at the party, how far she would go for Samuel Montrose's drugs.

After her death, the police never found Samuel to question, never looked that hard, never dispensed any kind of justice. Katherine had overdosed on almost pure heroin, but it was treated as a suicide. If Chadwick wanted to blame others, the cops' eyes said, then perhaps he should look in a mirror.

And now, Ann dared to believe in Samuel's brother, even at the risk of her daughter. How could Chadwick accept that? If he were John, wouldn't he be demanding full custody of his daughter, too?

"Race brought a gun to school," he said.

Ann nodded. "Another student tipped me off. The gun was . . . I forget what the policeman said. A .38."

"Why?"

"Did Race bring it? He denied it was his, wouldn't give me any explanation. I can't imagine he meant to use it, but of course I had to expel him. You can imagine the panic it caused with the parents."

"You still don't regret taking him."

"Honestly, Chadwick? Of course I have moments when I regret taking him. But that's not fair to Race. Until the gun incident, two weeks ago, Mallory was the one who usually got them in trouble."

"He was supplying Mallory with heroin."

"Race is no dealer."

"Ann, he was armed again tonight. He almost killed me."

"No. Race was a good student—angry, always struggling to fit in, but not a bad kid. When he was expelled—he took it calmly. He just left. Mallory broke everything in our house. She ran away to be with him."

"And a few days later, Mrs. Montrose was murdered."

"Goddamn you, Chadwick." She hit his chest, but she wasn't Norma. She had no experience, no talent for hurting. Chadwick clasped his hand around hers.

"The police want to talk to Mallory," he guessed. "That's

why you called. You need to get Mallory away from the police."

"Chadwick, she's only fifteen. She's gone through so much already. You of all people—you have to understand."

"You weren't honest with me."

"I didn't know where else to turn."

"Do you think she saw the murder?"

"No. No, of course not."

"But the police do?"

"I didn't say that."

"You're scared."

"Well, no shit—"

"Your hand is trembling."

She looked up at him, those gray-blue eyes pressing on his heart with the weight of Niagara.

Then she wrapped her fingers around the back of his neck, and pulled him into a kiss—her lips unexpectedly bitter, like nutmeg. "Take my daughter away, Chadwick. Keep Mallory safe. You owe us that."

"The police—"

"Trust your heart for once, you big idiot. What is the right thing to do for Mallory?"

She traced his jawline, stood on tiptoe to kiss the scratches Norma had put on his cheek. "I promised myself our senior year that I would never say I loved you. I would never sink a good friendship. I am such a damned fool."

Chadwick had an unwelcome image of Mallory in the BART rail pit, her eyes those of the little girl, curled in the black leather chair on Mission Street.

Then he glanced into the locker area and saw someone there—David Kraft, watching them, just long enough to register what he was seeing. Then he was gone, back down the stairs.

Chadwick pulled away from Ann. "I should go."

"Norma knows about the affair," she told him. "In case you were wondering. She knows we were planning to break the news that night. After I told her, she didn't speak to me for almost two years. Now—it's funny. Over time, you realize how hard it is to really get someone out of your life."

"I'll call you from Texas," Chadwick muttered. "Dr. Hunter will send you a report."

"Norma doesn't blame us anymore for what happened to Katherine, Chadwick. She's gotten over that. Why can't you?"

Chadwick closed the Japanese curtain behind him and walked downstairs. David Kraft and the after-school attendant fell silent as he passed, but neither acknowledged him.

On the tire swing, the last two children were chanting a jump rope rhyme—*Cinderella, dressed in yellow*—spinning in a circle of light and moths as they waited to see if their parents had truly forgotten them.

5

Until Race tried stealing his money, Samuel was having a good week.

The children at work would run up to him when he came in the gate, their basketballs scattering behind them. They would herd him toward the bench, plead for a story, push each other aside for the chance to climb on his knee—sometimes two on each leg, until he told them they were going to squash him like a jelly sandwich, and they would giggle. They'd ask for Anansi, or Brer Rabbit, or Pandora's Box. He would always oblige. Whatever they wanted.

After all, this was Samuel's dream. He'd gone to college so he could work with kids. Make a difference. And now here he was, doing what he'd always wanted.

Only sometimes the mask would slip a little. He'd be preparing his lunch in the staff lounge, watching the microwave, or chopping carrots—and he would find himself staring at his own hands, but they were not his hands. They were Talia's—long slender fingers, scarlet polish, gold rings.

He knew that was crazy. He would stare at the blade of the kitchen knife, and watch it cut through the orange flesh of the carrot, making little yellow bull's-eye targets, and he would remember the way Talia chopped vegetables for stew. *You hold the blade like this, okay, honey? Cut away from your body.*

He would imagine Ali, the worst boyfriend, between Talia's legs at night, banging the headboard and calling on the Lord as he climaxed, her children giggling in the next room and trying to keep quiet, because they knew the man had fists—Ali could peel the metalwork off the side of their house, he could damn well peel their heads off.

Except in the vision, Samuel saw himself under that big man—sour breath against his cheek, his belly crushed under Ali's weight, a hipbone grinding into his thigh. And Samuel would have to put down the knife, very carefully, and talk himself back to reality, thinking, *Come on, now. Samuel has made good out of his life. He has survived. Stop it.*

Talia was dead. He was alive.

It didn't matter if he had trouble keeping that straight, now and then, or if he sometimes got distracted when the kids asked him questions, or if he let the smile slip a few too many times. He would be moving on soon enough.

The moment he dropped the last letter in the mailbox, he knew he had done the right thing. He'd settled for too little too long, trying to keep things stable for Race's sake. But the prize had always been there, ripening, waiting to be taken. He'd thought about it for years. And now that Laurel Heights was ruined for Race, anyway—fuck it.

He and Race would scrape San Francisco off the bottom of their shoes like dog crap. They would move to a new country, make a new start. Mexico. El Salvador. Some place hot enough to bake the bad thoughts out of Samuel's head.

All Samuel needed was to find the girl—that was the key. The old leverage wasn't enough anymore. Zedman had made that clear when he tried to buy off Talia. But the girl—Zedman wanted the girl safe. And Samuel could control that variable. Yes, he could.

He took off from school early Friday evening, tired but content, got in his old battered Civic and drove back to Berkeley, to his condominium in the hills.

The place was much too expensive—one of a cluster of brown and blue townhouses just above the Caldecott Tunnel, in an area still bald of trees from the Oakland Hills fire. Samuel had looked up at these hills all his life. He had watched them burn in '91—the horizon rimmed with fire, ash snowing down even as far as the metal Santa Claus on his roof in West Oakland, the smell of burning wood and plaster permeating the city for days. Then he had watched the rebuilding—the gaudy new homes bought with insurance money, the gleaming new apartments on the blackened hillsides. He had loved these condos from the time they were wooden frames, back in the days when he had been rebuilding, too, re-creating himself from scratch. He had fantasized about living here, far above everyone else—a castle in the ashes.

His neighbors were all young and rich. They drove Land Rover SUVs, kept shih tzus, wore North Face hiking clothes but never went hiking. Every morning they said hello to Samuel with polite, nervous smiles, wondering how the hell he had managed to buy his way into their company.

Soon, he could tell them all to fuck off. On his way out of town maybe he'd swipe one of their nasty-faced little dogs, take it to West Oakland, find a pit bull for it to play with. Mail what was left back to the owner. Sign it like he'd signed the letters to Zedman for the last nine years. *Love, Samuel.*

He was thinking about that possibility, smiling to himself, when he pulled into his carport space and saw the mud-splattered mountain bike next to his back gate.

He felt in his pocket, fingering the new blade he'd bought to replace the one that was now at the bottom of the Lafayette Reservoir.

He entered the backyard, found the sliding glass door open. Inside, the television was playing, sitcom angst mixing with the AM talk show from the bathroom radio, the top 40 station on the bedroom boom box—all the voices Samuel left on, twenty-four hours a day, to drown the noise in his head.

The bedroom windows were open, looking out on the view that was half Samuel's rent price—Highway 24 directly below, a ribbon of lights slicing its way through the hills, down into the Berkeley flats, toward the blanket of fog that covered the Bay.

Race was kneeling by the bed, his back to the door. He was going through Talia's leather satchel, pulling out money, a gun next to him on the sheets.

"You need allowance?" Samuel asked.

Race lurched around, his eyes swimming. His fingers curled around the gun.

Samuel wasn't worried about that. The gun wasn't any different than the pillow Race used to carry around when he was two, or the toy car he'd had when he was five—just something to hold tight.

"What happened to your nose?" Samuel asked. It looked like somebody had grafted his left nostril with a strawberry, then smashed it.

"I need money," Race said.

"You can try asking. I never said no to you, have I?"

Race pressed his lips together, trying to keep from sobbing. He rubbed his nose with the back of his wrist.

"Momma's dead," he said, like he hadn't already known that for a week.

"Yeah," Samuel agreed. "And you know damn well who's going to take the blame, you don't get your girlfriend over here, let us talk things out."

"I need to get to—Texas, somewhere. I need a plane ticket. Mallory—"

"What you talking about? Where is she?"

"Gone."

"What you mean, gone?"

Race told him. He described the man at the café who'd busted his nose, Mallory running off. Then afterward, watching from a distance, how he'd seen Mallory in handcuffs, forced into the man's car, a couple of BART cops watching. Race knew the man—the one who used to work at Laurel Heights, who now worked at a school for fucked-up kids in Texas.

But Race didn't have to tell Samuel that.

Samuel knew the man, too. And he knew what this meant for his plans, losing hold of Zedman's child.

Katherine's father, who'd moved away, who Samuel had tried so fucking hard to let go, to believe he'd been punished enough.

He got a warm feeling, like a ski mask rolling over his face.

He remembered the whimpering sounds Talia had made, the magnolia smell in her hair. He looked at Race and saw that same guilt, same amber eyes as Talia's, and Samuel knew he had to swallow back the rage. Swallow it quickly before it killed him.

The stereo was playing a song he didn't like—some Britney Spears shit. He slammed his fist against the speaker. He picked up the whole unit and threw it—smashed it into the wall with the cord flying behind like a rat's tail.

That felt good.

He stared at Race, thinking how handsome the boy would look, so much like his oldest brother, if he would only clean himself up. Race didn't need to smell like sour milk, wear that ratty jacket, go around town like a transient from Talia's to Nana's to God-knows-where. He should be living here. He should make something of himself. Samuel had sacrificed so much for him. So much.

He swallowed again, but there was only so much he could do to counter the rage when he saw the pathetic way Race was holding that gun, like he could ever shoot anything.

"What you looking at?" Samuel demanded.

"You killed Momma," Race whimpered. "This money— it's hers. Ain't it?"

"What you going to do with that gun? You going to fly down to Texas and shoot somebody? You going to kill people for that girl, huh?"

"I got to help her."

"You got to do shit."

Samuel slapped the gun out of his hand. He picked it up, and for a dangerous second the gun seemed to be working against him—seeking flesh like a dowsing rod.

Samuel hated that moment, hated Race seeing the loss of control in his eyes.

He pressed the muzzle of the gun into the mattress and fired, over and over, screaming obscenities that were drowned out by the noise, until the magazine was empty.

His hand burned. The sheets smelled like ozone. There

was a black ragged hole in the mattress, all the way down into the box spring.

Stupid, he told himself. *The neighbors will call the cops.*

But he knew the neighbors weren't home yet. They all worked late in the city. Nobody in the condos this time of evening but a couple dozen shih tzus.

When the ringing in his ears died down, he heard the television sitcom still going in the next room, the AM radio bitching in the bathroom.

Race was curled up in the corner by the nightstand, his hands grabbing at his hair. He was shivering, a line of mucus glistening on his upper lip. When he cried, he made wet, drowning sounds.

Samuel felt his mind tearing in half.

His rage drained away, replaced by a deep protectiveness—a benevolence toward Race so strong it made him want to cut himself to prove his love.

He had tried so hard to protect his family. He had sent Race to Laurel Heights for the opportunities, not for revenge. And yet when the girl had gotten too close to Race, Samuel hadn't stopped them. He had expected them to become friends—he *wanted* it.

Then at Talia's house . . . he'd been heartbroken to learn that Race had discovered the body, that the police wanted to talk to him. Samuel didn't wish any of that on Race. Nobody should make that kind of discovery.

But at the same time, Samuel had anticipated it. He had left Talia there to be found. He had wanted Race to see her— the whore stripped of her ability to run away, to fail them, to lie. And he had spilled the girl's necklace into the blood, too, imagining that a police technician would pick it up with tweezers, watch it glimmer in the light, read the inscription.

For the first time, Samuel understood why he'd done that. He understood the pattern his subconscious had been weaving—the dark net taking shape under the tightrope.

Chadwick. Everything else had just been practice.

Funny, how you could build up to something all your life and not even realize you were doing it.

He knelt beside Race, stroked his hair. The boy looked five years old, shivering, his eyes glowing with fear.

Samuel imagined one of those nights long ago, after Ali did his business. He imagined Talia—or was it Talia?—stumbling out and holding Race, and saying, *It's all right, honey. I'm okay. We going to get you out of here. You going to a good school. Samuel's going to help you. Ali's not going to touch us no more.*

And Samuel had taken care of Ali.

Samuel always protected his siblings—because if he didn't, who would?

Years before, he'd tried to send his sister away to protect her from Elbridge, and when that didn't work, he'd taken Johnny Jay's gun out of the welder's box in the garage, waited in the bushes down the street for Elbridge to come home—Elbridge, who always walked home the same way from the pool hall, who had plenty of enemies and wouldn't be missed.

Samuel couldn't leave his sisters and brothers alone. He couldn't bear to see them hurt, any more than he could bear for Katherine to die, his only friend—the only one who ever understood the darkness inside him.

He touched the side of Race's face. "Where you think you were going?"

"After Mallory."

"No. I got a better idea."

"You'll kill her."

"Now, you listen to me, Race. I'll take care of you, but you got to listen. Nobody else going to get hurt. Not your girl. Not you. Not anybody who matters."

And Samuel painted a picture for him—simple and pretty. Lots of money, a new home in a faraway country, he and his girlfriend together, Samuel watching out for them, taking care of them. Samuel told him how it would work. He wanted Race to understand, to appreciate how beautiful it was. Race was a bright boy. He could figure the math.

"You can't," Race said. "They'll catch you."

"You crash here for a few days, all right? Nobody think to

look for you here—last place in the world they look for Race Montrose. You wait for me. Your girlfriend going to be okay."

Samuel could see in his eyes—Race desperate to buy into the dream. Samuel knew he was terrified, knew he wanted to run. But Samuel wasn't worried about that.

In the end, Race would come to him the same way the schoolkids did—crowding onto his lap to hear a story. Samuel could make him believe whatever he wanted. He would make the girl believe, too. And when it was time to change the story—to write the girl out of it, Samuel would make that go down easy. Race would get over it.

Because kids have survival instincts. They're like animals. They know who cares for them, who to trust. They won't climb onto just anybody's lap.

"Stay here," Samuel told him. "And Race, I know your hiding places. Don't skip. Understand?"

"Yeah."

"Now go wash your face. And while you're in the bathroom, turn up the radio. It's too quiet in here."

Race stood, still shaky, and wiped the blood and mucus off his lip. He went to do as he was told, leaving Samuel staring out the window, down across the valley where the highway cut through like a bleeding artery, spilling bloody brake lights into the Bay.

Chadwick had disrespected him again.

If Samuel ever doubted God had a plan for him, he didn't doubt it anymore.

He had been given a sign. He must not leave without settling every score. He must not leave one brick on top of another in the rubble.

And, praise God, Samuel would obey.

6

"Zedman!"

Mallory wanted to yell something back. She chewed on all the bad names she could call this bastard, but she was thinking about what had happened to that last kid who used the F-word.

The instructor yelled her name again.

Mallory didn't look up. Boots crunched on the gravel.

"Simple instructions, Zedman." The guy bellowed like he was talking to somebody across the river, like he wanted all the buzzards circling this fucking place to hear him. "I say your name. You say, 'Here, sir.'"

Mallory's nausea was getting worse—the cold shakes, razors in her gut. She told herself she was sitting down on purpose, to protest, but the truth was she wasn't sure she could stand. The pain had never been this bad before. Her whole body was turning to ice and melting from the inside. She needed a fix. She had fantasies about Race finding her, busting in with a semiautomatic and taking her away. But Race wouldn't be coming. He was in worse trouble than she was.

It was hard for Mallory to control the shaking, but she decided she wouldn't throw up again. She wouldn't give the instructor the pleasure.

The instructor's assistant, a young blond dude, started yelling at Mallory, too—"Get over here! Get off your butt and get on this line!" But that was just background noise. Mallory knew the real threat was right in front of her.

She looked up, just so she wouldn't have her face in puking position.

The black guy hadn't gotten any prettier. He was huge—maybe not as tall as Chadwick, but wide, built like a tank, black T-shirt and camo pants and combat boots like a character from one of those arcade games Race liked.

She imagined Race pointing a blue plastic gun at this guy, the instructor's head exploding on the video screen. Race giving her a warm bright smile, saying, *See? Ain't nothing.*

The thought made her feel a little better.

"I've got all day," the black guy said. "All day and all night."

Mallory looked at the other three kids. They'd already given up. They were standing on the line, holding their supplies. The fat girl had mascara streaks down her cheeks from crying.

The assistant instructor was pacing behind them, yelling in their ears whenever they moved or muttered or looked in a direction he didn't like. The boy who'd said the F-word had a gag taped in his mouth—a goddamn gag.

Screw that, Mallory thought. Screw her mother for sending her here.

There was *no way* her mother could've known what this place was like. No way a gag was legal. If she could get to a phone, she could call her mom. She'd thought of that in the airport, but Chadwick always seemed to know what she was thinking. He'd been too hard to get away from. Maybe this black guy wasn't as smart as Chadwick.

Finally, one of the other kids yelled at her, "Get up, Zedman!"

For the first time, the assistant instructor didn't shut the kid down, didn't even act like anyone had spoken.

"I ain't standing here all day for you!" the kid yelled. He was the overweight guy—the one with the acne and the greasy hair. "GET——UP!"

Hell with him, Mallory thought.

But Mallory had a new thought—maybe she *should* play along. Pretend. If she did, it would be easier to get to a phone.

One call to her mother, and she could swallow her anger long enough to apologize, cry a little, tell her what this place was like. Her mom would cave in. She'd bail her out. Mallory knew she would. And then Mallory could run away again—only this time, she wouldn't be found.

Mallory tried to get to her feet. It wasn't easy. Her head was spinning and her legs felt like bendy-straws.

She was standing, but she wasn't going to look at the black guy. No way.

"Zedman!" the black guy yelled.

Mallory muttered, "Here."

The black guy's feet crunched gravel. "Here, *sir.*"

Mallory bit back some cuss words. She concentrated on Race. She had to get back to Race. "Here, sir."

"I've heard kindergarteners louder than that. Are you a kindergartener?"

"HERE, SIR!"

Mallory was crying, but she didn't care. She just hoped she'd broken the bastard's eardrums.

"Fall in, Zedman."

Mallory staggered toward the line, stopped halfway, doubled over. The world thickened like maple syrup around her—everybody staring at her, waiting for her to die.

The instructors' eyes looked like her father's—cold disapproval, her last argument with Daddy, his insistence, *If you don't keep away from him, I will make him stay away. I can't stand this anymore, Mallory.*

She finally managed to get in line. She held out her arms and the assistant instructor shoved a bundle at her. He yelled orders until she was standing straight, holding her stuff with her elbows at a 45-degree angle, forearms level to the ground. The bundle wasn't that heavy, but standing there at attention, her arms got sore quickly.

The assistant instructor ripped the gag off the guy who'd cussed.

"I say, *Eyes front,*" the black dude bellowed, "you say, *Sir.* And you are looking at me. Eyes front!"

"Sir," they all said.

"Pathetic. EYES FRONT!"

"SIR!"

The black dude was getting off on his power trip, bullying little kids. It occurred to Mallory that one of these instructors might actually hit her. The idea sank in like the prick of a heroin needle—painful, but salty, pleasant in a sick way. Mallory would be able to show her bruises in court. She'd laugh when this place was shut down and all of these blowhards were dragged off to jail.

Just pretend a little while, she told herself. *Just get to a phone.*

"Ladies and gentlemen," the black guy said, "this is Cold Springs Academy. My name is Dr. Hunter. I own and direct this facility. While you are here, I direct you."

He didn't say, *I own you,* but that's what Mallory heard.

"You are now part of Black Level," Hunter said. "You are holding two sets of black fatigues, two pairs of underwear, one pair of shoes, one blanket, one bar of soap, one roll of toilet paper, and one toothbrush. Everything else—all other privileges—must be earned. Every rule must be followed. You will not advance from Black Level until you show that you have earned the right to do so. Is that understood?"

Mallory muttered, "Yes, sir."

Of course, not everybody did, so they had to say it again, yelling, "YES, SIR!"

"Run in place," Hunter said. "NOW!"

You've got to be joking, Mallory thought.

But the assistant instructor was yelling in her ear: "MOVE IT! KNEES UP! RUN!"

Mallory tried. She was sure she looked like a damn fool, holding this crap and jogging, feeling like she was going to puke.

Soon she was sweating, wishing she'd taken off her jacket. The air was cool, even cooler than back home, but it was drier, too. It burned her mouth and nose. The pain in her gut was unbearable.

Hunter called, "Halt!"

The second instructor was at the end of the line, yelling at the kid who'd had his mouth gagged earlier. The kid had thrown his supplies on the ground and kicked them away.

"I'm leaving!" the kid yelled. He had spiky hair, unnaturally yellow, and with his face all red and angry his whole head looked like a big match.

"F—" The kid stopped himself, remembering the gag. "Forget your Black Level. You can't make me stay here."

Match-Head started storming off, but quickly he realized he didn't know what direction to storm off in.

They were in the middle of a clearing about the size of a volleyball court, surrounded by scrubby woods. Workout equipment was scattered around—a balance beam, a tire obstacle course, a couple of cinder block walls of various heights. The only road led toward the big ski lodge–type building they'd passed on the way in, and that was a good quarter mile away. The van that had dropped them off was gone. The horizon was nothing but low puke-colored hills in all directions. Mallory knew from Chadwick that this place was somewhere in Texas—the absolute middle of nowhere.

Match-Head started to stomp up the road, then stopped in his tracks. A third staff member had appeared in front of him, like he'd been waiting in the woods. The new guy was holding something that looked like a canvas pup tent with a bicycle chain stitched through it.

Hunter said, "No one leaves except by working the levels. How you stay depends on you."

Then Mallory realized the canvas thing was a body sack. The bastards would chain you in it up to your neck.

Mallory glared at Hunter, not believing anyone would actually use that thing, but Hunter didn't look like he was bluffing.

Match-Head didn't move.

"Your supplies are on the ground," Hunter told him. "You won't get new ones."

Slowly, the kid turned. He went to the supplies and started picking them up.

The kid was crying. He was probably a year older than

Mallory, but there he was, crying. Mallory could still see the impression of the gag—red lines around his mouth.

When Match-Head was back in line, Hunter barked more commands—turns, forward march. Army stuff. None of the kids made any more fuss.

Mallory switched off her brain, tried not to think about the pain. She concentrated on her feet moving, on the commands of the instructors.

She hated her mother for sending her here. She hated Chadwick for catching her.

Most of all, she hated the memory his presence had sharpened—Katherine's face, her cold fingers on Mallory's knee, her smile when she said, *Hold it for me. I want you to, Mal. I love you.*

Mallory's definition of love had been formed that night. Someone makes you admire them, need them, want their approval, and then they abandon you, leave you holding... something. A necklace. Pain. Their blackest thoughts. Their path.

It had taken Mallory years to get angry about that. She had grown up deathly afraid she would end up like Katherine, but when she tried talking about it to her parents, her counselor, her teachers, she saw no reassurance in their eyes, just the exact same terror. They handled her as if she'd been infected, as if the silver necklace around her neck was a vial of nitroglycerin. They gave her doe eyes. They used gentle voices. If she threw a fit, they retreated. Just like Katherine—always turning to smoke.

And so Mallory had gotten angry. Fuck, yes, she would keep the necklace. She would be Race's friend. Fuck, yes, she would try heroin. She would validate their fear. She would leave them holding her childhood pictures, wondering what the hell had gone wrong. That was love.

"You will rest when it's time to rest," Dr. Hunter yelled. "You will work when it's time to work. You will do what you are told, and you will save your own life before you get out of here. That, ladies and gentleman, is a promise. You will find I keep my promises."

She tried to push away the anger, the desire to scream cuss words until they taped her mouth. She thought about home—about Race, and the world of trouble she'd left him in.

She couldn't be gone now

Every time she closed her eyes, she saw Talia Montrose—the ragged cuts, the way her fingers had curled into claws, the fat black fly walking along her eyelid. The sound that had come from Race's throat—the raw, hollow moan that was beyond pain—the sound of some animal that had never learned language. The look he had given her—not saying anything, not accusing, but knowing damn well it was all her fault. Her father had threatened to do something like this. And still she and Race had stayed together. They had run. They had slept in places too horrible to remember, on mattresses that stank of urine and grease. They had made awkward love—the first time, despite what their parents had thought—driven together by pain and fear and the need to believe there was something that could burn the image of death out of their brains. She had tried to comfort him. They had tried to make a plan. Race had pressed the money into her hand, said, "I can get more. I will. Keep this for now, until we're ready to leave."

She wanted to believe Race's beautiful vision—that they could run away together. Race had wonderful dreams, better than anything Mallory ever had.

But at the same time, she had delayed. She had dragged her feet, kept them from leaving Oakland. Part of her craved trouble the way she craved heroin—the way she wanted to lie down and feel the rumble of the BART tracks until the sky turned black and the world ended. Part of her wanted to follow Katherine into that darkened bedroom and close the door.

No, Mallory told herself. *Just survive. Just get out.*

And so she marched, the man with the body bag screaming in her peripheral vision, as if he'd always been there, waiting for her to step in the wrong direction.

7

Another week of pickups—New York, Utah, St. Louis, Belize. Chadwick chased a boy across a rooftop, collared him at the TV aerials, and dragged him down five flights of stairs by the scruff of his neck. He pulled a girl out of an underage prostitution ring after breaking a two-by-four over her pimp's head with a little too much relish.

Olsen did her job with quiet efficiency. She related well to the kids, treated them with the right mix of respect and firmness. She had no more nervous moments, betrayed no further scent of fear. She performed better than most of the young women he'd trained that year—always women, since Hunter's rules stipulated a male and female escort must work together on every assignment—but the whole week, she said maybe a dozen sentences off-duty. He could feel her slipping away, withdrawing from the job, just like so many others.

The dropout rate for new escorts was eighty percent. The work was just too intense. It didn't take long for the rookie to hit a job that really unnerved her—a situation that resonated in her nightmares like a diminished chord. For Olsen, for whatever reason, it had been the Mallory Zedman pickup.

They got back to Texas late Friday night.

Saturday morning, after four hours' sleep, Chadwick was sitting on the deck of the Big Lodge, proctoring a White Level study hall. He had his cell phone in his hand, tapping his thumb lightly on the numbers.

At the picnic tables behind him, a dozen white levels were

bent to their work—writing essays, studying for AP exams or SATs.

The morning was crisp and cool as the underside of a pillow, the sky scratched with high winter clouds, sunlight gilding the hills and the wings of redtail hawks. The white levels didn't seem to notice. They labored so quietly that a family of deer had gathered to graze the hillside not a hundred yards away.

The last year of his marriage, living in San Francisco, Chadwick had often fantasized about the Texas Hill Country. He had imagined starting every day here, teaching kids in this setting, reinventing young lives. Now here he was, thinking only about San Francisco.

He closed his eyes and concentrated on 1994, the year he'd started escorting.

Whenever the hot empty feeling started burning in his stomach, whenever he felt like kicking down a brick wall, it calmed him to calculate backwards through history, jumping from event to event like stepping stones, making a continuous line into the past. He could do it with centuries, or millennia, any measurement larger than his own life.

1894. Eugene Debs and the railway boycotts.

1794. Jay's Treaty.

1694...

He took a deep breath, turned on his phone, then dialed a number he'd never forgotten.

He circumnavigated a few secretaries at Zedman Development, gave them his name, told them he had news about Mr. Zedman's daughter.

When John finally came on the line, his voice was tight and familiar, as if Chadwick had just called five minutes before. "Well?"

"Mallory's safe."

"You call me now. You steal my daughter, and a week later you call. Your timing sucks, old buddy."

He was trying hard to sound callous, but Chadwick heard the emotion cracking through. He wondered if John missed their arguments about basketball and politics; if he found himself wondering how Chadwick had spent the millennial New Year's, or whether he could get through Thanksgiving without thinking of the way they used to spend it together—their two families, now irrevocably shattered.

"I didn't know about Race Montrose," Chadwick said. "I didn't know about the murder."

"And what—you want to apologize?"

"We need to talk about this, John."

"I'll only ask you once. Bring back my daughter."

"She's better off here. She needs help."

"Goodbye, Chadwick."

"Race Montrose brought a gun to Laurel Heights. Mallory said he needed protection. Did you threaten him?"

"I tried not to blame you, Chadwick. And then you take my daughter without asking, without even warning me. You know what? Fuck it. It *is* all your fault. Katherine's death, my wife leaving me, my daughter turning against me—that's all on you."

"I'm not your enemy, John."

"Yeah? Tell me you've been getting the letters, Chadwick. Tell me you've been living with it the way I have."

"Letters."

John's laugh was strained. "That's good, old buddy. I'm sure Samuel is laughing—fucking laughing his ass off."

"John—"

But he was talking to dead air.

Chadwick stared at the phone, the little LCD message asking if he wanted to save the number to his address book for easy redial. Just what he needed—a moral dilemma from his cell phone. Chadwick punched *yes*.

He made the rounds among the students, flexing his fingers, which suddenly felt frostbitten. The white levels were all on task—no questions. No problems. Nobody needed to go to the bathroom.

Chadwick moved his chair a little farther away on the deck, then placed another call—to Pegeen Riley, a woman he'd worked with before at Alameda County Social Services.

After five minutes with her, he tried the Oakland Police

Department, Homicide Section. He watched the deer graze until Sergeant Damarodas came to the phone.

"Well, Mr. Chadwick. Imagine my surprise." The homicide investigator's voice reminded Chadwick of a drill instructor he'd had at Lackland Air Force Base, a bulldog of a man who'd sing German drinking songs while the BTs dug trenches.

"Sergeant," Chadwick said. "Pegeen Riley from Social Services says you're in charge—"

"Yeah. She just called. Good woman, Peg. I'll be honest, Mr. Chadwick. Without her recommendation, I'm not sure you'd be on my Christmas card list."

"About Mallory Zedman—"

"You transported a material witness out of state. Pegeen says you used to be a teacher. You'd think a teacher would have better sense."

Chadwick tried to read the man's voice. There was something besides annoyance—a wariness Chadwick didn't quite understand.

"Listen, Sergeant, Mrs. Zedman is a worried mother. She's trying to do the best thing for her daughter."

"I've got another mother I'm worried about. Her name was Talia Montrose. She's got thirty-two stab wounds."

The wind rose. On the hillside, a thousand grasshoppers lifted from the grass and whirled like smoke over red granite.

"Sergeant, how much do you know about the Montrose family?"

"Enough to piss me off," Damarodas said. "I know the lady had six kids, maybe seven, depending on which neighbor you talk to. Not one of them's come to ID her body. I know the victim's mother is a head case, lives in a condemned building downtown, reacted to her daughter's death by asking me if I'd ever been off the planet. I know the youngest kid, Race, was sharing a sleeping bag with your little angel Mallory at his mom's house the week of the murder. Then your worried friend Mrs. Zedman paid God-knows-how-much money to have her daughter picked up and smuggled to your fine facility. What am I missing, Mr. Chadwick?"

"The girl says she and Race were at a Halloween party. They came home, found the body, called 911."

"And then they ran."

"They're fifteen-year-olds. They panicked."

"You want to explain why the 911 call came from a pay phone on Broadway, halfway across town? They were calm enough to get away from the scene before they called. The girl's voice on the tape—she'd practiced what she was going to say, Mr. Chadwick. How about you put her on the phone?"

"Not possible."

"Talia Montrose's house? Blood everywhere. Looked like a damn sprinkler went off. Wounds caused by a short, bladed object, six, maybe seven inches long. Fingerprints all over the crime scene. Blood samples. Hair samples. We'll get it all back from the lab in a day or so. In the meantime, I can tell you we're pretty sure Race and Mallory were the only ones staying at the house. Talia was staying with a boyfriend, getting ready to skip town, probably came home to tell Race *hasta la vista*. We think she had upward of twenty thousand cash on her person when she was killed. Except for a few bills stuck in the blood, all that money is gone."

Chadwick thought about the $630 he'd taken from Mallory's coat pocket—fresh new bills. "The Montroses aren't saints. Run the last name. Take a look at her kids. The oldest son—Samuel. He'd be an adult now."

"What would I find, Mr. Chadwick?"

Something in Damarodas' tone made Chadwick's scalp tingle. The detective was playing him, flashing a lure.

"All I'm saying, Sergeant— Mallory Zedman didn't bring trouble to that family. I don't believe she would get herself involved in a murder."

"Last week? I arrested a seventy-two-year-old grandmother, kept her dead boyfriend in a freezer, five different pieces wrapped in aluminum foil, so she could collect his Social Security checks. I didn't believe she'd be involved in a murder, either. I intend to fly down there and ask Mallory Zedman some questions."

"Cold Springs is a closed program. No exceptions."

"This is a homicide investigation, Mr. Chadwick. I've requested a court order from Alameda County."

"I wouldn't go that route, Sergeant. Dr. Hunter's lawyers have had a lot of practice. They'll turn your court order into trench warfare."

Chadwick watched the sunrise creep over the hill, melting the shadows from the hooves of the deer.

Finally Damarodas sighed. "Perhaps there's another thing you could help me with, Mr. Chadwick."

"Sergeant?"

"Something we found near Mrs. Montrose's body. Kind of an odd piece of jewelry to be stuck in the woman's blood."

Chadwick felt a distant rumble, like a train ripping through a dark tunnel.

"A silver necklace," Damarodas told him. "An inscription on it. I bet you can't guess."

The morning seemed colder—the air thickening, swirling to a standstill.

"What was your daughter's name, sir?" Damarodas asked. "Was it Katherine Elise?"

Chadwick took the phone away from his ear, knowing it was the wrong thing to do. Don't run away from this conversation. Don't hang up.

He heard Damarodas say, "Sir?"

Then Chadwick disconnected.

He wasn't sure how long he sat there, watching the deer graze the hilltop, before Asa Hunter came out to join him.

Hunter hooked a chair, pulled it up next to Chadwick's. "That bad, huh?"

"What?"

Hunter propped his combat boots on the railing, laced his fingers around his coffee cup. "You look like hell, amigo."

"Blame my boss. He works me too hard."

Hunter gave him the same skeptical appraisal he'd been giving him since they were both eighteen, working perimeter guard duty in Korat, Thailand. His expression posed the rhetorical question, *Where'd this big dumb white boy come from?*

"Listen, amigo, if I thought picking up Mallory Zedman would make you feel worse rather than better—"

"How is she doing?"

"Hit her assistant trainer yesterday. Day before that, she scratched and bit a white level. Day before that, kicked her counselor in the balls. Three solitary confinements. No extra privileges. Standard problems."

"Standard, if she's a rabid mountain lion."

Hunter's face could have been crafted from stealth bomber material—smooth hard contours, bald scalp so dark it seemed to drink the light. His eyes trapped you, studied you, released you only when they were good and ready. "The girl is resistant. We'll get to her."

"She talk much about why she's here?"

"You need to let the program work, amigo. You got enough..."

Hunter's voice trailed off.

A white level, a kid named Aden Stilwell, stood waiting at a respectful distance to be recognized. Chadwick called him forward. Aden politely asked if he could go inside and use the computer to look up a word. Chadwick reached into the bin of reference materials at his side and pulled out a dictionary. He explained to Aden how it worked. Aden looked at the book, mystified, then thanked Chadwick and walked away thumbing the pages.

Hunter smirked. "Hard to believe that's the same boy tried to run you over a year and a half ago, huh? Someday—that's going to be Mallory Zedman."

"Trying to run me over?"

"You know what I mean."

"I need to go back to San Francisco, Asa."

"You want to tell me why?"

Chadwick told him about the murder of Talia Montrose, Katherine's necklace at the crime scene. He told him about the letters John had mentioned from Samuel, the court order

Sergeant Damarodas had threatened to get to interview Mallory.

Hunter looked out toward the hills. He sighted a deer over the tips of his combat boots, as if calculating the best shot. "You think this young man—Samuel—he's trying to get some kind of revenge?"

"I don't know."

"For what—Katherine?"

Chadwick was silent.

Hunter sighed. "Look, amigo. Samuel Montrose was what—her drug dealer? So maybe you brought a little heat on him for supplying the drugs that killed her. Maybe he had to leave town for a while. So what? Guys like that—they have an attention span of three seconds. They use people, throw them away, forget about them. You're telling me he's spent nine years planning some kind of revenge scheme? That he'd kill his own mother to get at you? Doesn't make sense."

"Mallory is following the same path Katherine did, with this guy's little brother. That's a coincidence?"

Hunter's jaw flexed, as if he were chewing on something small and hard. Chadwick knew the warning sign. He'd seen Hunter do that in Korat, when an ARVN made a racial crack at Hunter's expense. Hunter had walked up behind him, real calm, yanked him out of his seat by the hair, and drove the Vietnamese's head through the hootch wall.

Years later, Hunter had taken Chadwick out to show off his new six-thousand-acre spread that would become Cold Springs—land he had bought with minority business loans and mortgages on three different houses and decades of blood and sweat, working on grants that had landed him an initial capital outlay of $5 million. When they'd gotten almost to the gates, county deputies pulled them over, said Hunter fit their description of a wanted rapist. Hunter's jaw had been going as he explained to them he didn't care if he was the only black man they'd seen all month. He was now the biggest landowner in the county, and they had best get used to it. He'd kept his cool, but he spent the rest of the afternoon down by the river, throwing his knife at a tree, impaling the blade three inches into the bark.

"This Samuel guy," Hunter said. "He got some kind of blackmail leverage over John Zedman?"

"I don't know. It's been a long time."

"You ever meet Samuel?"

"Once. Sort of."

"Sort of."

"I was picking up Katherine from a police station. She'd been busted at a party at the Montrose house. Samuel was in the next holding cell, staring at me. His eyes—you remember Galen, the arsonist kid we got a few years back, lit homeless people on fire in their sleeping bags?"

"That scary?"

Chadwick nodded. "After Katherine died, Mallory identified the Montrose house as the place they'd gone to get the heroin. The police looked for Samuel. As far as I know, they never found him."

Hunter's fingers made a claw against his camouflage pants, as if he'd caged something there. His jaw was still tight with anger. "Look, amigo, I've known you since before Norma, before Katherine, before God entered puberty. Am I right? I understand about guilt. I understand you help kids because you feel like you failed Katherine. But Mallory Zedman isn't your daughter. You start trying to salvage the past through her, then I made a mistake, taking her."

The bitterness in his voice stung like sleet.

Hunter was right, of course, about knowing him. Only Ann had known him longer. That was one of the reasons Chadwick had accepted this job, when his life was at its darkest point—just after Katherine's death, when it took him conscious effort just to get out of bed and take a shower.

With Hunter, Chadwick could almost believe that his adulthood was a shell—a layer of years that could be slipped off, set aside for a while, examined impartially.

"You can help the girl," Chadwick said. "That's why you took her."

"I've been telling you a long time, you're too hard on yourself: Katherine wasn't your damn fault."

"But?"

"But it wasn't her dealer's fault, either. Maybe I don't like that you're so ready to believe your daughter was corrupted by the poor black kid she was hanging out with. Maybe that's been bothering me a long time. Now you're telling me his younger brother is ruining Mallory Zedman."

"It's not about them being black."

"Isn't it? What do we teach here? Honesty. Responsibility. Katherine was responsible for her actions. Mallory is responsible for hers. Period."

"I can't just step back, Asa."

"This necklace—Katherine gave it to Mallory before she died, right?"

"Right."

"All that suggests to me—Mallory left it at the scene of the murder. Anybody's sending you a hate message, it's the girl."

"If you think she was involved, maybe you should turn her over to the police."

Hunter swirled his coffee.

Chadwick wondered if he saw something in the liquid— the faces of the thousand-plus kids he'd graduated, most of them rich, most of them white. He wondered if Hunter ever regretted the clientele he served.

With his charisma, his doctorate in education administration, his business experience after the Air Force, raising money for nonprofits, Hunter could've gone anywhere, been superintendent of any major metropolitan school district. He could've been a model for kids who grew up like he did— poor, scraping with gangs on the East Side of San Antonio, perpetually angry.

I don't want to go to work and see myself every day, Hunter had told him once. *You want to help somebody, you got to have a little distance from them. White kids, I understand. I can save their sorry-ass lives.*

When he said that, Chadwick got the uncomfortable impression he was talking about their friendship, too.

"Nobody gets access to Black Level," Hunter decided. "I allow one exception, the integrity of the whole program is compromised. On the other hand . . ."

He looked at Chadwick, seemed to be weighing unpleasant options. "This Sergeant Damarodas—he could be on our doorstep next week. Court orders, I can fight. But I need to know what I'm fighting and why. I don't appreciate being kept in the dark by this girl's mother."

"Like I said. Let me go back to San Francisco."

"You got a full slate of pickups, and you're going to have a new partner to train."

"What about Olsen?"

"She's asked for a different assignment. You probably guessed that."

"I'll convince her to stay on," Chadwick said quietly.

"Won't do any good."

"Asa, I've had four partners in the last five weeks. I'm not going to lose another one."

Hunter raised an eyebrow. "Why you making a stand, amigo? What makes Olsen different than the others?"

"Can I talk to her or not?"

Hunter gazed across the hills, at the land he owned all the way to the horizon. "I won't stop you. Now why don't you get some rest? I'll watch the class."

Chadwick was about to decline the offer, but his friend's expression told him it might be best not to argue. He left Hunter at the edge of the deck, the sunrise turning the steam from his coffee red.

Inside the main lodge, tan levels were doing their chores—scrubbing floors, cleaning windows, sweeping the enormous stone fireplace in anticipation of tonight's hard freeze.

When Chadwick came near, they stood at attention. He remembered each of them by name and pickup city, and by how each had performed during Survival Week, which Chadwick sometimes led. Sarah from Albuquerque, who couldn't light a fire; Lane from Rochester, who would eat anything no matter how slimy; Tyler from Houston, who'd never been camping and got the highest marks for survival in his team. Chadwick talked to each of them, told them they were doing a good job. He hoped his tone wasn't as weary as he imagined.

Hunter had a saying—staff members find their level, then dress to it. It was not a requirement, but it was a fact.

Hunter himself, like most of the drill sergeant types, tended to wear black. They felt most at home with the new initiates. They relished confrontation.

The hands-on learning buffs, the ranch hands, outdoor ed graduates who weren't quite up to Black Level—they wore the second-level color, gray.

The therapists, the part-time teachers, the studious ones who preferred to work with kids the way jewelers worked with settings—they all wore the fourth-level color, white.

But tan was the invisible third level. Tan levels did domestic chores, lived by quiet routine, combated nothing worse than boredom. They learned tranquillity through humility. They were kitchen patrol. They were toilet cleaners. They were not the center of the world. Their therapy sessions chased the most elusive byword in Hunter's program—Honesty.

Very few people on staff dressed to that level. And though his job had nothing in common with the level, Chadwick almost always wore tan.

Partly, he envied their invisibility. It wasn't something a giant like Chadwick ever got much of. If there were other reasons, Chadwick had never thought them through. Maybe that's why he was still wearing the color.

He walked down the north wing, past the gym, the cafeteria, the infirmary—all state-of-the-art facilities built with the bulging profits of Hunter's alternative-education empire. Eight years ago, when Chadwick started escorting, none of those amenities had been there. Now Hunter had five campuses in three different countries.

His apartment was in the staff dormitory on the second

floor. He didn't realize his hands were trembling until he started searching his key ring.

Every key at Cold Springs was identical except for the number, and Chadwick had never gotten around to color-coding them. He stopped at the only unique one—the gold key for the house in the Mission. He told himself for the millionth time he needed to remove it, put it in a box somewhere. He still owned the house, refusing to sell because under the terms of the divorce he'd have to share the money with Norma. But he hadn't visited in years. Had no intention of doing so.

And still, every time he took out his key chain—there it was. He could envision the green door with its brass knob, brass numbers above the mail slot. He could imagine opening that door, calling up the stairwell that he was home.

What had Hunter said about not trying to salvage the past?

He and Chadwick had walked away from Southeast Asia together with never a flashback. They'd seen children who'd stepped on land mines, shriveled Vietcong body parts strung on jute necklaces like Mexican *milagros,* dead GIs Huey-ed into base, their bodies cooked from napalm Chadwick's colleagues had loaded onto planes. None of that affected Chadwick much anymore. None of it gave him the shakes.

But when it came to San Francisco—the house in the Mission—his hands still trembled.

He put his keys back in his pocket, walked down the hall to Olsen's apartment.

He had to knock several times before she answered.

She stood in the doorway, squinting, the room behind her a yawning darkness that smelled of sleep and rye bagels she'd bought in New York.

"Glad you're up," Chadwick said. "Can we talk?"

"Are you crazy? I just went back to bed."

"Your room or mine?"

She scowled. With her buzz cut, her shapeless fatigues, her harshly plain face, she looked about twelve years old. Chadwick wondered why young women who tried to look butch always ended up looking frail and vulnerable.

"Your room," she decided. "It's probably cleaner."

The comment forced Chadwick to think about what his room would look like—and it was clean, but like a hotel room, not a home. He had never asked for new furniture since the early shoestring budget days of Cold Springs. He still had the particleboard desk, the hundred-dollar double bed, the Sears CD player. The corners of the sheets, the clothes on the shelves were folded with military precision, but there was little of personal significance—just a few pictures, and a few essential books. Herodotus. Mark Twain. David McCullough.

He opened the sliding glass door to the porch, let in the smell of cedar, the distant rush of the river.

Olsen examined the photos on Chadwick's writing desk. Her fingers hovered momentarily over the picture of Katherine—a young girl of eight, the summer they'd planted morning glories, her smile wide with amazement, the flowers making a raucously colored arch around her body. Mercifully, Olsen's fingers moved on. She picked up an old group shot of Chadwick with a bunch of Laurel Heights eighth-graders, all of them in colonial costumes.

Olsen looked up at the present-day Chadwick, then back at the photo of him with the powdered wig. "Anybody ever told you—"

"Repeatedly," Chadwick interrupted. "I look like George Washington."

Olsen managed a crooked smile. "And these kids in the picture—"

"Students. Former students."

"Why'd you quit?"

"My daughter was a student there," Chadwick said. "She committed suicide."

Olsen's lips quirked, like she thought he was kidding, and then, when she was sure he wasn't, she returned the picture to its place, carefully, as if it were a detonator.

"Katherine," she guessed. "What Mallory was talking about that night in the car."

"She took her own life while she was baby-sitting Mallory Zedman, overdosed on heroin while Mallory was watching

The Little Mermaid. Mallory was six. We were gone several hours longer than we should've been. Mallory put in the call to 911."

Olsen sank into a chair. She rubbed her palms on her cheeks, pushing up the corners of her eyes. "Christ, Chadwick. Okay. Fuck. I feel like a jerk now."

"As you can tell, I'm a lot of fun to be with."

"I've been mad at you for a week because you wouldn't talk to me about the Zedman girl. Wouldn't explain why you were acting weird. You left me in the car while you talked with her mom."

"So don't quit escorting. I need your help."

Olsen hunched over, laced her fingers together and stared through them.

Her hair gleamed in the light. Her skin had a yellowish hue to it, like half-churned milk. Once during the week, on the flight into La Guardia, a flight attendant had told Olsen, by way of a compliment, that she looked a lot like her father, then gestured at Chadwick. The comment weighed on Chadwick's heart like lead.

He remembered how many times he'd had to explain that he was Katherine's father. Yes—her, the Latina child. He'd learned to stare through people's momentary disbelief, their embarrassment and confusion. He remembered thinking that he would never be able to claim a resemblance to Katherine, so he would have to claim something else about her—common personality, or interests, or career. Someday, he'd thought, after she grew up, people would look at Katherine and think, *She's so much like her father.*

"I should have told you I was requesting a new assignment," Olsen decided. "It's not you, Chadwick. It's me. I'm not cut out for this work."

"I don't agree."

"Oh, please. I can't do what you do—not the direct intervention."

"That's the job you requested."

"I was unrealistic, okay? I wanted to be the rescuer, the

one who whisked kids out of trouble. I thought they'd respond to me because I'd been there. I was wrong."

She'd been there.

Chadwick remembered Olsen's interview, how she'd talked in vague terms about coming from a broken home, how that had gotten her interested in child psychology. Chadwick hadn't pressed her for details.

"You can't expect the kids to thank you," he told her. "The more a kid fights, the worse she needs us."

She shook her head. "The things Mallory said to me in the car while you were in the school...Not a thing about your daughter. Nothing about that. But vicious things. She reminded me—"

Olsen stopped herself.

Out the window, a trio of buzzards had gathered over the river, circling for breakfast.

"Kids like Mallory," Chadwick said, "they've learned they can make authority figures cave in if they just act outrageous enough. That's terrifying power for an adolescent. They love it, but they hate it, too. So they keep getting wilder, hoping to find the limits. They need to hit a brick wall—somebody who finally says, 'This is it. This is where you stop.' When a kid fights, she's testing to see if you're for real. Remember that. Remember you're basically dealing with a scared child, no matter how big or loud or out of control."

Olsen was staring at the picture of Chadwick in his colonial outfit—the Father of his Country. Chadwick suddenly hated the picture.

"Some of those things Mallory told me," Olsen said, "some of it was about you. You and her mother."

Chadwick made a conscious effort to keep his eyes on hers. He knew he should be open with her, like he should've stayed on the line with Sergeant Damarodas, like he should've confessed his secret to Norma, that cold night, so many years ago, before everything came unraveled.

But it was hard. It was like forcing his hand to touch a hot stove plate.

"I need to go back to San Francisco," he told her. "The

boy Race—I need to find him, ask him some questions. I'll have to do that during the workweek, between escorts. I'd rather have you with me than someone new. You, at least, know some of the background."

Olsen traced her knuckle along the frame of Katherine's photograph.

"That day in Oakland," she said, "you hesitated long enough for Race Montrose to shoot you. I almost watched you die, Chadwick."

It wasn't a question, not even an accusation. Just an expression of sadness, of concern, and before he knew it, he was putting his hand to the hot stove plate—telling her a story he'd never shared with Ann, or Norma, or anyone.

"In 1973," he said, "Hunter and I were in the Air Force, stationed in Thailand. We were eighteen years old, security police. Officially, the Vietnam War was over. Officially, none of us were even there. We spent a year in Korat, guarding planes that officially never dropped bombs on anybody."

He paused. He wasn't sure why he was telling Olsen this—a woman he'd only known two weeks—but something about her drew it out of him, like snake venom.

"Hunter and I were on perimeter duty one night. We'd had an intruder a few nights before—an NVA with a claymore wired to his chest whom we shot fifty yards from the fence—so we were both on edge. We were at the far end of the base, a hundred yards from anything, when this figure rose up from the rice fields only a few feet away, pointing a pistol right at us. I got off one round with my sidearm and Hunter opened up with his M-16 and the guy fell. Only later we found out we'd shot a local villager kid—maybe twelve, thirteen years old. The pistol was a piece of junk, wouldn't fire even if it had bullets. I don't know why he did it. Maybe an American had done something to his family. I don't know what the hell he was thinking. But when they brought his body into base, I could see the .38 hole I put in his chest, just above his heart."

Chadwick paused, listening to the rush of river, impossible to separate from the roar of blood in his ears. "I don't think about that kid often. I'm not saying I could've done something differently, or that I haven't had kids point guns at me in this job since then. But if I hesitated a little in Rockridge...now you know."

Olsen's eyes were molten glass—not yet hardened into anything definite. "Is that why you work with kids?"

"What?"

"Because of that boy. Is that why you became a teacher?"

"Maybe. Maybe partly."

"The pickup still bothered me, Chadwick, okay? Mallory Zedman bothered me."

"Don't run away from that."

"You don't understand me." She stopped, seemed uncomfortable with what she was about to say. "What you do—you go from crisis to crisis. You're always at the point of intervention. If I kept doing that, moving on from kid to kid, I *would* be running away. I need resolution—I need to help one kid at a time. That's why I've requested a counseling position. I've specifically requested Mallory Zedman."

Chadwick felt as if she'd passed her hand through his chest—gently, like a ghost's hand—and given his heart a squeeze.

"You'll be a good escort," he managed. "I want to work with you."

Olsen rose.

"I think you're a good person, Chadwick. But I can't. I'm sorry."

Long after she was gone—after the uncomfortable handshake and the good wishes and the smell of her soap and rye bagels dissipated—Chadwick stared out at the long shadows the morning sun was slicing from the woods, and he felt the full weight of the problem he had willingly hung around his neck—Mallory Zedman.

There was no difference between that name and the .38 Smith & Wesson revolver locked in a case under his bed, the colonial photo on his desk, or the old house key in his pocket. Some things, once they are slipped on your chain, can never be removed.

8

Mallory dreamed she was six years old, sitting shotgun in the old Toyota, waiting for Katherine.

Her teeth chattered. She sat on her hands, pressed her back into the cracked vinyl seat, tucked her chin into her collar, but still the night cold pervaded her clothes—working its way into her jacket, under her T-shirt, slithering against her skin like dry-ice vapor.

The dashboard rattled to the music on the radio—a stiff pulse of bass and drums, wild-voweled Australian voices chanting about coming home. She could smell the lemon air freshener Katherine hung from the rearview mirror to hide the cigarette odors from her parents.

At the top of the sidewalk, the Montrose house looked just the way it had—metalwork curling up the yellow walls like oil fire smoke, the door wide open. In the front yard, four palm trees shot into the frozen orange sky.

Then the scene shifted, as cleanly as a holographic picture, and her dad was behind the driver's seat.

Mallory knew, with the logic of dreams, that she was now ten years old as well as six, and her parents had just gotten divorced. Her dad had spotted her walking home from school, pulled her into his car to explain—to apologize for being mean, for yelling, for making her mother run away with Mallory a few months before, the sleeves of Mallory's pajamas trailing from a hastily packed suitcase.

"I didn't mean to scare you," he said, his hand clamped on her wrist, his eyes like a madman's.

Her mother's words rang in her head, *Stay away from him, Mallory. I'm sorry, but we both have to. I'm afraid he'll hurt . . . someone.*

Her dad told her the divorce hadn't been his idea. Her mother was keeping them apart. Her mother had bad ideas about how to raise her. He wanted custody of her. He wanted to be with Mallory. Didn't she want that, too?

And Mallory knew full well what her parents had been arguing about, the night her father hit her mother. She remembered their words through her bedroom wall, the sound that ended the yelling—like a sheet of Styrofoam cracked over a knee.

She asked her dad, "Why do you hate Race?"

His eyes closed, his fingers still biting into her wrist. He put his forehead on the steering wheel and started to cry. His weeping scared her more than the look in his eyes, or the grip of his hand, or even the sound of him striking her mother.

The dream shifted again and it was Pérez, her dad's bodyguard, behind the wheel. Mallory was fifteen—her last weekend visit to her dad's, their last huge argument, just a few weeks ago.

Pérez had been driving her to school on Monday morning—Mallory trying to ignore him, trying not to concentrate on the baseball-sized fear that swelled in her gut whenever her dad left her alone with this man.

A lot of her friends' parents had au pairs, or drivers, or personal assistants. But nobody had a Pérez—someone with no soul behind his eyes.

Usually, he would take her straight to school, toss her overnight bags onto the curb without a word and leave, her friends watching from behind the fence, coming up to her afterward and saying, "Shit, Mal. That guy carries, doesn't he? What is your dad—like the mafia? That is so cool."

And her hands would curl into fists, because these were the same friends who asked if she was "done" with Race yet, if she was tired of slumming, hanging with the homeboy.

But the morning she was dreaming about, Pérez took a detour.

He pulled over in front of the Mill Valley Safeway, and when Mallory demanded what he was doing, he said, "You bring your father nothing but grief. I'm telling you right now, you better stop."

"Fuck you," she told him.

But his eyes absorbed the words like they absorbed everything about her. It was as if she were just a shape in a storm cloud, not worth treating as human.

Then she was ten, and it was Pérez holding her wrist. Then she was six, and Pérez was pointing at the Montrose house, saying, "Wasn't for them, you little whore, your dad would be okay. He won't tell you that, but I will."

"I'll tell my father you talked to me that way," Mallory said. "He'll fire you."

"You say anything," Pérez said, "your boyfriend's going to be scattered off the Farallon Islands for shark chum. You understand me?"

And she knew—the same way she knew Dr. Hunter wasn't kidding, or Leyland, or any of the damn Cold Springs instructors—she knew Pérez was serious.

"Your dad wants to be with you," Pérez said. "He has it all planned out. But these people—they mess him up, keep a gun to his head; he still tries to solve it peaceful, because he doesn't want to hurt you. And what do you do for him? You disrespect him. You say you don't want to come for weekends anymore. You know what I think?"

Katherine was hurrying down the sidewalk of the Montrose house now, her breath steaming, a brown paper bag in her hand. Six-year-old Mallory was bouncing in her chair, worried that Katherine would run straight into Pérez.

"I think you better change," Pérez told her. "Cut that boy loose, before we do it for you."

Ten-year-old Mallory tried to yank away her hand from Pérez, but now the grip was her daddy's—and as much as she feared her father, and hated him sometimes, she didn't want to hear him cry. She didn't want to leave him forever.

A voice was calling from the Montrose house, someone standing on the porch, calling to Katherine. Someone had been in the doorway of the house that night, watching Katherine leave, telling her goodbye—visible only for a second.

Why hadn't Mallory remembered before?

She tried to look, to see who it was, but the shape made her afraid.

"I will make him stay away," her father was saying. "I have to."

Something was out of place. Something was wrong with Pérez's words, and her father's. Something about the shape in the doorway.

Then Katherine opened the door of the Toyota, sank into the driver's seat, straight into Pérez's body.

And Mallory's eyes snapped open.

Instructors were yelling, rousting her out of her sleeping bag. Their flashlights cut arcs across the darkness, illuminating the cinder block walls of the barracks.

"Get your lazy butts up!" Leyland shouted. "You think this is a resort? You think this is Club Med?"

The cold had been no dream. It was worse than the night in the Toyota, worse than any cold Mallory had ever known, because she'd been in it for days. Her whole body ached from shivering.

She didn't want to leave the small pool of warmth that had collected in her sleeping bag.

Fuck the drill sergeants. She wasn't going to move.

But Leyland and another instructor dragged her to her feet, tossed her a shirt that smelled like a dead animal—her own smell. They forced her to get dressed in the dark, reminding her that she was wearing the same dirty black fatigues as yesterday because she'd refused to wash them in the river when they'd told her to.

"You are here," Leyland announced to them all, "because *you* have a problem."

He walked back and forth between Mallory and the others, watching them fumble with their clothes.

"You are here because you failed your family," he said, "not the other way around."

Mallory's fingers were too numb to work the zipper. Her

breath seeped out as mist, as if trying to expel the remnants of her dream.

The cinder block cabin that passed for their dormitory had no electricity, no heat, no running water. Mallory remembered bitterly, a million years ago, how she'd hoped to find a phone. There was no goddamn phone. There was no goddamn outside world.

"This is not about your parents," Leyland told them. "This is not about the bad breaks you've had in your overprivileged young lives. THIS IS ABOUT YOU!"

If he only knew, Mallory thought bitterly.

She couldn't get rid of Pérez's image—those brown eyes staring straight into her like a coroner, or a dentist, someone with no interest in her beyond the point of a scalpel.

The instructors herded them outside, called out their names—Zedman, Morrison, Smart, Bridges.

It wasn't light yet, but Mallory knew it was five o'clock sharp. That's what time they always came.

A full moon glowed through the dead oak branches, making bulbs of Spanish moss look like silver fur. The air smelled of frost and wood rot, and the hills were moaning faintly, the way they did all night.

Nothing to worry about, the instructors had told her about the moaning—just a billion tons of granite contracting with the temperature drop. But Leyland had smiled maliciously, as if he knew that Mallory stayed up wide-eyed at night, ashamed to call for help, to admit that she was terrified of ghosts. How bad did Texas have to be, that even the hills groaned?

"Move it!" Leyland said.

They began to run, taking the course Mallory had come to know too well, even in the dark—a half mile through the woods, down steep timber steps hammered into the mud. The run didn't warm Mallory up. It just made her sweaty, let the cold stick to her body and the wind pierce her flimsy clothes.

The edge of the sky was turning pink by the time they got to the riverbank.

Past the obstacle course, Mallory could see her goal: the cliffs at the river, outcroppings of rock that the instructors called the Mushrooms. To Mallory, they looked like scar tissue, swollen and raw and pink.

If all four black levels made it there, across one hundred yards of holl, the instructors had promised they would never see this obstacle course again. But they hadn't come close—not yet.

How long had they been doing this—a week? Ten days?

Every day, Mallory would rebel. Every day they would slap her down, lock her up for a while, then put her right back on the treadmill.

She no longer faked cooperation. Now she tried to resist every way she could—sitting out, yelling, hitting, kicking. If she just acted up long enough and hard enough, eventually they'd kick her out of the program, call her mother and tell her Mallory was hopeless.

She knew what the body sack felt like now. She knew how many bricks made up the wall of the solitary confinement room. She knew what duct tape felt like over her mouth.

She had been mad so long that she'd started to feel like a burned-out lightbulb. Still, she had to keep at it.

The counselors stood at the far end of the obstacle course—young guys in white sweats, ready to head-shrink the kids when the physical torture was over. Mallory had seen enough TV to recognize the good cop/bad cop setup—the instructors bullied them around; the counselors played like their friends, gave the kids a little kindness, then cracked open their insides like rotten pecans.

Screw that.

But Wilson, her would-be counselor, Wilson was no longer in the lineup. She'd kicked him in the nuts at their first meeting, and he hadn't been back since. Dr. Hunter was probably still looking for a replacement crazy enough to deal with her.

"Line up!" Leyland raised the whistle to his lips.

This was the time to make trouble. To resist his command. She could run for it, or hit somebody, or just sit down and not do the course.

But her eye started twitching—remembering the body

sack, the insults the other kids hurled at her whenever she made the team suffer for her bad behavior.

For every infraction, Leyland made her pay hard. But when she cooperated, even a little—he gave her perks. Five minutes extra sleep. A new bar of soap. Lemonade instead of water.

She hated it—but she felt a flicker of pleasure when he paid her even the smallest compliment, when he said, "That's more like it, Zedman," and filled her cup with watery pink swill she wouldn't have washed her toilet with back home.

No, she thought. *Don't cooperate.*

But the whistle blew, and Mallory hit the mud on her chest, started crawling under the rope net.

Leyland yelled, "Don't you touch my ropes, Zedman! Don't let your dirty back touch my ropes!"

Then he turned and yelled at Morrison, who was lagging behind.

Morrison got in trouble almost as much as Mallory. Not because Morrison was a rebel, but because she was a weak fat slob who could never make the course. She'd taken all the abuse the instructors could dish out, but every day she failed to get even halfway. They all had to wait for her while she tried repeatedly, and cried, until finally the instructors walked her through and punished the whole group for what she couldn't do.

Mallory was grateful for her, though—grateful that there was another girl in the group. Grateful that Morrison sometimes took the instructors' abuse instead of her.

Mallory's elbows felt like spikes going through her skin, pulling her along through the mud.

"Move, Zedman!" another instructor yelled. Always a new voice—another anonymous demon with a pitchfork. "This is what you ran away for, isn't it? You're all grown up now! Take care of your own life!"

Mallory clenched her teeth to keep from screaming obscenities.

She got out from under the rope net and started the tire gauntlet.

The two boys in her unit—Bridges and Smart—were

already ahead of her. Smart was the kid with the spiky yellow hair, the one who'd gotten his mouth taped for cussing the first day. Ever since then, the instructors had had a good time calling him Smart-Mouth, like that was some hysterical joke.

Bridges was the fat kid with the bad acne, yet somehow he was always the first one under the ropes.

Mallory didn't know their first names. She didn't care.

Behind her, Leyland yelled, "Come on, Morrison!"

Mallory could hear Morrison sobbing, which was predictable, like every other damn thing in this place. Every day—yelled awake, drilled to death, fed bread and water for breakfast. Then the damn counselors pulled them aside for the "program"—lectures nobody wanted to hear, followed by chances to talk nobody ever took. And then there would be the slave labor—building a new dorm for the next group of victims.

What would Race think of this? Mallory tried to imagine him here. Race would fight the instructors, she decided. He would succeed where she failed.

She slowed down on the tires. The new assistant instructor got in her ear, yelling at her to keep her knees up. Mallory didn't look at the guy, but she could tell it was one of the older kids—the ones they called white levels. No one would ever brainwash Mallory like that.

She tried to keep her mind on Race. The guilt swelled up in her again—the knowledge that she had left him, didn't even know where he was staying now, or if the police had caught him.

Everything had gone horribly wrong. Her mom finding the gun in the locker—somebody must've told her to look, but Mallory couldn't figure out who. Then the argument with her mom, running away to Race, that nightmarish week at Talia's. The Halloween party, coming home and finding the body. Then afterward . . . hiding out with Race, holding him while he cried, making love in the stairwell of that abandoned apartment building.

It had all been a mistake—even the sex.

She understood now why they called it *losing* virginity.

She had lost something of herself, and what had she gotten in return? She didn't even feel what she had wanted most—closer to Race.

She tripped on the last tire, fell flat on her face. She turned over, wheezing, her eyes stinging with mud, and stared at the canopy of cypress branches above. The white level's face hovered over her, hollering at her to get up.

She got to her feet, managed not to take a swing at the kid. She'd tried that when—yesterday? She'd popped some instructor in the eye and paid for it with four hours in solitary, locked in a lightless shed until she'd started to see spots like jellyfish floating in the darkness.

She jumped up to the balance beam—still thinking about Race, and Pérez's words. *If it wasn't for those people, your dad would be okay. They keep a gun to his head.*

Mallory wasn't stupid. She'd never met Race's older brother but she knew Samuel had supplied Katherine's drugs. She understood why her dad wouldn't like her hanging out with the Montroses. But still, the hate in his voice when he talked about them...it was way beyond fear for Mallory. It was murderous.

And the idea that he was planning something, that the Montroses were keeping a gun to his head—what the hell did that mean?

She'd tried to talk to Race about it, but he'd gotten really quiet.

He admitted his brother had been a dealer, a real bad-ass. He told her how Samuel used to beat up his mother's boyfriends—grown men, twice his size. Samuel had made Race work as a spotter for cops on the street corner. The same year Mallory had been starting kindergarten, Race had been working the drug trade.

But that was a long time ago, and Race had been adamant—Samuel wasn't in the picture anymore. He wouldn't say where Samuel had gone, but Mallory was pretty sure Race was telling her the truth—on that point, anyway.

What bothered her, the more she thought about it, was something Race had told her after they'd made love, when she'd asked if there was any relative he could go to—anybody he trusted.

He had propped himself up on his elbow, stared over her shoulder long enough for a BART train to blare past outside the grimy window. "Insanity runs in my family, Mal. There's nobody I trust. Nobody."

He opened his palm. His nails had cut deep crescents into his lifeline.

Ever since that night, she'd been thinking. Little things, like the fact that she'd woken up the morning after Halloween, crashed on a couch in an abandoned house, and Race hadn't been there. He'd come back soon enough, bringing donuts and beer for breakfast, but she had no idea how long he'd been gone. And after that they'd walked together to his mother's.

That didn't mean he'd killed Talia. Of course it didn't.

But if the police questioned her, if they visited Cold Springs and pressured her the way the instructors did, told her it was her ass, or her boyfriend's—what would she say? Would she have the courage to lie? To be Race's alibi?

She was falling behind on the course. She hit the parallel bars, arm-walked across, caught up with Smart and Bridges, who were throwing themselves uselessly at the wall.

"Let's go!" Leyland bellowed. He'd traded places with the white level—let the white level chew out Morrison for a while. "This is a *little* wall, Zedman. My grandmother trains on this wall. Get your sorry butt over the top. LET'S GO!"

Mallory knew the wall wasn't more than six feet high, but it felt a lot taller. She could get her fingertips to the top, but there was no way she had enough strength to pull herself up. She slammed into it anyway, grabbed the top, felt the blisters break on her hands from where she'd done the same thing the day before. She ended up sprawled on the ground, staring at the gray cinder blocks. Her whole damn life came down to cinder blocks—sleeping in them, climbing them, building with them. The instructors would have her eating cinder blocks pretty soon.

Smart and Bridges weren't having any more luck than Mallory. Smart wasn't strong enough. Bridges was too damn fat; he could get his meaty hands around the top, but then he'd climb about two feet and hang there like a sandbag before falling on his butt.

Mallory got up and tried again, hating the wall, wanting to bust it down.

Morrison came up next to her, huffing and sobbing, and Mallory realized that nobody had walked her up this time. She'd made it herself. Mallory didn't know why, but she liked that Morrison had beaten the bastards, shown them she could get this far.

Mallory looked down at her raw hands. She was about to throw herself at the wall again, then she stopped.

She remembered a time in second grade—Mrs. Sanford's class, Laurel Heights, the new kid Race huddled under the sand table because the boys had teased him about wearing the same shoes five days in a row, asking him if his mom had ever heard of Goodwill. And Mrs. Sanford not seeing any of it— blind to what was going on right under her nose, just like every teacher. Just like Mallory's mom.

Mallory had scooted under the sand table with Race and apologized to him, even though she hadn't done anything. Right there, they'd formed a friendship, writing their names for each other on the sandy cement. They'd ganged up together and become the terrors of the class.

"Hey," she told Morrison. "Come on!"

She laced her fingers together, made a foothold. Morrison looked at her like she was from Mars.

Morrison had lost all traces of that heavy mascara she'd worn on arrival, but her eyes were still swollen from constant crying. Her stringy hair had been dyed four different colors and was matted to her cheeks so it looked like several different animals had crawled on her head to die.

"Don't mess with me, Zedman," she muttered, but she didn't put any heart in it.

The instructors were still yelling, but they weren't yelling specifically at Mallory or Morrison. Mallory felt as if she'd suddenly created a bubble of neutral space, the drill sergeant crap flowing right around her.

"I'm serious," she told Morrison. "Screw Leyland, okay? Come on!"

Morrison hesitated, then, awkwardly, put her foot in Mallory's cupped hands. She almost fell trying to get her balance, but she got her hands on the top of the wall and held on. Mallory's raw blisters hurt like hell, but she kept her fingers laced together and stood, pushing Morrison's leg up. It was like trying to balance a barbell on one end, but Mallory kept pushing and suddenly Morrison was at the top, and then over the wall with a painful thump.

Mallory had forgotten how good it felt to smile.

Bridges and Smart were staring at her like they were sure she'd just signed their death warrants.

Leyland shouted, "Keep it moving, Zedman!"

And Mallory heard something new in his tone—approval. That's what they wanted. They wanted team cooperation.

Mallory was about to offer Smart a boost over the wall when a whistle blew two times—that sharp signal that meant "faces to the wall." Black levels weren't supposed to see anyone but their own team. They weren't supposed to make eye contact with any visitor. Smart and Bridges turned so their noses were touching the cinder block.

Morrison scrambled around from the other side of the wall to join them. Her whole left side was caked with mud, but she gave Mallory a strange look that made her feel they had a new understanding—an alliance.

"Wall!" the white level screamed.

Mallory made the mistake of glancing back before complying, and when she did she saw Dr. Hunter and his visitors.

One was a young black woman. From her street clothes, and Hunter's body language, it was obvious she was getting a tour—maybe a parent, or a reporter. The other newcomer was the butch-looking blond woman who'd been with Chadwick, the day they'd picked up Mallory.

What was her name—Owens? No. Olsen.

She was dressed in white sweats. She joined the line of counselors at the end of the course.

Then Mallory understood what she was doing here—she

was going to replace Wilson, the guy Mallory had kicked in the balls. The realization was like a drink of acid.

Leyland was yelling at her now, telling her to get her nose to the cinder block, but she didn't.

Olsen smiled at her—but the smile seemed cold. She seemed to be examining Mallory like an exhibit, a piece she'd added to her freak collection.

No way was Mallory going to have that lady as her counselor.

"To the wall, Zedman!" Leyland shouted again.

Dr. Hunter stopped talking to his guest. If he stepped in, it was all over. Mallory would be forced to obey, bent into any damn G.I. Joe position Hunter wanted, and—if Mallory didn't get another slap in the face like seeing Olsen—Mallory might even grow to accept it.

She couldn't believe she'd been concerned with Morrison, felt good that the fat slob had gotten over the stupid wall. Mallory realized she'd been on the verge of giving in to the program, of cooperating.

Seeing Olsen again, she had a target for her anger. Mallory remembered the plane trip—how Chadwick had reassured her, treated her with firmness but respect, which had somehow been a worse trick, a worse lie than if he'd treated Mallory like these bastard instructors did. Chadwick had tricked her into thinking that Cold Springs wouldn't be so bad. Chadwick had manipulated Mallory's mother into sending her here—Mallory's mother, who'd always liked Chadwick, who'd shown him more affection than she'd ever shown Mallory. Chadwick had probably sent Olsen here to keep an eye on her.

"Zedman!" Leyland yelled.

Hunter's guest asked him something too quiet to hear, and Hunter answered, "Watch."

Mallory took a step forward, then another, her whole body trembling. She would not be an exhibit. She would not play their game.

One of the boys, Bridges or Smart, yelled, "Zedman, get back here!" They knew Mallory was about to earn them extra hours of drill time.

They'll make good white levels one of these days, Mallory thought, but not me.

She stepped toward Olsen. *"You* did this to me!"

The drill instructors were still yelling, but out of the corner of her eye she could see the enforcer, the staff member with the body bag who was always on the periphery, ready to move as fast as the Grim Reaper whenever things got out of hand. The bag was for Mallory. The whole force of the camp would come down on her if she didn't obey.

But Mallory couldn't. She had remembered herself now.

"Fuck you!" she shouted at Olsen. "Tell Chadwick—tell him I'm glad Katherine's dead. Tell him I said that! You tell him!"

A white level pinned her arms, held her back while the guy with the body bag came forward.

She hated that she was crying, but she couldn't stop it. If they put her into that bag, she would find a way to kill herself. She would never run their damn obstacle course again. She'd die if she spent another day in solitary.

Mallory kicked as they fastened her legs.

"You lied!" she screamed at Olsen.

Olsen said nothing.

Mallory's only satisfaction was the sadness in her eyes, as if Mallory had really damaged her. But on second thought, Mallory wasn't sure if that look in Olsen's eyes was new.

The gag went over Mallory's mouth, the enforcer and the white level dragging her toward the cinder block shed under the cypress tree, where she would be spending more time in the dark.

The whistle blew. The course resumed without her. And Hunter and his guest went back to their conversation, Hunter gesturing toward Mallory as if she'd just provided a testimonial for the program he was trying to sell.

9

Norma's house on Telegraph Hill was a peeling wedge of white stucco, like a slice of bride's cake, scrupulously preserved until it had petrified into something inedible.

She hadn't always thought of it that way.

Years ago, fresh from her first big commission, she'd loved the house John had found for her. It was spacious, clean, quiet, secure—everything the townhouse in the Mission had not been.

Now, however, she dreaded coming home.

She spent the afternoon at Laurel Heights, working with Ann and the school board and David Kraft—Katherine's old friend, her first boyfriend. Norma sat in meetings about rebuilding the school, gave updates on the fund-raising, and every time David smiled, she thought about her daughter—how she had never graduated, never gone to college or had a job. Then Norma drove home to her beautiful empty house, her ears still ringing with the sounds of children.

She was torturing herself needlessly. She knew that.

But she wanted to help Ann. She found herself neglecting her paying accounts, spending way too much time on the pro bono work for Laurel Heights.

Whenever she talked it over with John—who still knew more about the school's finances than she did, had set up all the accounts—he seemed mystified by her commitment.

Of all people, John said, *you should be rooting for her to fail. What has she not taken away from you?*

Norma understood what was on the line for Ann. She'd

seen it in the faces of the board members—Ann was in trouble. Families were worried about the school's dilapidated facilities, the program that seemed stuck back in the late 1970s when Ann had seized the helm, and the amount of time it had taken Ann to meet her capital campaign goals. Parents had heard about Mallory's problems, the weapon that had been found on campus—and they wondered uneasily if it wouldn't just be easier to move their kids elsewhere.

If Ann's building program finally succeeded, she might turn things around, head the school until she retired, leave a permanent legacy. Otherwise, she had given her entire professional life to Laurel Heights. What would she have to show?

Norma also had less altruistic reasons for helping.

When she thought about jackhammers breaking up the playground, bulldozers plowing a muddy path up the side of the hill, trampling the azaleas and hydrangeas that had been there for eighty years—she felt a dark satisfaction, the same satisfaction she felt sitting up at night, in her bathroom, counting sleeping pills in her palm, wishing she possessed her daughter's courage.

She couldn't end her life. It wasn't in her nature. But she could bury her memories of Laurel Heights—raze the place that had gobbled up all of her ex-husband's time, ruined her marriage, failed Katherine so miserably. She could help replace it with something clean and huge, empty of history, just like her house.

It started to rain as she turned on Greenwich. Red-faced tourists huffed up the hill, their cameras wrapped in plastic bags, *Bay Guardian* newspapers wilting over their heads. The Rastafarian flower seller who sometimes gave Norma free roses was hastily loading bouquets from the sidewalk into his van.

When she saw the black BMW in front of her house, her heart developed a caffeine flutter.

She pulled into the driveway.

John came out her front door, smiling into her headlights.

She shouldn't have been surprised. John and Ann both had keys. Mallory, too—for that matter. Hadn't she made it clear to all of them—this was their home as well as hers? She wanted them in her life. She wanted to be neutral ground, a conduit through which they could interact.

And today was Wednesday—her night for dinner with John. But that shouldn't have been until later, and they usually met at a restaurant.

So what was he doing here?

At least Pérez didn't seem to be with him. That's one thing she had put her foot down about—John was never to bring that man to her home.

Pérez scared her on some instinctive level. She knew he was Mexican, but his military bearing, his cruel eyes, brought back too many childhood nightmares, stories her grandfather would tell her about Castro's soldiers.

She pulled her satchel out of the car, tossed it to John. "You were cleaning house for me, I hope?"

Despite the smile, he looked tired, angry, as if he'd just gotten through yelling at someone. "Like you need house-cleaning. Five years, Ms. Reyes—when are you going to move in?"

She punched his arm. "What are you doing here?"

"Come and see."

Inside, candles on the dining table. A takeout Chinese dinner—white paper boxes, chopsticks, an uncorked bottle of Chardonnay. The doors of the back deck were open on the rainy evening. The Bay glowed below, the soft neon of the city illuminating the wake of the Sausalito ferry.

Music was playing—not John's favorite classical. He knew that would remind her too much of Chadwick. He'd picked Los Lobos, *La Pistola y el Corazón*—music she'd once daydreamed to. She must have told John she loved this album. She should have been flattered he remembered.

But the music brought back memories of the bougainvillea out her old kitchen window, Katherine playing in the backyard, Chadwick grading papers at the yellow Formica table, massaging her ankle with his toes. She swallowed back her sadness. "I hope we're talking Szechwan."

"Only four-pepper items."

"Ay, qué buena. What's the occasion?"

He pulled out her chair, poured her some wine. Only after she'd sat, allowed him to serve her some chicken and peanuts, did he say, "I'm apologizing."

"For what?"

"Mallory being taken away. You knew. You didn't tell me."

Norma felt heat collecting in her cheeks.

"It's okay," John said. "I was mad all week. Then I realized—Ann put you in a hell of a position. You couldn't betray her confidence. Wouldn't be fair of me to expect that, would it? Just promise—if I ever put you in a bind like that, force you to choose between us, you'll tell me. Okay?"

Norma took a shaky breath.

Something bothered her. Behind the diplomatic, carefully rehearsed words, John seemed . . . hungry. Grasping.

"I'm sorry," she said. "If it helps, I told her she was crazy."

"Mallory's my child, too. Yet I'm allowed no say in this?"

His smile seemed dangerously thin.

Norma thought about the night of the auction, John and Chadwick sparring drunk in the school playground—how ridiculous they'd looked. It never would've occurred to her to be scared of John Zedman.

Then again, she'd never been scared of anything with Chadwick. As mild-mannered as he was—come on, you'd have to be nuts to challenge a guy that big. That feeling of safety, of immunity from danger—she'd taken it totally for granted until she became single again.

Now, alone with John, she felt a little shiver of fear up her spine, even though she knew that was absurd. The guy was one of her oldest friends.

She speared a chunk of chicken, nudged the fleck of red pepper off it. The food was too spicy even for her. It wasn't much of a meal, or an apology. More like a gourmet punishment.

"I thought you forgave me," she told John.

"I do. I'm just wondering—you know. You let her call

Chadwick? I mean—what was that...temporary insanity, Norma?"

She folded her napkin, got up from the table, picked up her plate. "Thank you for dinner, John."

"Whoa. I'm just trying to sort through things. Okay?"

"Don't lay a guilt trip on me. I'm not—"

She stopped herself.

"You're not Ann," he finished for her. "I know that, Norma. God, I can see that."

She went to the kitchen counter, set her plate down.

"Come on," he coaxed. "Finish eating."

She poured her wine into the sink, froze when she felt John's breath on her shoulder. "What was it like—" he asked, "seeing Chadwick again?"

She turned.

"He did come to the school," John guessed. "He saw Ann...privately?"

Some deep instinct warned her not to share what David Kraft had told her—about Ann and Chadwick kissing in the office. As much as the information had angered her, as much as she wished she could commiserate with someone, something in John's eyes told her that subject was dangerous.

She put her hand lightly on his chest. She thought of how she'd raked Chadwick's face when she'd seen him, how she'd cried, later, as she scrubbed and scrubbed his blood from underneath her fingernails.

"Mallory needed help," she told John.

"Ann took her away from a police investigation. Now they think my daughter murdered that Montrose bitch. I'm going to get custody, Norma. I'm going to take Ann back to court until she hasn't a dime left to pay any lawyers. You know Mallory will be better off with me, don't you?"

"A minute ago you asked me to tell you if you ever put me in a bind."

His breath smelled of wine and peppers. In the background, Los Lobos were singing words Norma knew he couldn't understand—about the power of a gun.

He put his hand on the small of her back, his fingers spreading out to encompass as much of her as he could.

"John," she said.

"Why are you punishing yourself, Norma? Why are you still alone, after nine years?"

Heat spread out across her rib cage. Not excitement, exactly—more the thrill of skidding on an icy road.

How many times had she wished that Chadwick were more like John? And now here was John, pressed against her—kissing her, his lips burning from Szechwan—and all she could think of was Chadwick, about the ravenous sadness that had made her lash out at him, claw his face, because she needed to be certain he was still real.

"Hey," she murmured. "Knock it off."

John ran a finger up her spine, sought her lips again.

All she had to do was pretend—just a little.

She pushed him away. "I'm serious, John. Stop."

His eyes came back into focus, glowing with anger. Then he stepped back, managed that self-deprecating smile he did so well.

"I guess I got a head start on the wine," he said. "Sorry."

"I think you should leave now."

"Okay. Sure."

He gathered up his coat, looked at the bottle of wine like he was thinking of taking it, then picked up his briefcase instead. Norma hadn't noticed the briefcase before. She wondered why he'd brought it to dinner.

"I'll call you," he said. "I guess you're busy with the auction."

"It's next Friday. Yeah."

"If I can help—"

"I've got it under control."

He lifted his fingers in an anemic farewell. "It'll be nine years exactly. Hard to believe."

He gave her one last smile, as if his reminder hadn't been calculated to wound her.

She watched the taillights of his BMW disappear down Telegraph Hill. Then she walked to the balcony. A cruise ship was passing under the Golden Gate. Rain pattered on her deck, filling up her empty flower boxes.

She cleared the Chinese food from the table so she wouldn't have to smell it. She turned off the music, then she went to her home office and stared at the dark computer screen, the empty crib of the fax machine. Everything just the way she left it.

Like what— Like John would steal her credit card numbers? Hardly.

So why did his visit tonight bother her so much?

His romantic advance was nothing new. He'd tried that twice before, never so forcefully, but she had to put it in perspective—the guy was lonely. He was dealing with a divorce a lot fresher than hers. She was a safe target. And yes—the anniversary of Katherine's death was next week. Norma wouldn't be the only one who'd have trouble dealing with that.

John understood "no." Norma could handle him, as long as she was fair. She had to do a better job with that. She had to stop playing games with the guy. Why had she let it go so far?

She took a long shower, and thought she heard John clunking around in the kitchen, but she knew it was her imagination. Then she remembered she hadn't locked the front door, hadn't even closed the glass doors to the porch.

She knew there was nothing to be afraid of—this was hardly a high-crime neighborhood. But her heart beat faster anyway. She turned off the shower, heard nothing except the rain.

She pulled on her terry cloth robe.

It was pouring in earnest now—a rare event, especially this time of year. Rain sheeted off the awnings, drummed on the roof.

She stepped into the living room in bare feet, her hair wet and cold on the back of her bare neck, and she saw him—a lean black man silhouetted in the doorway of her deck. No, not a man. A teenager. Norma backed up and seized the phone as the boy came toward her. He was wearing a mud-splattered T-shirt, jeans drenched up to the thighs with water, and a tattered camouflage coat.

She dialed 911.

"Ms. Reyes," the boy said. "Wait!"

She tripped over a chair, backing into the hallway. The emergency number was ringing.

"Ms. Reyes," the boy said. "It's me."

She realized she knew those eyes, the red hair, the strange set to his mouth and jaw, as if he'd been pulled lengthwise when he came out of the womb. She heard herself say, "Race?"

The emergency operator was on the line.

"Please," Race said. "Please, just listen."

"911 switchboard," the operator repeated. "What is the nature of your emergency?"

Norma's fear was turning to anger. How dare Race—of all people.

She said into the phone, "I have an intruder in my house."

"No," Race said. "No. Listen."

Norma had spent years trying to follow Ann's advice—trying not to blame this boy for what his family had done. And Race had made it easy for her, most of the time. He seemed to understand her hatred. He countered it with politeness, went out of his way to treat her with respect. The older he got, the more Norma had grown to like him, and she was angry at herself for allowing that to happen.

Mallory would have been a good kid, would've gotten past Katherine's death, except the Montroses had stayed in their lives, like carbon monoxide, slowly poisoning her.

The Montrose bitch. Had John been so wrong, calling her that?

Norma remembered a few months after Katherine's death, just after Chadwick had left for Texas—Talia Montrose showing up at Laurel Heights in her pink pants and cheap satin blouse and bleached hair, looking like a hooker—her mouth trembling, but her eyes defiant, full of vengeance she had no right to want. She asked for an application for her youngest boy. And four days later, when Ann broke the news to Norma that she was actually accepting the child—Norma exploded. She'd brought up the affair with Chadwick—forced the truth out of Ann. They'd said horrible, hurtful things. Then they didn't speak for two years.

All of that was the Montroses' fault, and Race wasn't any better than the rest. He had brought a gun to school, gotten himself expelled. He'd gotten Mallory involved in drugs, and a murder.

Why would he come here now?

"Ma'am?" the operator was saying. "Can you safely exit the house? The police are en route. Is there a window or a door—"

"Please, Ms. Reyes," Race pleaded. "You got to listen. Please."

The boy was shivering. He was more frightened than she was. He looked like he hadn't eaten in a week—his eyes jaundiced, his lips dry and cracked.

Her maternal instinct stirred, unwanted, the way it used to when Mallory would come over to escape her parents' arguments. She would sit at the dining table, right there, and let Norma stroke her hair while she sobbed.

Norma took the phone away from her ear, punched the *off* button.

"You had better explain yourself," she told Race. "What are you doing in my house?"

His chin started quivering. He sat down on the couch, smearing it with mud and leaves, running his fingers through his red hair. "Don't say I was here. Please—don't tell anybody. Okay? You have to promise."

"Race, I can't promise that. The police are looking for you."

"My mother..." he said. "She was murdered."

The words came out like they'd been cut from him, and suddenly Norma remembered her first reaction when she'd heard Talia was dead. She had thought, *It serves her right.*

Now, she realized how heartless that had been, how little Race deserved the pain.

"I'm sorry, honey," she said. "I really am."

"Mallory was with me. My momma—she was..." He

curled his hands as if trying to grasp the image. "She was stabbed..."

"Honey," Norma said. "You need to go to the police."

"No! No police. I know who they're gonna blame. You got to listen to me. She ain't going to be satisfied until they're both dead."

"Who, honey? What are you talking about?"

Race swallowed, held out his hand and watched it shake. Norma got the uneasy feeling he had been talking about his dead mother—as if Talia were whispering things in his ear.

"The money," he said. "Check the money, you don't believe me—"

Then he stopped. Norma heard the sirens a half second later, a long way off, but getting closer.

"Race," Norma said. "Stay with me. Talk to them..."

But he was out the back door faster than Norma would have believed possible—over the deck railing, the fence, then down the hillside, skidding across the black plastic tarp that was supposed to keep the slope from turning into a mudslide on nights like this. He plunged through a wet clump of manzanitas and disappeared over a ridge that dropped ten, maybe fifteen feet, straight down to Columbus Avenue.

When Norma turned, she realized the police had been closer than she realized. Red lights pulsed through her windows, casting blood-colored squares onto her ceilings.

John stopped at the Palace of Fine Arts. He couldn't face the Golden Gate Bridge traffic yet. He knew Pérez would question him, pester him as soon as he got home—and he wasn't ready for that.

He paced under the huge dome of the pavilion—the pink Grecian columns lit up for no one, the park desolate and empty, cold rain falling outside.

He set up his laptop on a trash can.

He didn't realize how on edge he was until a vagrant slipped from the shadows, attracted by the glow of the screen, and wheedled, "You got a little extra, mister—"

John's .22 was in his hand, the muzzle pushed under the old man's grimy, bearded nose, John saying, "You want something?"

"Whoa!" The bum's eyes went completely schizoid, skipping right off the top of reality like a river rock. "Whoa, fuck."

He backed away, white palms melting into the darkness. Not until he was a tiny smudge of shadow on the far side of the lake did he yell, "Happy Thanksgiving, asshole!"

John expelled a laugh that sounded crazy, even to him. He slipped his gun back into his coat pocket.

He was going to shake to pieces. He was a test plane at the edge of the sound barrier, the bolts of his wings starting to rattle loose.

Oh, God, Norma. What had he been thinking?

He shouldn't have seen her tonight. He'd told himself he needed to check her computer one more time, just for insurance. He needed to make sure the passwords hadn't changed.

But that wasn't why he'd waited for her, why he'd picked up dinner and lit candles and put on her favorite music.

He'd been hoping for the courage to tell her the truth. He thought if he looked straight into her eyes, he could confess what he had been sucked into, how hopelessly entangled he'd become. He would explain that his motive had been pure—he just wanted to save his daughter.

Norma would understand instantly. She'd grip his hands across the table, her face beautiful and compassionate in the candlelight. She wouldn't condemn him, wouldn't call him a monster. She'd talk the problem through with him until he figured out another way to save Mallory, and himself.

It would be so different than it had been with Ann—that last horrible argument of their marriage, when he'd tried to tell her about the letters from Samuel, only to have the conversation deteriorate into one more shouting match about why Ann should quit her job, why they should put Mallory in another school, get her away from Race. Finally, his patience had snapped—his years of frustration and rage discharged in a single brutal slap across his wife's jaw.

There could be no forgiveness for that. No second chance.

Once you lose control, women never trust you again. Norma had made that clear tonight, with the fear in her eyes.

He stared at the computer screen, the wireless connection accessing a bank account halfway around the world.

Bitterness tasted like cheap whiskey on his tongue.

Why the fuck not?

The calls had all been made. The setup was perfect. All it took now was a single e-mail.

"He ain't going away," Pérez had warned him that afternoon. "You throw more money at this Samuel, play his easy fuck—you think he'll ever leave you alone?"

Pérez had been loading his gun at the kitchen table, pushing nine-millimeter cartridges into the magazine with the care of a pharmacist counting pills. "All I need is two plane tickets, Boss. I got a friend can help. We get the girl back, teach this Chadwick a lesson. Then you call this son-of-a-bitch Samuel's bluff. He shows his face, I blow him the fuck away."

Pérez's plan had appeal.

But it wasn't the real reason John was hesitating.

He hated to admit it, but he had begun to see the wisdom in what Ann had done, calling Chadwick. At least Mallory was out of danger. At least she was far away from the Montroses. And after all these years, dreaming of destroying Ann, now that it was within his reach, he found it hard to do.

John could close the laptop, drive home.

The police he could handle. He had started pulling strings already on the Talia Montrose problem, letting a few well-placed friends in Oakland know that a certain homicide sergeant needed help distinguishing a concerned citizen from a suspect. The only person to fear was Samuel. And what could Samuel do to him—expose his past sins? That meant nothing to him anymore, as long as his daughter was safe.

The screen asked for a prompt.

How long would it take—ten minutes? Less. He had planned so well.

Across the Bay, the Sausalito ferry was coming back from its final evening run. He imagined his father at the Embarcadero docks, forty years ago, sitting on his toolbox, wiping the grease off his forehead with the back of his hand while he waited for the boat. He would be bone-tired, having worked repairs since six in the morning, but he'd still have energy to sit with John, tell him stories about the Pacific War. When the ferry docked, he would have exactly ten minutes, from 7:50 to 8:00, to do a final check on the engine before sending it back across the Bay, where it would dock in Sausalito for the night.

"That boat is no fool," his father would tell him, tousling John's hair so he would smell like engine grease for a week. "Works here, but sleeps up north with the rich folk."

He would flash his crooked teeth, the front two broken in a bar fight years ago, but John would see the sadness in his eyes, the spirit that had been broken when John's mother left.

John had promised himself he would never turn into his father.

He would be one of those rich folk across the Bay. He would keep his family together. As a boy, he assumed that if he just managed the first part, the second part would take care of itself.

He took out his cell phone, stared at the number that had been sent with the last letter.

Call when it's done, the letter said. *The number will only work one time. Punch in 12 23. Then hang up. I will call you back.*

12/23. John wasn't blind to the meaning of that. It had been Katherine Chadwick's birthday.

He dialed as he'd been told, then hung up.

Even though he was expecting it, the sound of the return call made him jump.

"Hello, John." The voice was distorted. It could've been a man or a woman or a child.

Still, John was finally talking to the ghost—the one who had turned his life into hell all these years.

"I'm not going through with it," John said. "Do what you want. You won't get a dime."

There was a rushing, distorted sound in the background—maybe a highway, or a river. John wasn't sure.

The ghost said, "You think you're safe from me, John? You think I've forgiven you?"

"I don't care anymore."

"That's brave. You know what your daughter did today?"

"She's out of your reach, you bastard."

"She ate one slice of bread," the ghost said. "Drank some river water. She screamed at her instructors in the obstacle course, got put in a sack, John. A big burlap thing with a chain through it. Duct tape on her mouth. They locked her in a small room with no windows for two hours."

John sank to his knees, the phone pressed against his ear, his forehead bowing toward the pavement that smelled of pigeon crap and rain.

"I can get to her anytime, John. Do anything I want."

All his confidence drained away. Mallory was a little girl again, shivering in a huge black recliner, waiting for him to rescue her, her eyes accusing him for being gone so long.

"Please," he said. "Leave her alone."

"You have your instructions, John. You're going to cooperate. You know it's for the best. That is what we all want, isn't it? We all want a happy ending. Don't we?"

"My daughter—"

"She's asleep now. In a little cinder block cabin. She's shivering. No heat. She's hungry. They yell at her every morning, noon, and night. If you had custody, you could sign your name to some papers and have her home. Or do you want me to take care of her for you?"

"I'm online now."

"That's good. The problem is, you used up your one call. Do what I told you. I'll be in touch. And John—you don't have any leeway left. Understand me?"

The line went dead.

John looked up at the screen of his laptop—the screensaver etching orange curlicues in the darkness.

He thought of his father's eyes, as bright as shattered glass, staring out at the lights of Sausalito as if they were patches of ship wreckage, burning on the Okinawan Sea.

Then John began to type.

10

"Kindra Jones—Chadwick," Hunter said. "Mix it up."

They shook hands, Chadwick trying to hold down his feeling of wariness, thinking about how many times he had replayed this scene with different women.

Kindra Jones was lithe, athletic, her hair in cornrows. She had perfect Nefertiti features, her long neck inclined slightly forward. Black horn-rimmed glasses, gold stud in her nose and clothes that seemed randomly chosen from dryers at the laundromat—camouflage and corduroy; olive, brown, muddy blue.

She had a firm handshake and a cocky smile that Chadwick immediately liked—and then, just as immediately, dreaded, thinking that she was destined to be another coin lost in the wishing well.

"Jones is from California," Hunter put in. "You'll get along fine."

As if all Californians were one happy family. But Chadwick nodded politely. "Where from?" he asked her.

"Alameda," Jones told him. "And Sacramento. And a few other places. Papa was a rolling stone."

She wasn't old enough to know that song, and the fact she did, almost made Chadwick smile.

Hunter gave them a quick briefing—the dozen clients he needed to schedule for pickup, twice that many gray and tan levels to process out to the other facilities. Business was good. The escort service couldn't afford downtime.

"And now, Ms. Jones," Hunter said, handing her a stack of

files to read, "if you would excuse me, I have a few things to go over with Chadwick."

"See you," Jones said, and her smile suggested she was really looking forward to starting work.

When she was gone, Chadwick said, "Promising."

"Yeah," Hunter said absently. "BA in education. Good recs. I'm sure you'll drive her away."

"Cynic."

Hunter pushed aside a paper plate of half-eaten cafeteria food—turkey, cranberry sauce, pumpkin bread. He switched on his main monitor, began rewinding a green-tinted surveillance tape.

Chadwick said, "You left the staff party pretty early."

Hunter waved the comment aside. "Come here. I want you to see this."

Chadwick pulled a chair around the side of the desk. He watched the tape rewind—ghostly figures moving backwards, bars of silver static.

Truth was, he'd been glad to leave the party himself. It had been the first time he'd seen his ex-partner Olsen since she'd quit escorting. He wasn't good at avoiding people, even when it was clear that was what Olsen wanted. She'd stood chatting with a group of other counselors, wearing her new white uniform, trying not to make eye contact with him, which wasn't easy. Given her basketball player's stature, the two of them had easily been the tallest people at the party.

"There," Hunter said, stopping the tape and letting it run forward.

The camera angle was Black Level Clearing Three—looking down from a tree branch just outside the barracks. It was a night-vision shot, so everything in the picture glowed. Black Level students were being mustered in for dawn exercises. The instructor was Frank Leyland. Counselors shouldn't have been on duty yet—they usually didn't join the fun until after morning drills—but Chadwick recognized Olsen. She stood with her back to a mesquite tree, her blond hair and white fatigues blurred in the film like a bleach stain.

Mallory Zedman stumbled out of the barracks.

An assistant instructor was right behind her—yelling, though there was no sound. Mallory kept turning away from him, refusing to get in line. Then Olsen came up, put her hand on Mallory's shoulder, said something. Mallory reluctantly got into formation.

Leyland paced back and forth, issuing orders, lecturing—like any morning inspection. Then Mallory detached herself from the line. She stepped toward Olsen with something in her fist, something that glinted.

Olsen didn't see her coming until Mallory was on top of her. Then it was too late. Mallory's arm flashed and then she ran.

Chaos in the line. The kids broke in every direction. Olsen staggered, clutching her shoulder. The assistant instructor ran to Olsen's aid. Leyland started after Mallory.

Hunter hit the pause button, froze Leyland mid-stride, canted forward like an Olympian statue.

"Kitchen knife," he said. "She had it in the sleeve of her sweatshirt."

"Black levels eat in camp. They don't go anywhere near the cafeteria. Where'd she get it?"

"A staff member must've gotten careless, left it somewhere. I find out who, I'm going to grind them into rebarb. The point is, the Zedman girl is resourceful. And determined."

"I just saw Olsen at the party. She said nothing about this."

"She insisted we not make a big deal about it. Got three stitches and a tetanus shot and she wants to keep working with Zedman. The girl has spirit, amigo. I can see why you wanted to keep her."

Hunter hit another button on his surveillance console, brought up a live shot.

It was like looking into a well—just a shaft of gray brick. Mallory was sitting with her back against the door, as if to keep anyone else from coming in. She was mumbling something. It could've been a lullaby, judging from her expression.

As if she knew they were watching, she stopped singing and looked straight up at the camera. Her eyes were like a marathon runner's in the middle of a course, just when the real pain was setting in.

"Has she eaten?" Chadwick asked.

"Been two days. We'll have to force-feed soon." Hunter's tone was dry. Force-feeding was one of the extreme measures even he disliked. "I'm not saying we haven't dealt with worse..."

"Let me talk to her," Chadwick said.

Hunter sat back in his huge leather chair. He stared at the only photo on his desk—his father, the Reverend Asa Hunter, Sr.

Hunter often professed dislike for his father, had run away when he was fifteen, joined the Air Force when he was seventeen. And yet there was the Reverend's picture—the implacable African Methodist Episcopal who had turned his son into the most biblically well-versed atheist in the world.

"I spoke with your friend at Oakland Homicide," Hunter told Chadwick. "Sergeant Damarodas."

"Since when is he my friend?"

"They identified two people's blood at the scene. Talia Montrose's. The other—smaller amount. They're assuming the attacker. DNA says chances are a billion to one the attacker was related to the victim."

"Samuel Montrose?"

"Police are still looking for the younger brother, Race. They still want to talk to Mallory. Damarodas thinks she may have seen the murder."

"You reconsidering giving him access?"

Anyone besides Chadwick probably wouldn't have sensed Hunter's uneasiness, it was so slight—as hard to see, as insubstantial as a tripwire.

"You know a guy named David Kraft?" Hunter asked him.

"A friend of my daughter's. Works at Laurel Heights now."

"Damarodas talked to him—wanted to get some background on you, Katherine, that necklace they found. David Kraft said he used to date your daughter. He admitted that

once, to score some pot, he took her to this place he knew—
the Montrose house. He's the one introduced them."

Chadwick flexed his fingers, which suddenly felt stiff and
swollen. "There's no point bringing all that up now."

"So I told Damarodas. Except, according to Kraft, your
daughter took an instant liking to the dealer, Samuel. She
dumped David Kraft pretty quick after that, but he claims
Katherine and Samuel got involved—heavily involved. Ro-
mantically."

On the surveillance screen, Mallory was serenading her
knee, prodding it with her finger as if there were a tiny bug
there.

"The night I told you about," Chadwick said, "the one
time I saw Samuel. I was taking Katherine home from the
Oakland police station and she told me about him. She said
she was in love. She was going to run away with him."

"That's why you came to see me," Hunter guessed. "You
needed to get her out of there, bring her to Texas. And then,
before you could, she committed suicide. That's why you're
afraid of Samuel. You think he holds you responsible for her
death."

Chadwick said nothing.

Hunter leaned forward. "I don't like this, amigo. I don't
like finding things out about you from a homicide cop."

"Asa, I didn't tell anyone about Katherine and Samuel.
Not even Norma."

"And now the police are going after a student of mine to
frame some poor black kid."

"Frame?"

"The cops aren't buying the Samuel Montrose angle.
They're not going to expend any effort to find the guy. Easy
money is on Race."

"Damarodas said that?"

"He didn't have to. Maybe I'm reading between the lines
here, giving Damarodas too much credit, but the man sounded
like he was warning me. Said he was coming down here—
even gave me a date, a week from Monday."

"You going to let him in?"

"Not if I can help it. Thing is, Damarodas hinted that John Zedman was throwing his weight around, having lunch with the chief of police, shit like that. I got the impression they're trying to cut a deal—drop accessory charges against Mallory if she provides testimony against Race Montrose. Damarodas told me Talia Montrose sold her house for twice what it was worth just before she died. Damarodas is pretty certain John Zedman worked that deal—paying her off for some reason. That's all being overlooked by Damarodas' superiors. I don't think the sergeant was completely happy with that."

"We're agreed on that point."

"So I'm asking you again—is there leverage the Montroses might've had on John Zedman? Anything he had to hide?"

"I don't know." Chadwick held his eyes. "But Damarodas didn't have to wait so long to visit. He didn't have to warn you, either. It's almost like he's giving us time to find out."

Hunter's gaze shifted to the monitor. He tapped his knuckle on Mallory Zedman's forehead. "I don't like this, Chadwick. This kid would sell us south in a minute. When you talk to her, you tell her I'm going to save her sorry butt anyway. She's going to go through the program. She's got no choice about that."

Chadwick managed a smile. "Thank you, Asa."

"She wants to tell you something, fine. But don't make it into a deal. This is about compliance to authority, not co-opting."

Chadwick studied the unrelenting face of Reverend Asa, Sr., and wondered if that were a quote from him. He said nothing.

"Keep to the weekly schedule. I gave you a pickup in Menlo Park Thursday. Kindra Jones goes along with you—we'll treat it as standard time on the job. But you'll have the day in the Bay Area, just in case you wanted to do anything. Understood?"

"You're the best, Asa."

"I'm flying down to the Playa Verde campus for a couple

of days," Hunter said, "but you've got my number. You find out something, I'm the first one to know. Are we clear on that?"

His tone was even, but the set of his jaw, the veins standing out like a root system on his bald scalp, made Chadwick think of the afternoon, long ago, when Hunter had thrown his knife at a live oak tree, over and over, until his hand blistered and the bark of the tree erupted in wet white splinters.

"We're clear," Chadwick promised.

As he left, three people were staring at him—Hunter, the Reverend and the glowing apparition of Mallory Zedman, singing him a soundless lullaby.

11

Her left wrist was cuffed to the picnic table.

Olsen sat next to her, a large trail of Mallory's spittle glistening on the shoulder of her fleece jacket.

It was too cold, too late in the afternoon for anyone else to be using the deck. Deer grazed the hillside. Mesquite smoke scented the air. The junipers crackled as ice expanded in the joints of their branches.

Chadwick sat across from Mallory, slid her a plate of food.

She scowled at the turkey and dressing. "What is this— Thanksgiving?"

"Yes. You need to eat."

She shoved the plate back toward him. "Like I've got a ton to be thankful for. Thank you, Chadwick. Thank you, Miss Bitch-sitting-next-to-me-with-the-plastic-handcuff-collection."

"Mallory," Olsen warned.

The girl turned away.

Olsen removed her wristwatch and set it on the table next to the plate of food. "Ten minutes. That's all you have to be here."

"He ruined my goddamn life. He slept with my mother, made Katherine kill herself. He brought me here. *You* helped him. Why the fuck should I listen to you?"

The deer on the hillside raised their heads. Their hindquarters twitched.

"Set aside the anger," Olsen told her. "Put it away for ten minutes and listen."

Mallory grabbed the fork from her dinner plate. She wedged it under the handcuff and tried to pry it loose, but the fork was cheap plastic. The tines snapped. She threw what was left at Chadwick.

"Ten minutes without an outburst," Olsen said. "Starting now."

Olsen looked at Chadwick, and he realized that her deadline—the maximum time she would tolerate—was an edict meant mostly for him.

He told Mallory about the police investigation into Talia Montrose's murder—the bloodstains, Sergeant Damarodas' visit, the fact that Race and she were both wanted for questioning. Mallory kept her eyes on the mist curling up from the turkey.

"Dr. Hunter will protect you if he can," Chadwick told her. "But we need to know what you saw that night. What you did."

"Nothing. I didn't do anything."

"Who killed Mrs. Montrose?"

"I don't know. I don't want to."

"Mrs. Montrose's killer was probably related to her," Chadwick said. "Was it Race?"

"No. Goddamn you. No."

"One of his brothers?"

Her face darkened. "You mean Samuel. Race told me . . . Race swore Samuel was gone. Like, permanently gone." She yanked on her handcuff. "Anyway, why the hell do you care? You'd love them all dead."

"Three minutes, Mallory," Olsen promised.

"Just lock me up," Mallory murmured. *"Fuck* you."

The watch kept ticking. It had a transparent face, exposed gears that reminded Chadwick of his father's repair shop.

He wondered if the closet in the Mission house was still full of old clock parts. He remembered Katherine playing hide-and-seek there, surprising him by leaping out of the woodwork, smelling of dust and oiled copper, wrapping her arms around his neck.

"Mallory, did your father ever say anything about Samuel?"

The question drained the color from her face. "No. Why would he?"

"Your dad bought Talia Montrose's house. He gave her a lot more money than it was worth. Maybe he was paying her to go away—to get Race away from you. But I think there was more to it than that. I think someone in the Montrose family was blackmailing him."

Mallory's attention seemed to be focusing on smaller and smaller things—the design in the paper plate, the grain of the table.

"Talia Montrose should've had a large amount of money on her when she died," Chadwick said. "The police found nothing. When we picked you up in Rockridge, you had over six hundred in cash."

"Race got it."

"Where?"

"He just said . . . I don't know. I don't remember what he said."

"What about your necklace?"

Her hand crept up to her neck. "I don't—I left it . . ."

"You left it at Talia Montrose's house. It was found next to her body."

"No. I was with Race. We came into the house, and his mother—she was lying on the . . ."

A tear made its way down her cheek. She brushed it away like it was coming from somewhere else—like an insect or rain.

"Time's up," Olsen said.

"I'm going back to San Francisco," Chadwick told Mallory. "Tell me where to find Race."

"So you can turn him in?"

"So I can talk to him."

Mallory moistened her lips, and Chadwick got the uncomfortable feeling she was deciding whether or not to lie.

"Mr. Chadwick," Olsen said, her fingers covering the watch.

"His grandmother's," Mallory said. "She lives in downtown Oakland, off 14th."

"The police have already checked there."

"Yeah. But that's where he'd go. That's the only place he could go."

Mallory's eyes were intense green, just like her father's. "Make sure he's okay, Chadwick. He didn't do anything."

Chadwick promised nothing, but he got the uncomfortable feeling he'd made an irretrievable bargain—one that cuffed him to the table more firmly than Mallory's plastic wrist restraint.

He looked at the hillside, where the deer had gone back to grazing. He wondered if the grass tasted any different on Thanksgiving.

"I'll do what I can," Chadwick told her. "If you concentrate on the program."

"I hate the program."

"Start small." He remembered the little girl who used to steal white meat as soon as it was carved, then go running, giggling wildly, through the house as her father pretended to chase her. "You like turkey. Eat some."

Mallory looked at the plate of food, now cold. She picked up a half-moon of turkey, bit off a piece. She started to put the rest down, then changed her mind and took another bite.

Olsen said, "I'll cut your restraint. When you're done, we'll take you back to the Black Level barracks."

As Mallory ate, Chadwick motioned to Olsen. She followed him as far as the sliding glass doors.

"She's hiding something," he said.

Olsen crossed her arms, the shoulder bandage crinkling under her jacket. The skin around her eyes tightened. "The girl's whole life, people have betrayed her—Katherine, you, her parents. Now she's wondering if Race has lied to her, too. Of course she's hiding something."

"You don't approve of me talking to her."

"Your priorities are wrong. You're more interested in torturing yourself about your daughter than helping Mallory."

He felt anger building in his stomach, but mostly because he was afraid she was right.

"You're making progress with her," he said. "I'm impressed."

"You know why? I told her I'm not leaving, no matter what. She can't push me away. I learned that from you."

She looked nothing like the young woman who had been so afraid at the Rockridge café. There was determination in her eyes, absolute conviction that she was going to help this kid. Chadwick remembered why he had chosen her as a partner in the first place—she had a good heart. Heart wasn't something you could fake. It wasn't something you could train for. And it wasn't something she had learned from him.

"Watch out for her," he said.

"She stabbed me. Of course I'll watch out."

"No. I mean, keep her safe."

"You're worried about somebody coming after her? Is that what you're talking about?"

"I don't know. It's just a feeling."

She looked back at Mallory, but seemed to be looking through her—straight into the past.

"I'll stick by her," she promised. "That's my job."

Chadwick knew she didn't mean it as an accusation, but he remembered her words the day she'd quit—that his job was a form of perpetually running away. He felt the same wistful resentment he'd felt on the plane, when the flight attendant had assumed they were father and daughter. "You identify with her."

"Yes."

"I remind you of someone, too, don't I? Not a good memory. That's really why you couldn't work with me."

She said nothing.

"Can I ask who it was?"

"You could," she said, "except for two things."

"What?"

"I told you your priorities are screwed up. I can't very well admit that maybe mine are, too."

"What's the other reason?"

She raised her eyebrow, as if that should be obvious. She tapped her wristwatch. "Your time is up."

She walked back to the picnic table, where Mallory Zedman was eating a cold Thanksgiving dinner in the fading afternoon light.

12

On Monday, Chadwick and Kindra Jones took a flight to Boston. They picked up a thirteen-year-old who'd been expelled from his middle school for dealing Ecstasy and flew him to the Green Mesa facility in North Carolina. An easy job. The kid knew it was either Dr. Hunter or Juvenile Hall.

Jones had dressed in another corduroy and flannel montage, her freshly braided cornrows glistening with styler. She spent the plane trip arguing with the kid about whether Lauryn Hill or Dr. Dre was the bigger musical genius. Chadwick, who had no opinion, read two chapters of a Theodore Roosevelt biography.

He called John Zedman from Raleigh-Durham International and got voice mail. He left a message, telling John he was coming to town and wanted to meet.

He called Laurel Heights and got the secretary, who told him Ann was in a meeting with Ms. Reyes—no interruptions.

Tuesday morning, he and Jones transferred a gray level who'd been diagnosed anorexic to Bowl Ranch in Utah. Again, Jones fell into easy conversation with the kid, this time about the death of reality television. Between flights at DFW, Chadwick called both the Zedmans and failed to get them. On the last call to John's house, a man with a slight Spanish accent answered the phone.

Chadwick gave his name, and the man was silent so long Chadwick thought he'd hung up.

Finally the man said, "This is Emilio Pérez. Let me give you some advice."

"I'd rather you put your boss on the phone."

"You come out here, you'd best be returning the girl."

"That's not open for discussion, Mr. Pérez."

"Mr. Z? He remembers how you used to be a friend—only reason he hasn't let me hang you on a meat hook yet. Me? I got no sentimental problems. I know what you are. I know your game. You show your face, I'm going to make Talia Montrose's murder look like a quiet death."

The line went dead.

Kindra Jones came back from the TCBY, handed him a cup of yogurt with rainbow sprinkles and a pink plastic spoon.

"Got chocolate for me and the kid," she said. "Figured you for a vanilla man."

Wednesday evening at Bowl Ranch, Chadwick stared out the lodge window at miles of red sandstone—rock formations and stunted junipers marbled with snow like a Martian Christmas.

He thought about Mallory Zedman on the porch at Cold Springs.

He heard Olsen's voice in his mind—Olsen, whom he'd accused of running away from her fear.

From the moment he turned the first shovelful of dirt onto Katherine's coffin lid, Chadwick had known he would be moving to Texas. He would devote his life to pulling troubled kids out of crises, rewriting his failure with his daughter, over and over again. He told himself the job had been hard penance. In the years since, he had seen his share of suicides. He had been shot at, spit at, cursed and sued by the very parents who hired him. He had changed lives, delivered a lot of kids into Hunter's care.

But emotionally, escorting was safe—a brief, scripted performance where success was easy to measure, not much different than his history classes at Laurel Heights, or the way his own father had dealt with children—as appointments, gears to be oiled, chains to be balanced, with care and skill, but no particular emotional attachment. Chadwick could help kids on that level. He could do it brilliantly.

But when it came to permanent commitment—living with

a child, letting her see you warts and all, unscripted and stumbling and unsure, staying with her no matter what, whether she screamed or stabbed or turned away—Chadwick had never been good at that, even with Katherine. Especially with Katherine. He had failed his daughter. And nothing he had done in the nine years since—not all the escorts he had made, all the children he had pulled from horrible situations—atoned for that.

The next morning, when they got to the San Francisco rental car counter, Chadwick asked Jones if she was up for a little sightseeing.

She gave him an easy grin. "Noticed you got us in here on the earliest possible flight, and the pickup isn't until tonight."

"A few courtesy calls."

"Uh-huh. You want to tell me what about?"

"Preferably not."

She lifted the car keys from his hand. "In that case, I'm driving."

At first, Chadwick was impressed by Jones' command of the terrible Bay Area traffic. After a few blocks, he realized Jones was the *reason* for the terrible traffic. Curbs were loose guidelines for her. So were sidewalks, pedestrians, traffic lights, medians, other people's bumpers.

After twenty minutes of death sport on Highway 101, then weaving through downtown playing kill-tag with the bike couriers, Jones found an open stretch of Van Ness and shot north. She fishtailed onto California, sent coffee-toting students and medical workers diving for cover, and slammed the car into fourth gear for the final half mile.

"This is it," Chadwick warned. "This is it. That was it."

Jones swerved onto Walnut, pulling over a red curb and crunching into a trash can two doors down from Laurel Heights.

Chadwick exhaled for the first time in a mile and a half. "You hardly killed anyone."

"Just jealous," she said. Then she pointed with her chin. "What's going on over there?"

Half a block up, across the street, a local CBS satellite

news van was cranked for business. The reporter's back was to them, the cameraman filming in their direction. The backdrop for their news spot was Laurel Heights School.

A cold feeling started to build in Chadwick's chest.

The auction would be tomorrow—the first Friday after Thanksgiving. Maybe Ann had arranged some publicity. But the thermometer banner that had hung in front of the school was gone. It didn't seem right they would take that down before the final fund-raiser, especially with the press coming.

Jones slid down her black horn-rims, checked out Laurel Heights, tall and cozy on its hill. "That's your old school, huh? Think they could afford a paint job in a neighborhood this snooty."

"You want to come in?"

"And do what—talk to the custodians?" Kindra leaned back in the driver's seat, propped open an April Sinclair novel on the wheel. "No thanks, Chad."

Before he could respond to the unwelcome nickname, he saw Norma hurrying down the steps of the school. From the stiffness of her shoulders, the way she held her rolled-up newspaper, Chadwick knew she'd been arguing with someone.

She froze when she spotted the news van, then kept walking toward her Audi, which sat directly across the street.

Chadwick got out of the car.

"Hey," Jones shouted after him, "we get paid hourly, right?"

Norma was chirping off her car alarm when Chadwick caught her.

Her makeup was smeared from crying, her hair a chaotic swirl of black, her wrinkled dress and overcoat two mismatched shades of red. The furious set of her mouth made her look like she was walking through a dust storm.

"Oh, so you're the cavalry, again?" she demanded.

"What?"

She thrust the newspaper at him. "Good luck."

A-1, below the fold, the headline read: *$27 Million Scandal Unfolds at Bay Area School.*

"The boy was right," Norma said. "He told me to check,

and I'll be goddamned, but there it wasn't—the entire account. Gone. Transferred to fucking Africa."

"What? What boy?"

"Race Montrose. Goddamn it, Chadwick, I sat on the information for a *week*. I gave her a chance to explain. I couldn't be quiet anymore. This isn't a fucking clerical error."

The television reporter was watching them now, mumbling something to his cameraman. Chadwick felt as if he were bleeding, as if the scratches Norma had put on his face three weeks ago in Ann's office were reopening.

"You called the media?" he asked. "You told them Ann stole money from her own school?"

"Fuck the media. I told the police and the board. Only two people had access to that account, Chadwick. Ann and me. You think I'm going to fail to come forward on this? You think I'm going to risk jail time on top of a ruined career? *Chíngate.*"

"Two people. What about John?"

"Oh, no, no." Norma's hands flew in front of her like a warding spell. "Don't try that. You know goddamn well John didn't need that money. He wouldn't risk his career."

"And Ann would?"

The anger in her eyes turned brittle. "I will not do this. I will not have another argument with you about the Zedmans."

"What did Race tell you? How did he know about the money?"

"No," she repeated. "I will not—"

The reporter called, "Ms. Reyes? Norma Reyes?"

Norma's lips started trembling.

Chadwick stepped toward her, some involuntary reflex telling him to protect her, despite all their history. The familiar rose scent of her hair made him feel hollow, hungry in a way he did not want to admit. He cupped his hand around her arm. "Get in your car. Come on."

Norma pulled away. "Go back to Texas, Chadwick. Just . . . get away, all right?"

She slipped into her Audi, started the engine and pulled

away from the curb, almost clipping the reporter's leg. The faint scent of rose remained on Chadwick's clothes.

"Sir?" the reporter asked.

Chadwick walked across the street. The reporter followed him, his cameraman lumbering behind.

"Sir? Excuse me—"

Chadwick turned on the reporter, made him back straight into the camera lens.

He couldn't have been more than twenty-five. Whatever hard-edge attitude he'd put on that morning along with his foundation and rouge crumbled immediately.

"Leave," Chadwick told him.

"But—"

"Now," Chadwick said, rolling Norma's newspaper into a tighter baton. "Or I show you why I prefer print."

"Ah," the reporter said.

He scurried back to the news van, pulling the cameraman along by his belt loop, hissing at him, "You weren't filming? What do you *mean* you weren't filming?"

Another minute and they were packed and gone.

Chadwick glanced at his rental car.

If Kindra Jones had watched the exchange, she gave no sign. She was still reading her novel, chewing gum, bobbing her head to whatever music she'd found on the radio.

Chadwick looked up at Laurel Heights.

It seemed impossible that potato-print pictures could still hang from clothespins in the windows, that children could still shriek with delight on the playground. If $27 million had really vanished, the place should collapse. The yard should be silent, the gate draped in black.

The color and energy of Laurel Heights suddenly made him resentful, the way it had nine years ago, when the world had also failed to stop.

He took a deep breath, then walked up the steps of the school.

* * *

Ann would not allow her knees to shake. She would not let her hands tremble, or her voice quiver.

She told herself she must stay in control. This was her school—her legacy. They would not take Laurel Heights away from her with their well-meaning concern, their polite questions, their uncomfortable silences.

They sat in a semicircle—an impromptu Star Chamber made from student desks: five board members and Mark Jasper, the president, who until today had been Ann's biggest supporter. David Kraft, poor David, who'd been up forty-eight hours straight, trying to help her figure out the disaster, was slouched against the radiator in the corner, his eyes bleary, the tails of his dress shirt untucked.

"So you don't know." Mark Jasper spread his hands. "You have no idea."

He'd come straight from his art studio, smelling like turpentine, his polo shirt and faded jeans flecked with paint from whatever million-dollar commission he was completing.

His expression was calm and sympathetic, but Ann knew better than to trust his friendship. Mark was the archetypical Laurel Heights parent—a liberal artist who doubled as a cutthroat businessman. As much as he professed to love Ann's idealistic vision for the school, if he began to consider her a liability he would orchestrate her firing with as little remorse as an auto plant manager ordering a layoff.

"I'm cooperating with the police," Ann told him. "We're working tirelessly on this."

"Tirelessly," he repeated. "I wish we could give the school community a better answer than that, Ann. This is a lot of money we're talking about."

The other board members studied her—their faces morose, anger smoldering under the surface. She knew what they were thinking. She had pushed, and pushed, and pushed this capital campaign, let it drag on for ten years. She had insisted that the new building was the answer to the school's falling enrollment. She had bled the school community with constant fund-raising. And now, $3 million shy of her goal, the final auction tomorrow—this had happened. A crater, blown right in the middle of her career.

It was her fund. It must be her fault.

"You asked Norma Reyes to give you a week before she told anyone," Mark said. "Even us. Is that correct?"

"Mark—it was Thanksgiving weekend. I didn't want to cause a panic if it was some . . . mistake. I didn't want—"

"And then when Norma informed you, this morning, that she *had* to tell this board, and the police, you asked her for yet more time. Is that correct?"

The floor was sand, eroding under her feet. Out of the corner of her eye, she saw Chadwick appear in the classroom doorway—a tower of beige, his expression as grave as that of the members of the board. Her mind must be playing tricks on her—lack of sleep, too many days of stress. Chadwick was in Texas. But it made sense that he would appear to her now, like some Jacobean ghost.

Mark cleared his throat. "Look, Ann, the administrative leave—"

"I'm not taking administrative leave."

From the playground came the sounds of the second-grade PE class—Red Light, Green Light. Laughter and the coach's whistle.

Ann wanted to be down there with the children. She wanted to be in the classrooms, reassuring her teachers, who had woken up this morning to reporters' phone calls.

There was an answer, if she just hung on long enough to find proof. She knew where the blame lay—oh, damn yes, she knew.

She was not a violent person. But when she comprehended the extent of John's evil, how completely she'd underestimated his capacity for hate, she wanted him dead.

"I'm afraid we have to insist," Mark told her. "I mean, look, Ann—"

"I have a school to run." She closed her fists. "I will not take administrative leave when the school most needs me. If you want to fire me—fire me. Until then, you all will have to excuse me. The middle school returns from the park in fifteen minutes, and I'd appreciate it if you put these desks back into rows."

She walked out, conscious of their eyes on her back, conscious that Chadwick wasn't in the doorway anymore, David Kraft falling in beside her, saying, "Ann? Ann?"

"David, please—you'll have to excuse me."

"Is there anything—"

"*No*. No, dear. There isn't. Please."

"They can't fire you, right? I mean, that's nuts, right?"

She kept walking, leaving David behind at the stairwell.

She pushed through the Japanese curtain into her office, wishing for once that she had a door to lock, blinds to pull over the window, anything to hide behind.

Chadwick was sitting in her visitor's chair, his eyes topaz blue, his clothes layered like wind on a sand dune. He looked so much like a natural formation that she could fancy he'd always been part of that chair—a trick of the shadows, waiting for the right light to delineate his features on special occasions—the day he'd asked for a leave of absence to go to Texas, the day he'd announced he was quitting, the day he'd picked up Mallory.

Only then did it hit her why he might be here, and her concerns about the school faded to nothing. "Mallory—?" she said.

"She's fine," he told her, though his tone suggested he was glossing over plenty of problems.

"Then why—"

"Talia Montrose's murder. I came out hoping to clarify things. Then I met Norma and the CBS news team on the street."

Ann sank to the edge of her desk in front of him. She pressed her palms to her eyes.

God, what she wouldn't give to be in a different place—the faculty retreat house at Stinson Beach, walking the shore, watching the lights of fishing boats out on the horizon. Or in the redwoods, or at the Russian River—all those camping trips Chadwick and she had talked about taking, some day when their lives were aligned. This was the second time she had seen

Chadwick in a month, after nine years dreaming about re-union—and they were stuck here, the same place they'd said goodbye, in the office where she'd mediated crises for most of her adult life.

"John stole the money," she said. "No one believes me."

"You have proof?"

"He set up the account. There was a voice authorization clause—Norma tells me this, but I swear to God, if I ever knew it, I'd forgotten. John made it so I was the main signatory. I could . . . I could transfer funds to another account with just a phone call, as long as the new account was also in my name."

"But you didn't call."

"The bank says I did, a week ago, requesting a transfer of funds. It was a woman's voice. She had the right numbers. Knew the balance and how all the funds were allocated. They got an e-mail that appeared to come from Norma, confirming the withdrawal. The money was electronically transferred to a new account in my name, then transferred overseas to a numbered account in the Seychelles Islands. Have you ever tried to get information out of a bank agent in the Seychelles, Chadwick? Don't bother. And the bank agent here? The one who took the call? He's done business with John for years. You figure it out."

She didn't realize she was crying until Chadwick offered her a handkerchief, a pure white square of linen.

How many guys still carried a handkerchief in their pocket? She wondered if it was a tool of his new trade—did he need it on a daily basis, the way he needed Mace or plastic handcuffs? She wiped her cheeks.

"The minute I open my mouth about John . . . The board, the police—they all see it as a weak defense. Bitterness. Of course I would blame him. They don't believe me."

"I'll talk to him," Chadwick said.

"What for? You know why he did it—to ruin me. To get custody. One more year, Chadwick, and Mallory turns sixteen. She can refuse treatment, sign herself out of any program. If

John gets her now, I'll never have another chance to help her. I'll lose her forever. Just like Katherine."

Immediately she wished she could retract the comment.

He turned his head, as if from an icy gust. She wished she could kiss him, like she had the last time he was here, when the whole world had momentarily shifted into perfect balance. But he'd pulled away from her that time, and she'd ended up feeling cheap and desperate.

He was so unlike John. He was a grounding wire, a steel-beamed foundation, and even though she knew she didn't need a man to feel safe, something about Chadwick made her want to fold up inside him, take off the mental armor she had to wear as a leader, a professional, a mediator, and let him protect her.

Back in the old days, back in high school—that's the very feeling that scared her away from romance with him. She could be his friend, but she'd known instinctively that if they got involved, she would never become who she needed to be. She would become his shadow.

And ever since then, she'd been attracted to the wrong men—volatile, flashy ones, men who required her to be on her toes, to be calm and steady to balance them out. She remembered the day she'd met John—her first year as a kindergarten teacher, at a Noe Valley school long since defunct. He'd been dating a single mother whose child was in her class, and he'd come to the school picnic in Golden Gate Park, stood against a eucalyptus tree, and started lighting Kleenexes on fire for the children—throwing them into the air as they ignited—a dangerous and wildly inappropriate magic show. She'd known he was trouble, and known she would marry him, at almost the same moment.

What was wrong with her, that she had to marry the wrong person before she could recognize the right one?

"A woman called the bank," Chadwick said.

"John has plenty of secretaries."

"Maybe."

But she could tell he wasn't comfortable with that explanation.

She thought about Norma, about the e-mail that had supposedly been sent from her computer. The past week, Ann had had her moments of doubt. Was Norma's friendship, her apparent forgiveness of Ann for stealing her husband, all a ruse leading up to this—one huge moment of revenge? But that was insane. Norma wasn't a plotter. She couldn't hide her anger that well.

Chadwick said, "Did Talia Montrose have any connection with John?"

"What do you mean?"

"Race Montrose warned Norma about the money. He knew this was going to happen."

Hearing Race's name again made her shiver. It brought back the day she'd pulled the dull black pistol out of his lunch bag, the smell of gun oil mixing with pencil shavings and bologna and mayonnaise.

"I don't see how," she said. "John hates Race. The Montroses are the last people he would tell anything."

"Why did Mrs. Montrose send Race to Laurel Heights?"

"I told you—"

"Race is gifted. She wanted the best for him. And yet the morning before she was murdered, she sold her house, cashed in her checking account, and was getting ready to leave town, maybe without her son. Why?"

Ann wanted to rise to Talia's defense. She knew that Talia, in her better moments, really did care for her son. But she also remembered the parent conference Talia had come to stoned, the many other conferences she'd failed to make, the paperwork she never sent in. She remembered the time Talia had changed her phone number and forgotten to tell them—Race having an allergic reaction to a bee sting at school, an ambulance en route, and no emergency form on file from the mother. She remembered one particular argument between Talia and John, when they'd brought the fifth-grade People in Profile show to a standstill—Mallory and Race on stage, dressed up like Susan B. Anthony and Booker T. Washington, while John and Talia yelled at each other in the back of the room about which of their children was the bad influence. It had been such a nightmare Ann had blocked out exactly what Talia had said that night, but she'd been critical of Laurel Heights, as if she'd put Race there against her will. Almost as if it had been someone else's idea. Two days later, John and Ann had had the final argument of their marriage. He had struck her, permanently shattering any illusion that they should stay together for Mallory's sake.

"Talia wasn't perfect," Ann said. "But if you're thinking she would make any kind of deal with John, forget it. They hated each other."

"Race got a scholarship?"

"A half scholarship."

"That's what—eight thousand a year?"

"Roughly."

"She always pay on time?"

"I don't see what that's got to do with anything, but yes. Quarterly installments. Always cashier's check in the mail. It was never late."

"Her handwriting on the envelopes?"

"My god, do you want me to dig one out of the files?"

His eyes stayed locked on hers, and she began to understand why he was asking.

Talia had never been late with a tuition check. Not once. And she'd never shown up to pay in person. It was always a cashier's check, never a personal check.

"Typed," Ann remembered. "The envelopes were always typed."

"Postmark city?"

"You're suggesting someone else was paying the bills for Race?"

"I'm suggesting someone was blackmailing John, taking his money, turning right back around and using it to fund Race's tuition at Laurel Heights. Talia went along with it, but I don't think it was her idea."

"That's crazy."

"If you wanted to punish John, really drive him over the edge, can you think of a better way than putting his daughter together with Race Montrose, after what happened to Katherine?"

"I stand by what I said before— Race did not corrupt Mallory."

"But he knows something about the missing money. He tried to warn Norma. I think John wasn't sure who was blackmailing him. He guessed it was Talia. He finally got tired of it, scared enough for Mallory that he wanted to make a final settlement, so he offered to buy Talia's house for a huge amount of cash. Talia went for it, didn't bother to tell him she wasn't the blackmailer. The real blackmailer came along, got mad at her for making the deal, and killed her."

"But blackmail? Christ, Chadwick, blackmail for what?"

His eyes fixed on the interior window, where the board members were now walking by.

Ann didn't turn to look. She half expected Mark to walk in anyway and fire her on the spot, but no—Mark Jasper wouldn't confront her that way. He'd call her tonight at home, chickenshit style, and tell her not to bother coming back in the morning.

"The capital campaign money," she told Chadwick. "If the Montroses found out that John was going to steal the school's money to discredit me—if they had some kind of proof, that could be what they were blackmailing him about."

Chadwick pinched the lining of his coat. He said nothing, but Ann began to doubt her own theory. If Race's tuition had been paid for with blackmail money—then the blackmail had been going on for nine years. How could you pressure someone for nine years over a plan he hadn't yet executed? What leverage could anyone hold over John for that long, ever since...

She remembered her conversation with the policeman from Oakland. "Katherine's necklace. It was left in Talia's blood. Some kind of message?"

Chadwick's eyes were deadly still, their very brightness making them seem cold. "I intend to ask John, when I see him."

She thought about that necklace around Mallory's throat—remembered how hard it had been, letting her wear it after Katherine's death, but they'd been afraid that if they forced her to take it off, it would damage her even more, take away the linchpin that let Mallory cope with what she'd seen. Mallory had clung to it, insisting that Katherine gave it to her. And so, since Mallory was six years old, Ann hadn't been able to look at her own daughter once without thinking about the night of the suicide, without seeing the words Chadwick had inscribed on that silver charm.

"John has ruined me," she said. "The Montroses aren't the problem, Chadwick. They did not steal the school's money."

"If Race knows who did, he may be in more danger than any of us. It may be why he brought that gun to school, to protect himself, and why he ran from the police. And if he told Mallory what he knows..."

Every joint in Ann's body had turned to ice. She went behind her desk, sat in her chair, and began shuffling papers—admissions forms, auction flyers, purchase orders—none meant much now.

Down the street, she could hear the whoop of the upper- and middle-schoolers coming back from PE at the Presidio, the unmistakable hormone-induced yells of adolescent girls—Mallory's classmates, her peers.

"The upstairs students will be coming in," she said. "I need a few minutes alone. All right?"

Chadwick rose. "I'll find Race. I'll find out what's going on."

She tried not to look at him, tried to concentrate on her paperwork as the middle school kids began to come in a few at a time, racing each other down the hall, playing tag and throwing backpacks.

"Just tell me one thing, Chadwick. Will you?"

He waited in the doorway—an enormous pillar of sand hovering on her periphery.

"The night of the auction," she said, "before the police called—you were about to tell John and Norma, weren't you? You would've told them about us?"

She didn't look, but she could sense him struggling with

what to say. Then he left, silently, his presence no longer blocking the door.

She held his linen handkerchief up to her mouth.

The children were arriving in force now, streaming past her window, high on fruit juice and snack food, yelling and slamming their way into class. Teachers passed by, glancing into her office with concern, wondering if they would have a job tomorrow, or if they would spend Christmas reading the classifieds.

Ann felt as if she were moving, rather than them—that her office was racing down a road as dark and cold as the one back to the Mission, years ago—racing back toward her daughter where she sat curled in the black leather chair, staring at an empty doorway.

Chadwick found David Kraft sitting at the bottom of the school steps, lighting a cigarette for Kindra Jones.

"Damn," Kindra told Chadwick. "Thought the cannibals ate you, man. We're out here getting run over by a herd of puberty."

"Things got complicated. You two know each other?"

"Do now," Kindra said. "The man has cigarettes."

David took a last puff on his, then flicked it, smoldering, into the dusty millers. "I suppose I'm out of a job, sir? Is that what Ann said?"

"Don't do that."

He knitted his eyebrows. "You mean smoke?"

"Don't call me 'sir.' Kindra, would you start the car, please?"

"Whoa, Chad. Somebody piss on your Roosevelt biography?"

He looked at her.

"I'll start the car," she decided. "Man, you got to lighten up."

Chadwick reached into the dusty millers and retrieved the cigarette butt. He pinched it dead and tossed it into David's lap.

David looked a little worse for wear than when Chadwick saw him three weeks ago—like he'd been stuffed in an overhead compartment on an international flight. Still, he gave Chadwick the same reverent look, the sad eyes of an unrequited admirer. "Sir, did I do something to offend you?"

Chadwick mentally counted to five before answering. "David, did you have access to the Laurel Heights accounts?"

"No, sir. I just made alumni phone calls. I coordinated the auction—of course they'll cancel it now, but I coordinated the donations. I didn't have access to the money."

Chadwick remembered David at the auction nine years ago—a gawky teenager with a raging case of zits, waving his red flag to mark the high bidders.

"You still live in the East Bay?"

"Yes, sir. I've got a place in Berkeley. My parents', really, but they make me pay rent."

"Your name came up in '93, when the police were looking into Katherine's death," Chadwick told him. "I suppose you know that."

David's ears and neck turned bright red. "Like I told you—I wanted to write—"

"You introduced Katherine to Samuel Montrose. You took her there to buy drugs from him. After she broke up with you, you knew she was seeing him, getting hooked on heroin, talking about running away. And you said nothing."

David rubbed his finger in the ashes on his shirttail.

"I took her there once," he said, his voice tighter now. "That's all. I never went back. You can't make me feel guiltier than I already do."

"Seen Samuel recently?"

That got his attention. Chadwick couldn't quite read the look in his eyes—apprehension? Fear?

"No," he said. "Of course not. Not for years. If I had—"

"You would've told someone. You're awfully anxious to be helpful, David. You called Sergeant Damarodas and told him all about my daughter—gave him the connection between my family and the Montroses. You called the media about the embezzlement."

"What? I didn't—"

"Must've called the papers yesterday afternoon," Chadwick said, "before Norma even notified the board, just to make sure it made this morning's paper."

David's face became darker, harder, as if invisible hands had decided to remold it. Chadwick had seen this often with kids he picked up for escort—a sudden chemical change for battle mode, the moment they realized Chadwick couldn't be convinced or conned into letting them go.

"You know what?" David said. "I should've left this place years ago, but I kept *fucking* coming back. This school failed Katherine. You failed her. When I talked about writing you a letter? That's what I wanted to put in it. I hope the banks foreclose on Laurel Heights. I hope they bulldoze this place to the fucking ground."

And David Kraft, his old pupil—who'd blushed his way through the Declaration of Independence in eighth grade, who'd dated his daughter and had the adjective *poor* put in front of his name in high school more than any other descriptor—brushed the dead cigarette off his lap and headed upstairs, with all the determination of a fireman heading into a burning building.

13

A week after she'd talked to Chadwick, Mallory couldn't believe how much had changed. Once she'd allowed herself to go with the program, it had been like turning a boat downstream. Suddenly, she was racing.

Her team had finished the obstacle course. They'd built an entire new barracks for the next group of rookies—the first thing Mallory had ever constructed with her own hands. Then, yesterday, they'd graduated to the job of demolition. They'd been given sledgehammers and told to destroy the barracks they'd been sleeping in.

Like a snake shedding its skin, Leyland told them. *Time to grow.*

Mallory hated to admit it, but she loved knocking down the walls. She got in a few good smashes with the sledgehammer, and pretty soon she could loosen the cinder blocks enough to kick them down with her feet.

She didn't even mind sleeping in the open. The outdoors wasn't much colder than the barracks, and they'd earned new sleeping bags—good down ones, no more cheap cotton.

Tomorrow, they would start training for Survival Week. None of them knew what that meant, exactly, but the white levels talked about Survival Week like it was sacred. Their anticipation was contagious.

She still missed Race. She was scared for him, and angry with him, and worried that he might have lied to her. She was worried about her dad, too. But mostly, she was relieved she'd handed the problem over to Chadwick, the way Olsen had advised her to. Chadwick would take care of things. He'd make sure Race was safe. He'd check on her dad. Chadwick could even handle Pérez, if he had to, she was sure of that. The thought of Chadwick was like touching metal—it discharged the static energy for a while, let Mallory go about her day.

The nights were worse. She would wake up in the dark, the hills groaning, the raccoons fighting over scraps in the trash bin by the river, crying like mutant babies. She'd shiver in her sleeping bag, feeling every pebble under her shoulder blades, watching the black mesh of cypress branches cat's-cradle the moon, and she would feel absolutely certain somebody had been watching her while she slept.

She knew that was crazy. Her fears were as dumb as the ghost stories they used to tell at summer camp, back in the redwoods when she was little. There were no camp ghosts at Cold Springs. If there had been, the drill instructors would have put them to work busting cinder blocks. And yet she lay awake, thinking about Talia Montrose's torn body.

Chadwick's questions had dislodged something in her mind—something about Race's brother. She wasn't sure what. But it was there in the back of her skull, growing like a salt crystal.

When she fell asleep again, she would be back in the old Toyota, watching Katherine come down the steps of the Montrose house.

She would force herself to look at the figure on the porch—the one who'd said goodbye to Katherine before slipping back through the dark doorway.

Today, she had exhausted herself, throwing herself into the work, hoping that at night, she wouldn't dream, wouldn't wake up until the instructors rousted her out of her bag.

She spent the afternoon knocking down the last walls, pretending every brick was her mother's face—transferring all the anger she'd thrown at the program back to her mother, where it belonged.

She worked shoulder to shoulder with Morrison, but neither of them talked. That was okay with her, since the few times they got to talk they always got in a fight. When they were silent, they worked together pretty well.

She was getting stronger. The heroin shakes were gone now—the razors in her gut turned into an empty hunger that she could usually ignore. Her hands were like leather gloves, the blisters peeled away. She sweated a lot and probably smelled like crap, but there'd be the river tomorrow—the coldest bath in the world, and a chance to wash her clothes.

She was working so well she didn't realize it was time to fall in for evening sessions until Leyland started yelling at them.

Even Leyland's voice had changed over the last week. He sounded more like a PE coach, less like a demon. Not that Leyland wouldn't slap her down to size in a second if she didn't toe the line, but that didn't bother Mallory anymore. Leyland's voice had become an involuntary reflex inside her body.

The jog back to base camp was half a mile—from the destroyed barracks through a stretch of flat scrubland, wooded with soapberry trees and whitebrush and nopalitas, things Mallory wouldn't have known how to name a month ago. Now, from Leyland's survivalist lectures, she knew she could wash her clothes with those fat yellow soapberries. She knew the thorns on a whitebrush were all show—they didn't hurt a bit. And the white powder that collected in the joints of the nopalitas cactus turned red on contact with human skin— Apache war paint.

Another cold front was blowing in. Their stretch of mild sunny days was about to come to an end.

It still amazed Mallory that she could look up and see the weather changing—a curve of blue clouds like a seining net pulling south, blotting out the sunset. The sky in San Francisco was never so dramatic. The weather back home was more like her mother—mild and sweet and spineless.

"Rain tonight," Leyland announced, jogging beside her. "Get to try your pup tent."

"Yes, sir."

"We're spoiling you, Zedman."

"Yes, sir."

They passed the stables and the pasture, and Mallory stole a glance at the horses—a bay filly, a sorrel mare, a black and white paint...she couldn't remember the name for that one's coloration.

They kept jogging, past the solitary confinement shed, then the damn gravel clearing where she'd been initiated into Black Level a zillion years ago. Each time she passed the place she felt ashamed and angry about that first day. She was pretty sure that's why the instructors took this route.

Another hundred yards, and she could see the counselors gathered at the base camp, on a ridge overlooking the river. The wind was swirling spear grass and dust across the granite, and the temperature had dropped.

Mallory tried to prepare herself for seeing Olsen.

With her short blond hair and her pale complexion, Olsen didn't look anything like Katherine Chadwick. Didn't even act like Katherine. But when she talked to Mallory about turning her life around, she got the same hungry look in her eyes that Katherine had had, the moment she unhooked the clasp of her necklace.

That scared the hell out of Mallory.

She was afraid of liking Olsen—starting to trust her, then waking up one morning to find Olsen gone, replaced by some other counselor who didn't give a damn.

But so far, Olsen had stayed with her, even after Mallory attacked her with the knife. Once or twice in group therapy, Mallory had been tempted to tell Olsen about her dream, to see what she'd say.

No, Mallory told herself. *You open up your head, they'll see how crazy you are. They'll keep you back.*

She listened hard to the other kids' stories. She'd learned about Morrison getting beat up by her stepfather. She'd learned from Smart about the drug scene in Des Moines—unbelievable that they had meth labs there, not just farmers and corn. Smart had been busted when his bedroom exploded while he was at school. Mallory had learned about Bridges,

who'd been to two other boot camp schools before this one—
"A kid died at one of them, so I had to leave."

Then, last night, Mallory had shared for the first time.

It was a stupid thing to do, telling her life story to kids
who didn't even know her. But it was hard to explain—like
she was on the light end of a scale, getting higher and higher
the more the others put out, so the whole camp felt uneven,
and Mallory felt like she stuck out, like she was rising above
everybody.

Maybe the program was starting to get to her—all the talk
about how she was responsible for what happened to her, how
it was whining to blame everyone else. She hadn't let go of the
anger toward her parents. Not at all. But San Francisco did
seem another life—two thousand miles away.

So Mallory had told them a little about herself. She'd told
them about Race—how they'd gotten to be friends in the second grade, how they found a lighter once in the Presidio, and
set an acre of grassland on fire while the rest of the class was
playing capture the flag. Did they get expelled? Of course not.
Her mom was the goddamn headmistress.

It was a stupid little story, but the team had liked it, which
was such a relief to Mallory that she almost told them what
was really on her chest, the thing that had been sitting on her
heavier than any of the damn cinder blocks—her suspicion
that maybe, just maybe, she'd slept with a murderer.

The base camp was set up on a shelf of red granite,
pocked with erosion pits as big as dinosaur footprints. The
largest depression, about the depth of a bathtub, served as the
team's fire pit, but there was no fire yet. The team would have
to make one from scratch—and they only got to do that after
the counseling session was over.

Their rolled-up sleeping bags sat in a neat row in front of
an easel with a chart board—the program's four big concepts,
each written in a different color marker:

Accountability
Competence

Honesty
Trust

Below that was a line, then the night's two activities, in what Mallory knew was Olsen's handwriting:

1. *Take responsibility for a lie you got away with.*
   Tell what the truth was.
2. *Postcard.*

The second item made Mallory nervous, because she didn't understand it.

Olsen stood next to the board, waiting for them, a clipboard tucked under her arm, her hands hidden in a huge beige overcoat that reminded Mallory of Chadwick. The other counselors were a few feet away, counting out pens and postcards from a plastic sack.

The team fell out to their sleeping bags. They sat cross-legged, backs straight, hands in their laps. First, Olsen asked them to brainstorm on the word *accountability*, which was old-hat now, automatic stuff. Then she asked for volunteers to tell about a lie they'd gotten away with.

Silence.

"Anything," Olsen said. "Even something small."

She was looking at Mallory.

"I don't know," Mallory murmured. "I can't think of anything."

Smart and Bridges and Morrison looked equally glum.

Wind curled the chart paper, tugging at the paper clips that held it in place. A drop of rain splattered the *y* in *Accountability*.

"Never lied, huh?" Olsen sat down with them, motioned for Bridges and Morrison to scoot in and make a circle. "You want me to start?"

The black levels stared at their shoes.

Mallory felt sorry for Olsen, having to deal with them. Mallory would never be a teacher. She'd never work with kids.

Olsen grabbed her ankles, pulled in her legs. "I never knew my dad, okay? I grew up with a stepdad, and he left my mom and me when I was eight. When I was in college, I hired somcone to look for him."

Bridges asked if Olsen meant her real dad or her stepdad.

"My stepdad," Olsen said. "I wasn't interested in finding my biological father. Never have been. I don't know why. Anyway, I found out what had happened to my stepdad, but when my mom asked, I just told her he had died. She believed me. I think she was relieved to know that's why he had never come back. But I was lying to her."

Even Smart, the goddamn ADHD poster child, was paying attention now.

Morrison said, "What was the truth?"

Olsen raised her eyebrows. "First you guys tell me your lie."

They all looked away.

Smart-Mouth mumbled that he'd been taught liars went to hell, so he never did it, seriously. That brought a groan from Morrison. Smart snapped at her to shut up.

Bridges gave them some lame story about a time he'd told his mom he was going to a sleepover, but he was really with a girl. Mallory knew the biggest lie was that that had ever happened.

Mallory found herself watching Olsen. She didn't know why, but she felt a cord of understanding between them—small but warm. She wanted to hear what had happened in her story.

"Last week on Thanksgiving," Mallory said. "I lied to Chadwick."

Olsen tried to keep that standard counselor expression on her face, but her eyes had gotten nervous. "What did you lie about?"

"My friend Race."

Bridges said, "The guy helped you burn down that park?"

"Yeah. I told Chadwick I was with Race at this . . . really important time. I was kind of like Race's alibi. I kind of lied."

"I don't get it." Smart was shaking his head. "What do you mean *kind of*?"

Mallory looked at Smart—with his newly buzzed orange hair and that ugly gash on his lip where he'd hit the obstacle course bar, and his glazed eyes—IQ 89, maybe, with the wind at his back. She looked at Morrison, and Bridges. All of them waiting for her to spill her guts.

Suddenly she felt ashamed, angry, as if she'd exposed herself. She'd betrayed Race to get Olsen's favor. "Of course you don't get it, Smart. You're an idiot."

"Hey!"

"Whoa," Olsen intervened. "Mallory, stop. Time out."

Mallory counted silently back from twenty. A drop of rain hit her eye and made her blink.

"You want to finish your story now?" Olsen asked.

Mallory shook her head. She was mortified they'd think she was crying.

Olsen let the silence build, waiting for her to fill it, but she wouldn't.

"Anybody else, then?" Olsen asked.

But the possibility of openness had evaporated. Smart and Bridges and Morrison all stayed mute.

Mallory waited for Olsen to stop the session. She could've called over the instructors, told them the team wasn't cooperating, gotten them all put to bed with no fire, no dinner. Instead she said, "Let's move to the last activity. Break out, one-on-one."

The other three black levels scrambled up and found their counselors. Mallory stayed where she was.

Olsen asked, "You sure you don't want to tell me anything?"

"I'm sure."

"About Race?"

"Forget it. I was like digging for something to say, okay? It was stupid."

Olsen let it pass. She pulled a postcard off her clipboard and gave it to Mallory. The computer-printed label read:

Mrs. Ann Zedman
200 Coit Dr.
San Francisco, CA 94611

The left half of the card was blank.

"This is your first chance to write home," Olsen said. "It'll also be your last chance until you finish Black Level. You don't need to say much. Just tell her you're okay."

Mallory stared at the blank half of the card.

Six square inches of white had never seemed so huge.

She pictured her mother the last time she'd seen her—eyes swollen from crying, hands over her temples to push back the headache, screaming at Mallory to stop. And Mallory, in a haze, taking the hammer from the kitchen cabinet, breaking dishes and coffee mugs, following her mother down the hallway, smashing her framed childhood pictures on the walls, turning pots into shrapnel, yelling that the last person her mother should be scared of was Race.

It was like something that had happened to another person, but the memory didn't make her feel sorry. All that anger was still inside her. Her mother was never there for her. She was always running away—from her father, from Mallory, from everything except her precious fucking school.

What did Olsen expect her to do? Dash off a quick note, *Hi, Mom. I Love You.* Smiley faces and little hearts on the i's—something that her mom could file away in the office, in that fat manila folder labeled *Zedman, Mallory*?

Over by the fire pit, Bridges was crying. Mallory would never have figured it—but there he was, bawling like a two-hundred-pound baby.

Smart was sitting at the edge of the cliff, hunched over his postcard, writing every word like it was part of his obituary.

Morrison sat stone still, her face pale, her pen frozen over the card.

Mallory handed Olsen back the postcard.

"I can't do it," she said. "Lock me up."

There was something in Olsen's eyes Mallory hadn't seen in so long she didn't recognize it at first—sympathy.

"Come on," Olsen said, gentle but firm.

They walked back down the path in the growing dark, the rain sprinkling their clothes, until they got to the split-rail fence of the horse pasture.

Mallory knew there was a white level tailing them, ten or twenty feet behind—there was always an instructor on duty, keeping an eye on things—but somehow that didn't matter. It felt like she and Olsen were alone.

Olsen leaned against the rail, pulled a plastic bag out of her overcoat—apple slices. She pointed to one of the horses, the bay filly. "I bet that brown one would come over if you offered it something."

Mallory felt her cheeks get hot.

One of the pictures Mallory had smashed at her mother's house had been a kindergarten drawing of a horse. The panel she'd done for the auction quilt that year—that had been a horse, too. She'd been obsessed as a little girl, and probably would've continued to be obsessed, if it hadn't been for Katherine's suicide.

After that night, Mallory was the girl-who'd-touched-a-dead-body. And girls who touch dead bodies don't get to play with toy horses. They sit in the corner of the classroom and draw dark pictures, while the teacher hovers over them with concern. Those girls grow up fast, learn bad habits, make bad friends with the kids everybody else snubs. They start dating early, and set things on fire. And of course their parents divorce. That goes without saying. Girls who touch dead bodies don't have time for horses.

"No thanks," she said.

"Come on," Olsen said. "These apples have been in my pocket for hours. Who else is going to eat them?"

Olsen plopped the bag on the fence, split the zip-lock, and the filly immediately pricked up its ears. Its mane and tail were silky black, its flank so velvety brown it was almost red.

"I'm not writing the postcard," Mallory told Olsen, "if that's what you're thinking."

But she dug her fingers into the bag and fished out an apple slice—warm, slippery, marbled with brown. She held it over the fence and the horse clopped toward her, its velvety nose snuffling.

The filly was huge, its shoulders higher than Mallory, its hooves the size of steam irons. It was nothing like the cute little drawings Mallory had made as a kid. The real horse was all muscle and twitch. Dangerous, powerful. The thing's snout was warm with mucus and saliva, and it breathed steam on Mallory's palm as it lipped up the apple. Mallory told herself it was disgusting.

She fed it the rest of the apple slices, one at a time, stroking its muzzle between bites.

Olsen propped her foot on the bottom fence rail. "You know about Gray Level, Mallory? You choose a ranch skill to master. One of the options is horsemanship. You could do that, if you wanted."

The filly nuzzled the empty plastic bag, then bopped Mallory gently under the chin.

"Why're you telling me that?" Mallory asked. "You into horses, or something?"

"The truth?" Olsen asked.

"Yeah."

"I don't know a damn thing about horses. They scare me. I wasn't even sure they liked apples."

A smile tugged at Mallory's lips. "I suppose I have to write that postcard now."

"After I brought you to see horses and didn't even freak out? You pretty much owe me, yeah."

"Why is it so important I write my mom?"

"It's not important to me. It's important to you. The people in your life never go away, Mallory—not when you run, not when they hurt you. You have to find a connection with them that works. You have to start somewhere."

She brought out the postcard and the pen, offered them to Mallory.

The horse sniffed to see if this was another offering of food, and then, disappointed that it wasn't, snorted into Mallory's hair.

Mallory took the postcard, suddenly liking the idea of sending her mom something that had horse snot on it.

She wrote, *Dear Mom, I'm fine. I'm sorry for trying to hurt you.*

She signed her name and gave the card back to Olsen. Her hands only trembled a little. Olsen dabbed the raindrops off the card, then slipped it into her coat pocket.

"So where was Race?" Olsen's question was as unobtrusive as the patter of rain on the grass. "If he wasn't with you, where was he?"

"I told you, I was just talking. It's nothing."

Olsen crumpled the plastic bag and stuffed it in her pocket along with the postcard. "It's the fourth thing to master, Mallory, the last of Dr. Hunter's concepts. *Trust.*"

"Yeah? What's the end of your story?"

Olsen stared at her.

"The thing with your stepdad," Mallory said. "The lie you told your mom. That's got something to do with why you're counseling me, doesn't it? I remind you of something that happened to you."

Olsen's eyes were blue, but they reflected the blackening sky. "You'd better get some sleep, now, kiddo. Big night tonight."

"Don't you mean big day tomorrow?"

Olsen hesitated, and for a weird moment, Mallory thought she knew about her dreams, knew how Mallory sometimes woke in a cold sweat.

"Just get some sleep. We'll talk again soon enough."

That night after rations, Mallory was allowed to build the fire.

She set tinder around the brace, trying to keep it dry from the cold drizzle that was falling.

She thought about Katherine, and wondered what she'd be doing now if she were alive. Maybe Katherine would be here at Cold Springs, helping kids the way Olsen was.

She got the fire to smolder, then flicker, then finally blaze.

Mallory cracked a branch of mesquite that looked like a

wishbone. She tossed the short end into the flames, stared at
the red outline of the other piece, which now resembled a
crutch.

> *Accountability.*
> *Competence.*
> *Honesty.*
> *Trust.*

14

The man who opened John Zedman's door had a pencil goatee, the build of a middleweight, and a Mexican snake-and-eagle tattoo on his forearm. He reminded Chadwick of Norma's cousins in L.A.—the ones who threw hand grenades into empty police cars.

"You must be Pérez," Chadwick said. "I've heard wonderful things."

"Don't take warnings real well, Mr. Chadwick, do you?"

No hesitation. No confusion about who he was talking to. Pérez's eyes glowed like magnifying glass light on kindling.

"This is Miss Jones, my partner," Chadwick told him. "We want to speak with John."

"You carrying?"

"We fly for a living," Chadwick said. "Be a little hard to pack pistols."

Pérez produced a nine-millimeter from the back of his belt. "I don't have that problem. Come on in."

Chadwick glanced at Kindra. "Told you, you should've waited in the car."

"After sitting on my butt an hour last time? Shit, Chad. Even this clown's more interesting."

"I'm being hospitable," Pérez warned. "So shut up and come in."

All traces of Ann had vanished from the house. No orchids in the windows, no kentia palm under the skylight. Her folk art no longer cluttered the coffee tables. The mantel was bare of photographs. Everything was stark white and black and decidedly John.

Debussy on the stereo, postmodern paintings on the walls. The only sign Mallory had ever lived there was the old kindergarten quilt hanging by the fireplace, its glass frame cracked, a huge triangular shard missing at about the level of a man's fist.

Pérez stopped Chadwick by the sofa and turned him around, made him open his overcoat. Then he studied Jones, who could've concealed six or seven weapons in her baggy flannel and corduroy layers.

"You ain't frisking me, Juan Valdéz," she said. "Just get over it."

Apparently Pérez decided she wasn't worth the trouble.

"Walk," he said. "Mr. Z's on the back deck. Go straight—"

"I remember," Chadwick said.

They went through the kitchen, Pérez flanking them, putting himself at just the right angle to maximize Chadwick's discomfort. His presence brought back combat instincts Chadwick hadn't used in years—memories of hand-to-hand training at Lackland, waiting for a baton strike from any angle, trying to widen his peripheral vision.

"You want to not breathe on my cornrows?" Kindra told Pérez.

John Zedman stood on the back porch, talking on his cell phone, the Pacific Ocean glittering behind him. The wind coming up from the headlands smelled of sea foam and wet redwood. He registered their presence and held out his fingers, as if to catch a baseball.

"Yes," he said into the phone. "Subdivided into twenty-acre lots. Correct."

It was noon, but John still wore pajama pants, a linen dress shirt open over a tank top. He paced, barefoot, across the wooden slats of the deck. A coffee cup sat on the railing next to a plate of Eggo's.

His hair had thinned, gone gray at the temples. His face looked drawn, as if he'd been fighting the flu. He'd put on weight in the gut and his eyes were bloodshot. Chadwick had somehow anticipated that John would look better than he had in the early 1990s—that affluence would've oiled him up like a machine. But each year seemed to have been leeched out of John from a painful incision in a vein.

John hung up, punched some buttons on his cell phone, as if doing a calculation. He seemed in no hurry to speak.

"Tell your doorman to put away his pea-shooter," Chadwick said at last.

"I don't think so," John said. "Pérez has a pretty good sense of who's untrustworthy."

"Twenty-seven million stolen from Laurel Heights, John—from the fund you set up."

John set the phone down on the railing, picked up his coffee cup. "You've got some fucking nerve coming here. Ann embezzles, and you complain to me."

"Stop playing games."

John held his hand toward Pérez, who stood motionless in the doorway. "Am I playing any games, Emilio?"

"No, sir."

"There you are then. Emilio is the most humorless man I've ever met. He would know if I was playing games."

"Have you seen Samuel Montrose?" Chadwick asked. "I mean, actually seen him?"

John's reaction was immediate and negative—like a man with a severe food allergy. His face became blotchy. "Pérez—did you offer Chadwick any coffee? And Miss—"

"Jones," she said. "No. Your man was too busy showing off his little gun."

Chadwick kept his eyes on John. He wished Kindra had stayed in the car like he'd asked. He wished Pérez would go inside. John was too stage-conscious with other people around. Chadwick would never get a straight answer this way.

"How long has the blackmail been going on?" he asked.

"No. We're not going to have this conversation."

"Your money has been putting Race Montrose through school. You arranged to buy Talia Montrose's house. Now you've stolen Laurel Heights' capital campaign money. I don't think you did it just to get back at Ann, or get custody of Mallory. I think your blackmailer put you up to it. What did he promise you, John—that he'd go away?"

"I had about three minutes to give you, Chadwick. I'm afraid you just used it all."

"I'll keep Mallory safe," Chadwick said. "I promise that."

John laughed bitterly. "He can describe her day, Chadwick. He can tell me what she had for breakfast and where she slept and every punishment you put her through."

The deck swayed under Chadwick's feet. "Who said this? When?"

"You meant a lot to me once. That's dead now. Get the fuck out of my house."

"Talk to me, John."

"Tell me one thing," John said. "Straight to my face. Did *you* get any letters? Did Samuel contact you even once?"

"No."

John looked away. "You should've lied, Chadwick. You should've told me yes."

"I can help you. I understand—"

"You understand nothing. You ran, Chadwick. I stayed here. I've had to deal with your shit as if it were mine. So don't tell me you understand. You don't have the first fucking clue."

"John, this is your daughter—"

"My daughter, Chadwick. Yours is dead, remember? Yours is dead, and you don't get a second chance with mine."

Chadwick's body didn't belong to him anymore. His fingers gripped John's shirt, crumpling the fabric, lifting John as if forcing him to see Chadwick eye-to-eye.

"Hey, Chad." Jones' voice, a half octave higher than usual. "Um—somebody wants to break in."

Dimly Chadwick became aware of Pérez, the muzzle of his nine-millimeter an inch away from Chadwick's temple. Through the roar in his ears, he heard John say, "Emilio, back off."

Pérez lowered the gun.

Chadwick set John down, let go of his shirt.

He stepped back, the anger draining as quickly as it filled

him, leaving him ashamed and hollow. "I don't want to be your enemy, John."

"You stole my wife, then my daughter, and you're not my enemy? Get the fuck out, Chadwick."

He turned and poured his coffee into the wind, the liquid curling like a brown silk shroud as it fell.

After Chadwick left, John stood at the railing, staring at the half-eaten toaster waffle, at his own reflection in the yellow glaze of the Fiestaware plate.

He looked like a plague victim.

Worse. He reminded himself of his father in the last year of his life—slugging down gin at El's Tavern, bemoaning the wife who'd left him and the son who'd grown to fear him—until his liver had finally turned to clay.

Men who don't let their anger out eventually get warped inside. John knew this. They get twisted. They drink, or fight, or seek even darker consolations.

Chadwick had seemed larger, dangerous in a way John never would've imagined before.

He had always been so reserved. How could anybody be that way all the time? How could they not let their feelings break out somewhere?

"Boss," Pérez said.

I don't want to be your enemy.

"The money," Pérez said. "You already sent the account numbers?"

"No. Not yet."

"Don't."

John looked up. "My daughter. Samuel will kill her."

"Samuel Montrose isn't the blackmailer. Blackmailer is that asshole Chadwick. You see the look in his eyes when he grabbed you?"

If Pérez hadn't said it, John might have let the moment pass—he might have let the doubt play in his mind, then evaporate. But Pérez saw it, too.

How could the blackmailer have described Mallory's day

at Cold Springs so well? Why had Chadwick been spared the blackmail letters, and John had not? Most importantly, who knew about that one mistake John had made, nine years ago, that had been the grounds for the blackmail?

As much as the nightmare haunted John, he had always suspected the blackmailer couldn't be Samuel.

It had to be Chadwick.

Katherine's suicide had derailed Chadwick's plan to steal Ann from him. Chadwick was left alone, bitter, cut off from his past. Naturally, he would look for someone besides himself to blame, someone to hate. He would look at John, who still had his wife and child, and Chadwick would grow angry. If Chadwick couldn't be happy, then neither could John. The blackmail had destroyed John's marriage. Now John was close to losing his daughter. This wasn't the work of Samuel Montrose. This was the work of an embittered friend, who'd just looked John in the eye and claimed he wanted to help.

"Let me take care of this," Pérez said. "I'll get your daughter back. I'll deal with Chadwick. Let me call a *compadre* of mine."

John's hands trembled. Chadwick—his oldest friend.

His daughter's life.

The taste in his mouth was like arsenic. His reflection in the yellow plate stared up at him—sour, hard, old. Getting old alone. Without his daughter, or his wife.

"What do you need?" John asked Pérez.

And for the first time that John could ever remember, Pérez smiled.

15

Downtown Oakland steamed with eucalyptus and car exhaust and burning peanut oil from Chinese buffets. On Broadway, Asian women pushed strollers past the vegetable stands. Jackhammers echoed in the canyons between buildings. Businessmen chatted under the red and gold awnings of dim sum restaurants.

Jones turned on 12th Street and found a nice illegal parking spot by a construction zone, where the plywood walkways were decorated with murals of César Chávez and Malcolm X.

The address for Race's grandmother was across the street—a ten-story brick building that should've been condemned for earthquake safety decades ago. Or maybe it had been condemned. Half the windows were boarded up, the other half open to the air, like cells in a rotten honeycomb.

"What's this kid's name again?" Jones asked.

"Race Montrose."

"And he's not a pickup."

"Just a kid I need to talk to."

She chewed her gum, then nodded. "Okay. We're getting out of the want-to-tell-me phase, into the pretty-much-have-to-tell-me phase. What the fuck's going on, Chadwick?"

He had been waiting for a confrontation. All the way across the San Rafael Bridge, Jones had been too calm, driving almost like a human being—both hands on the wheel, speedometer not a mile over eighty. She hadn't even rammed the drivers who cut into her lane.

"I'm sorry about what happened in Marin," he said. "You don't have to come in this time."

"Aren't we supposed to be partners?"

Behind the horn-rimmed glasses, her eyes were tranquil, almost sleepy. False advertising.

"You're right," he said.

He told her about Katherine and Samuel Montrose, Mallory and Race, Talia Montrose's murder. He filled in what she hadn't heard about the missing millions from Laurel Heights, the fact that Race had tried to warn Norma before it happened.

The information seemed to weigh her down with a heavy, quiet anger that reminded him a lot of Asa Hunter.

"You're telling me somebody who lives here"—she lifted her hand toward the apartment building—"forced your rich friend in Marin to steal twenty-seven million from his ex-wife's posh school? Do I have that right?"

"There's a connection between the money and the Montroses. Race knows what it is. That's all I'm saying."

"This boy is black."

"Yes."

"Dr. Hunter—he knows you're doing all this on company time?"

"He knows."

"So he figures something doesn't add up. He's afraid this Race kid is going to end up in jail for murder and your friend Zedman is going to skate. He's trying to decide whether or not he wants to protect Mallory."

"Something like that."

Jones blew a bubble and bit it. "Day I interviewed? Hunter showed me that girl. She was exhibit A for how to use a straitjacket."

"He showed her to you?"

"He was touring me around and shit. Your old partner—tall, blond crewcut—what's her name—"

"Olsen."

"She was there, going down to counsel the girl. Should've seen the way Mallory blew up at her. Those two have a history?"

He remembered Olsen and Mallory on the Big Lodge porch, Mallory's spittle gleaming on Olsen's shoulder. "No history."

Kindra frowned. "The police looking for a murder suspect in the juvenile category, I know who I'd nominate."

A biplane droned overhead, dragging a yellow banner for a local microbrewery. Chadwick thought about the days when he could look up at a small plane and not wonder if it was some kind of threat, some lunatic with a canister of nerve gas. That kind of simplicity seemed as distant as Katherine's life, as the days he could come to Oakland and not think dark thoughts about the Montrose clan and the part they played in Katherine's death.

"I'm not saying Mallory's an innocent victim."

"But you've got a stake in saving her," Kindra said, "because of your daughter, right? And you've got no reason to help the Montroses."

"I'll ask Race for the truth, encourage him to talk to the police."

"And if he doesn't, there's always the plastic cuffs."

Chadwick was silent.

"Hunter won't let you turn him in?"

"That's not why."

"You promised Mallory?"

"No."

She raised her eyebrows. "Don't tell me it's because you don't trust the police to be fair. I hear that from a white man, my whole world image is going to shatter."

"If I turned Race in, I'd be doing it for the wrong reasons."

The biplane hummed and tilted and arced away over Lake Merritt.

Jones opened the car door. Her anger stiffened her movements like chain mail, but she gave him a punch in the leg that might almost have been an apology. "You're starting to interest me, Chad. Let's go."

The building's doorway was filled with a smelly green mound of blankets that might have contained a human being.

Chadwick and Jones stepped over it and began climbing the dark stairwell.

"How do you know where we're going?" Kindra asked.

"Mallory said fifth floor."

"The cops so hot to find this kid, how come they're not staking this place out?"

Chadwick had wondered about that. As shorthanded as all police departments were, especially when it came to tracking juvenile offenders, he had half expected to see some surveillance on the street. Maybe they were too late. Maybe Sergeant Damarodas had already apprehended the boy.

Out every broken window on the fifth-floor hallway was a million-dollar view—afternoon light on the water, patina hills rimming the horizon, wind sweeping white sails across the Bay. Inside, the scene was twenty-first-century dungeon— peeling wallpaper and crumbling brick, carpet worn down to fungus patches on an otherwise bare concrete floor.

They walked to the only visible door—a cheap sheet of particleboard, Motown music seeping from the uneven crack at the bottom.

Chadwick knocked. Then again, more loudly.

A black woman in her sixties opened up. She was short and pudgy, but she had Race Montrose's luminous eyes, his delicate mouth. Her hair was permed and gelled into a ginger-colored hydra, pieces of aluminum foil stuck in the curls. In her grimy pink sweat suit, she looked like she'd just run from a burning beauty salon.

"Mrs. Ella Montrose?" Chadwick asked.

"You that man," she said.

"Ma'am?"

"One with the stick. Big stick." She showed him the length of the imaginary implement with her hands, glared at him like she was making the most reasonable accusation in the world.

Then the smell hit him—rum fumes rippling off the old woman as thick as gas station air.

"My name's Chadwick," he said. "This is Ms. Jones. We're looking for Race."

The old woman jabbed a fat knuckle at Kindra. "You that girl, too. What you mean, bringing a big pet like this inside, where people live? Ain't I tole you before?"

Jones pointed at Chadwick. "This pet here? Yes, ma'am— he's mostly housebroken. You know where Race is at?"

Ella Montrose raised her hands in front of her face and pushed the air away. "No, no. NO GODDAMN DEALIN' in my home. I'm a CHRISTIAN woman!"

She started to close the door, but Chadwick pressed his palm against it. "Ma'am, Race is in trouble. We need to talk to him."

Her murderous look reminded Chadwick of Samuel, that night nine years ago at the Oakland juvenile detention center. But whatever circuitry once connected Ella Montrose's brain to her face had long ago melted. On Ella Montrose, a scowl held no more menace than the eyes on a moth's wings.

"You two ain't real," she told him. "I reach in the photo book and pull you out. Just like my Talia."

"Ma'am," Chadwick persisted. "Is Race here?"

"I'm not going to no home. I'm not crazy."

"It's about Mallory Zedman."

The name seemed to set off a ripple in Ella Montrose's facial muscles. "Seen too much when he was small, that boy. You stay away from him, you hear? Go back in the picture book."

"Hey," Jones said. She dug a twenty out of her pocket, held it up between two fingers, then spoke slowly and clearly, as if to a child, "How about you go down to the Jiffy Liquor, buy yourself some lunch, okay?"

"Ms. Jones—"

Chadwick's reprimand was cut short by a young man's voice, coming from somewhere deep inside the apartment. "Nana?"

Ella Montrose licked her lips. "He kill you, I let you in. You got to go back into the pictures, okay?"

"Take a walk, Nana," Jones suggested gently. "Get you some Bacardi."

"Christian woman," Mrs. Montrose mumbled. "Girl got no business—a pet that size."

She snatched the twenty, pushed past Chadwick into the hallway, and made for the stairwell. The aluminum foil in her hair glinted as she passed the empty windows.

Chadwick looked at Jones. "In the future, no bribery. That woman is ill."

"So now she's ill and twenty dollars richer. We going in or not?" Her voice was harsh and brittle, as if the old lady had unnerved her more than she cared to let on. She held the door for Chadwick.

On the other side was no apartment—just an enormous loft space, vast open floor and ceiling supported by white concrete columns, huge windows pouring in light. A living room area had been set up in one corner, a bedroom in another, so it looked like a third-rate furniture showroom rather than a place someone would live. Cheap jasmine incense burned somewhere. A boom box played "Mustang Sally." Strung between two columns was a water-stained pink sheet; behind it, Chadwick could see the lanky silhouette of Race Montrose getting dressed.

Race yelled, without alarm, "Nana? You okay?"

He pushed aside the sheet. He wore his camouflage jacket, bare-chested underneath. Black jeans. One black Nike on his foot, the other in his hand.

He stared at Jones and Chadwick. Then he dropped his shoe and bolted.

By the time Chadwick realized Race was going for a gun—a semiautomatic resting on the windowsill—it was too late to back off. Race grabbed the gun, but with a six-foot-eight wall of white man coming down on him, the boy abandoned all intention of fighting. He started out the window, hooking his leg on a rusty fire escape as Chadwick grabbed his arm, Race pulling away, putting his whole weight on the railing.

The metal groaned under Race's feet, the fire escape peeling away from the wall, taking the boy with it. Chadwick's grip slipped to the boy's wrist just as Race's legs lost contact with the rail and his chest slammed into the side of the building.

Race Montrose hung, five stories up, twisting in slam-dunk position, the gun still clenched in his free hand.

He looked down at the line of dumpsters in the alley below, about the size of pillows, then up at Chadwick. He made a wild and heroically stupid effort to aim the gun at Chadwick's head.

"I tend to drop people when they shoot me," Chadwick told him. "Let it go. I'll pull you in."

Race was sweating, making his wrist hard to hold.

"I don't know anything," the boy said. "I swear to fucking God."

Chadwick tightened his grip. Kindra was right behind him, her hands latched to the fabric of Chadwick's coat, as if that would be enough to keep him from falling. She was muttering words of comfort and support: "Shit, oh goddamn shit. Crazy mother-fucking idiot."

"We just want to talk," Chadwick told the boy. "Drop the gun."

He could feel his own pulse against Race's wrist bones, the semiautomatic's line of fire wobbling back and forth across his forehead.

The gun clunked against the dumpster below like a timpani strike. Chadwick pulled him inside.

"Damn!" Jones exhaled. She kicked the boy's bare foot. "Damn, little man! The hell you thinking? You born stupid or you study on it, huh?"

Race huddled against the wall, pushing his back against the bricks. He was skinnier than Chadwick remembered. His breastbone was concave and hairless between the folds of the camouflage jacket, his eyes soft, on the verge of tears.

"I don't know nothing." His voice trembled. "Didn't say nothing."

"We're not going to hurt you," Chadwick said.

"Yeah. You just come from Texas to help me, like you helped Mallory."

Chadwick scanned the area where they'd ended up—a

sunny corner of the loft that passed for Race's bedroom. A cheap cotton sleeping bag was spread out on the cement floor next to a scatter of CDs, clothes, loose ammunition. Three cellophane-covered library books were stacked neatly against the wall next to a better sleeping bag—a green down one, rolled up in a red bungee cord. Chadwick stared at the down bag, trying to figure out why Race wouldn't use that one instead of the cotton one, then wondering where he'd seen the bag before—the green fabric, the red cord around the middle.

Faded letters were marked next to the zipper, *AZ*. It was Ann's old sleeping bag, the one she'd brought to the faculty retreat at Stinson Beach, when they'd looked at the stars together.

"Was Mallory staying here?" he asked.

Race's eyes darted around, as if he'd missed something he should've seen. "I was just—keeping the bag for her. You know."

Chadwick knelt down, picked up one of the library books. It had been checked out from Laurel Heights: a Thomas Jefferson exposé about the DNA tests on his black descendants. Chadwick had read it himself about a month ago. The book under that was by Howard Zinn, the bookplate inside inscribed, *Donated by Ann Zedman*. The third title was *Black Athena*. "You keeping these for Mallory, too?"

"Why you say that—you figure I can't read?"

"Mrs. Zedman told me you were gifted."

"So gifted she kicked me out of school."

"You blew that. You brought a gun on campus."

"The hell I did."

"It just appeared in your locker?"

Race rubbed his nose with the back of his wrist. "You ain't gonna believe me anyway. Listen, I got friends coming over, man—they going to drill a hole in you the minute they see you. You going to kill me, you better do it quick." He cut his eyes toward Jones. "That what you brought her along for? She your nigger gun?"

"Watch your mouth, little man," Jones said. " 'Fore I put my boot in it."

Race scowled, but he had to blink to keep from crying.

Chadwick picked up a bullet from the tangle of clothes, turned the brass in his fingers. "You prefer guns over knives, Race?"

The boy hugged himself tighter.

"Your mother was stabbed to death," Chadwick continued. "Six- or seven-inch blade."

By the front door, the radio kept playing—Marvin Gaye, ridiculously happy music in the big empty space of the building.

"You think it was me?" Race asked. "That what you think?"

"Police found two people's blood at the scene. Attacker and victim. DNA says they were related."

Race put his forehead down, rubbed it against his knees. "No. No, no."

"Mallory's dad says he's been getting blackmail letters from your brother Samuel. That true?"

The boy was shivering.

"Hey, little man," Jones tried, her voice softer now. "Come on. Just answer him."

Race said something into his knees.

"What?" Chadwick asked.

"I said yeah. Samuel sent those letters. Said Zedman was gonna get his."

"Get his. For what?"

Race glared up at him. "You know for what . . . your kid. She used to come around. Slumming and shit. Samuel didn't want to fall for her, but he did, and then you go and keep them apart. And she kills herself, and the police are all like—she was infected. She was poisoned. How you think that made him feel?"

Chadwick felt Kindra Jones staring at him.

Out the open window, the sun flooded from behind a cloud, cutting a yellow arc of light down the side of the next building. A jackhammer pounded a five-beat cadence. The loose fire escape bobbed and swayed on its bent ladder, ten feet out from the window.

"Why the Zedmans, then?" Chadwick asked. "If Samuel was mad at me, why take it out on them?"

"You left, man. Not so easy to get to you. You didn't have nothing left to steal. Zedman—that was different. You all a piece of the same world, man—Laurel Heights. All that shit. Samuel hates all of you."

"And yet he sent you there."

The look in Race's eyes wasn't anger, exactly, but a memory of anger, as if he were hearing a story whispered over a telephone. "He used to say it was my duty. Show them up. Improve myself. But he hated the place. After they kicked me out—he said fuck it. Those kids—I used to come home crying. They'd ask me what kind of car my momma drove. And what was I supposed to say? My momma take the bus? She drive whatever her boyfriend's driving? They used to ask why I wore the same shoes every day. And I got to look at them like, 'This is the only pair I have.' And they just stare at me, okay? And then they talk over me, the rest of the day. Improve myself? So I can be like them? Hell with that."

"What'd that Zinn book say about the Revolution?"

"Said it didn't have nothing to do with freedom principles and Locke and Hume and all that shit. Said it was rich white landowners escaping their debts from England and setting themselves up to get even richer and more powerful."

"What'd you think of that?"

"I think the book was written by a rich white man. So the Revolution must've worked."

Chadwick smiled in spite of himself. "You must've had some interesting discussions in history class. Mrs. Zedman was right."

" 'Bout what?"

"You. She believed in you. Still does. Told me you were one of the smartest kids she'd ever had at the school."

He dug his finger against the cement, sketching invisible cursive letters.

"You really hate Laurel Heights?" Chadwick asked.

"Said so, didn't I?"

"Then why did you warn Ms. Reyes?"

He lifted his finger, as if the floor were suddenly hot. "What?"

"You showed up at Ms. Reyes' house last week, told her to check on the school's money. The next day it was gone. Why did you try to warn her?"

"She's lying."

"Eight years of your life, Race. Mrs. Zedman was always in your corner. Maybe you were mad at her for expelling you—maybe that's why you went to Ms. Reyes instead, but I don't think you wanted the school destroyed. Whoever did that, get away from him. You don't owe him any loyalty."

"Samuel protected me. He was good . . ."

"Thirty-two stab wounds, Race. Your mother was murdered and no one protected her. The truth."

"Mr. Chadwick," Kindra said.

Her expression was hard, full of angry sympathy for the kid. "We got that other appointment, you know?"

Chadwick glanced around the loft, trying to recapture his feeling that Race was a dangerous person. He had needed to believe that, almost as much as he needed to believe Samuel Montrose was dangerous. But he saw only a young man who needed less help than most of the kids he worked with each year—whose circumstances were harder, maybe, but not because of anything he had done.

Chadwick could understand Ann's desire to help him—he could understand why she'd wanted him at Laurel Heights. But he wondered if Ann had done Race any favors—if Asa Hunter wasn't right about the boy being corrupted by the girl, and not vice versa.

"Your grandmother said you saw too much," Chadwick said. "What did she mean?"

"Nana don't know what she's saying, half the time."

"If you want to talk," Chadwick said, "if you want to get out of here, you want anything—call."

He took out his business card. He kept it extended until Race took it.

The boy looked up, his eyes red, but the look of defiance was starting to re-form. "What's this Cold Springs place like?"

"Strict," Chadwick said. "You go through levels, have to learn survival skills out in the woods. Learn a trade on the ranch. Most kids get their GED. Some get college credit."

"Mallory out in the woods?" Race wiped his nose with the back of his hand. "I can't see that. Texas—I thought that was like desert."

"Not this part. Green and hilly. There's a river. Rainy and cold this time of year."

Race seemed to be imagining it, stretching his mind around a new alien planet.

"Keep the card," Chadwick said. "Call me."

Race glanced at Jones. "Whatever, man. Fuck you, anyway."

But Race called them before they got to the door. "Hey, Chadwick. You asked why Samuel didn't come after you? Ask yourself what would hurt you worse than leaving you the way you were, okay? See how gifted you are."

Back at the car, by silent agreement, Chadwick took the wheel. His hands were numb, his vision tunneled to the stripe in the road and the feet of pedestrians in the crosswalk. He didn't look at Kindra, didn't pay much attention when she took out her cell phone and had a hushed conversation with somebody named Clarisse, something about whether or not King Hunan still served coconut chicken. Blocks later, after she'd hung up and they were well into Berkeley, she said, "Pull over. You're dropping me here."

"What?"

"Just do it."

He wedged the car into a loading zone on College and Ashby. Kindra opened her door, put one foot outside, turned back.

"I got some friends in Teach for America," she told him. "They live right down the street. We're going out to dinner now—that'll give you a few hours to yourself."

"Why?"

"Because it beats me slugging you," she said tightly. "What were you thinking—messing with that boy's mind?"

"I wasn't."

"Oh come on, Chad. 'You want anything, call.' Please. His mama's dead. You saw his grandmother. That kid has been jerked around enough without your false sympathy."

"I meant what I said."

"I liked you better when you were honest—when you were worried you'd turn him in and feel good about it."

Down the street, the distant white Campanile of UC Berkeley glowed in the afternoon light. Chadwick wished he could explain to Kindra, but he knew he couldn't. Race Montrose and his dead mother tore at his soul, his conscience.

"Race wasn't telling the truth," Chadwick said. "I had to press him."

"You think—" Jones stopped herself, bit back her words.

"What?"

"Forget it."

"What were you going to say?"

"You pushed that kid until he told you about his brother. You get what you want—you get to take the guilt for your daughter. All the guilt you can eat. You push him and now you think he's lying. Maybe you should've pushed your rich friend as much as you pushed that kid."

"Zedman?"

"You left him, Chad. He told you to leave, so you did. Real question you didn't ask the kid—what the fuck is the blackmail about? They been messing with Zedman for years, haven't they? And I think you got an idea what your friend was into. The man wanted to tell you, too, but he couldn't do it with me and that crazy asshole, Pérez, there. You ask me, you ran from the hard choice, and you're a fool if you don't go see him again, try to get him alone. That's why I'm going out to dinner. Give you a chance to do something right for a change. Now get lost. I'll meet you—what, about nine. Montgomery Street station."

Chadwick waited for his stomach to stop twisting. She

was right, of course. He was starting to understand, and he didn't want to.

"You all right on BART?" he asked.

Jones sighed. "Yeah. Of course."

"Ashby is the closest station from here," Chadwick offered.

"I know that."

They stewed in silence.

"Look," Kindra said. "I come from a big family. I got little brothers, too, okay? I guess seeing Race just tugged at me a little more than I realized. I didn't mean to razz you."

"That's okay."

"You could come to dinner with me and my friends," Jones offered, without enthusiasm. "Forget what I said."

"No thanks."

"All right." Jones' voice was suddenly tight again. "No problem. Nine o'clock."

She got out and slammed the door.

Chadwick watched her push through the pedestrian traffic toward a Chinese restaurant, and disappear inside. He pulled away from the curb and headed back toward the Bay Bridge, telling himself he had no destination in mind, but knowing exactly where the road would take him, whether he wanted it to or not.

16

John Zedman dreamed of a blasted-out apartment building—the kind of property he would purchase only if he were preparing it for the wrecking ball.

In the dream, he stood high up on one of the top floors, the interior walls stripped away, the windows gutted so that the night wind ripped through his jacket and sweater. In the distance, the lights of the hills shimmered like birthday candles.

He was holding his .22 pistol to Chadwick's forehead—his old friend Chadwick, who had lashed their lives together like burning galleons, slept with his wife, destroyed his family.

Chadwick knelt before him, eyes downcast, waiting for John's decision.

John's trigger finger tightened of its own volition, like wet rope contracting in the sun.

He woke up and his hand hurt from squeezing on the gun, but it wasn't a gun. He was holding a Laurel Heights yearbook. He had fallen asleep looking at pictures from Mallory's kindergarten year, the only year they'd all been together—Mallory, Katherine, Ann, Chadwick. All of them alive and well at the same school. Nineteen ninety-three. Snapshots from the end of time.

John remembered thinking, in 1993, *We can take care of this.*

He remembered his confidence, the giddy feeling that came from riding a wave of financial success, feeling as invulnerable as a god or a sixteen-year-old driver. But the memory was cold and empty. That had been some other man, someone who had withered and died the same night as Katherine Chadwick.

Even those last hours at the auction, buying Chadwick a drink, sparring with him on the playground, John had had a sense of foreboding. He'd known then that his life would come to this—his family disintegrated, his friends gone, replaced by hirelings.

All he cared about was Mallory, but the past nine years he'd had another child to nurture—his own guilt growing inside him, a burden so huge it sometimes flipped into anger, made him drink and smash picture frames and lash out at the only people who mattered. He had hit his wife. He had threatened his daughter. He had done much worse.

He wanted to explain to Chadwick that he didn't hate Race Montrose. He had paid for Race's tuition willingly; he'd felt almost relieved when the first blackmail letter came, years ago.

He was a father, goddamn it. He understood that the child was not to blame. He hadn't held a grudge against the boy, at least not at first.

Even when Mallory and Race got out of control, when Race Montrose had ruined his daughter, taught her to shoot up drugs and call her parents filthy names and unlatch windows at night to escape, John had tried to save her peacefully. He'd offered Talia Montrose money rather than unleashing Pérez. He'd been sure, then, that the letters were from Talia. He couldn't explain it, any more than he could explain how he knew when a buyer would close a deal, but he had sensed the voice of an angry mother behind those letters. So he had met with her face-to-face, treated her like a human being. And his plan had gone wrong. He had misjudged fatally.

He swallowed the cottony taste from his mouth, stared out his living room window at the sunrise until he realized with sickening disorientation that it was the sunset. He had fallen asleep after a Valium and half a bottle of wine—that same damn Chardonnay he'd meant to share with Norma Reyes—

and after all that, he hadn't even managed to sleep the night. He'd taken a nap. A goddamn nap, like an old man.

He sat up. Someone was tapping a carpet tack into his left temple.

On the table, a silver lighter and a packet of tissues sat in a ceramic ashtray—the only piece of Ann's ceramic collection she'd forgotten to take when she moved out. Or maybe she'd left it on purpose. *You keep the ashtray, John. Figure it out.*

John didn't smoke, didn't know anybody who smoked, but he kept the ashtray on his coffee table. He picked up the lighter, dug a tissue from the pack.

John sparked the lighter. He held his tissue to the flame and threw it in the air. It erupted into an orange tangle of thread and disappeared, the ashes so small they might have been dust motes.

Children loved that trick. Women, too, smiling even as they scolded him: *You'll give them bad ideas.* The problem was the tissue went too fast. Less than a second, and the show was over.

He tossed the lighter back in the ashtray and went out to the deck. The surf pounded cold and steady below. The wind was picking up. The day had been warm, but that was changing. The winter was remembering itself.

He almost called for Pérez to fetch him a coat, then he remembered Pérez was gone on his errand.

The thing in his stomach—the child-sized burden of guilt—began turning, kicking its small feet. Even if Chadwick was punishing him, even if the worst was true—how could he blame Chadwick? He deserved everything he got. Why had he told Pérez to act?

The safety of his daughter, he reminded himself. That made it necessary. He had to protect his daughter.

He had already planned their escape.

He would keep the money in the Seychelles account. Pérez would rescue Mallory, bring her to him. This time, he wouldn't wait for the courts to let him have his daughter. He would take her.

Fathers kidnapped their own daughters all the time. He

read the papers. And most of those fathers did not have his resources.

Why hadn't he done this years ago? Cowardice. The need to be vindicated in his hometown, to win against Ann, to show he was not a quitter. But fuck all that. He and Mallory would just start again elsewhere. They would create a new home, a new life. If Chadwick could escape the past, then so could he.

He tried to taste the impending success of his plan, the way he could have years ago, but now it was salted with doubt. The FBI had already called—a special agent named Laramie who wanted to talk to him tomorrow about the Laurel Heights fund. Just procedure, his friends in the County Sheriff's Department assured him. But the Sheriff's Department could not protect him from this. He would have to be cool. He would have to be the consummate actor, the man who unloaded worthless blocks of real estate for billions, leaving the buyers certain they had discovered the next hub of a commercial renaissance. No more slip-ups. No weakness. He just had to get through a few more days alone, until Pérez came back with his daughter and the news that an old friend was dead.

He heard the distant rock-tumbler sound of car tires pulling up his drive, and he felt a spark of hope that it was Pérez. But that was impossible. Pérez would still be on his way to Texas.

Then, a warmer sensation hit him—Chadwick was coming back to apologize. Of course he was. John had heard the brittleness in his voice when he was last here. Chadwick wouldn't let things stand the way they were. He understood now how much John was suffering—what Chadwick had pushed him to. He would come back, and they would make amends. John would say, "It's a good thing. I was about to have you killed." And Chadwick, simple old Chadwick who always needed John to lead—he would wonder forever if John had been joking.

The doorbell chimed.

John went to answer it, a hopeful smile forming on his lips for the first time in weeks.

* * *

The begonias in front of the house had been dying for a long damn time—dried leaves and flowers crusted so thick the new pink blooms looked like insects trapped emerging from their shells.

Samuel usually wouldn't have noticed, but he'd been thinking about Katherine all week. And those begonias were the kind of thing she got jacked up about.

He knelt down, picked a few of the withered petals, broke the cobwebs between the planter and the wall. Katherine whispered inside his head, talking the way she'd talked the last night she came to the West Oakland house—about dead morning glories and palm trees freezing and how she wanted to drift away into a garden somewhere and never come back.

Was Samuel going crazy?

Way he saw it, when somebody important died—didn't matter if you loved them or murdered them—you'd better take something from them. You'd better eat a little bit of their soul. Otherwise they were just gone—couldn't help you, couldn't change their mistakes—and thinking about that made Samuel uneasy. His mind started teetering on its high wire, the safety net down below unraveling in the darkness.

He looked up at John Zedman's door, felt his anger building again.

The week hadn't been easy. Between Zedman calling, trying to weasel out of the deal. Then Race betraying him, talking to that bitch Norma Reyes. Samuel didn't like people running from him, trying to slip out from under his control. If they did that too often, the way Talia had, they'd force him to pin them down for good.

He rang the doorbell, heard it fill the house with a long, tuning fork hum.

Down in the driveway was the blue sedan he'd rented—nondescript, nice big trunk, backed up as close to the house as Samuel could pull it. Cost him a shitload of money, renting it for two weeks, letting it sit in a parking garage near his condo, but Samuel hadn't known when he'd need it, and he knew he'd need it at a moment's notice. Tonight, the investment would pay off.

He heard somebody coming to the door, saw a shadow on the glass.

He slipped the DVD disc out of his left coat pocket—in case he got John. His other hand stayed in his right pocket, tightening around the grip of his pistol, in case he got Pérez.

John Zedman opened the door. His expectant, waiting-for-his-mistress kind of smile faded quickly.

"Hey," Samuel said.

"What are you doing here?"

John had been drinking, that bad boy. His eyes were bloodshot, his nose webbed with capillaries. The way he stood blocking the doorway—nervous and pale, glancing down the street like he was looking for the cavalry—Samuel knew Pérez wasn't there. John had sent him away, maybe, so he could have time alone to think. Or better yet—maybe John was hoping Chadwick would come back.

"I'm with the prize patrol," Samuel told him. "Invite me in."

"Why the hell should I?"

He raised the movie disc. "It's about Chadwick."

John's eyes latched on the DVD—not understanding, but hungry to, like an addict, like Katherine, the last night she'd visited.

He stepped back from his doorway.

There was a faint burning smell in the living room—the back windows were open to the sunset, the ocean turning the color of beer.

"Well?" Zedman demanded.

"Talk to me about the money."

Zedman stole another glance at the DVD. He rubbed his fingers on the tail of his dress shirt. "You've got bad information. I don't know—"

"—what I'm talking about? Not what you said when you called Friday, John. Not what you said at all."

Disbelief took over Zedman's face slowly, gripping it like

a shot of novocaine. Samuel knew what he was thinking: *This couldn't be who I've been afraid of.*

Samuel had expected that. He was used to being underestimated.

"Chadwick sent you," John said. "Is that it?"

"Sorry, John. Working this solo, and you don't even get why, do you?"

Zedman looked old and bent in that wrinkled tank top, those baggy pajama bottoms—like he should be using a walker.

"I'll see you buried," he said. "I'll call the police—"

"And tell them what, John—how you stole twenty-seven million? How we know each other?"

Zedman's fists balled, his face turned the color of his dying begonias. "You couldn't do this alone. You wouldn't have the first clue."

"You know, for a millionaire, you're a stupid fuck."

Zedman charged him, but Samuel had been expecting that, too. His gun was already out of his pocket.

He pistol-whipped John across the left cheek, slammed him into the side of the fireplace.

John clawed his way up, but Samuel smashed the butt of the gun into his mouth, sent him back to the carpet.

Shit, he told himself. *Slow down. Not here.*

Zedman was kicking his legs feebly, trying to get up again. His upper lip had split open, blood making a stalactite down his chin, spattering the white bricks of the fireplace.

Samuel stared at the spots of blood, but he wasn't thinking of John Zedman. He was remembering Talia's house on a cold night with his little brothers yelling and stomping in the bedroom, Talia's music going in the kitchen while she argued with Ali. And Katherine coming in the door, crying, her lips cold when she kissed his cheek, saying: "This has to be the last time. Please. The last time, I promise. They found my stash."

She told him why she was crying, why her father had gone to Texas, why she wanted to die—and Samuel tried to keep his anger from showing. Not just anger at Chadwick, but at Katherine, too. She was leaving him, after all that had happened. So he got her what she asked for, but something special, the uncut Colombian white, telling her, "This batch is a little weak."

Standing on the porch, telling her goodbye, he had looked down at the little blue Toyota, dented up and smoking like a two-dollar pipe bomb, and saw the little girl's face in the window, just for an instant—the little girl who was Race's age. Samuel thinking, *They get to leave. They drive across the bridge and leave us like a zoo exhibit.*

Samuel and Race and the rest of his family alone—unprotected, with Ali treating their mother like a side of beef to be tenderized, and ripping down his real father's metalwork, then coming around at night to Samuel's little sister, same way Elbridge used to do, only this time, who would take the gun out of Johnny Jay's toolbox? Samuel had to. If he didn't, who would?

So he watched Katherine and the little girl drive away in the old blue Toyota, and he was thinking, *No. You will not leave me behind. I will never let you go.*

John Zedman had made it to his knees. He hunched over the fireplace, his smashed mouth swelling, his lips red and wet as a whore's. "I'm b'eeding. You hit me."

"Get up," Samuel told him.

"Won't get . . . the money."

Samuel scooped a pack of Kleenex from the table, tossed it at Zedman. "Put that on your mouth. Then get the fuck up."

Zedman pressed the whole wedge of tissues to his lip. Samuel watched the blood soak through, knowing that he should be moving things along, that time was not on his side, but Katherine's voice was still in his head, talking about flowers coming back after you tried to kill them, pleading with him that Zedman had paid enough already. Samuel should get the account numbers and leave. He could be on a plane tonight, him and Race. They could watch the sun come up tomorrow over Puerto Vallarta. Why add more voices in his head?

He looked at one of Zedman's paintings, the glass turning gold in the sunset, and the reflection he saw wasn't his face. It was Talia—frightened, uncertain, always ready to scurry into the darkness like a cockroach. Samuel lifted his pistol, fired a round into the reflection.

When the ringing died down in his ears, he said quietly, "Get to the bathroom, John. You got one upstairs, right?"

John was still blinking from the gunshot. He had the look of a Black Level kid—that moment when the enforcer brings out the bag for the first time.

"What are you going to do?" he asked. "The disc—you said it was about Chadwick."

Samuel had forgotten all about the DVD. Now he held it up, trying not to smile at his own private joke. "You want to see a movie, John? Get on upstairs—I'm sure you got a player in your bedroom, right?"

He twitched the barrel of the gun toward the stairs.

Unsteadily, Zedman rose, the Kleenex keeping the blood from dripping too much—a crooked trail across the living room, up the carpeted stairs, Samuel thinking all the way that this was not as neat as he'd planned. He wouldn't have time to clean this shit up.

Let him go, Katherine whispered. *Get the numbers and just leave.*

At the top of the stairs, Zedman hesitated.

Samuel said, "Don't."

"Wha'?"

"Whatever you were just thinking. 'Less you want to be shot in the back."

Zedman swayed, then turned left, into the master bedroom.

Wasn't Samuel's kind of room. High ceilings and no windows. Too many pictures on the wall, too many mirrors. A good television, though—DVD player, sure enough. Through the open bathroom door he could see a big square tub, maroon tiles.

"Mallory," John said. "Tell me she's safe."

Samuel went to the television, slipped the disc in the machine. When the movie came on, Zedman's face got sleepy with bewilderment. Then he began to understand, gradually. Samuel could see it in his eyes.

"Please," John said.

"Tell you how they do it at Cold Springs," Samuel said. "Cold Springs's all about compliance. You earn privileges by doing exactly what you're told. You understand what I'm saying, John?"

"The account numbers are in my computer. I can show you."

"Oh yeah, but see—I'm too stupid to work this all by myself, right? I wouldn't have the first clue."

John's eyes were moist with defeat, shame. He was ready for the gag, for solitary confinement—for whatever punishment the instructors threw at him. He said, eagerly, "It just takes a phone call. The account numbers, I can show you. The password on the computer—it's Ferryboat*, with an asterisk, last character. Capital F."

"Get in the bathroom."

Zedman hesitated, and Samuel advanced on him, forcing him back step by step until Zedman stood in front of the toilet.

"Well?" Samuel said. "Use it."

Zedman looked at the pot, then back at Samuel. "What?"

"You heard me."

"I—I can't."

Samuel pressed the gun against Zedman's shoulder. "You already bleeding all over the place, John. I don't want any more to clean up later, you understand me?"

John took a piss—a good long one. Samuel was amused by the little shriveled thing he used, too. I mean, damn. All that self-importance, all that strutting—it made sense when the man dropped his drawers.

"You do that real well, like you've been practicing," Samuel told him. "Now get in the tub."

"You'll never get the money, if you kill me."

"Why would that be, John? You ain't told me the whole truth about those codes? Is that cooperation?"

Zedman stared at the water swirling in the toilet.

"I heard you a woman-slapper, John. You want me to hit you again, remind you how it feels? Get in the tub, bitch."

He pushed Zedman back, watched him stumble into the tub.

"Stay on your knees," Samuel said. "I like that."

Samuel pulled the shower curtain closed as much as possible, making mental notes about the tiles, how the blood splatters would go.

"Don't," Zedman said.

Samuel turned on the shower, watched the way it splattered in John's half-dazed face, rinsing the blood into a pink swirl—like Talia's bathroom, Talia's blood, only Zedman was still alive, still listening.

"Your daughter's life, John. I haven't decided if you get to keep that privilege, yet. You think you've cooperated?"

John's lips were moving, making sounds, but nothing intelligible came out. For a minute, Samuel was afraid Zedman might've broken completely.

Then Zedman said, "Pérez. I told him . . . I thought . . . he's going after Chadwick—"

Samuel stared at him. And then he got it, and he started to laugh. He filled up the bathroom with laughter, had to sit on the pot, it was all so funny. He looked down and saw that poor Zedman wasn't sharing the joke.

"Yeah, I got you," Samuel said. "And?"

"It wasn't Chadwick's fault. It was mine. Please stop him. Don't let Pérez . . ."

"Noble, John. What does it take for you to make an enemy and have it stick? Man fucks your wife, steals your daughter— brings all this on you, and you want to save his life now, after you told your Mexican to kill him? Man. Money makes you crazy, John. I guess it does."

In the next room, the DVD was still playing—bright and cheerful sounds, music from a fairy tale.

"The real account number," John promised. "A password. The right one."

The wound on his mouth was still bleeding—ragged and pink like a fishhook gouge.

Zedman told him the password, the account number, the name of the bank. He told him the exact amount, the agent who could make the transfer. And Samuel knew he wasn't lying this time. He was broken. He was ready for the next level of training—as pliable as his goddamn weak daughter.

"You can't remember all that," Zedman muttered. "Let me out of here. I'll write it down. I'll take you downstairs—"

"Oh, I'll remember," Samuel promised. "I'm brilliant, see? Everybody says so."

Then he came over to the tub, knelt, pressed the gun to John's heart—imagining the pattern it would make, like red wings on the tiles behind him, imagining Katherine's pleading, the fairy-tale music going, evoking impossible images like Talia being alive, Samuel being in charge—realizing his dreams, getting through college, teaching kids, protecting his family once and for all.

John Zedman closed his eyes. His lips trembled so violently it was hard to tell if he was just afraid, or if his body was involved in some terrible, desperate prayer.

Samuel was filled with benevolence. Good old John. Paying his dues at last.

He said, "I'm thinking about letting you go, John. Would you like that? Would you give me anything for that?"

And they knelt there together, at a moment of endless possibility, the shower soaking Samuel's sleeve and running off John Zedman's thinning hair, John's heartbeat so strong Samuel could almost feel it in the grip of his gun.

17

Chadwick told himself he had no destination in mind, but it wasn't true. He fell back into a pattern as old as his adulthood—south on 101, exit on Army Street, up Van Ness to 24th.

He knew he shouldn't go to the Mission District. He shouldn't indulge in the past. But seeing John, then visiting the East Bay, had put him in a frame of mind for examining old wounds.

Some of the townhouses on San Angelo Street looked the way he remembered them—muddy facades, windows curtained with bedsheets, the stoops decorated with hubcaps and bilingual City Council election posters, Spanish graffiti. Other townhouses had been renovated by invading dot-commers—painted mauve and burgundy and teal, dandified with gingerbread trim and high-tech security systems. No cars out front—those would be parked in a guarded lot somewhere close by, safe from keying and window-smashing by angry blue-collar residents being driven out by the skyrocketing housing prices.

Chadwick pulled in front of his old home, which nobody could have mistaken for dandified. The street level, which had once been his father's clock repair shop, was boarded up, anarchy signs and gang monikers scrawled across bricks and plywood and window frames. The steps up to the second-story porch were littered with takeout wrappers. A beer bottle sprouted from the mailbox.

Chadwick slid his key in the lock—almost wishing it wouldn't work—but of course it did.

The green door swung open on the interior stairwell, the air dark and stale as sleeper's breath.

Chadwick tried the light switch. The electricity still worked—regulations required that of Chadwick. The management company must not have been changing the lightbulbs.

He climbed up to the living room, ran his fingers over the chocolate wainscoting, stared at the coal-burning fireplace that had not worked since he was a child. On the mantel, islands of light dust marked the places where clocks had stood, years ago.

Thin evening light filtered through the branches of the enormous bougainvillea in the backyard, making yellow streaks across the kitchen floor. Chadwick had always loved that bougainvillea—the pink snow of petals that had filled the yard every spring. He opened the window, stared past the empty clotheslines, the patch of weeds that had once been his garden, the toolshed, the broken fence, over the backs of the stores that faced Mission, their tar roofs painted silver and their vents pouring out the charred smells of *cabrito* and hamburger.

He thought about Norma at the oven, cursing her burned raisin bread. It was one of the few memories he could conjure about her that did not cause pain.

A portable stereo sat on the kitchen counter, a Brahms CD in the carriage from Chadwick's last visit, maybe three years ago. He'd dropped by between escort jobs, supposedly to inspect the property with a mind toward finally selling it, giving Norma her half that the divorce decree demanded. His property manager had begged him to do so. He'd tried to impress Chadwick with the incredible market, promising him an easy million for the old house. But in the end, Chadwick had decided nothing.

He could never live in this house again. But he couldn't bear to sell it, or even lease it. He certainly couldn't bear to give any money from the sale to Norma. She had hated this place, blamed it for her unhappiness, cursed him for trying to raise Katherine here. Their last argument as a married couple, just a month after Katherine's suicide, had been about this house.

And so the place stood heretically vacant in a zero-vacancy real estate market. Instead of making him lots of money, it took most of his meager income in property taxes. It was his one luxury—his one indulgence.

He pushed the button on the stereo, let Brahms play.

He walked into the front bedroom—his old childhood bedroom, later Katherine's. It was stripped now, the only piece of furniture a wooden chair where Chadwick had once sat and told stories to Katherine. A woman's red coat, probably Norma's, was draped over the chair back. Chadwick wondered how long it had been there.

He remembered Katherine's bed in the corner, the crisp white sheets, the headboard he had painted—little pink stars, a cow jumping over a smiling moon.

Chadwick remembered the imprint Katherine's slender body had left on the sheets, the tarnished heroin spoon discarded on the floor, the police lights pulsing in the windows. A female plainclothes officer kneeling next to the black leather chair in the doorway, holding Mallory's hand while the little girl chewed on a silver necklace, sobbing if anyone tried to take it away from her.

Chadwick sat heavily in the wooden chair, in the middle of the empty room, surrounded by his memories.

Piano Quartet No. 3.

Chadwick closed his eyes. He thought about the number three, tried to strip away the years, imagining himself in 1903, then in 1803, trying to think of major events for those years.

When he was in high school, he used to sit by these windows and watch the younger kids play basketball across the street. Even then, he knew he wanted to be a teacher. He and Ann would someday teach together. He had enlisted in the Air Force for the education money, pure and simple, knowing that his parents couldn't provide college tuition even if they'd been inclined to do so. And later, after discharge, with Norma harping at him to get a business degree, he'd studied history instead, because it was the opposite of everything his father stood for—his father who spent his life oiling chronometers, making time go forward as smoothly and flawlessly as possible—no drama, no breaks, never a surprise. Certainly nothing ever went backwards.

Thinking about his father, Chadwick instinctively checked his watch. Seven o'clock. Nine o'clock in Texas. Mallory Zedman would be bunking down for the night. Hunter would be in his office, catching up on paperwork. Olsen...where would she be? Her room in the Big Lodge, or out for drinks in Fredericksburg, perhaps—a counselor's big night out.

It bothered him, what John had said about his blackmailer describing Mallory's day.

Chadwick had tried to dismiss the comment at first. No one got on the Cold Springs campus without Hunter's approval. Security was tight. And even if John was telling the truth, and the blackmailer had said something, it could've been a bluff—some facts recounted from daytime talk shows where boot camp schools got plenty of lurid publicity. Hell, some of that publicity Hunter had generated himself.

But Chadwick kept returning to what Kindra Jones had said—about how he should go back to confront John. She was right, though part of him wanted to stay bitter, to leave John to his fate.

John thought he had a monopoly on suffering?

Race Montrose was right: What could anyone do to Chadwick that was worse than leaving him alone?

Chadwick heard light footsteps on the stairs. He thought he was imagining it, but then the Brahms piece ended, and the creaking didn't.

"House isn't vacant!" he yelled. "I've got a gun."

Norma appeared in the doorway, looking embarrassed, still wearing her wrinkled red dress from that morning. She raised her hands in surrender.

"I was...just driving past. Saw that car in front."

Almost a decade since they'd been divorced, and Chadwick was surprised how quickly he still picked up on her signals. Her statement wasn't so much a lie as a request that he not ask. He read the truth—Norma came here often. The coat on the chair was not from many years ago. He remembered she'd been wearing it that morning, which meant she'd been here once today already.

Chadwick suddenly realized that if he'd stayed in San Francisco, he would've made the same pilgrimages, torturing himself, hating that he was drawn back to the source of the wound, but returning to this empty room nonetheless. How much Norma must resent him for not selling the property—how much easier it would've been for her if he hadn't kept this shrine open for visitation. Better it be painted mauve, trimmed with gingerbread, sold to some young business grad whose definition of history was any amount of time longer than a Super Bowl commercial.

"I found Race Montrose," he told her. "Claims he never talked to you."

"He's lying."

"The boy is scared. He told me his big brother Samuel has been extorting John for years. Stealing the school's money is the final act."

Norma shivered, hugged her arms. "You're sitting on my coat."

Chadwick tossed it to her.

She stepped into the room, pacing, her eyes on the floor. "I know about Samuel. The real story—that Katherine wasn't just getting drugs from him, that they were in love. I heard it last week, from David. He felt sorry for me, that I didn't know this about my own daughter. How do you think that made me feel?"

A lowrider cruised by on San Angelo, the bass of its stereo loud enough to rattle the house's windows.

"David Kraft is a disturbed young man," Chadwick told her. "He wants the school razed, preferably with all of us inside."

"So we're going to shift the blame again?"

"No."

"Because what I think? I think you knew about Katherine and Samuel a long time ago. That's why you went to Texas the week before she died—you didn't know what to do. So you ran to Hunter. You and Hunter came up with some fucking scheme to send my daughter to that... *place*. And meanwhile you don't tell me shit. Not only are you sleeping around behind my back—you are hiding things about *my* daughter. And if I'd known... if you'd bothered to fucking tell me..."

She pushed the air away, a gesture that reminded Chadwick a little too much of the crazy old woman Ella Montrose, mother of a murdered daughter.

"That night of the auction," she told him, "I knew you were going to confess something. I thought you were going to tell me about your fling with Ann. But now I'm trying to believe it was something more important—that you were finally going to tell me the truth about my daughter. Maybe bring me into the problem so we could solve it. If that were the case, I could almost forgive you, Chadwick. I could almost forgive you for being too late."

Her eyes were hungry. She seemed to be asking forgiveness, rather than offering it.

Chadwick wanted to tell her she was right. He wanted to buy her amnesty by agreeing with her, but the words wouldn't come.

Norma sensed his hesitation.

"You think Samuel holds a grudge," she said. "He loved Katherine and he blames us for Katherine's death. All of us who failed her—you and me, Ann and John. The school, too. But what's bothering you is that he started with John. Why he went after the school's money and left you alone. That's it, isn't it?"

Chadwick didn't reply.

Norma traced her fingers down the wall, following the faint line of grime that marked the place where Babar the Elephant once hung. "What I want to say now—I'm afraid to say."

"Norma Reyes, afraid to speak?"

"You're going to put it down to spite. When Race came to see me, he said, 'She ain't going to be satisfied until they're both dead.' *She.*"

"Mallory? She'd probably complained to him about her parents."

Norma shook her head. "I've been thinking about why Race would come to me. Why *me,* why not somebody else? You see it, don't you?"

"Norma..."

"Ann needed the money. When I told her about the embezzlement, she wasn't shocked. She was...nervous. Calculating. Her biggest concern was buying time. I don't think she meant for anybody to find out until after the auction, when the fund was complete. After that she'd have two weeks over Christmas break to leave town, nobody at school, nobody checking up on her. A head start."

"Norma, you're talking about Ann—"

"You were fucking her—you don't know her at all. She puts on a brave face, but she's in desperate shape. Her school's sinking. She'd been taking a salary cut every year to mask how bad it is. She's frantic about not having enough money to fight another custody battle, scared she's going to lose her daughter. You don't know what that will do to a mother, Chadwick, the fear of losing your child."

"Don't I?"

"No." Norma's tone was as sharp and proprietary as a barbed wire fence. "Being the mother is different, *pendejo.* You *don't* know."

Chadwick studied her face—the familiar wisp of black hair looping over her ear, the half-moon curve of her chin.

"I have a job tonight," he said. "I need to go."

"Who you rescuing this time—some drug addict? Some kleptomaniac?"

"I'm stopping by John's house first. Anything you want me to tell him?"

Norma's face reddened. She turned toward the hallway, her face in the sunset. "Don't go there. It won't help."

"Good seeing you, Norma."

"I'm serious. I keep thinking about the two people Ann might want dead, like Race said. The two who stood in the way of everything she wanted. You know what she wanted, don't you? She wanted you."

"Turn off the stereo, will you?"

"Ann is the one who brought you back here. Think about that, Chadwick."

He was at the bottom of the stairwell when she called him one last time. Against his better judgment, he turned to look up at her, and in that moment he could imagine it was ten years ago, fifteen years ago. She could've been reminding him to get milk at the corner grocery, or tossing him Katherine's jacket and mittens, laughing because he and Katherine had once again forgotten them.

"I'm not bitter, Chadwick. I'm empty. You understand the difference? The difference is you see more clearly when you've got nothing left."

Chadwick opened the door of the house, stepped out into the growing gloom of the evening. Down the block, he could hear the lowrider cruising, its stereo setting off car alarms all across the neighborhood like a bloodhound flushing quail.

By the time Chadwick returned to John's house in Marin, it was full dark, the fog settling in over the hilltops.

No cars in the driveway. No lights in the windows.

Chadwick thought it unlikely that John would've gone out, given his frazzled demeanor earlier, but there was no response when he rang the bell.

After two more tries, he felt the weight of the silence build on him, the need to do something. He tried the door. Locked.

He went around to the side window—the one that John always used to leave unlatched, even when Ann scolded him for doing so. It was latched, but easily undone with Chadwick's penknife. He jimmied it open and slipped inside.

He moved through the house, sensing that there was no one here, but feeling he should call out, just in case—make a pretense of respecting John's property.

He couldn't make himself call. The silence was too heavy.

In the foyer, the voice-mail button was blinking on the phone. Chadwick hit *redial*, tried Mallory's birthday for the pass code, and was rewarded with four new messages—one from a real estate client, one from a reporter asking about the Laurel Heights scandal, one from an FBI special agent named Laramie, confirming an appointment for the next morning. The last message was the shortest, a voice Chadwick recognized as Emilio Pérez, saying simply, "Everything's cool. I'll call you."

Chadwick hit the *save* button, hung up the phone. He turned on the living room lights and noticed the blank space on the wall—a space where he was sure a framed painting had hung that afternoon. He went over, touched his finger to a nickel-sized hole. It could've been where a mounting hook had ripped loose. Or it could've been a bullet hole.

He scanned the floor—found a wet spot by the fireplace where the carpet had been scrubbed. And another, closer to the stairs.

Chadwick's throat tightened.

At the base of the stairs, he heard music, very faint, like a television going softly in one of the bedrooms above.

He went upstairs, wishing for the first time in years that he carried a gun.

In the master bedroom, the television was playing a cartoon. John's bed was made, fresh pajamas neatly folded on the pillow. Nothing out of place that Chadwick could see. No sign of a struggle. On the nightstand was a picture of Mallory at about six years old. Chadwick could tell, from the brilliance of her gap-toothed smile, it had been taken before Katherine's suicide.

Chadwick walked to the bathroom, flipped on the light.

There was no shower curtain on the rod, only a few rings. A small red puddle glistened on the tile floor. Chadwick had just put his shoe in it.

He stepped back, making a red spot on the beige carpet.

Chadwick backed away, left another bloody print, fainter than the first.

His survival instinct was telling him to get the hell out.

A sudden burst of music from the television cartoon startled him. Marimbas, trumpets, a loud "Ha-ha!" He reached to turn it off, but his hand froze.

On the screen, fish danced in swirls of bubbles.

Sebastian the Crab was singing "Under the Sea."

Chadwick made it to the bed just as his legs failed him.

He saw himself nine years ago, ejecting a video cassette of this movie, cracking it against the mantel after all the police had gone, tipping over the television and ripping cords out of the wall and picking up the black leather chair and throwing it against the wall until the Romos next door started shouting curses and pounding on the Sheetrock.

Now he stared at the "on" light of the DVD player, the flashing green circular icon that meant continuous replay.

He could barely pull out his cell phone.

His finger hovered over the 9 for 911, but he didn't dial it. He knew who that would summon—John Zedman's local police. John Zedman's lackeys.

Instead, he scrolled back through his recent calls, to an Oakland number he had dialed two weeks ago—Sergeant Damarodas, the only homicide detective he knew.

18

Floodlights.

Mallory knew that wasn't right. There was no stadium in the woods—nothing brighter than stars and the campfire. But when she woke up to Leyland's voice, rain drumming on the canvas roof of her pup tent, there were blinding lights outside, down toward the river, like a goddamn UFO had landed.

"Move it!" Leyland was yelling. "This is your lucky day, Zedman! Show me your enthusiasm!"

"Yes, sir!" Mallory croaked.

It couldn't be five o'clock yet. Mallory's body told her she hadn't slept at all.

She struggled into her clothes—damp and sour from yesterday, still smelling of horse—then she stumbled out to find the line. Morrison, Smart and Bridges were already at attention, standing in the freezing downpour, letting the rain drip off their noses.

Something is wrong, Mallory thought.

She spotted Olsen, a half-dozen other counselors and white levels, even Dr. Hunter—all with grim faces, all wearing fatigues. Too many people.

Fear kicked Mallory in the gut. Had her team messed up somehow?

"Fall in, Zedman!" Leyland yelled.

Mallory joined the line, forced herself to stand straight, eyes forward, trying not to blink in the rain.

"Black levels!" Dr. Hunter said. "Who is responsible for getting you here?"

"We are, sir!"

"Who is responsible for getting you out?"

"We are, sir!"

"First step is accountability," Hunter chanted. *"You* are the problem. *You* are the solution. You must accept that. You must take the blame if you fail. Do you understand?"

"Yes, sir!"

"Are you accountable?"

"Yes, sir!"

"Are you ready to move on?"

This was a new question—not part of their litany—and the black levels hesitated. It sounded as if Dr. Hunter was offering them a choice, and choices were not something black levels trained for.

Mallory answered first. She shouted, "YES, SIR!"

"That's funny," Hunter said. "Rain must be affecting my ears. I didn't hear you all. Are you ready to move on?"

This time they all shouted, "YES, SIR!!!"

"We will see," Hunter said. "Eyes front."

He called Leyland forward. As the rain pattered down on the red granite, Hunter grabbed a mess of ropes and metal clasps from one of the white levels and started fitting the gear around Leyland's waist.

What the hell? Mallory wondered.

"Accountability isn't worth a dime without courage," Hunter told them. "You need courage to remove yourself from your old patterns; to tell your so-called friends to take a hike; to face the people back in the real world and convince them you aren't the worthless heap of self-pity you were when you came into this program. We will see if you've got courage, ladies and gentlemen. You will not leave Black Level until you know that nothing—NOTHING—can test you worse than I can test you."

Mallory's ears were ringing. Did he say *leave Black Level?*

Hunter finished fitting the straps and hooks around Leyland's chest, then Leyland started putting a similar harness on Hunter. The black levels stood there, watching—like this was normal, standing outside in the icy rain in the middle of the night watching your instructors tie each other up.

It dawned on Mallory that the gear was some kind of climbing equipment—and her excitement turned to apprehension. Courage was something she knew she didn't have. If she'd had courage, she never would've wound up here. She would've figured out a way to help Race.

Your so-called friends.

Leyland finished putting the harness on Dr. Hunter. They double-checked each other's straps.

"Now," Hunter told them. "In partners with your counselor. The job you do may be the difference between life and death. Do it right."

Olsen came up to her—tossed her a harness. "After you, kiddo."

Mallory did her best to fit Olsen. Her hands felt numb, the straps sluggish going into the metal buckles. Olsen's clothes were as wet and cold as her own, smelling faintly of sweat and campfire smoke.

One of the instructors yelled, "You don't want to be last! You DO NOT want to be last!"

"Doing fine," Olsen assured her. "I won't bite you."

Mallory got the last strap secured around Olsen's thigh.

Olsen checked her work, grimaced. She lifted a strap Mallory had forgotten to fasten. Mallory's face burned with embarrassment, but she finished the job.

Olsen picked up the other harness and started weaving it around Mallory's torso—tugging hard on the straps, making them tight around the shoulders, like she'd done this a million times before.

They weren't the last ones finished. Bridges took forever getting his counselor hooked up. But finally, everybody fell into line.

"Too slow," Hunter told the group. "Let's make up for lost time."

Leyland blew his whistle and led them on a run—down the familiar path to the river, rain spiking in their faces, kids slipping in the mud, instructors yelling. Just like old times.

They passed the obstacle course, the Mushroom Rocks, and then came to the banks of the river.

The whole forest was lit up fluorescent silver, striped with rain.

Floodlights burned in the branches of two enormous cypress trees, one on either side of the river. Strung between their trunks, maybe forty feet in the air, were three thin cables like power lines. Below this the river raged, swollen and glistening like an enormous, melting slug.

"That bridge," Hunter yelled over the growl of the rapids, "is the only way across."

What bridge? Mallory started to ask. And then she realized Hunter meant the ropes.

All her confidence drained out of her.

"There is no going back," Hunter continued. "You will be here until you make it across—if that means tonight, or a week, or the rest of your life. So watch and learn."

Hunter tossed Leyland a safety helmet.

Leyland put it on, clipped himself to a climbing rope, and Hunter took the other end.

"This is the belay," Hunter told them. "This is your lifeline. I will not do this for you. I will not catch you if you fall. You and your counselor will spot each other. So pay attention."

Leyland began climbing handholds Mallory hadn't even noticed before—knobs no bigger than drawer handles going all the way up the trunk of the cypress.

He ascended effortlessly. At the top he stepped onto a tiny platform—just a couple of boards nailed between the base of two branches. He hooked himself to a new line, dropped the climbing rope, then started over the rope bridge—his feet on the bottom cord, hands on the middle, a safety line tied to the top. He shimmied his way across the river, to a platform in the opposite tree.

Mallory no longer felt the cold. She no longer felt the thousand pounds of rain soaking into her clothes. Her mouth was dry and hot as beach sand.

I can't do that.

She had always been scared of heights. She couldn't even

look out the windows of Race's grandmother's apartment. Now she was certain she was going to fall and die.

"One pair at a time," Hunter said. "Your counselor will spot you. Then you'll return the favor. Volunteers?"

No one spoke.

"Zedman and Olsen," Hunter decided. "Thank you."

Mallory's eyes widened. "I didn't—"

But Olsen was already stepping up to the tree.

A white level explained the belay gear. He told Mallory she would be climbing first.

"No," she said. "Not first, please."

The white level frowned, started to repeat the order.

"It's okay," Olsen interceded. "I'm ready to climb."

Mallory didn't like the idea of holding Olsen's lifeline any more than she liked climbing. How the hell could Olsen trust her, after everything she had done? Her shoulder couldn't be fully healed from the stab wound Mallory had given her. But Olsen didn't act scared.

The white level fitted Olsen's helmet, hooked her to the line and made sure it was secure. He showed Mallory how to wrap the belay cord around her waist. Mallory would be responsible for spotting Olsen as she went up, taking up the slack, making sure she didn't fall. Then Olsen would spot for her, from the top platform. Simple.

Right, simple, Mallory thought. *We're both going to die.*

Olsen said, "Belay on?"

"On belay," Mallory said.

"No," Dr. Hunter chastised. "You got her life in your hands, girl. Say it like you mean it."

"On belay!"

"Climbing," Olsen called.

"Climb on!" Mallory said.

Mallory watched her ascend, even more swiftly than Leyland had. Soon, she was at the top, reversing the ropes so she could hold belay for Mallory.

There was no way Olsen would be able to stop her falling, holding her rope from way up there. The platform and Olsen looked so tiny.

Mallory got hooked up, stepped to the tree. *This would be a good time to wake up,* she thought.

She yelled that she was climbing, heard Olsen's distant voice shouting back to climb on.

Mallory got ahold of a slippery knob, pulled herself up. She tried putting her foot sideways on the footholds, pushing with her legs. That worked pretty well. About five feet up, she slipped and banged against the slippery wet bark of the tree, but she didn't fall. She just dangled. Olsen had taken up the slack.

Mallory found a foothold and continued climbing.

Her progress was maddeningly slow. Her fingers ached, her forearms burned. The strap of the safety helmet cut under her chin. There was nothing but tree trunk and rain and the unforgiving floodlights in her eyes. Her vision telescoped to the smallest details—canyon patterns in the bark, the gray plastic half-moon of the next handle, the blood seeping from the cut on her right hand. After a million years, she reached the base of the platform; she hauled herself up next to Olsen.

"Good job," Olsen told her. "Excellent."

She was trembling, and Olsen's praise made her want to sob like a baby. She hooked herself to a new line, then lowered the climbing rope to the ground.

Looking down made her stomach spin—the other black levels the size of dolls, their heads all bent upward, watching her.

The platform seemed to shift under her. She grabbed Olsen's leg.

"You're not slipping," Olsen promised. "It's vertigo."

"I'm going to die. I can't do this."

"Yeah, you can," Olsen said.

"I'm scared of heights."

"You're connected to the cowstail. You'll be fine." Olsen pointed to the rope bridge—the small top wire that ran above the bottom two. It was red, and impossibly thin, and Mallory's lifeline was now connected to it.

"Cross slowly," Olsen instructed her. "Small movements. Slide across, don't step. If you slip, you'll just hang there. Take your time getting back up. You saw the ropes take Leyland's weight. They'll take yours."

"Christ, have you done this before?"

"Counting tonight?" Olsen asked. "Once."

"Oh, shit."

"Language," Olsen warned her.

"Language? I'm about to die here and you tell me 'language'?"

"Let's go. I'll help you up."

Mallory knew her fingers were leaving permanent gouge marks on Olsen's arms, but Olsen didn't complain.

She coaxed Mallory to the platform edge, said encouraging things Mallory couldn't even register as words, and somehow got her to step out over nothing.

"Good!" Olsen said. "Slow—just take it slow."

The rain was worse now—needling her face, reducing her vision to nothing. She slid one foot out on the bottom rope. The feeling was like a trampoline, only worse. Every vibration in the line was an earthquake.

She knew the others were watching her—the black levels, Olsen, Leyland, Hunter.

Mallory wanted to do well. She took another step, exhaled, the cord cutting into her soles.

"Good!" Olsen told her. "Your right hand. Just slide it out a little. Now the left."

Mallory measured her progress by inches, memorizing the feel of the cord, the braid pattern under her hands. Olsen's voice was the only thing keeping her heart beating.

About halfway across, just when she was feeling like she might make it, she stepped wrong. The rope slipped from under her foot and the world did a mad pirouette on a floodlight. Mallory found herself hanging, unable to find the lines, the river twisting and churning below, hungrily waiting to swallow her.

She was too terrified even to scream.

"It's okay!" Olsen shouted. "It's okay. The foot line is right next to you."

"Where?"

"Right hand. Extend it."

Mallory tried, but she was still swaying in the void. Her hand found nothing but air and rain. She saw Olsen on the platform above her. Then the rope turned and Mallory was looking at Leyland in the opposite tree, his face stern. He was gesturing for her to come on.

Mallory extended her hand again, found a cord.

"Good!" Olsen yelled. "Now slowly—take your time. Put—"

There was a sound like Velcro ripping, and Mallory dropped a millimeter, the pit of her stomach threatening to yank out the bottom of her shoes.

"What—what was that?" she yelled.

Olsen's voice—for a terrible half second—wasn't there.

"Mallory, other hand," she called, the new urgency in her voice making Mallory's joints freeze. "Both hands on the line. Now."

Mallory tried, but her arms wouldn't obey her. The rain stung her eyes. She swung and saw Leyland, his face now pale.

"Mallory!" Olsen shouted again. "You need to get back up."

"I can't!"

"Other hand!"

"I can't!"

Leyland came into view again, frantically hooking cables to his harness, his left foot already out on the bridge.

There was another Velcro rip, and Mallory dropped another millimeter, her one good handgrip on the slick rope slipping away.

She could hear confused voices below now—Dr. Hunter, the other kids shouting through the storm.

This isn't happening to me. It isn't.

She realized her shoulder didn't feel so constricted now. The belt around her waist was loose. She was unraveling in midair.

"Please, God..." Her voice didn't sound like her own.

"Right above you!" It was Olsen. "No—I mean left. The rope, Mallory! It's right there."

"Where?"

She felt the line trembling through her harness as Leyland worked his way toward her—too far away. Much too far. *This isn't happening to me.*

Another ripping noise, and then the foot line bowed against her forearm, and she grabbed it, shaking off a string of raindrops into her face. She got her other hand on the line. Olsen was yelling encouragement, urging her to hang on.

Then Leyland was there, lifting her up with one arm, making sure her feet found the bridge. He crushed her against him with one arm, and they slid together—across the river. Even after they reached the opposite platform, after Leyland had threaded an emergency line around her waist and rappelled her to the ground—Mallory still felt the world swaying. She crumpled onto all fours, soaked and shivering.

"Just get me down," she mumbled, her eyes squeezed shut. "Get me down."

"Zedman, you're all right now." Hunter's huge hand was gripping her shoulder. Then his tone hardened. "Leyland, what happened?"

"Look," Leyland said. He tugged lightly on Mallory's back strap—something she couldn't see, didn't want to see.

Hunter snapped, "Get it off her."

Mallory's hands curled in the moss and the wet leaves. Her vision went black and she vomited, heaving all the terror out of her body, everything she had ever feared—from Talia Montrose's torn body to her father's fists to Katherine leaving her, disappearing into the yellow house with the dark doorway and the ivy made of iron.

"Zedman." Hunter's voice was smaller now, like it had been compressed to fit in the barrel of a gun. "You're all right, Zedman. Look. The harness ripped."

And she looked up, saw him holding the strap that had almost killed her, the rip sprouting tufts of orange synthetic fiber.

"It's okay," Hunter said. "The main thing is you're safe."

But she could hear the anger in his voice, and she could see the strap as well as he could—the truth that no amount of reassurance could make all right. The tear line was perfectly straight—the strap had been cut.

19

The Marin County Sheriff's Office found no body at John Zedman's house, no sign of forced entry except for Chadwick's.

They couldn't locate John Zedman, nor his car, nor his driver, Emilio Pérez. Zedman's only two neighbors on the cul-de-sac had seen or heard nothing suspicious in the past twenty-four hours. But then, they hadn't noticed Chadwick drive up, or Sergeant Damarodas' arrival twenty minutes later, or the caravan of sheriff's vehicles with lights flashing that followed. As Chadwick figured it, their ocean views were so expensive the neighbors lost money every time they looked street-side.

The splatters in John's bathroom were definitely blood. The hole in the living room wall was definitely a bullet hole.

Past that, Detective Prost of the Marin County Investigations Division wasn't prepared to say. He was much too busy enjoying Chadwick's company. Even after an hour of interrogation, Prost was not anxious to let him go.

"So your relationship with Mr. Zedman," Detective Prost recapped for the twentieth time. "You wouldn't characterize it as friendly."

"I'd characterize it as irrelevant," Chadwick replied. "There's blood in his goddamn bathroom. Maybe you ought to try looking for him."

Prost reached across the kitchen counter, helped himself to some of John's gourmet coffee.

Prost didn't look at Sergeant Damarodas, who was leaning

against the refrigerator behind him, but Chadwick could feel the tension between the two policemen. Citing the need for interdepartmental cooperation, Damarodas had politely insisted on staying, and the local cops moved around him with a flustered kind of annoyance—the way pedestrians move around public modern art.

"Mr. Chadwick," Prost said. "John Zedman's ex-wife was your employer at Laurel Heights. Correct?"

"The answer was yes an hour ago," Chadwick said. "It's still yes."

"You and Mrs. Zedman keep in touch since?"

"Not really."

"No? So after nine years of not keeping in touch, she calls you out of the blue to help kidnap her daughter—"

"Escort," Chadwick corrected. "Legally escort. At the custodial parent's request."

"Escort." Prost nodded neutrally. "And at the time of the escort, two weeks ago, did you speak to John Zedman?"

"No."

"Yet this afternoon, you visited him."

"That's right."

"By your own account, there was an argument. You accused John Zedman of causing his ex's financial troubles—the ones that made the headlines this morning."

"I discussed the matter with him."

"The friend you paged to come up here, the lady waiting outside—Ms. Jones? She implied it was a little worse than a discussion."

Chadwick caught Damarodas' eyes.

In some ways, the sergeant had been less than Chadwick expected from talking to him on the phone—not over five-ten, cheap suit, pale skin and brown hair and facial features that reminded Chadwick of an overgrown field mouse—but his eyes were startling blue and sharp. The message in those eyes was a silent warning, *No*.

"John and I had a discussion," Chadwick told Prost. "That's all."

"I see. So when you came back this evening and broke

into Mr. Zedman's house—you did that just to check on Mr. Zedman's welfare. Do I have that right?"

"Detective, we've been through this. Unless you're charging me with something—"

Prost spread his hands. "Oh, you're free to go anytime, Mr. Chadwick. Tom!"

A bored-looking deputy poked his head in from the living room. "Sir?"

"Mrs. Zedman get here yet?"

"'Bout five minutes ago."

"Show her in."

Chadwick's hand closed into a fist. "You made Ann Zedman drive up here?"

"Escorted her," Prost corrected. "Strictly voluntary."

"She has enough to deal with."

"Why, Mr. Chadwick, I thought she'd be concerned—father of her child, and all."

Chadwick shoved back his chair and rose to his feet. "You son of a—"

Damarodas cleared his throat. "Been a long night, Mr. Chadwick. Let me walk you out."

Prost was about to add something when Ann came into the kitchen, her expression like a highway crash survivor's—one of the commuters in the fifty-car pile-ups on the Grapevine who go wandering through almond orchards in the fog.

"Ann?" Chadwick said.

There was a three-second delay before she focused on him. "I just—Two calls in a row. Mark Jasper, forced leave of absence from school. Then the detective here. John's blood . . . ?"

"Don't do this now," Chadwick told her. "I'll take you home. Get some sleep. Get a lawyer."

"No, no. That's not . . . I mean, that's not necessary, is it?"

"No, ma'am," Prost said. "We have some coffee, if you'd like."

Ann gazed blankly around the kitchen that used to be

hers. "I haven't been in...so long. He changed the counter-tops."

Prost smiled sympathetically. "Have a seat, ma'am. Mr. Chadwick, thanks for your time."

Chadwick didn't move. He needed to believe that Ann was unshakable. Even after Katherine died, after he'd quit the school and given up all hope of having Ann in his life, he needed to know she was still at Laurel Heights, working with children, dreaming about the ideal school. As much despair as Chadwick had encountered working for Cold Springs, no matter how many terrible situations he'd walked into, how much proof he accumulated that the American family was dying a slow and painful death, he needed to believe that Ann's optimism survived. Now her fragility paralyzed him and he saw that he had relied on her too much, been intoxicated by her faith too long, to believe that she could be broken.

In the space of twenty-four hours, her life's work had been stolen from her. Her soul had spun off balance. If Detective Prost harbored the same suspicions Norma Reyes did, he'd have Ann admitting to anything.

"Let me stay with you," he tried again. "You don't have to—"

"It's all right," she murmured, not looking at him. "You go on."

"Sound advice," Prost agreed. "And by the way, Mr. Chadwick, just as a formality, I should tell you it'd be a bad idea for you to leave the Bay Area for the next few days."

"I'm flying to Texas in the morning. You know that."

"Yes, I do." Prost smiled, as if nothing could've suited him better. "I suppose I knew that."

Chadwick took a step toward the detective, but Damaro-das' fingers closed around his arm like owl talons. "Right this way, Mr. Chadwick. Easy to get lost in a house this big."

Damarodas steered him past the evidence techs in the living room, into the front yard, past the police vehicles and the news vans to Chadwick's rental car, where Kindra Jones was sitting on the hood.

When she'd returned his page, Kindra had been waiting

for him in a Montgomery Street coffeehouse, pissed off and impatient after three cups of house blend. Her mood hadn't improved when he'd told her the situation, and that she'd either need to wait for him there indefinitely or find a taxi to Marin. "I'm charging the cab to Hunter," she'd said. "And you're explaining it to him. Goddamn, Chad, I said *talk* to the man."

As Damarodas and he neared the car, she slid to her feet. "This joker arresting you?"

"This joker is not," Damarodas said. "Miss—"

Chadwick made the introductions, then suggested that Kindra start the car.

"No. Uh-uh. I've been waiting for you all night. Somebody's going to tell me what the hell is going on."

Chadwick filled her in the best he could. "Just so I know," he told her, "what exactly did you say to the police?"

"What did I say—" Kindra's eyes narrowed. "Oh, wait— they did not sucker you with that, did they? I didn't tell anybody jack shit, Chadwick. Police will fuck with your mind every time."

"That's a gross overgeneralization," Damarodas commented.

"Fuck you," Kindra told him. "Fuck you, *Sergeant, sir.* Now if you'll excuse me, the car's starting to sound better."

She slammed the driver's side door behind her.

Damarodas took out a cigarillo, poked it in his mouth, and slumped against the side of Chadwick's car. "Your timing, Mr. Chadwick—remarkable."

"The blood. Is it John's?"

"It's fresh," Damarodas said. "Within the last few hours. Past that—they'll run DNA, toxicology. This was Oakland, I'd say a week or two for results. But Marin County? They're not exactly backlogged with cases. Maybe twenty-four hours, they'll know. Doesn't mean I'll find out, unless somebody decides to tell me something."

Chadwick felt the cool force of his eyes. He realized Damarodas probably got a lot of confessions.

"John Zedman was an old friend," Chadwick said. "I would never hurt him."

"Yeah, well . . . we won't get into the fact that the majority of murders are between old friends. Why did you call me?"

The lights of the police cars raced red and blue circles across the windows of the cul-de-sac. The news van people were packing up shop, the cameraman looking disappointed he hadn't gotten any shots of a gurney being wheeled out.

"Someone left that movie playing for me," Chadwick told Damarodas. "The same video that was playing the night my daughter died. Someone left Katherine's necklace near Talia Montrose's body. Someone's trying to pry up sanity with a crowbar, Sergeant, and I don't know what to do about it."

Damarodas lit his cigarillo.

"Let me give you a scenario, Chadwick. Just because, well, I'm thinking if I was a suck-up asshole like Prost—sorry, did I say that aloud?—but a halfway decent homicide investigator, too, and I knew what I know about you, and I read the newspaper about this school you used to work at Laurel Heights going down in a scandal—here's what I might think: I'd think Ann Zedman is having financial difficulties. She plans a scheme to embezzle from her own school. Except things start going wrong. Maybe her daughter knows about the plan, tells her boyfriend, Race. Race tells his mom, Talia, and Talia decides to grab a piece of the action. Mrs. Zedman decides the safest thing is to shut Talia up permanently."

"Ann Zedman is headmistress of a school. You saw her. You figure her for a knife-murderer?"

"For the sake of argument, let's say Mrs. Z doesn't do it herself. She calls somebody she trusts, somebody who's already got a beef against the Montrose family. You savvy?"

Chadwick looked out at the fog, at the lamppost like a hanging tree in front of the empty Zedman house. "Go on."

"Mrs. Z continues with her plan. She's waiting for the whole thirty mill to be collected before she makes the transfer, but her friend Norma Reyes finds out what's going on. The kid Race tells Norma, 'cause after all, it's his mom that got killed. So Mrs. Z plays scared and innocent, asks Norma to please wait just a couple of days. That gives Mrs. Z time to cover her tracks. Reyes doesn't want to turn in her best friend, but somehow the ex-husband, John Zedman, finds out, and he doesn't share Norma's qualms about making trouble. Maybe he's even got some kind of evidence that could tie his ex-wife to the embezzlement. You're Mrs. Zedman's accomplice. You come over and try to make him see reason. But he's angry and he's stubborn. So you come back later and kill him."

"And then call the police?"

Damarodas shrugged. "Smart cover. That's what I'd think, if I were Prost. Now here's the rub: A young fellow Laramie from the FBI Financial Crimes Section talked to me today. SFPD's already given the embezzlement investigation over to him. Hell, half the City Council sends their kids to Ann Zedman's school. The locals don't want anything to do with that mess. So Laramie's already working on following an international transfer of stolen funds. He's smelling a career-starter case against Ann Zedman, maybe with a murder or two thrown in. He comes to me on the Talia Montrose homicide, reminds me that it's going nowhere by itself—nobody really gives a damn about a poor strung-out black woman from Oakland. He asks for my cooperation. Then John Zedman, who Laramie wanted to interview, disappears in a little red grease spot. You know Laramie will be talking to Prost, if he hasn't already. If you leave the state now, Mr. Chadwick, how long do you think it'll be before you're the focus of a federal investigation?"

Through the windshield, Chadwick could see Kindra Jones tapping her watch.

"You believe that bullshit?" Chadwick asked Damarodas.

"Me?" Damarodas took a puff from his stench-stick, making the tip glow. "Hell, no. Me, I think somebody's messing with your mind. And I'll tell you something else for free. That kid David Kraft? He seemed pretty damn anxious to make the Zedmans look bad. Loved them almost as much as he loved you. He told me there'd been rumors at Laurel Heights about John Zedman way before this embezzlement scandal broke, back when Kraft was still a student—rumors that when Zedman was working development for his wife, he was structuring the accounts in . . . let's say in some truly creative ways. Taking advantage of the tax-free nonprofit status, being a little loose about what money belonged to Zedman Development and what belonged to his wife's school. You get what I'm saying?"

"I never heard anything like that."

"Yeah, well, maybe young Kraft is full of shit. On the other hand, maybe he shared that information with somebody else years ago, and that somebody looked into it. Maybe that's where the blackmail came from."

Chadwick liked the idea about as well as the smell of the cigarillo. "You told Laramie this?"

"Not yet. I'd like to have a candidate for blackmailer, first."

"Samuel Montrose."

"I *might* believe that. I checked the police records, like you suggested. I talked to some old-timers in the department. Your friend Samuel had quite a juvenile record. A dozen arrests for drug dealing. Possession. Accessory to murder in two different drive-bys. Never did any time. He was a freelancer with the drugs—got himself on the wrong side of several gangs. Something else interesting that might go in his column—1988, when the kid was just ten years old, his stepdad Elbridge Montrose was shot to death a block away from his house."

"Stepdad?"

"Yeah. There was another husband before that, I guess. Point is, I talked to the guy who worked the '88 case, retired now. He remembered that the oldest boy Samuel was a suspect. Seems Samuel didn't get along with the late unlamented Elbridge. There was some evidence the stepdad had been hitting the mom, maybe even molesting the kids. No charges were ever brought in the murder. A few years later, about the time your daughter knew Samuel, another one of Talia's boyfriends disappears—guy named Ali Muhammad, like the boxer, only backwards. Word was he was abusive to the kids, too." Damarodas sighed. "Now you take all that into consideration, I might go for the idea that Samuel Montrose was holding you responsible for your daughter's suicide, maybe the Zedmans, too, because they were your best friends, and easier to get to than you. If he cared about Katherine the way he cared about his little brothers and sisters, maybe Samuel held a grudge. I'd buy that Samuel Montrose killed his own mother because she tried to strike a deal with John Zedman, then he punished the Zedmans by arranging the embezzlement. No need for Samuel to be a financial whiz kid—he just sticks a gun to Zedman's head and tells him to figure out the details. That were the case, I'd say now Samuel's got his hands on a lot of money and is having a good laugh while all the people he hates are at each other's throats."

Chadwick stared into the sergeant's blue eyes. He promised himself that he would never make the mistake of underestimating this man.

"You say you might believe your scenario," he told Damarodas. "So what's stopping you?"

"One little thing, my friend."

Chadwick was silent.

"When I looked at Samuel Montrose's sheet," Damarodas said, "there were only juvenile records. They'd never been sealed, because Samuel Montrose never petitioned for them to be. He has no adult sheet, though; as far as the Oakland PD is concerned, Samuel Montrose is still out there somewhere. Then I got the bright idea to check with some other municipalities."

Damarodas' eyes burned into him. "Hayward, late 1993. A body washed up on the beach just in time for New Year's Eve. Three gunshot wounds to the chest. One in the mouth, which gave it the mark of a gang killing—the way gangs treat rogues dealing in their territory. The victim had been wrapped in a sheet, weighted down, thrown into the Bay, but the ropes had slipped and the body floated up. You want to guess who that body was?"

"A mistake," Chadwick said. "It had to be."

"No mistake," Damarodas said. "Fingerprints. Dental. The mother herself ID'ed the clothing and personal effects. I checked everything. Samuel Montrose is dead. Has been for nine years."

20

Chadwick barely remembered the pickup in Palo Alto, the parents looking scared and nervous about handing over their rebellious teen to a pissed-off black woman who'd had seven cups of coffee and a six-foot-eight zombie with blood on his shoe.

It was a long flight back on the Texas red-eye, but the trip went unexpectedly without incident. After sleeping like the dead for six hours, Chadwick stood on his dorm room balcony in the Big Lodge, listening to Mozart, watching the rain clouds crack open and admit a fleeting spill of afternoon light. He was trying not to think about John Zedman.

Down below, tan levels were stringing Christmas garlands from their art therapy class on the railings of the deck. A pair of armadillos scuttled their way toward the river on some armor-plated tryst.

Chadwick tried to think in numbers, but the only one that would come to him was his age, forty-seven.

Nineteen forty-seven, the 22nd Amendment. Eighteen forty-seven, the Mexican War.

Seventeen forty-seven.

He got stuck, thinking William Pitt and the colonies, not coming up with a good event.

Finally, he went back inside, rolled the glass door shut. On his desk, Katherine's picture smiled at him—an eight-year-old girl wreathed in morning glories.

A knock at the door. Asa Hunter came in without waiting for permission. Kindra Jones tailed him.

"She blames herself," Hunter said tersely. "She's trying to cover for you."

"It was my fault," Chadwick answered. "Going back to Zedman's was totally my idea."

"Goddamn it, Chadwick." Hunter chopped the air in front of his face like he was trying to wake him up. "What happened to me being the first to know, huh?"

"I have to talk to Mallory."

"AND you got the nerve to make a request like that. God Almighty."

Kindra looked like she wanted to say something, but Chadwick caught her eye, gave her a mute warning to stay silent.

"I had to defend you," Hunter fumed. "Marin Sheriff's Office called, asked what was your background before Cold Springs. Did you have some grudge against John Zedman? How did you handle your daughter's death? What was I supposed to tell them?"

"They say anything about the blood?"

"It's John Zedman's. They're treating his disappearance as a homicide."

Chadwick felt the air particles slow, like a whirlpool changing direction. He thought about the fear that had been growing in the back of his mind—something about Pérez's phone message: *Everything's cool. I'll call you.* As if he'd been sent on a mission, maybe to retrieve Mallory. As if John had tried to preempt something his blackmailer was doing. The last time John had tried something like that, Talia Montrose had been butchered.

"Asa, I have to see Mallory. She may be in danger."

"The only danger is whether we disrupt her program with news like yours."

"I heard about the cut harness on the rope course."

"It wasn't cut," Hunter snarled. "I checked it myself. I looked at every harness, every rope, every goddamn piece of equipment we own. The harness broke."

"Along a straight line."

"It can happen. It *did* happen. The gear was distributed randomly. There's no way anyone could've targeted her."

"Anyone who wasn't there, you mean."

Hunter raised a finger like a gun. "Don't push it, amigo. My program is safe. It was an accident. Mallory Zedman *will* finish Black Level. Her group's in the wilderness now. I won't let you disturb her any more than I'll let the police."

"Someone's got inside the school, Asa. Someone who's working with the black levels. John Zedman said they could describe Mallory's day."

"Not possible."

"The girl knows something. I think she was being used as leverage to make John cooperate. Now that he's gone, the blackmailer may have what he wants. In which case, the girl is expendable."

Hunter cut his eyes toward Kindra Jones, as if deliberating whether to ask her to leave.

"Jones says you let that kid go," he told Chadwick. "Race Montrose."

"As I recall, you wanted to make sure the boy got a fair shake."

"Not at the expense of losing you. Not if it comes down to a choice between you and some kid in Oakland—"

"I couldn't turn Race in."

"He lied to you, Chadwick. You understand that? What makes you so sure you didn't cause another murder by letting him go?"

Chadwick couldn't answer. He'd been plagued by the same thought, agonizing about it the whole plane trip back, ever since he realized Race had given him a snow-job about Samuel being alive.

At the very least, he should've told Damarodas that he'd tracked down Race. But Chadwick's gut still insisted the boy wasn't a killer. Letting him go had been the right thing to do. Free, Race might yet make some good decisions. There were no good decisions to make in a jail cell.

"Mallory needs to know what's going on," Chadwick insisted. "I owe that much to her parents."

Hunter balled his fists. He seemed to be searching his memory for a boxing routine that would fit the Quartet No. 14 in G Major. Failing to find one, he said, "Ten minutes. Clearing Six. And Chadwick—don't make me regret this."

After he'd left, Jones sank onto the edge of the bed. "I don't think I want to see Hunter that mad again."

"He's got a lot at stake."

Kindra gave him a look he couldn't quite read. "Yeah, I suppose he does. Almost thought he *wanted* me to quit in that debriefing."

Debriefing.

It hadn't even occurred to Chadwick, but of course it was one week since Kindra had signed on board. Hunter would've done his standard debriefing to ascertain if, by some miracle, she was interested in staying with the job, or if he needed to keep his perpetual ad open in the educational journals.

The thought of losing another partner, on top of everything else, made Chadwick want to fly back to Oakland and take a high dive off Ella Montrose's fire escape.

Finally he mustered the courage to ask: "You moving on?"

The Mozart kept playing, bright and incongruous.

Jones looked at the CD player with distaste. "And leave this—the fun, the danger, the good taste in music? Naw, Chad. I'm still your partner. Just don't let me drink that much coffee ever again, all right? I feel like a fucking rocket engine."

Chadwick's throat tightened. He felt more grateful for Jones' vote of confidence than he cared to admit.

Before he could figure out how to tell her that, she kicked him not-so-gently on the shin. "Come on, man. Let's get out of here 'fore Amadeus give me hives."

21

"Any questions?" Leyland asked.

We're too damn tired to ask questions, Mallory thought. But she said nothing.

The four black levels stood in a semicircle, looking at the habitat Leyland had constructed—a neat little burrow, scooped out of the soft ground next to a fallen tree. The roof was woven out of branches, covered with leaves and moss.

Mallory didn't love the idea of sleeping in a hole in the dirt, but night was coming with a hard freeze, and she was ready to do anything if it meant getting to sleep.

The other black levels looked just as ragged—Morrison, who'd spent an hour starting her first fire without matches, only to have it die in the kindling stage; Smart, who'd run himself into a record twelve trees during the blindfold compass activity; and Bridges, who'd been practicing remedial knife-throwing with Leyland most of the afternoon and still sucked at it pretty bad. Mallory had proven much more skilled—she could impale the blade on target four times out of ten, which Leyland told her was damn good for a beginner.

The day had been a friggin' marathon, even by Cold Springs standards, and Mallory couldn't help but wonder if Leyland was overcompensating for what had happened the night before—driving them so hard they wouldn't have time to think about Mallory almost dying.

If that was his goal, he'd succeeded. All of them were ready to drop. Even the two counselors—Baines and Olsen—

who were the team's designated cheerleaders, looked like they'd just swallowed raw crayfish.

Of course, they had. For dinner, Leyland had made them demonstrate how to catch, shuck and gulp the slimy things out of the river as a survivalist meal. That had been pretty funny, until Leyland reminded the black levels that tomorrow it would be their turn. Tomorrow, each of them would strike out on their own—no food, no shelter, no help for twenty-four hours. So they'd better learn how to fend for themselves.

"All right," Leyland said. "If there are no questions, go forth and build."

Mallory moved toward the nearest fallen tree, which she'd been eyeing all through Leyland's talk, but Bridges beat her to it. "Mine, Zedman. Get your own."

"Working as a team," Mallory mumbled.

"Screw you."

The comment would've been enough to get Bridges punished, if Mallory reported it. But she moved on. It wasn't worth fighting about.

Morrison was down by the river, eyeing a rotten log. Smart stood at the north end of the clearing, getting chewed out by Leyland for God-knows-what.

Mallory studied a jumble of car-sized limestone boulders at the base of the hillside. There were lots of nooks and crannies that might serve as ready-made caves.

She tried not to think about what Olsen had told her earlier—a casual comment that the wilderness wasn't as complete as it appeared. That there was a road only a half mile away, toward the setting sun.

Why had Olsen told her that? To make her feel better? To tempt her? Or was it Olsen's idea of revenge for Mallory giving her the silent treatment?

It had been days since Mallory thought about running. In truth, she couldn't imagine going back to San Francisco—to Race, to Laurel Heights, to her parents. But the nightmares still pressed in on her: Talia Montrose, Katherine, the sound of her harness ripping, the dizzying jolt of free fall through the rain.

Mallory was so tired of being scared. She felt a sudden powerful urge to confide in Olsen, to get everything off her chest, to tell her the crazy things she'd been thinking. She should accept the fact that the accident was just an accident, like Hunter said. These people would take care of her. She truly wanted to get through Black Level. She wanted to work with horses all day. She wanted to learn to ride.

But she couldn't escape the feeling she'd been betrayed up on the rope bridge. She was in danger. Olsen and Leyland and Hunter had failed her, just like Katherine had, and tomorrow they would abandon her, send her out into the wilderness by herself. She knew she was being childish, but she'd snubbed Olsen all day, trying to let her know how badly she'd been scared. When she thought about last night, the old heroin hunger twisted her gut. The old anger flared up. And she considered Olsen's road.

Mallory tried to put away the idea. She trudged off toward the rocks, collecting branches as she went.

Before long, the last rays of the sun were cutting through the woods, the shadows of the trees and the limestone boulders as thick as India ink.

She worked so intently she didn't hear Olsen until she crouched next to her.

"The rock is a good idea, Mal, but you're on the cold side."

Every muscle in Mallory's body tensed. She picked another branch, laid it against the rock.

"Been in the shade all day," Olsen explained. "The other side has been baking. It'll let off heat for several hours into the night."

"I've already built the shelter."

It was a pretty bold description for the meager thing she'd constructed—a ragged line of branches propped against the rock face. She'd seen card houses that were more substantial.

"Tomorrow night," Olsen said, "when you're on your own, try the warm side."

Mallory bit back a retort.

She added a new branch, which promptly slid down and knocked over half the lean-to.

Mallory wanted to scream.

How could they send her out on her own tomorrow? How could they believe she was ready?

Olsen picked up a branch, offered it to Mallory. "Listen, kiddo, about last night..."

Her voice trailed off.

Mallory looked where Olsen was looking and saw Leyland talking to two people—outsiders in what should have been a closed camp. With a feeling of vertigo, worse than spinning in the floodlights the night before, Mallory realized it was Chadwick, tall and gaunt in his beige coat, and that young African-American woman she'd seen that morning at the obstacle course. Leyland was pointing in Mallory's direction, Chadwick's eyes met hers, and Mallory had a premonition that one of her nightmares was about to come true.

Chadwick didn't know any better way to tell her, so he gave her the news as straight as he could.

Mallory stared at the shelter she'd been building.

She looked healthier than she had seven days before. Her eyes were no longer dull. Her hair had been shaved and was starting to grow in again, its regular blond color. She was filling out her black fatigues better.

Her hands dug into the limestone gravel. "My father isn't dead."

"We don't know that he is, sweetheart. The police—"

"Race told you Samuel was alive? Race said that?"

"Race was scared. He told me what I wanted to hear."

"You're lying."

"I was there," Kindra said. "Man's telling you the truth. You really want to help your parents, maybe you should do the same, huh?"

The sun was going down so fast Chadwick could see the shadows rise from the ground, swell over Kindra's and Olsen's legs like a tide. He could feel the temperature dropping, or maybe that was just the force of disapproval emanating from Olsen. She hadn't said a thing, but he had no doubt how she felt about him being here, interrupting.

Mallory dropped pieces of gravel onto her shoe, as if she were counting money. "Race never told me Samuel was dead, but I think . . . I think maybe he tried to. He said when he was about six or seven—we figured it must have been just after Katherine died—he watched a drug dealer get shot. Race was playing in this abandoned building when this guy came in, so he hid between a couple of crates, in the dark. The next thing he knows a couple of other guys show up, gang members maybe. They start to argue with the first dude."

"Race saw this happen?"

"Nobody saw him. They start arguing, and the first guy pulls a gun, but he never gets to use it. The other guys shoot him three, maybe four times. They wrap the body in an old piece of canvas and drag it away somewhere—maybe to their car. Race didn't see. He never said anything to anybody. He was scared the killers would come back and get him. He made me promise not to tell." She looked up, her eyes defiant. "I think he was talking about Samuel. Race watched his own brother get killed."

Silence except for the river; Leyland's voice at the other end of the clearing, telling one of the black levels how to insulate with moss.

"What about Race's other brothers?" Chadwick asked.

"No way," Mallory said. "He's only got two others—twins, go by initials, like TJ and JT or ET and TE or something. They're in jail—armed robbery, I think. Been there for years."

Chadwick thought about what Norma had told him, Race's comment that the person to be afraid of was a *she*. "Any sisters?"

"One that I know—name's Doreen. I've met her. If you're thinking she's dangerous, you're crazy. She's like a year older than me and stupid as dirt. Lives in L.A. She's eight months pregnant."

"That leaves Race."

"Race wouldn't hurt my family. He wouldn't hurt my father."

"Mallory, there was a video playing in your father's bedroom last night. *The Little Mermaid*."

The meaning of his words seemed to sink in slowly. Her hand crept up to her throat.

"Did you tell Race about that video?" Chadwick asked. "Could he have told someone else?"

A tiny orange butterfly cartwheeled across her face, then floated toward the boulders. Mallory didn't even blink.

"Mr. Chadwick," Olsen intervened. "I think that's enough questions."

She tried to put her hand on the girl's shoulder, but Mallory pushed it away.

"You don't know everything," Mallory said, her voice trembling. "None of you do. I was with Katherine the night she died. I know what happened. I swear to God, if my father is hurt..."

Chadwick waited. He felt as if the last decade of his life were being compressed into this moment—the sunset streaming into the woods; the cold thickening in the air; the black levels rustling in the clearing; and Olsen and Kindra Jones standing next to him.

Then the wind changed. He tensed, the hairs on his neck suddenly standing on end.

"What?" Kindra asked, bewildered.

The loud SNAP echoed off the rocks, like a tree branch cracking.

Black levels stopped working, puzzled faces turning toward the rocks—toward Chadwick.

Another frozen heartbeat, then he yelled, "Get down!"

He bowled into Mallory, crushing her against the side of the boulder as a second SNAP threw a spray of gravel into the air where Chadwick had been standing.

"What is it?" Mallory screamed.

"Quiet," Chadwick ordered. "Don't move."

In the clearing, kids were screaming. Leyland was barking orders, repeating Chadwick's command to get down.

Kindra had scrambled behind a tree, pulling one of the black levels to the ground beside her.

Chadwick pushed Mallory further against the base of the boulder. Olsen crouched nearby, also trying to become one with the rock.

"Stay with Mallory," he ordered.

"Where—"

"Just do it."

Chadwick pulled Mallory's knife out of her leg sheath, rose to a crouch. He felt his pockets and realized he'd left his cell phone back at the lodge, two miles away.

Shit.

He looked around the clearing. The young counselor, Baines, was thirty yards out, crouching behind a rock that provided him absolutely no cover. Baines was hugging the med pack—which meant he had the emergency phone, the group's only contact with the outside world.

Chadwick snapped his fingers, then put his hand to his ear, miming a phone. Baines just stared at him, pleading silently.

The young man, Chadwick realized, was in shock.

Yes, idiot, it's a gun. Someone is sniping at us.

Chadwick caught Kindra's eyes, gestured toward Baines, then made 9–1–1 with his fingers.

She understood immediately, started crawling in Baines' direction.

Good girl.

Another shot rang out, and down in the clearing, a small rock exploded into a dust cloud.

The sniper was on top of the boulder pile, about twenty feet above Chadwick's head.

Kindra got to the med pack, pulled Baines into better cover, began to search for the phone. In another fifteen minutes, they might expect some help—too late for any of them.

A fourth shot.

Whimpering, one of the black levels huddled farther into her newly made lean-to, as if the branches would hide her from bullets.

Bile rose in Chadwick's throat.

The sniper was using a high-powered rifle. He had picked his location perfectly, made sure the sun was at his back, in the target's eyes. And he was shooting at Chadwick's kids.

Chadwick gripped the hunting knife, made sure Olsen was still on Mallory, then worked his way around the boulder.

Another shot, and a black level yelped—a boy's voice, crying out in pain. Chadwick's stomach turned to a lump of hot coal.

He leapt from one rock to the next, keeping low, moving in the direction of the firing. Behind him, Leyland's voice barked, "Baines, med kit, goddamn it!"

Chadwick couldn't hear Kindra talking on the cell phone. He could only hope that was happening.

Finally, he'd circled enough so that the sun was at his back. He felt soundless, an enormous, silent shadow in the dying light.

He glimpsed the shooter—a camouflaged leg first, then a boot. He made out the shape of the man lying half hidden in a clump of grass atop the limestone ridge, the ideal vantage point over the entire riverfront. The sniper wore a ski mask. His rifle was scoped. Three clips of ammunition lay at his side. He could shoot any of them. They should've all been dead.

The man fired again into the clearing.

Chadwick reached for his knife. Twenty yards, over gravel and leaves and open ground. He weighed his options, remembering his combat training—hating that he knew exactly what must be done.

The shooter sensed his presence just as Chadwick gripped the knife by the point. The rifle barrel swung toward Chadwick, but the knife was already flashing, impaling itself in the man's abdomen. The man's gun discharged into the air, as Chadwick moved in with the speed of a truck.

The sniper tried to stand, but Chadwick ripped his gun away from him, kicked him in the face and sent him toppling over the ridge, onto a boulder below, from which he rolled out of sight. The rifle was now in Chadwick's hand. A streak of the shooter's blood stained his pants.

Chadwick scrambled down the side of the hill—his heart hammering, his breathing rasping loud in his ears.

Black levels were starting to come out of hiding, despite Leyland's commands to keep down. Kindra Jones held the phone, staring wide-eyed in disbelief at the thing that had fallen into their midst, but when she saw Chadwick she managed to say, "State troopers. On the way."

The sniper was crumpled on a ledge of limestone like an altar. He was making wet noises as he clawed for the knife in his side. Chadwick looked down into the glazed brown eyes behind the ski mask. The sniper's arms were exposed—Latino skin, the edge of a tattoo on one forearm.

Pérez, Chadwick thought.

His vision went black.

He clamped one hand around the sniper's shirt, dragging him off the ledge, slamming him into the trunk of a tree. The man screamed, began pleading in rapid Spanish that Chadwick couldn't understand. He didn't want to understand.

Leyland was next to Chadwick, trying to pull him off. "Hey, man, wait—"

But not even Leyland had the strength to stop him.

Chadwick tore off the mask.

The sniper was not Pérez. It was no one Chadwick knew. He was young—maybe thirty, Hispanic, with the build and haircut and hardened face of an enlisted grunt. His eyes were glazed with pain, the knife still buried in his abdomen.

Chadwick held the man against the tree, staring at his face until Olsen snarled, "Chadwick—for Christ's sake. I *need your help.* Smart is wounded."

Chadwick paused, then dropped the sniper. The man crumpled into a ball at the base of the tree and curled over to shelter the knife, as if anxious that no one should take it from him. There was blood—a lot of blood.

The boy named Smart lay on the ground nearby, two other Black Level kids hovering over him, Olsen putting pressure on his arm to stop the bleeding.

Chadwick yelled at Baines for the med pack, then ordered

Leyland to watch the sniper, though it was obvious the man wasn't going anywhere.

"He shot me." Smart was trembling. "He shot me."

"Take it easy, son," Chadwick told him. "You're going to be fine."

Chadwick worked quickly, automatically. The wound was not bad—a small rivulet carved into the skin by the bullet's path. The high velocity of the weapon had helped, reducing the amount of damage.

By the time Chadwick had dressed the wound, Smart was actually smiling weakly at the humor the other black levels were throwing out. Smart-Mouth was going to be okay. The kid was tough. He was going to have a nice scar to show the girls back in Des Moines.

Sirens wailed in the distance.

Chadwick felt Leyland tug his sleeve, stepped aside to let Leyland take over. He walked back toward the sniper, only to find Olsen kneeling over the man. Seeing Olsen's eyes, Chadwick wondered if she would go into shock before the sniper did.

"He's going to die," she said.

"No, he won't," Chadwick promised, but when he looked down at the young sniper's pallid face, he was not at all sure about that.

The state troopers arrived, then a fire truck from Fredericksburg. While they waited for the ambulance for Smart, and the firefighters tended to the sniper, a state trooper finally asked the obvious question—a question that rage and shock and concern for Smart had completely driven from Chadwick's mind.

"Is everyone accounted for?"

Leyland started to say yes, but Chadwick put the back of his hand on the instructor's chest. A feeling like an ice pick cut through him, and he finally realized what had just happened.

"Everyone is not all right," he said. "We have one missing."

Mallory Zedman was gone.

22

"Get down here," Chadwick said into the phone. "Now."

"I can't... what time is it?" Ann Zedman sounded bewildered. "Chadwick, I can't. I have a meeting with my lawyer at eight in the morning. This time tomorrow night I could be in jail."

"Maybe you didn't hear me," he said. "Mallory's gone. A man came after her with a high-powered rifle."

"Stop," she pleaded. "Please—I can't be more worried than I already am. But if I leave town, I'll only make things worse."

"I may have killed a man tonight, Ann."

In the night sky, the Milky Way shimmered like frost. Chadwick wished he could shut down the lights of the Big Lodge, turn off the flashing police car lights at the front gate. He wished he could send inside the counselors and white levels who stood milling around, shivering in their nightclothes, hungry for news. He wanted to be alone with Ann's voice and the stars.

He turned from Olsen and Kindra Jones, both watching him from a few yards away, and moved farther into the darkness, the frozen grass snapping under his feet.

"Ann, I can't see straight about this anymore. No one here knows the history. I need you."

"Chadwick—oh, God. If you'd told me that a week ago ... a month ago."

He felt her despair pulling at his ear, as if they were children, speaking through a wall with cups and string.

"I'll try to arrange something," she said at last, when he didn't answer.

"Call me with flight information I'll meet you at the airport."

He gave her his cell phone number.

"Just find Mallory," Ann said. "Please ... if I lose her ..."

Chadwick tried to say something reassuring, but Ann had already hung up.

Down the gravel road, at the limestone-columned gates of Cold Springs, Asa Hunter was talking to the sheriff and a plainclothes detective. He turned, wearing that same look of cold anger he'd had years before when he'd impaled the blade of his knife in a live oak. He saw Chadwick, motioned him forward.

Chadwick wasn't worried about the sheriff—old Bob Kreech was as easy to understand as a water moccasin. But something about the plainclothes officer was wrong. He looked too young. His suit was too nice.

"Mallory made it as far as the road," Hunter told Chadwick. "They found this."

He held up a compass—the cheap plastic model all black levels were given for Survival Week training.

"They found fresh tire ruts nearby," Hunter said. "A large vehicle pulled over. One guess, she flagged down a truck, hitched a ride."

One guess, Chadwick thought.

"The shooter?" he asked.

"Dead." Sheriff Kreech studied Chadwick, waiting for a reaction.

"Chadwick's a hero," Hunter said. "He protected our kids."

The other man—the young plainclothes officer—was staring at him.

Something clicked in Chadwick's brain.

"You're Special Agent Laramie," he said. "From San Francisco."

The young man smiled thinly. "You're a difficult man to catch up with, Mr. Chadwick."

Chadwick had worked with the FBI on runaway cases a few times. He'd seen enough to know that when agents smiled, it was generally not a good sign. "The shooting was only an hour ago," Chadwick said. "What did you do—teleport?"

"I got in this afternoon. Booked the flight right after yours." Laramie asked, "You don't know the shooter?"

"No."

"His name was Julio de la Garza. ID in his pocket identified him as a Mexican national. I made some inquiries. Guy was ex-military. Had an interesting career before he was discharged—torched a house full of rebel sympathizers down in Chiapas, turned out to be Mayan schoolchildren. Last few years, he's been living in the Mission in San Francisco. Your old neighborhood, isn't it, Mr. Chadwick?"

"A long time ago."

"Would it surprise you to learn that there were two shooters?"

Laramie's eyes were bright, almost glassy, but intently focused on Chadwick. With that little smile pulling up the corners of his mouth, the special agent could've been a kid playing a lethal video game he understood intuitively.

Hunter said, "Sheriff found casings at a different spot about twenty yards away—second guy was flanking the first, probably took a hike when you sent his buddy airborne."

"Pérez," Chadwick said. "The second shooter was Emilio Pérez."

"Employee to Mr. John Zedman," Laramie said. "Now why would you think that?"

"Pérez was sent to retrieve the girl. Maybe to kill me, too."

"You can prove this?"

"Pérez is still out there. He's got Mallory or he's looking for her. He might not even know his boss is dead yet."

"Missing," Laramie corrected. "Not dead. Slip of the tongue."

Chadwick felt his fists curl. "Pérez and the girl didn't get along, Mr. Laramie. If Pérez finds out his boss is dead—that he's suddenly unemployed and he's got a young girl who's un-deliverable merchandise—"

"Look," the sheriff interrupted, raising his hands. "I'm telling you, I ain't convinced these shooters were *after* anybody. Two idiots in the woods with rifles during hunting season—that ain't exactly a first. These guys spotted an oppor-tunity to make some mischief and they took it."

No one contradicted him. The silence made it clear enough nobody believed him, either.

"You didn't see a second shooter," Laramie told Chad-wick. "You didn't have any visual ID on this Emilio Pérez, or whoever it was."

"No."

"The second shooter just disappeared."

"Possibly with the girl," Chadwick said. "And we're standing here talking."

"Hell, the girl left under her own steam," Sheriff Kreech insisted. "Who wouldn't?"

Hunter's neck muscles tensed, but he said nothing. He had to live with Bob Kreech, even if Kreech had been elected sev-eral times on a promise of closing down Hunter's campus to "safeguard the community."

Laramie kept his eyes locked on Chadwick. "The firing started while you were still in sight. How long exactly were you out of sight from the rest of the group, would you say, while you did your act of heroism?"

"What are you getting at?" Hunter said. "Chadwick did nothing wrong."

"No," Laramie agreed easily. "Just that he appears to be real good with a knife. Woman in Oakland, Talia Montrose—"

"Get the hell off my property," Hunter said.

"We can't put this conversation off much longer, Mr. Chadwick," Laramie continued, ignoring Hunter.

"Phone my lawyers in the morning," Hunter told him. "Until then, Agent Laramie, get the hell out."

Laramie picked a clump of Spanish moss off the tree branch above him before replying. "I'm here to help, Mr. Chadwick. Think about it. I'll be back tomorrow."

He walked to one of the police cars, twirling the ball of moss between his fingers.

"Mr. Hunter," Kreech said, "perhaps you'd give me another few words in private?"

The sheriff knew damn well that Hunter's title was Doctor, but he stubbornly resisted using it. Chadwick turned before he could lose his temper, walked back up the road to where Olsen and Jones were waiting.

"What?" Jones asked.

Chadwick filled them in.

"Where does the fucking FBI get off?" Jones asked. Her eyes burned with pride for her partner. "You took that guy out with a hunting knife. He deserved it."

Olsen was not burning with pride. Chadwick got the feeling she shared his discomfort.

"Two shooters," she said. "They could've killed you and Mallory—all of us. So why didn't they?"

Chadwick had no answer.

"We've got to find her," Olsen said.

Kindra pushed her on her bad shoulder—the one Mallory had stabbed. "We? Girl, you're the one who lost her."

Olsen winced. "Smart was hurt. I didn't think—"

"You got the last part right."

"Kindra," Chadwick said. "Check a car out of the pool. Meet me at the gate."

Kindra waited for Olsen to return her challenge. Olsen didn't.

"No problem," Kindra told Chadwick. "I'll try to get us something fast. Something *dependable*."

She turned and stormed off.

Hunter and Kreech were still talking by the sheriff's car. Special Agent Laramie sat in the back seat of the police car, talking on his cell phone.

"You warned me on Thanksgiving," Olsen told Chadwick, "you told me to watch out for her. And I promised her I wasn't going to leave her for any reason."

"This isn't your fault."

"I want to go with you. I want to help."

"They need you here. Leyland will have his hands full calming down the other kids."

"It won't matter. He'll cancel Survival Week."

"No," Chadwick said. "Hunter won't. He'll want them back in the woods as soon as possible. Order restored. The program goes on."

"That's crazy."

"That's Hunter."

Water was dripping from the roof of the Big Lodge, slower and slower, thickening into nubs of ice.

"I failed her," Olsen said. "Out on the ropes course, when Mallory started to fall. I understood how you felt, that day you almost let Race Montrose kill you. I just stood there . . . I let Leyland handle it. I should've been out on the ropes. I froze."

"She'll be all right." Chadwick tried to sound more confident than he felt. "I'll find her."

Olsen pulled her collar tighter around her throat. "Damn weather. I move to Texas and it freezes over."

The police lights pulsed on the back of her coat as she walked away.

Hunter shook hands reluctantly with the sheriff, then turned and came over to Chadwick. They watched the police cars disappear down the road.

"I don't have to tell you this is a nightmare for the school," Hunter said. "A kid escaping—that's worse than the shooting. Compromises the whole program."

"We both know those were no hunters in the woods."

"Maybe. Maybe Kreech knows it, too. We also know how much the lazy SOB will follow up. He never wanted us in this county. He'd be delighted to have us shut down by a scandal. As for Laramie, he doesn't give a damn about the girl. He's already on to the main course—you."

"It's up to us to find her."

Hunter glanced at Chadwick.

"This is what I do," Chadwick reminded him. "I find kids and I bring them in."

"You're in enough trouble," Hunter reminded him.

"If Mallory got a ride, the driver might've stopped for the

night. There aren't too many options out here. I need to get moving."

"And if this Pérez got her?"

"Let's hope like hell he didn't."

Hunter pondered that. "I'll need to call the mother. Get her approval."

"I've already done it."

Hunter scowled.

"We'll go by standard policy," Chadwick promised. "Treat it like any pickup on a runaway. Jones goes with me."

Hunter's boot traced two lines in the gravel before he nodded.

"Chadwick, in case you were wondering, I'll back you up one hundred percent. They try to get to you, my lawyers are at your disposal, but you have to watch your ass."

There was a new darkness in Hunter's eyes—the look of someone who'd just seen something evil and was trying to burn it out of his mind. Chadwick realized that Hunter's conversation with the sheriff and Laramie had not been about Mallory—not entirely.

"They asked you to sacrifice me," Chadwick guessed. "Make me the scapegoat and spare the school."

"No one asked me anything," Hunter said. "I'm just telling you, I'll stand by you, but we play this very, very carefully."

Chadwick hesitated, then took Mallory's compass from Hunter's outstretched hand. He went to find Kindra Jones and—for the first time in many years—to load his .38 service revolver.

23

In the wee hours of morning, the little town of Fredericksburg pretty much shut down.

A single lonely street lamp burned in front of City Hall. Banners for an art and wine festival sagged over the intersections, and the darkened limestone storefronts made the shopping district look almost like the city fathers wanted it to—a quaint Old West village. Main Street was a pastiche of white picket fences and barbed wire, grapevine arbors and prickly pear cactus, rose gardens and restored log cabins, B&Bs and Mexican restaurants—the Western and German and South-of-the-Border influences all wrestling for the soul of the town, and all of them losing to the tourists.

At three A.M., Chadwick was parked on the north end of Milam, the heat from his car hood shimmering in the cold. He was staring at the lighted cross on the hilltop just outside of town, wondering if it had been put there as a personal insult to those who had lost their faith.

Kindra Jones came out of the motel office across the street and walked to the car.

"Nothing," she reported. "You?"

Chadwick shook his head. He handed her a cup of truck stop coffee.

Chadwick's belief in his own strategy was unraveling. He'd been operating on the best-case scenario—that Mallory had run when the shooting started, somehow evaded Pérez, and managed to hitch a ride at the road. He assumed a local would not have picked her up, knowing as they did the nature of Cold Springs kids and being familiar with their black uni-forms. A trucker might have stopped, but few used that road except for local deliveries, which meant they would've pulled in somewhere close by for the night. Either way, Chadwick was assuming that Mallory would've gotten away from her driver at the first opportunity. That made Fredericksburg, or some hamlet around there, the logical place to search.

So far he and Kindra had come up dry. And at dawn—when rides out of town got easier to find—Chadwick's odds of finding her would get very long indeed.

All this assumed the best-case scenario: that Mallory was on her own. If she was with Pérez, the task of finding her could be hopeless.

"There's another strip of motels on the west side of town." He tried to sound enthusiastic about meeting more sleepy night clerks.

Jones raised her coffee cup. "Nowhere but up."

As they drove, Chadwick kept an eye out, like a patrol cop—scanning doorways, sidewalks, alleys. Down by the creek off West Schubert, local teenagers clustered around a couple of pickup trucks, having an impromptu party. As Chadwick drove past, some of the kids stuck their joints and beer bottles behind their backs, as if that made them invisible. He knew they'd spotted the Cold Springs logo on the side of the car—every kid in the area knew exactly what that meant—and he suddenly felt like a dogcatcher.

"I was Mallory, that's where I'd be," Jones said. "I'd ditch whoever picked me up soon as I got to someplace there were lots of people. You're a runaway girl, the last person you trust is somebody who'd pick up a runaway girl."

Chadwick looked over, surprised by the insight. "Confession time?"

Kindra grinned. "Okay. I got an inside track. I ran away a few times."

"Your folks come after you?"

"Nah. I did some stupid things. Some of the things you have to do to make money on the streets—then I came home on my own. See, back then, that was our boot camp. We didn't have to pay two thousand a month to learn reality. Momma just *boot* you outside."

She laughed, and Chadwick couldn't help smiling.

The anger that had been coiling around inside him all night, like a stripped high-voltage line, momentarily untwisted.

He looked back at the kids at the creek, debating whether he should stop to talk to them. He tried to picture Mallory hanging out with these teens from Fredericksburg. She would've fit in about as well as Race did at Laurel Heights.

Chadwick drove on.

"What about you?" Jones asked.

"What about me, what?"

"How'd you grow up?"

"My reality school was the Air Force—Thailand, right at the end of the Vietnam War. Me and Hunter."

"That must've been some fun."

She said it in the tone that young people used, like the Vietnam War was a TV rerun she'd seen and enjoyed on Nick at Nite.

Chadwick remembered how he used to react to his grand-dad's stories about World War II—listening politely, unable to comprehend, and his grandfather giving him that empty stare, frustrated by what he could not share.

Time is the best revenge, he thought.

The next few blocks, Chadwick thought about Korat, and the service revolver now chafing in its shoulder holster. He thought of Julio de la Garza, the Mexican sniper in the woods, his throat warm and taut under Chadwick's grip. The memory was not pleasant, but there was something focal about it—a clarity that kept Chadwick's raging emotions in check. He would not lose Mallory Zedman. Eight years of finding children, of making sure they were safe—all of that meant nothing if Mallory Zedman was lost.

They searched another strip of hotels, then the only convenience store that was open twenty-four hours. No luck.

At five A.M., they pulled in to an all-night pancake-and-diesel restaurant at the junction of Highways 290 and 87—

their last-ditch hope before doubling back. The waitress, who'd been on duty all night, had no recollection of anyone resembling Mallory Zedman.

"A young girl I would've remembered," she said, looking Kindra over. "We don't get many of them."

Her voice indicated that she was thinking about something other than Mallory.

The high-voltage line in Chadwick's gut made a sparking, vicious knot.

"You know what?" he told the lady. "We're staying for breakfast."

Over Kindra's objections, he sat down at the counter and waited until the waitress, sour-faced, pushed two menus across.

They had the restaurant to themselves except for three young truckers at a window booth. Once it became apparent that Kindra and Chadwick were ordering food, the truckers fell silent, staring at them.

"Chadwick," Jones murmured. "We don't have to—"

"Sit down," he said softly. "Order something."

He stared at the off-color pictures of eggs and bacon, the smiley-face pancake meals. He tried to convince himself he was hungry.

One of the truckers said, "Nigger," just loud enough for the comment to slice the air.

Chadwick looked up. None of the truckers were looking at them, but one of them—a guy wearing a green bowling shirt—was grinning at his pals.

"Forget it," Jones said tightly. "Ain't worth it."

But Chadwick's nerves were too raw to forget. He rose.

"Hey," Jones insisted softly. "They're rednecks. They don't change—it isn't worth trying."

Chadwick walked toward the window booth.

Jones cursed, then fell in behind him, muttering, "Or if you insist..."

Green Shirt's smile melted as he realized just how big Chadwick was, and saw the bulge under the shoulder of his coat—the gun Chadwick was making no great effort to hide.

"The lady needs an apology," Chadwick told him.

"Shit, man," Green Shirt said, sliding his words sideways, so as to make himself invisible to criticism. "Apologize for what? Get a little brown sugar, it turns your head."

Chadwick grabbed a fistful of his hair and yanked him out of the booth, over his friends, spilling him onto the floor like so much laundry. The other two men pressed themselves against the window.

"Get up," Chadwick told him. "Apologize."

"Jesus, man—"

"Chadwick," Kindra said, then she turned to the truckers, her voice urgent and polite. "Look, gentlemen—Mr. Chadwick here has had a rough night. I would humor him. Really."

Suddenly, she and the truckers were unlikely allies—the common enemy being Chadwick's rage. Chadwick knew this, knew he should be in control, but he no longer cared.

"You were out of line, Eddie," one of the guys in the booth offered. "She's right."

Eddie with the green shirt got up from the floor, wiped the spit off his mouth. He tried for a tough-guy look, but the fear kept melting it off his face. "Sorry. I'm sorry. Okay?"

Chadwick walked back to the counter, but the waitress had reclaimed their menus. "I think y'all should look elsewhere for breakfast," she told them primly.

"Good idea," Kindra answered. "That's an excellent idea."

She didn't have to worry about Chadwick arguing. The fight had gone out of him.

They walked to the car, leaving three terrified truckers and a sour old waitress with something to talk about for weeks. Another local publicity triumph for the staff of Cold Springs.

Chadwick got behind the wheel, stared through the windshield. The sun wasn't up yet, but the east was lightening, turning the color of wolf fur.

"I appreciate the sentiment and all," Kindra said, "but don't fight my fights, okay?"

"That wasn't for you. If it was for you, it might've been excusable."

She spread her hands. "Okay. Whatever, Chadwick. Remind me not to grow up my kids the Air Force way, huh? It sure as shit doesn't work."

Chadwick didn't respond. He was trying to get up his nerve to call Hunter and admit defeat, formulate Plan B.

Then his cell phone rang.

Chadwick picked it up, expecting Ann with flight information.

Instead Mallory's voice said in his ear, "You passed right by me. You're supposed to be this great tracker of kids."

Brave words, but her voice didn't sound taunting. It was broken as static.

"Where are you, Mallory?" he said. "How'd you get this number?"

"It wasn't genius work," she told him. "I called Cold Springs. I got your voice mail. Your recording gives your cell phone number. Listen—I've got a problem."

"Yeah, you do."

"I mean a bigger problem than running away. Pérez is after me. He's trying to kill me."

"Tell me where you are. I'll protect you."

"Where have I heard that before?"

"What's your other option, Mallory? Running?"

"What the hell was I supposed to do—sit and take a bullet? Look—I'll make a deal with you. I'll tell you where I am."

"You're at Town Creek, with that crowd of teenagers."

"Not anymore. I'll meet you. But you've got to come alone. Promise you'll listen to me. Then you can decide if I have to go back to Cold Springs."

"There can't be any *if* to that."

"But you have to listen to me first. You've got to promise you'll hear me out. Agreed?"

Chadwick thought about it, but despite trying hard, he couldn't see any downside.

They agreed on the all-night convenience store back in Fredericksburg.

Mallory hung up without a goodbye.

Kindra said, "You're negotiating with that girl?"

"I'm bringing her in."

"Rendezvous at a convenience store? What's that about?"

"I still owe you breakfast, don't I?"

Jones closed the car door with a curse word. "Twinkies at the Kwik Mart. Be still, my heart."

Chadwick started the engine and they headed east, back into town.

24

The convenience store interior was lit up fluorescent blue—the color of laundry soap. It smelled of junk-food grease and overboiled coffee.

Mallory Zedman slumped on a plastic bench in the back corner, next to the automatic teller machine and the Texas Lottery slips. She was wearing clothes she'd obviously stolen from someone's laundry line—a pink "Stock Show & Rodeo" T-shirt, a quilt-patch jacket, boy's jeans that were too long—but she still wore her standard-issue Black Level sneakers.

The night cashier was a large bleached-out woman, chewing colorless gum. She scrutinized Chadwick and Jones as they walked in, decided pretty quickly she didn't like Jones, then gave Chadwick a critical look, nodding with her chin toward Mallory in the back. "You her father? You'd better be. That's what she said."

"Thank you for letting her wait here." Chadwick was careful not to confirm Mallory's lie. "We've been searching all night."

The cashier snapped her gum. "Girl that young shouldn't be out at night. A daddy ought to do better."

"You're right, of course."

Mallory looked terrible, even allowing for the two days she'd spent in the woods for Survival Week. As Chadwick and Jones approached, she started moving her shoulder blades as if she had an unreachable itch.

"What's she doing here?" Mallory demanded. "I said alone."

"Ms. Jones is my partner," Chadwick told her.

"I don't like her."

Jones laughed. "Well, for that matter, honey—"

"Whether you like her or not is immaterial," Chadwick cut in. "You can explain yourself to both of us."

The store door jingled. Chadwick pivoted on his heel, watched a bleary-eyed trucker come in to buy a cup of coffee. Chadwick waited until the man had left.

When he looked back at Mallory again, her eyes brimmed with all the emotion a teenage girl could muster—fear, loathing, resentment, embarrassment. The whole hormonal cocktail.

"Explain myself," she repeated. "Pérez is trying to kill me. Consider myself explained."

"Where did you see him?"

"You mean after the woods?"

"You saw him there?"

"Yeah," Mallory said. "I mean—he was wearing a ski mask, but it was him. He was up in the rocks with some other guy. They were shooting. Pérez saw me, started after me. I figured, screw that. I ran. When I got to the highway, I was sure he was going to come out right behind me, but he didn't. I flagged down a truck. The driver brought me here. I hung out with some local kids for a while and they told me a big Mexican guy had been showing around my picture, offering money. They recognized me from the picture. I guess it's the most excitement those hicks have seen in a while."

"You think Pérez is here to kill you."

"He had a goddamn gun. He was shooting. What the hell do you think he was doing?"

"I think he was sent to bring you home—to your father's. If he was here to kill anybody, I think it was me."

Mallory looked stunned, as if Chadwick had suggested she liked country-and-western music. "You think my father—"

"Mallory, your father's been living on the breaking point for a long time. He believed he was protecting you."

The front door jingled again. The cashier said "Morning" to another customer.

Mallory stared sullenly at the cuffs of her stolen jacket.

"Hey, girl," Kindra said. "The cops think Chadwick killed your dad, you understand? He's in trouble."

"Jones," Chadwick said.

"Man's done nothing but help you. Now it's time you helped him."

"My father wouldn't—"

"Who is it?" Chadwick asked. "Who blackmailed your father?"

"I told you I don't know."

"But?"

Her face colored. "Maybe I didn't tell you everything."

Then, like a period at the end of her sentence, a bullet hole punched into the plastic wall of the teller machine next to Mallory's head with a heavy *thunk*. The woman behind the counter screamed.

Chadwick slammed Mallory sideways, into the cover of the snack food aisle. He drew his gun as another bullet hole blossomed on the blue plastic bench where Mallory's chest had been.

There was no sound except the puncture. A silencer.

The cashier abruptly stopped screaming.

Chadwick clutched Mallory against him, his back pressed against the end-cap, making tortilla chip bags crinkle. Kindra was crouching next to the window, behind a drink cooler. Her face was like a boxer's, the corner of her eye twitching, anticipating the next blow.

Chadwick pointed his gun barrel emphatically at the floor. *Stay there.*

Kindra nodded.

"Make this easy, Chadwick," Pérez said from the front of the store. "Give me the girl. I'll let you walk."

Chadwick murmured in Mallory's ear, "Stay." He waited until he felt her nod.

Releasing her, he crawled to the far side of the aisle— looked up a row of glinting junk food toward the front. He could only see the fat cashier, paralyzed against the cigarettes, gaping at someone Chadwick couldn't see. Pérez.

"I'll give you to ten," Pérez bargained. "Because I like you, Chadwick. Then I open up, and I don't really give a shit who goes down with you."

Chadwick crawled to the far end of the store, came to the front, then rose up into a sideways crouch, using an iced bin of soft drinks as a shield.

He had miscalculated. Pérez was much closer than he'd realized, doing exactly what Chadwick was doing—sneaking around. Pérez was turning in Chadwick's direction, and for a quarter second Chadwick was too startled to move—long enough to die had Pérez not been distracted by a loud THWACK-FIZZ at the storefront—the sound of a full can of beer slamming into the window. Pérez fired.

The glass shattered as Chadwick discharged three rounds into Pérez's chest—insanely loud, the force of the blasts knocking Pérez all the way to the welcome mat. He landed on his back, his arms trying to curl up, his knees trying to rise.

Chadwick stepped forward, kicked the pistol out of Perez's hands.

Pérez's eyes were open, fish-eyes. There was no blood.

Outside, the street was still empty, dark, and quiet.

The convenience store cashier inhaled like a cadaver coming back to life. "Lord Jesus . . ."

Jones called out, "Chadwick?"

"It's okay," he called.

Jones came up, dragging Mallory, who was frantically trying to pry Jones' hand off her wrist.

Chadwick flipped aside Pérez's coat, knocked on Pérez's shirt with his knuckle, felt the hardness of Kevlar. "He came prepared. Got the wind knocked out of him. Probably broke some ribs. He'll live. Thanks for the beer, Jones. Stupid move, but thanks."

"Next time I'll let you get killed, I promise. So what do we do with him?"

The cashier made another inhale. "I'll call the police."

"No!" Mallory said. Her eyes implored Chadwick. "No

police! Please—you promised you'd listen to me. We have to . . . we have to talk."

"We can't leave him," Jones said.

Chadwick didn't like any of his options, but after his conversation tonight with Kreech and Laramie, he liked the idea of the police the least. Handing Kreech this situation would be like handing the sheriff a Mensa test. As for Laramie, Chadwick had a feeling the special agent would find a way of using Pérez to hang Chadwick, not the other way around.

"I'll handle him," Chadwick told the cashier. "I'll bring him to the proper authorities."

"Ain't my business, but—"

Then her pale eyes fixed on the revolver still in Chadwick's hand, and she decided against finishing her comment.

"Our car is out front," Chadwick told Mallory. "Jones will make sure you get in."

"Where are we going?"

"A friend's," Chadwick said. "You and Pérez, me and Ms. Jones—we need to have a nice long conversation."

25

"You need help with the box?" David Kraft asked her.

Ann was staring at the tarnished brass hand bell, wondering if she should take it. She remembered the old headmaster, a grizzled ex-hippie named Luke, handing it to her her first day on the job, telling her it had been a gift from Pete Seeger, back in the 1960s, when the teachers at Laurel Heights used to take the high-schoolers on field trips to civil rights protests and try to get the whole class arrested. They had helped Seeger sing, "If I Had a Hammer."

Bell is yours now, Luke had told her. *Ring it if you want, man.*

Was it hers, or the school's? After twenty years, how could she tell the difference? Cleaning out her office was worse than the divorce. Leaving John had been in the middle of the night, a hastily packed suitcase and Mallory. Everything else John had taken care of for her—throwing it out, smashing it, burning it.

No . . . she wouldn't think about John. She wouldn't think about the night before last, in their old kitchen, surrounded by policemen, telling them too much.

"Ann?"

David shifted uncomfortably in the doorway, his wet blond hair raked back from his face, his expression like a first-grader's, hungry for approval. Ann found it ironic that the board couldn't find anyone else to be her watchdog. She was contagious, virulent. Only a former student would take the risk—a young man who'd worked the very first auction, who'd been there from the start to the end of her grand dream to re-build the school. David Kraft, sad-eyed and apologetic, would be the last one to see her at Laurel Heights. He'd watch her pack up her personal effects, make sure she didn't steal any files, or the school silverware, or markers out of the supply cabinet.

She put the bell back on the desk. Let the next headmaster use it. Think positive—there would be a next headmaster. There would still be a Laurel Heights.

She took one more look around her office—her desk, which had never been bare before; the window that someone had left open overnight, turning her papers, now the school's papers, moist with fog; the halls outside empty and silent, all the students on winter break.

She told herself she wasn't officially fired yet, but in her heart, she knew it was over. She had only one more choice to make—her lawyer's office, or the plane to Texas.

She pressed her coat pocket and felt the electronic ticket receipt—purchased with her last working credit card.

I need you, Chadwick had said.

For years, she had wanted him to say that. If she were honest with herself, the hope of reclaiming him had been part of the reason she'd called for his help with Mallory in the first place. Now her daughter was gone. She had paid too dearly for Chadwick to need her.

She hefted the cardboard box, found it sadly light—a few framed pictures of Mallory; the postcard she'd sent from Cold Springs, a dozen precious words spotted with tears or rain; a potted orchid; a scrapbook of photos the faculty had made for her last Christmas; and the Japanese curtain that had hung on her doorway forever—folded up, smelling of a thousand colognes and perfumes from every parent who had ever walked through it.

David stepped aside for her, held the door to the staircase that led down the side of the building. The playground was de-serted—motionless swings, a scatter of milk crates and crum-pled juice containers, a clutch of dodge balls in a puddle of rainwater.

David stopped her at the middle landing.

"Um, sorry," he said. "I'll need the keys."

Before she could swallow her shame, or even put down the box, the door behind them creaked open and Norma appeared at the top of the stairs.

"He calls me," Norma said, pointing at David. "Tells me you're packing up. Ann, what the hell's the idea?"

David looked sheepishly at Ann, rubbing his arm as if Norma had punched him. "I just thought Ms. Reyes should know—"

"Shut up," Norma said. "Thank you for calling. Now get out."

David's face mottled. "I'm supposed to watch her. The keys—"

"I'll get the keys."

"But—"

"Take your nose and put it in someone else's ass for a change, *pinche* weasel. GET OUT!"

Norma raised her purse like a blackjack and poor David fled.

As his car screeched away down Cherry Street, Norma said, "He's poison, you know. The little bastard."

"You're too hard on him."

Norma glared at her. "Where is it?"

"Where's what?"

Norma sifted her hand through the cardboard box. Then she reached into Ann's coat pocket and pulled out the airline receipt. "San Antonio," she read. "Chadwick's idea?"

"I have to. Mallory is missing."

"And you think running to Chadwick will bring her back?"

"You should be happy I'm leaving."

Norma blinked. "You think that's what I want?"

"Isn't it?"

Norma reread the receipt, clutching it as if she wanted to rip it in half. Then she carefully refolded it, pinching the creases.

"Oh, Ann . . . I'm not happy." Her voice was as wilted and

defeated as the orchid in Ann's box. "I'm ashamed as hell. When Chadwick was here...the Laurel Heights money...I told him I thought you'd stolen it."

Ann stared out at the playground. She tried to remember where the new art room would have been built. The library. The theater. Larger classrooms flooded with sunlight. Ten years of work, convincing skeptics, prodding the school board and pleading for extensions when the money was slow in coming. Ten years carrying a dream uphill.

"You thought I would do that?" she asked Norma. "Steal from the school?"

"That's not what I want to think. I want to think you're a stupid damned optimist. You asked me not to say anything about the money because you really believed you could fix the problem. Just like you admitted Race Montrose to the school. Just like you're going to Texas now because you love Chadwick and you believe he can save your child and you don't see why going to him makes you look guilty as hell."

"You could stop me. You could call the police."

Norma closed her eyes. "You didn't do it, did you?"

"What?"

"Race Montrose, his family." There was an edge of desperation in Norma's voice. "You didn't keep the Montroses in my life to hurt me."

"Norma...of course not."

Ann longed to put down her moving box, to open her arms to Norma, reassure her friend, but she wasn't sure she had the courage. She wasn't sure she could keep going if she set the box down now.

A foghorn bellowed—a ship passing under the Golden Gate. She had always found it so easy to forget how close the ocean was, how tightly it hemmed them in.

"When Race came to me," Norma said, "I tried to figure out why. And you know what? He was operating like you. He was apologizing, even though he'd never done anything to me. It was some kind of olive branch—for Katherine. You mentored him, Ann. He's learned to be like you. And the problem is ... I need that stupid optimism of yours. If you go to Texas, I've got a feeling I'm not going to see you again."

Ann tried to say something—to tell Norma her fear was ridiculous. But the look in her eyes, the look of a friend betrayed, closed her throat.

Norma dropped the flight receipt in the box. At the bottom of the steps, she picked up a wet dodge ball, threw it across the abandoned playground with such force it rattled the chain link fence on the opposite side, making the ivy shiver.

26

The gateway to the Allbritton ranch was a giant concrete horseshoe, flanked by American flags and wilted cardboard signs that read GOD BLESS AMERICA. A black mare was pushing up one of the signs with her muzzle so she could get at a patch of icy grass outside the metal tube fence.

Chadwick didn't bother calling from the security intercom. He knew the code, and he knew the only person at home would be the person they needed to see.

They drove in past acres of meadows studded with cactus, bright yellow stables, a lone ranch hand in the riding circle, morning mist wreathed around his boots as he trained an Arabian for the halter. Next to Chadwick in the passenger's seat, Mallory craned her neck to watch.

Chadwick turned uphill, into the circular drive of the ranch house.

The horse-head door knocker was plated gold. Chadwick had to bang a few karats off it before Joey Allbritton finally opened up, his pale Neanderthal features squinting in the sunlight, his boxer shorts and a tie-dyed T-shirt giving off a stench like day-old pizza boxes.

"It's six in the—" His eyes got wide.

"Hello, Joey," Chadwick said. "Staying straight?"

"Yes, sir," he blurted, an old reflex. Then his face broke into a lopsided grin. "Chadwick? Are you really here?"

Chadwick had a momentary fear that Joey was going to hug him. Joey was a bear of a kid—a teddy bear, now, though he hadn't always been so. And his bad breath was the stuff of legends.

Chadwick rethought the word *kid*. Joey had to be at least twenty now.

"Your parents?"

Joey shook his head. "Kuala Lumpur. Or what day is it? Maybe Singapore. Doesn't matter. Dr. Hunter need another horse?"

"No. No horses." Chadwick gestured toward the car. "I have a problem. Need your help."

"Anything." Joey looked toward the car, saw Mallory in the front seat, Jones and Emilio Pérez in the back—Pérez blindfolded, his mouth duct-taped. "Um...what kind of help?"

Chadwick didn't water anything down. He told the story, explained they were baby-sitting a would-be assassin and needed a quiet spot to talk to him.

"This guy shot at you?" Joey asked.

"Yes."

"He messed with Survival Week?"

"Yes."

Joey's eyes danced with excitement. "This guy is vulture meat. Let me get my shoes."

Minutes later, they were following Joey's truck through the back acres of the ranch, past grain silos, fields tall with uncut sorghum. Like many local families, the Allbrittons did some farming, but they had apparently made the decision not to harvest their crops this year. With prices so bad, it was cheaper to leave the corn and sorghum and wheat standing. Chadwick had even heard rumors in town that some locals were plowing out huge mazes through the fields, charging admission for city folk to wander through. The profits promised to be much greater.

Joey's truck turned at the edge of a creek, rumbled down a dirt road to a barn set in a stand of live oaks.

Chadwick remembered the barn from his first trip to the ranch, three and a half years ago, when he'd picked up Joey for Cold Springs. The building was even more dilapidated now.

Its roof sagged, and the once red walls had faded to dirty pink, paint peeling off in ugly patches like diseased skin.

Joey checked inside, then waved to Chadwick that the coast was clear.

"Walk with me," Chadwick told Mallory.

He got her out of the car, leaving Jones to guard their guest of honor.

Inside the barn was a half-collapsed hayloft, a rusted pulley system hanging from the rafters. Spread out on a couple of hay bales was a sleeping bag—Cold Springs regulation issue, the kind white levels were allowed to take with them upon graduation. On the floor nearby was a Cold Springs gear bag. Chadwick guessed that if he were to open it, he would find all the supplies in order, just the way they were supposed to be for dorm inspection.

"Um, I just dump all my old stuff out here," Joey said. "I don't come out here much."

"Yeah, sure," Mallory muttered.

"What?" Joey asked defensively.

"This will do fine," Chadwick interposed. "Thanks, Joey. Go tell Miss Jones she can bring in our guest. It would be better if you waited outside. Better still if he didn't overhear your name."

"Yes, sir." Joey gave Mallory one more look, his eyes lingering on her Black Level shoes.

When he had gone, Chadwick told her, "Now would be a good time."

"For what?"

"Back at the store, before Pérez came in, you wanted to tell me something."

She stared at the Cold Springs gear bag, her cheeks turning red. "Nothing."

"Nothing?"

Mallory stripped off her stolen quilt-patch jacket, pitched it across the hay bale. In the sleeve was a tear Chadwick hadn't noticed before—a perfect hay-colored circle, just above the wrist. A bullet hole.

"That kid Joey," Mallory said, "he's a Cold Springs graduate?"

Chadwick nodded.

"That's what I'm training for? To be like him?" Her voice trembled, as if all her fear from their encounter with Pérez was just now coming to the surface.

"Joey runs his parents' ranch," Chadwick told her. "He manages a five-million-dollar budget, provides the horses for Cold Springs, knows more about animals than most ranchers twice his age. You could do worse than end up like him; you didn't know him before Cold Springs."

Mallory glanced over, trying to feign disinterest. "Why? What'd he do?"

"Last time I was in this barn, taking Joey into custody, those hay bales were stacked with fertilizer explosives. Pipe bombs. A box of grenades and an AK-47 Joey'd bought at a flea market. He was planning to blow up his high school—this was six months before the shootings at Columbine. If Joey hadn't gone to Cold Springs, he would've *been* Columbine. He would've been national news, and dead."

The barn door creaked open and Mallory instantly tensed, like she was bracing for a blow.

Kindra Jones dragged Pérez inside, still blindfolded and gagged, hands cuffed behind his back.

Chadwick pulled him to the middle of the room and said, "Sit."

Pérez remained standing.

Chadwick kicked his legs out from under him, and Pérez fell.

Chadwick knelt, stripped off the blindfold. Pérez's eyes blazed like a cornered wolf's.

"You're in the middle of nowhere," Chadwick told him. "Scream all you want."

Then he peeled the tape off Pérez's mouth.

Pérez just kept glaring at him.

Chadwick had stripped him of the Kevlar, thrown it into the woods off Highway 90. Now Pérez wore only his camo pants and T-shirt, which had rolled up to his ribs, revealing one of the massive bruises left over from Chadwick's gunshots, like an injection of chocolate under the skin.

"You could've killed us last night in the woods," Chadwick said. "Why didn't you?"

Pérez let the silence build. The tape had left a thin red rectangle around his mouth that didn't match the square of his goatee. Finally he said, "What happened to the guy I was with—Julio?"

"Dead," Chadwick said.

Pérez bunched his shoulders, straining against the cuffs. "He was a good man. Had a wife and kids."

"He torched a building full of schoolchildren. Last night, he shot a fifteen-year-old boy."

"Julio wasn't going to kill nobody. He was just supposed to pin them down, keep them busy."

"While you killed me and got away with the girl."

Pérez shrugged. "You surprised me. Moved too fast."

Chadwick knew he was lying. Pérez could've had him cold. In the woods. And then again this morning, in the store.

"What about the girl?" Chadwick asked. "You mean to kill her, too?"

Pérez turned hard eyes on Mallory, who instinctively slid closer to Chadwick.

"She belongs with her father," Pérez said. "I wasn't going to hurt her. I follow Mr. Z's orders."

"And now?" Chadwick asked.

"What do you mean?"

Chadwick waited until he was sure Pérez wasn't faking ignorance. But his look stayed flat and steady. He really didn't know what had happened in San Francisco during his absence.

"John Zedman is missing," Chadwick told him. "Presumed dead."

Chadwick gave him the details, but Pérez seemed to be withdrawing into some memory of his own—some long-ago insult that could still make him furious.

"You son-of-a-bitch." He struggled to kneeling position, his face beading with sweat from the effort. "You worked it together—you and this nigger bitch, didn't you? You killed him. Now you're gonna pin it on me."

"Yo, Juan Valdéz," Kindra said. "You call me 'nigger' again, I'm gonna tape up more than your mouth. Understand?"

Pérez studied her with contempt, but he didn't try to get up. He looked at Mallory. "They killed your father, and you just stand there? You and that nappy-ass boyfriend of yours—you see what you brought down?"

"I'm going outside," Mallory said. "I won't listen to this."

"Yes, you will," Chadwick said.

Her mouth trembled. She could've been six years old again, accusing a classmate of stealing her dessert.

Chadwick suppressed the urge to let her leave, to protect her from Pérez. Some instinct told him that he needed the two of them in the same room, listening to each other.

"Pérez," he said, "the person who murdered John is the same person who blackmailed him, the same person who murdered Talia Montrose. I think you came to Texas planning to shoot me, and take the girl back to her father, but you had second thoughts. Something started nagging at you. Something told you I wasn't the right guy."

"How the fuck you figure that?"

"Because if you didn't have reservations, I'd be dead."

The fire cooled a little in Pérez's eyes. He sat back on his haunches, still straining against the handcuffs, but as if it were an exercise in frustration rather than getting free.

"I told Mr. Z—when he paid off Talia Montrose, I told him it wasn't her. She knew about the blackmail. She knew who it was. But she didn't have shit for leverage. Real blackmailer was somebody she was scared of."

"Samuel Montrose is dead. It isn't him."

"Race." He turned on Mallory. "That goddamn punk is fractured in the head. I told you—"

"No," Mallory insisted. "He isn't crazy."

"You ain't got the sense to see it."

"You said you would cut him into pieces." Mallory's voice rose a half-octave. "He brought the gun to school because of

you, and got expelled—and then his mom was murdered...
It's all your fault. *You* killed her. You killed my father."

Pérez was laboring mightily to hold his tongue. And, with
a small twinge of surprise, Chadwick realized that Pérez
did not hate the girl. His eyes were full of disappointment,
bitterness, resentment—but not hate. Not the contempt you
might show for someone you planned to kill. Pérez reminded
Chadwick more of himself, in the days when he argued constantly with Katherine.

"Your dad was good to me," Pérez said tightly. "I
wouldn't hurt him. You think I'm the problem, then I pity you.
I couldn't hurt him as much as you did."

Mallory took a step back, retreating. She ran into the hay
bales and sank onto Joey Allbritton's sleeping bag.

"Mallory," Chadwick said. "Tell us what you were going
to say this morning—about the person who blackmailed your
father."

"I wasn't..." She looked toward the barn door, as if con-
templating escape, but Jones was there, silently guarding the
exit. "It's just... the Montrose house. Katherine had taken me
there before."

"You mean before the night she died?"

"Twice before that. But the last time, the night she died—
that was different."

"She was depressed," Chadwick said. "She was about to
take her own life."

"It was more than that." She was shivering, her breath
turning to mist as if all the cold air in the barn were condens-
ing around her. "The first two times, she went there to see her
boyfriend, Samuel. I was too young to understand it then, but I
remember her smelling good—she would borrow perfume
from her mother. She would smell like roses."

Chadwick had a sudden, painful memory of Katherine,
the night he picked her up from the Oakland police station—
the smell in the car a profane mix of Norma's perfume and
heroin smoke.

"The last time she took me," Mallory said, *"that* night,
she didn't wear perfume. She wasn't excited."

"Of course," Chadwick said. "She was clinically depressed."

"No. That night, Katherine went for a different reason. She said she needed to talk to somebody. She never said Samuel. I think she went to see someone else, somebody who gave her the drugs that killed her."

The silence was long enough for the tremor to reach every part of Chadwick's nervous system. "Who?"

Mallory took a quick glance at Pérez, making sure he was still bound. "Please—I don't know."

"Your father's life may be on the line, Mallory. He might still be alive."

"I know that. Christ, I *know* that."

"Tell me what you're leaving out."

Her eyes glittered with tears—sea-colored, like her mother's, but permanently seared with afterimages no fifteen-year-old should have.

"I don't know," she pleaded. "Just let me go back to Cold Springs, all right? I never wanted to run. I swear to God, I want to finish Black Level. I *need* to go back."

Chadwick looked at Jones. She mimed a push, a silent suggestion that he needed to back off the girl.

"So what now?" Pérez asked. "You kill me?"

Chadwick imagined giving Pérez over to the local deputies—the same deputies who had stopped Hunter on the road years ago looking for a convenient rape suspect. The same deputies who had been known to let illegal immigrants have accidents with doors, stairwells and nightsticks before turning them over to the INS.

Chadwick thought about his other options.

"You bring me in, man," Pérez said, "you know what's going to happen. I'm gonna have to sell you to the cops. You're gonna have to sell me. You think either one of us is going to get a fair shake?"

"Put the blindfold back on him," Chadwick told Jones. "The gag, too."

Jones hesitated only for a moment, then she did what she was asked.

Chadwick went outside, talked to Joey Allbritton, got directions to the kind of spot he needed.

"You get what you wanted from that guy?" Allbritton asked.

"As much as I could get."

"And you'll turn him in now, right?"

"Thank you, Joey. It was good to see you. I wouldn't mention this to anyone."

"Good to see you, too, sir. Tell Dr. Hunter I'll come out to help with horse training anytime."

"I will."

"Seriously. Anytime."

When Mallory came out, Joey clamped his hand on her forearm.

"Chadwick will take care of you. Chadwick saved my life, okay? Trust him."

Mallory murmured something, tried to pull away, but Joey held her.

"I mean it, black level," he said. "Trust him."

He let her pull away then, and she walked toward the car, stepping gingerly around rocks as if each might be a land mine.

As they drove back down the muddy road, Joey's figure got smaller and smaller, but the rising sun spread his shadow into something enormous on the barn wall.

By eight-thirty, Chadwick and Pérez were several miles away, standing in the middle of a fallow wheat field far from any major roadways. Chadwick stripped Pérez of his shoes. Then he tucked something in Pérez's T-shirt pocket. Only then did he ungag him and cut his arms free.

Pérez ripped off his blindfold. The gun in Chadwick's hand dissuaded him from taking any other liberties.

"So now you kill me?" Pérez asked.

"I advise you to walk that way, toward Fredericksburg. Be careful and polite once you get there. Avoid the local police. I put enough money in your pocket to get new shoes and a bus ticket back to Monterrey. That's where you're from, isn't it?"

Pérez's jaw tightened. "Just like that?"

"Just like that."

Pérez looked across the wet field, at the buzzards circling over the treetops a half mile east. "How do you know I won't come after you? Or the girl?"

"Because we're even now. And because if you give me your word you won't, you won't."

Pérez thought about that. He dug in his pocket, pulled out the money Chadwick had gifted him. "You and the girl—you aren't safe anyway. You know that, right?"

"Go back to Monterrey," Chadwick told him. "Start over."

"Don't trust her, man."

"You should hit town by nightfall. Be careful of the locals."

Pérez looked like he wanted to say more. Then he refolded the twenties, put a new crease across Andrew Jackson's face, and stuck the cash back in his pocket. "Go with God, Chadwick. You'll need the help."

And Chadwick left him there in the empty field, the turkey buzzards starting to circle above him hopefully.

27

Jones drove toward Fredericksburg like a tornado.

She swerved from a century oak a few seconds shy of crashing, cut across the edge of a field to reach the next farm road.

"This isn't L.A.," Chadwick said over the wind.

"I can't believe you," Jones yelled. "You just let him go."

"Forget Pérez."

Jones punched the accelerator. "He puts a bullet hole in the girl's sleeve, and now I should just forget him. What is that—some kind of bullshit machismo? You try to kill each other, and suddenly he's got honor?"

"What did you want—a hole in his head?"

"Better than *your* plan."

She spun away from a farm truck, found a straight stretch of blacktop, and shot down it, the speedometer edging sixty-five.

"Four hours," Chadwick said. "San Antonio and back."

"And then Hunter fires us."

Chadwick didn't respond. Jones knew his phone conversation with Hunter hadn't gone well. The idea of letting Mallory see her mother—even for a short time, even to coax Mallory into remembering more information on the possible identity of a murderer—had been about as appealing to Hunter as a cozy brunch with law enforcement.

"They're coming in the morning," Hunter had told him. "Laramie, Kreech, even Damarodas is here now. They're bringing a couple of suits from the County Attorney's Office.

I want *you* here. I want the Zedman girl back in the program and back in the woods. You take one step that does not lead her straight back to Cold Springs, we cease to act *in loco parentis*. Our legal ass is shredded, and you—"

About that time, Chadwick hung up.

Jones swerved onto Farm to Market Road 75. She slammed on the brakes when she found herself opposed by a freight train crossing the tracks.

She hit the steering wheel with her palms, let the horn blare for half a minute. "Damn!"

In the back seat, Mallory curled in the corner on Chadwick's side. She draped the stolen quilt jacket over her knees and arms like a shield.

"Your mother will be here at noon," Chadwick said. "She'll be worried about you."

"You mean she's lost her job and for once in her life she has nothing better to do. I want to go back to the program."

"Listen to the girl," Kindra said.

"You said Katherine met another friend at the Montroses' house," he told Mallory. "Somebody who gave her that heroin. You told me this, and then you want to slip back into the program and not be bothered?"

"I thought you wanted to help me."

"I do. I also want to know why you're afraid to tell me the truth."

Mallory shifted under her coat, her hands punching the fabric up closer to her chin. Chadwick realized that one of the things she was scared of was him.

"I'm not afraid," she said. "I just wish Pérez hadn't been wearing that bulletproof vest."

"Shit," Jones said. "That's the second thing she's said I agree with."

Train cars rumbled past—stacks of new automobiles glinting through the steel mesh siding, brown freight containers spray-painted with gangster love notes from Houston or the Rio Grande Valley or God-knew-where: MI CORAZON 4 E.P. LUPE N JOE SIEMPRE.

"John is dead," Chadwick said, feeling it in his heart for

the first time. "Ann's career is destroyed. Someone punished them to get at me, someone who knows every detail about my daughter's suicide. I'm not going to sit back and trust the police to figure out who."

"Fine," Jones said. She threw the car into Park. "Have fun."

"Kindra."

"Do what you want, Chad. Get yourself arrested for kidnapping. I'll walk back to Cold Springs."

She opened the car door and stormed out, heading toward the train as if she were going to take it on, *mano á mano.*

Chadwick reached over to the ignition, removed the keys.

"Stay here," he told Mallory.

"But—"

He got out, not waiting for her to finish.

The wind from the train was like asthmatic breathing; Jones was throwing rocks in the spaces between the cars.

"The girl told you what she needs," she said. "Why don't you listen?"

"She's hiding. She knows something that scares her."

"Yeah? So do I. In the last week, you've spent more time digging up your past than you have helping kids. You caught two people the cops want to see—that Race kid. Now Pérez. And you let them both go. It's almost like you don't want a solution. Like you get off on the pain. That scares me, Chad. It really does."

In the back seat of the car, Mallory sat still, watching them apprehensively through the glass.

Chadwick knew he could get to her. He could convince her to talk, but he needed more time. He needed Ann. Once Mallory was face-to-face with her mother, the problems in San Francisco would become real to her. She would remember what was important.

Ann was the most talented interviewer of children he'd ever known. Even if it was her own daughter, Ann would know what to say. She would get Mallory to open up.

And she would temper Chadwick's desperation—his feeling that every time he looked at Mallory, he was back at the house on Mission, about to leave for the auction, Katherine telling him, *"Don't worry, Dad. We'll be fine."*

He should have stayed. He shouldn't have allowed himself to be pressured into leaving. If he had talked to his daughter in private for just a little longer, he could've gotten the truth out. They could have reconciled. And Katherine would still be alive.

Now here was his second chance, and again he was being told to leave.

"I can't trust Mallory to someone else," he told Kindra. "I can't let her go yet."

She threw another rock, which pinged against a coal car. "Then you were wrong trying to help her."

"I had to."

"You're not getting me. You were wrong because you wanted to bury your grief about your daughter. That's why you decided to help Mallory. For a while, those two things went together. Now the girl wants to go on with the program. You want her to solve some goddamn mystery, but there is no mystery. There's just your past."

"It's her past, too."

"Maybe. But kids can put that aside. They can lock the most horrible memories into a box, pretend they happened to someone else, and go on with the present. Trust me on this, Chadwick—they have to. Now the girl's finally moving forward, and you don't want her to. It seems to me you've got a choice to make."

The last boxcar rattled through the crossing, sucking the wind behind it, tugging at Chadwick's coat.

"Her mother is coming to town," he said. "What am I supposed to tell her?"

"She ain't coming just for her daughter, is she?"

Chadwick didn't answer.

Jones threw the rest of her gravel at the train tracks. "That's what I thought. That's another choice you got to make, *without* the girl. I'll drop you at the car pool. Get yourself a set of wheels before Hunter sees you. Go into S.A.—take the night to work it out. Then get your ass back to Cold Springs in the morning before the cops arrive."

"I wasn't talking about—"

"You're blushing, Chad. Do what Kindra tells you. And while you're at it, ask yourself why you keep setting yourself up for hurt. Okay?"

He didn't object as Kindra lifted the car keys from his hand.

28

Norma sat on her patio, drinking hazelnut coffee and staring at her pile of disconnected phones. Three Touch-Tones, the office line, the fax, two powered-down cellulars. After coming home from Laurel Heights—wishing she had never gone, never picked up David Kraft's call—she had found twelve new messages from reporters and worried Laurel Heights parents and clients, even one from a heckler, telling her simply, "Go home, wetback." Norma had torn through the house, meticulously unplugging everything.

She couldn't afford the quiet. She should have been in her office, making calls, working to reassure the clients she still had left, but she couldn't make herself do it. Twenty-seven million, gone. Who would trust her with their money now?

Her lawyer had told her it could be worse. She'd gotten praise from the school board for blowing the whistle on the missing funds. The media, so far, had painted her as a good guy. None of the law enforcement agencies were seriously talking about pressing charges against her.

But John was still missing. The school's money had vanished—the bank in the Seychelles saying only that the funds had been transferred again, with proper authorization, to a numbered account at a different institution. Thirty families—one-fifth of the school population—had already announced they would be leaving Laurel Heights. The school was disintegrating. For the first time this morning, the *Chronicle* had run a front-page article speculating on a connection between the embezzlement and John Zedman's disappearance, and the story had been lurid and juicy enough to pop up in the national wire services. And Ann, goddamn her, had run off to Texas. Despite being crushed and humiliated, despite Norma's warning, Ann had flown to Chadwick with a hopeful light in her eyes. She was doomed, as permanently gone as John.

Norma watched tourist boats shuttle back and forth to Alcatraz. She thought of John—how he'd sold her on this house five years ago, convincing her that the price was a bargain considering the view. One and a third million to wake up every morning and stare across the water at a dilapidated prison.

Go home, wetback.

San Francisco and its political correctness—its racial sensitivity. Norma knew it was bullshit. White liberalism just drove the racism underground, made it more virulent, harder to root out. She remembered the looks people used to give Chadwick, when he'd say Katherine was his daughter. She remembered the time the Laurel Heights fourth-graders had been walking to the park, Norma talking to Ann along the way, just beginning to reconcile their friendship, and some guy had shouted from his car, wanting to know where they'd gotten the monkey. And only Race and Norma had instantly understood the insult—knowing that it was aimed at Race, the only black kid in the class. Norma had run after the car for a city block—screaming, throwing rocks. The jerk just sped up and disappeared. If he hadn't, Norma would've killed him.

Norma should've moved out of town years ago. Gone back to L.A., where people had the decency to set buildings on fire when they got mad.

But still she stayed in her empty house on her cold hill, in a town she'd never liked.

The anniversary of Katherine's funeral—nine years ago today. There would be no auction at school. No one to comfort her at dinner. No work to distract her. No Zedmans. No Chadwick. Soon, no Laurel Heights.

Norma knew what she wanted to do.

She fought against it—told herself it was no better than opening the medicine cabinet and counting pills into her palm.

But her last visit to the Mission—seeing Chadwick—had left her in pain.

Finding him alone in Katherine's bedroom had nagged at her. Oh, she understood the impulse, but still... it was intrusive, as if he were mocking her. It had thrown her off balance, made her say those bitter things about Ann.

She felt she'd missed something important about his visit—something she would've seen if she'd been thinking more clearly. She'd been so shaken, she wasn't even sure she'd locked the front door when she left.

She took one of her cell phones, slipped it in her pocket, and went back into the house.

On the kitchen counter was the Los Lobos CD John had played the night he'd visited. The cover illustration troubled her—a man and a woman dressed in Day of the Dead skeleton costumes, standing close enough to kiss, the man with an exposed, bright red heart, the woman with her arms crossed over her chest, a gun in her left hand. Had John been trying to tell her something? She couldn't help wondering if he had brought her Chinese food and wine because he'd wanted help, not romance. And she had turned him away.

She stared out at the balcony, remembering the rain, Race Montrose appearing in the doorway, drenched and frightened. A peace offering. Another message only partially delivered. *She ain't going to be satisfied until they're both dead.*

Where was the boy now? Where did he live, now that his home had been sold? She remembered the only time she'd ever given him a hug—in fourth grade, after chasing that car, how she'd hugged him and reassured him and told him to forget the shithead bigots in this world. He was better than them. The same words her father had told her, when she was small.

She traced her fingers along the Los Lobos CD, thinking of burning raisin bread in a Wedgwood oven, bougainvillea petals falling in the backyard as Carnaval music surged over the rooftops from Mission Street, Mallory jumping up to touch the arc of morning glories that had grown even taller than her father.

She grabbed her car keys and put on her coat.

On San Angelo Street, she found a parking spot a block up from the old middle school, deserted now for Christmas break. The air was cool and damp, the sidewalk slick with fog, but it was nothing like the hard freeze of nine years before.

She had just slipped the key into the lock of the townhouse when a man's voice called, "Hey!"

He stood in the middle of the street—a withered old Latino with a bent back and microscope lenses for glasses. He was wheeling groceries behind him in a little red wagon. Norma vaguely recognized him—a neighbor from ten years before, though she couldn't remember which floor of which building he rented. He'd complained about Katherine's music once, back in another lifetime.

"You still own that place?" he demanded.

She was tempted to say no, but having just put the key in the lock, she said instead, "Yeah."

"Well, what did you drop in there—dog shit?"

"Pardon?"

"Saturday night! Dog shit!" the man repeated.

Norma was too mystified to respond.

He persisted. "Look, were you here on Saturday night or not? I could smell sewage right through the walls for two days. Ain't so bad now, but damn. Happens again I'm gonna call the cops, get them down here with some Lysol."

The old man kept going, grumbling as he wheeled his wagon of groceries along the middle of the street.

Saturday night?

She'd been here that afternoon, as had Chadwick, but they'd both left before dark. She wondered if the man's bad eyesight might have caused him some confusion about the time, or the woman he'd seen, or maybe even which building smelled bad.

Transients might have found their way into the house. That had happened before. Each time they'd been pretty indiscriminate about where they'd gone to the bathroom.

Norma tried the door without turning the key. It was unlocked. She stomped loudly up the stairs, into the empty living room.

There was a bad smell, all right—but worse than dog shit. A dead rat. Rotten garbage. Something sweet masking it—almost like perfume.

She remembered one time, the Mexican restaurant across the fence had dumped their garbage in the alley for two months to avoid paying for pickup. By the time the police came, the smell in the neighborhood had been something like this.

She went in the kitchen and opened the window, but nothing wafted in except *taquería* smoke—*cabrito* and flank steak grilled with cilantro.

She peeked in the kitchen closet. Nothing but a decade-old roach trap. The oven was empty. The master bedroom and closet—nothing.

She walked into Katherine's room and a point of fear pressed like an ice cube between her shoulder blades. The only piece of furniture, Chadwick's old wooden chair, had been busted into kindling. The portable stereo was smashed, too—D batteries scattered across the floor, a cracked Brahms CD glinting in a square of sunlight near the window.

Vandals. But why wouldn't they have taken the CD player?

Norma swallowed back her desire to run. This was her house. There was no one here except her.

The smell wasn't coming from Katherine's room. She forced herself to move—back to the living room again.

The smell was strongest here. It seemed to be coming from the fireplace, but there was nothing there.

She stared around the empty room, remembering where the television had been, Chadwick's black leather chair.

Chadwick's father had sat in that chair during the last years of his life, watching out the window. He had shrunk to a frail, senseless old man, much smaller than his son, hardly moving except when his clocks went off on the mantel, every hour, driving Norma crazy.

The clocks.

Norma ran her eyes over the wainscoting, then moved her fingers along the wall until she found the crack. Hide-and-seek. Katherine's favorite hiding place.

Norma pressed the corner of the closet. The old door sprang open, and with it, the smell—excrement and cologne, rotten meat and baby powder and sour fear. Her eyes didn't understand what they were seeing at first—folds of crinkled plastic expanding, as if breathing, blue fabric and dark brown smears on pale skin, a crust of stubble and saliva on a cheek, a straight part in graying brown hair. She backed away and the thing twisted, tumbling out of its shower curtain as if to follow her—inanimate flesh that used to be a human face.

Norma stumbled backwards, fell, kicked at a dead hand. She was in Katherine's bedroom, then, pressing against the window, trying to claw it open, trying to breathe.

She had to get out.

But part of her refused to go into shock—the part that was inured to death, that dreamed of death all the time.

Stop, she said. *Stop.*

She did.

She turned, stepped back into the living room and stared at the thing.

It must've been there for several days, encased in plastic and doused in its own cologne, rotting, stiffening, in a place no one would ever look, in a house no one ever visited—no one except her.

Since Saturday, the day Chadwick was in town, the day Ann's embezzlement problem had been made public.

No. Chadwick would never do this. To kill in cold blood, to wrap the body and take it elsewhere. This house, of all places. That was the work of a monster.

But then, Norma believed in monsters. She had believed in them for nine years, had gotten close enough to see hers in the bathroom mirror, gripping a handful of blue and yellow pills.

John was dead. There was no longer room for doubt. No room for Ann's fucking optimism.

Norma heard Ann's voice in her head, pleading for more time. Don't call the police, not yet. But Norma had had enough of that. She wouldn't let anyone soften her. Never again.

29

Pérez's feet were bleeding.

He had walked for maybe an hour, but had only just hit the road, if you could call it a road—a two-rut path, sprouting weeds in the middle like a hairy spine. The gravel and mud were no kinder on his feet than the fields had been.

He tried to concentrate on the morning, which was really very fine—cold, but sunny. It made Pérez think of a winter day in Monterrey, back at his family's ranch. This place was greener, but otherwise much like home. Better than the fog of Mill Valley, that damn hilltop house of Mr. Z's.

Pérez stumbled along, cursing his luck.

He should've taken the clean shot at Chadwick when he had the chance, last night in the woods, but something had failed him—some unwanted twinge of conscience.

It bothered him that Chadwick had read him so well. Pérez wished he were the type who could track down a man who'd just released him—put a bullet in his head. But he couldn't do that. He couldn't even muster anger at Mallory.

He consoled himself with the thought of a payoff. Now that he understood the truth, the knowledge would be worth something. He could turn the tables. He could become Samuel. The idea made him smile.

It was God's will he had spared Chadwick's life. In return, Chadwick—the deluded bastard—had unwittingly given him knowledge, a way to make money. Chadwick was in enough danger—he didn't need Pérez's help to die.

Pérez would kill no more. He would demand his cut of the

millions, and he would get it. He would return to Monterrey a hero, live out the rest of his days on the ranch, free of debt.

His wife, Rosa, would take him back. He would be with his children again, two boys he had not seen since they were babies. They would be scared of him at first, maybe even angry, but eventually they would understand why he had left for so long, to provide for them.

He would spend the rest of his life making amends. He was still young. He would enjoy many winter mornings like this, in his own fields, teaching his children to ride and to shoot.

He was so focused on the horizon, wondering where the muddy path would lead him, that he did not hear the vehicle behind him until it was almost on top of him.

It was a new blue minivan—out of place on the country road. When Pérez saw the driver, he frowned. He had not counted on this—but he could handle it. Cool and dumb. He had not yet played his hand.

The van stopped. The driver's window purred down.

"What the hell you want?" Pérez demanded.

"You were not easy to find."

Pérez spat into the dust. "You got something to tell me?"

"You've walked far enough. You want a ride?"

Pérez thought about that, knowing he should refuse, but that would look bad. And his feet hurt. There was no danger here—just some bullshitting, some posturing, a test he knew he could pass.

He nodded, stepped around the front, and the van started moving forward, bumped gently into his legs.

Pérez glared through the windshield. He stepped back, not amused by the joke.

The van lurched forward again, and again bumped Pérez's legs. But Pérez didn't move out of the way. It was not in his nature to back down. He tapped his chest with his fingers. "What the fuck?"

And then he read the situation—a heartbeat too late—just as the driver punched the gas.

Pérez clawed at metal, felt himself being spun around like

a child in a blindfold game, and then he was looking at the cold blue sky, his arm held up by a barbed wire fence, several barbs sticking in the skin of his forearm. His legs were numb. He couldn't move.

He heard the van's door open and close. He imagined the porch of his ranch in Monterrey. He imagined that the steps coming toward him were his wife's.

The driver stood over him—an outline rimmed in the sunset. A voice from high above said, "I could've been gone by now, Emilio. But I wanted to see you kill Chadwick. You disappointed me."

Pérez imagined the sounds of the children he had not seen in so long. He saw the sunlight catching the edges of Rosa's cotton dress, triangles of red fluttering around her legs.

"And now you've figured it," the voice told him. "You and the girl both. I can tell in your eyes."

Pérez tried to speak, tried to tell Rosa he loved her, but no sound came.

"Let me help you out here, Emilio," the voice told him. "Let me give you a lift."

Pérez heard thunder. As his eyes went dark, he felt a small warm spot on his forehead, as if someone—perhaps a child—had planted a kiss there.

30

"You have two choices," Hunter said. "Your teammates left an hour ago. You can still log your solo trip, make the pickup area by noon tomorrow. Or you can sit it out, restart Black Level with the group below you. Do you understand?"

Hunter and Leyland studied her, measuring her, waiting.

Mallory's cheeks still burned from the dressing down they'd given her. They had wasted no time reasserting their authority, yelling twelve hours of freedom right out of her head. They gave her no apology or chance to explain, nothing to eat, no time to rest. They made her change into her spare set of Black Level fatigues—still stiff, still smelling of her own sweat and campfire smoke. Then they force-marched her across the river, through icy water up to her knees, all the way back to base camp, the exact place where Pérez had started shooting. Now she stood at attention, her pants cuffs freezing to her ankles, the wind making her eyes water.

It was crazy, pigheaded stubbornness for Hunter to bring her straight back to this clearing, as if nothing had happened, and offer her a solo hike the same day she'd returned from running away.

But she understood why he was doing it. Changing in the lodge, she'd overheard bits and pieces of his conversation with Leyland—about the police, the FBI, her mother. She knew Hunter was trying to protect her—to keep her in the program. And she wanted that. She wanted it badly.

She didn't even mind their drillmaster abuse. It was reassuring compared to running from Pérez, or being with

Chadwick—feeling so afraid and angry she'd almost confessed what she half remembered about the night Katherine died.

She wasn't safe —not here, not anywhere. At least in the woods she felt as if she were being given charge of her own fate. Hunter's word—accountability. Mallory liked the fact that Hunter had jogged her out here before giving her the choice, too. It made it clear what he expected her to do.

Footsteps crunched in the woods and Olsen appeared, jogging up the path from the main lodge, out of breath, a supply pack in her hands. No one acknowledged her, but Mallory could feel Hunter's disapproval radiating toward the counselor. Back at the lodge, he'd said her name through gritted teeth, wondering where she was, why she was late, as if Mallory's return was an appointment they'd planned for. Mallory realized they probably blamed Olsen for letting her get away in the first place—the chaos when Smart was shot, Olsen leaving her to tend him.

Hunter kept his eyes on Mallory. "Well?"

"I want to log the solo trip, sir."

Some of the tension in the air dissipated. Hunter nodded.

"Miss Olsen," he said. "Prep her and get her on the trail."

"Yes, sir."

Hunter and Leyland retreated toward the river.

"At ease, Zedman." Olsen forced a smile, but she looked like she hadn't slept any more than Mallory had. "We've got a lot to do."

"How is Smart?" Mallory asked.

The skin around Olsen's eyes tightened. "He'll be fine. His parents pulled him out. He's on his way back home to Iowa."

Mallory stared at the remnants of the shelter Leyland had built as a demo the night before. She told herself Smart's absence wasn't her fault. He wasn't her best friend, or even a friend at all. But the few weeks she'd known him seemed as important as all the years she'd been at Laurel Heights, and his absence hurt. After getting his mouth taped, getting his ridiculous torch hairdo shaved off, slogging through the obstacle course and the barracks-building and the ropes course—after all that, Smart had been whisked back home to goddamn Des Moines. He'd gotten shot because of her, and she had run in the other direction.

She wanted to cry. She hated the fact that she'd gone outside the program, caused a part of it to unravel.

"Come on," Olsen told her gently. "I've got a new piece of jewelry for you."

Olsen led her to the burned-out fire pit. She opened her pack, told Mallory to hold out her hand, then snapped a metal cuff around her wrist. The thing was dull gray, with a single, green blinking light the size of a pencil point. There was no visible latch, and it was too tight to slip off.

"GPS locator," Olsen told her.

"In case I run away again," Mallory guessed.

"All the black levels wear them for the solo trip." But Olsen's tone made it clear that the runaway factor had been discussed. Hunter's decision to send Mallory out hadn't taken so much trust, after all.

"We'll track your position," Olsen continued, "make sure you're moving in the right direction. But mostly this is in case of emergency—a broken leg, something you absolutely can't handle alone. If that happens, press the light. You'll need to use something pointed to do that—a stick, or your knife. The button will turn red, and Dr. Hunter will send somebody to extract you."

"Extract me," Mallory said. "Fun."

"It would mean starting survival training over from scratch. Not graduating with your team. And it might take us up to half an hour to reach your position, so the button is no substitute for being careful."

Mallory pulled at the bracelet, already wishing she had a hacksaw, but Olsen didn't give her time to dwell on it.

They started reviewing the basics of the solo trip—the first-aid pack, the emergency procedures. Mallory remembered it all. She knew how to use the snakebite kit, the epinephrine pen. She could dress a wound in her goddamn sleep. Her backpack would hold nothing but one ration bar, her med kit, and an ultralight Polarguard sleeping bag. She would be alone for twenty-four hours, heading east, directly away from the only public road, into the heart of Hunter's empty kingdom. She would cross the river once. And if she did everything right, sometime tomorrow mid-morning she would come across a small dirt access road used only by Cold Springs. That was her goal. Someone would be waiting to pick her up.

It didn't sound all that difficult. It was hard to believe the high-and-mighty Survival Week had boiled down to just this—a lot of preparation for a single day and night alone.

"Trust me," Olsen said. "It's enough."

She offered one last item—Mallory's survival knife. Except it wasn't really Mallory's. It was new. Hers had been borrowed by Chadwick, buried in the side of a sniper.

Mallory fingered the new blade. She remembered attacking Olsen—stabbing her in the shoulder with that stupid dinner knife she'd found. That seemed like it had happened to a different person, long ago.

She slid the hunting knife out of the sheath, pinched the clean new point. She balanced it, the way Leyland had taught her, then threw it at the nearest tree. It bit into the wood at a bad angle, like a loose tooth, and immediately fell out.

"Knife-throwing is just for show," Olsen promised. "You won't use it."

Mallory almost asked about Pérez. What if he came after her? What good would a blinking light and a knife do her then?

Olsen seemed to misread her expression. "You still mad at me?"

Mallory wasn't sure what surprised her more—the question, or the fact that Olsen truly seemed concerned to know the answer.

She *had* been mad at Olsen, after that night at the ropes course. It seemed a stupid matter now—the torn strap on her harness.

She had blamed Olsen for that.

She had spent years blaming everyone for everything.

Pérez. And Chadwick. And her parents. And Katherine—Katherine most of all.

I had reasons, part of her argued.

Her fears, her failures, her sorry excuse for a childhood—what if it *was* someone else's fault?

A small hard feeling started building in her—like Hunter's voice, like his crazy, pigheaded stubbornness. It didn't matter whose fault it was. She had no choice but to accept it and go on. She had a goal—Gray Level—and it didn't matter if they shot at her friends or made her father disappear or tried to kill her. If she didn't make this final trip, Katherine won, and she lost.

"I'm not mad," Mallory said softly. "Not anymore."

"That's good. I was worried about you, Mal. I'm glad you're all right."

It sounded like cheap throwaway sympathy, the kind anybody could say, but Mallory could tell Olsen meant it. She remembered that tenuous thread of understanding that had seemed to link her to Olsen during counseling sessions—that closeness that she'd been so afraid of.

"Whatever happened?" Mallory asked. "I mean . . . about your stepdad?"

Olsen stared at her for a moment, as if translating her question from a different language. "My stepdad?"

"The story you were telling us. That day in counseling."

Olsen bent down and picked up Mallory's knife. She looked at the blade, picked a tuft of splinters off the tip. "When I searched for my stepdad, I found out he was in jail, Mallory. He got a new girlfriend when he left my mom, and he was in jail for molesting a young girl, his girlfriend's seven-year-old daughter."

Mallory blushed. In a way, she was sorry she had asked. But also, she was awed that Olsen would tell her. It wasn't the kind of thing you told someone . . . unless you really trusted her.

"You didn't want to tell your mom that?" she asked.

"No," Olsen answered. "She would've gotten mad at me, refused to believe it. People like my stepdad, they don't become that way overnight. They repeat their pattern. Over and over. I didn't want my mother to know."

"Because... Oh."

"Not me," Olsen said. "Not me. But I have a little sister..."

She paused, weighing the blade just as Mallory had. "I *had* a little sister about your age, Mallory."

Mallory was silent, thinking about the story, liking Olsen sharing it with her.

"I need to tell you something," Mallory said. "A dream I had."

Olsen examined the knife absently. "Oh?"

Then Leyland's boots crunched in the leaves. "Time's wasting, counselor. Come on, Zedman—move! Long day ahead of you."

Hunter and Leyland were both standing over her. The moment for secrets was gone.

Olsen rose, gave her one last look of encouragement. "I'll see you on the other side, kiddo."

She turned the knife handle-out, and offered it to Mallory. Her hand was trembling, and Mallory knew it was from anger.

31

Ann Zedman didn't arrive on the noon plane from San Francisco.

When she finally appeared in the airport terminal, a little after one, she walked up from the wrong direction—from the ground transportation exit, trailing a small overnight bag on wheels. Her caramel hair was swept back in a ponytail, no makeup. Denim jacket. Green T-shirt tucked into faded jeans. She might've passed for a college student.

She stopped a few feet away, took off her glasses and folded them into the pocket of her T-shirt.

"I'm sorry," she said. "They sent me to the other terminal."

"The other terminal?"

Her eyes were puffy, hay-fever red. "I told you the wrong airline. It took me a while to figure out what had happened. I'm not thinking straight."

Chadwick had planned on being reserved when he saw her. He had prepared himself all the way into town, rehearsing how he would be. But he reached out his hand, and she took it, laced her fingers in his.

He told her the news about Mallory—that she was safe, that Pérez had only meant to take her back to her father. He left out the parts where Pérez tried to kill him, and Chadwick released him without bringing him to the police.

The good news seemed to kindle some light in her eyes, but she still looked shaken, more than ever like a kid who'd gone through Cold Springs—as if she'd been forced to reevaluate everything, deconstruct her life, put the pieces back together according to someone else's outline.

"Thank God you found her," she said. "But where...?" Her eyes scanned the gate area.

"She's back in the program. She wanted to go straight to the school."

"I want to see her."

"That's not possible now."

Ann unlaced her hand from his. "She's my daughter. You brought me all this way..."

"She's on Survival Week. Out in the woods."

"Are you insane?"

"They have her under surveillance. Most of the staff will be out patrolling the perimeter all night. She'll be safe."

"After what happened, you can promise me that?"

"Asa Hunter is on this personally. I've never known him to fail a kid."

Ann's cheeks colored.

Chadwick realized he'd sounded as if he were drawing some kind of comparison.

"So what am I supposed to do," she said. "Get back on the plane? I haven't taken a hotel room yet..."

She let the statement hang in the air.

Chadwick was suddenly ashamed of the plan he'd made—a reservation for her at the Hill Country Sheraton. Hunter had an account there, held admissions events in the ballroom, sometimes put his more important visitors up in the suites. Chadwick had booked a night for one, in Ann's name, figuring it was the least Cold Springs could do to compensate her.

He told himself he would not go up to the room with her. He would take no chance that his intentions would be misconstrued. But his right hand knew damn well what his left hand was doing. He had told Kindra about the hotel room, suggested that in case of an emergency, that's where Mrs. Zedman might be found. Implying that he might be there.

Kindra had said, "You scare me, Chad." But she'd agreed

to keep the information to herself, and to pick up Mallory personally when the girl emerged from the woods.

"Let's find a place to talk," he told Ann.

"No. I want to see Cold Springs."

"Ann—"

"I don't mean Mallory. Just the school. I want to see where you live. Isn't that allowed?"

Chadwick wanted to tell her there was nothing to see of him at Cold Springs. He'd spent his new career here in this airport, stepping on and off planes, flying from crisis to crisis, leaving as little mark as the changeable placards at the gates.

But instead he nodded, and made silent plans to cancel the Sheraton reservation later.

On the road to Fredericksburg, he tried to talk to her about John's disappearance, the missing school money, the Montrose murder investigation. He asked her what was happening in San Francisco. He told her about his conversation with Mallory and Pérez. But Ann participated in the dialogue the way a yarn-holder participates in knitting a sweater—giving material when asked, keeping her end of the line from going slack, but her mind nowhere near the task, paying no attention to the patterns he was struggling to create out of threads. She kept her eyes on the line of iron clouds rolling in from the north, sealing off the winter sun.

By late afternoon, the flatlands around San Antonio had rippled and swelled into the Hill Country, the highway shearing through fifty-foot ravines, curving under the shadows of granite peaks dotted with live oaks. In the valleys, cattle huddled for warmth, and swarms of blue dragonflies hovered over the watering holes. Mesquite smoke curled up from every ranch house chimney.

As they got into Fredericksburg, they passed the truck stop where Chadwick had assaulted the rednecks, the convenience store where Pérez had almost killed him. Chadwick pointed out the historic homesteads instead. The wildflower gardens, now dormant.

Another five miles, and they drove through the gates of Cold Springs.

"The property goes back over the tops of those hills," he told her. "Mallory can walk all day and just get to the middle."

But he saw what Ann was noticing—the surveillance cameras on the front gate, the wire fence cut free from brush and floodlit, just like a minimum security prison.

Inside the grounds, the only people visible were a group of gray levels, fixing a barn door down by the horse pasture, trying to get their work done before nightfall. Chadwick didn't need a forecast to tell him it would be freezing rain tonight. Possibly even snow.

Flurries weren't unheard of in the Hill Country, but they were rare enough to be talked about for weeks whenever they happened. The last time had been seven years ago. Chadwick remembered the lodge's aboveground water tank cracking wide open like a hatched egg in the cold.

He thought of Mallory out in the woods tonight. He decided not to discuss the weather with Ann.

The Big Lodge was deserted. Hunter would be out in his jeep, overseeing the solo treks, tracking the GPS coordinates of the black levels, keeping in touch via walkie-talkie with each counselor, who would be trailing his or her charge through the woods at a distance of half a mile, just in case. The black levels would feel alone—they would *be* alone. But the safety net would be there, invisible, in case something went very wrong.

Nobody was at the main desk, so Chadwick turned the logbook around and signed out a room for Ann in the staff dormitory, a few doors down from his. It wasn't much of a liberty. Parents stayed here from time to time, though usually not until the end of White Level, when the kids were getting ready to transition back into the outside world.

Tonight, with no other visitors and most of the staff working, they would have the dorm wing almost to themselves.

He showed Ann some of the empty facilities—the computer lab, the library, the gym. In the art therapy room, she picked up a red-clay figure from the table by the window—a limp human form that had been pulverized by a fist, its head caved in.

"I had a student last year," Ann said, "molested by her stepfather. The therapist did this—had her make an image of her abuser, then tear it apart. To empower the child."

"Good therapy is good therapy."

She set it down, pressed her hand over the boy's handprints stained on the butcher paper. "Somehow, I didn't expect Dr. Hunter to know that."

"Ann, his program works. It's strict, but it doesn't ignore the kid's needs. You did the right thing sending Mallory here."

She looked at her fingers, now stained with red. "Eighteen years, I fought to keep Laurel Heights alive. I believed kids were good, creative, able to make choices. And my school is dying. Meanwhile this...this kind of school is thriving. Should I feel good about that? When my own daughter needs a drill sergeant more than she needs me?"

Chadwick took the handle of her suitcase. He'd been up thirty-six hours straight now, and his blood was turning to helium. "Let me show you your room. It's not exactly five-star, but it's a place to sleep."

"Where do you stay? Let me see that first."

The light was fading outside when Chadwick opened the curtains of his dorm apartment. It seemed impossible to him that this was the same day he'd watched the sunrise in Fredericksburg with Kindra Jones.

As Ann stared at the books on his shelf, Chadwick excused himself. He went into his bathroom and splashed water on his face.

He noticed a streak of mud on his sleeve, a missing button on his shirt collar, a piece of hay from Joey Allbritton's barn stuck in his pocket. He'd gone to pick up Ann looking like this. He probably would've had food in his teeth, too, except he hadn't eaten all day.

He examined his wet face in the bathroom mirror, rubbed at the wrinkles, thinking for the millionth time that his eyes were too close-set, too comically mournful. His heavy jawline was starting to thicken into the slight jowls, making his resemblance to George Washington even more pronounced.

He shook his head.

You're almost fifty, he told himself. *You're not an adolescent.*

Back in the main room, Ann was sitting at his desk, looking at the picture of Katherine. Chadwick fought down a swell of resentment, as if Ann were trespassing. But of course, she wasn't. She'd taken that picture.

"Hungry?" he asked.

"Did I smell cafeteria meatloaf downstairs?"

"Afraid so."

"I'll pass."

His own stomach was knotting up, but he sat down on the bed across from her. Clouds continued to thicken outside, a cold metallic energy seeping through the glass window and the heated air of the lodge.

Ann traced her finger across the old eighth-grade class picture—the kids in colonial costume. Chadwick knew she could name each child, their parents, their siblings. She could list the colleges they had gone to, and what jobs they had now.

"I saw Norma this morning," she said. "She warned me not to come. Said I was a stupid damned optimist."

"My ex-wife. Always the diplomat."

Outside, the dusk dissolved the trees and the sky. An instructor's whistle blew three sharp notes, signaling the end of the tan levels' workday.

"And are you really happy here?" Ann asked. "Is this what you want to do?"

"Been a long time since I thought in those terms."

Heat kindled in her eyes. "And why is that?"

"This is where I need to be."

"Because you couldn't send Katherine here, so you had to come yourself?"

"Ann—"

"Katherine's suicide wasn't our fault, Chadwick. It's cost us so much time."

"You sound like you blame her for dying."

"I loved her, Chadwick, but not enough to give up our relationship. You shouldn't have left me. You shouldn't have spent the last nine years punishing yourself, punishing me."

"Was it my idea to put Race Montrose at Laurel Heights?"

"I didn't mean—"

"You called me—begged me to help, because you thought Mallory had been involved in the murder. Was that my idea?"

Ann stood, as if she were about to yell at him.

Voices came from down the hallway—two people talking, a man and a woman. Counselors, Chadwick thought, though he couldn't place names to the voices.

As they reached Chadwick's room, the man said, "I don't think he's here."

There was a knock on the door.

Chadwick and Ann locked eyes. He shook his head, and she tacitly agreed. Neither of them could stand company at the moment.

The woman's voice said, "Maybe he's on a pickup or—"

"No. Jones is here."

"Oh, right. We could ask her. Or maybe Hunter . . ."

The rest was muffled as they drifted down the hall.

Ann touched her cheeks with the back of her hand. "God. I haven't felt like this since I was sixteen. The high school broom closet."

"Who were you in there with?"

"None of your damn business."

"Rah-Rah Lucas," Chadwick guessed. "The butt-ugly football player."

Ann slapped him on the shoulder, and he grabbed her wrist. Their eyes met. He drew her down next to him on the bed, nestled her against his shoulder while she trembled, her tears damp on his shirt.

She pulled his chin down, found his lips. Chadwick felt himself borrowing her sense of direction, letting her guide him, as she'd so often guided him before.

She pushed him down on the bed, moved on top of him, her breath in his ear, her skin salty.

"How much of a loser am I?" she taunted, and bit his ear. "I wait thirty years for someone, and it's you."

There was a knock on the door once more during the

night, and they fell silent until the footsteps went away, trembling for fear of discovery like they were teenagers in a high school broom closet, or guilty adulterers in a sleeping bag at Stinson Beach.

For the first time in seven years, snow began to fall over the Hill Country, so quiet and natural that all the hot summers of the interim might never have happened.

32

It was goddamn typical. Not only had she gotten shot at twice in twenty-four hours, yelled at, sleep-deprived and starved. The minute they sent her into the woods for her wilderness overnight, she started her period.

The med kit had supplies for that, but Jesus Christ.

Mallory tried to imagine Leyland teaching them some survivalist tip for dealing with menstruation. *And, um, ladies, this is how the Indians used to do it.*

That thought lifted her spirits just a little, but the cramps were bad, like a rhinoceros using her pelvis for a skateboard.

She remembered her monthly ritual at Laurel Heights, ever since sixth grade, spending lunch break curled over in pain in the school office, tears streaming down her face, the other kids poking their heads in the door to ask if she was okay—her mom uncomfortable, having her so close, leaving it to the secretary to reassure the kids that Mallory just had a stomachache. Everything would be fine.

Her mom had never dealt well with female stuff. She was too damn busy being headmistress to be female. Maxi-pads? Trainer bras? Forget it. Mallory remembered how ashamed she'd felt, walking into the lingerie department by herself because her mom wouldn't take her, and then walking out again, scared of the salesclerk. Finally, Norma had taken her under her wing, bought her the right training bra—Norma Reyes, the woman who had lost her breasts to cancer. She could buy a bra, and her mom couldn't. Thinking about it still made Mallory angry.

Of course at the moment, everything made her angry. Her hormones were boiling over. Maybe all the women at Cold Springs were on the same cycle—her, Morrison, Olsen—all of them ready to tear somebody's throat out. Maybe Hunter had been wise to send them off into the wilderness for a while.

She skirted the base of a large hill, using a dry creek bed for a road. She wanted to avoid the underbrush—dense pampas grass and wild rye that grew waist-high on either side. Leyland had warned them about rattlesnakes. They were less active in winter, but they were still out there, living in the high grass.

How far had she walked? Miles, anyway. She hadn't known there were still open places like this in the world, where you could walk all day and see nothing—no people, no buildings, no civilization.

Her calf muscles were sore. Her knife chafed against her thigh. She'd eaten her only ration bar three hours ago, and now her stomach was a hole, slowly burning larger and larger.

Still, she'd felt proud of herself, for the most part. They had taken her compass away before she set out, but she'd used stick-and-shadow readings to find her cardinal directions. She was fairly confident she had remained on an eastward course, though the clouds had rolled in during the afternoon—and she could now only guess she was heading the right way.

Her stomach did a slow twist, trying to write the word FOOD on the back of her rib cage. They should've given her two ration bars. They should've taken into account she'd been on the run all night with nothing to eat, unlike the rest of the team. It wasn't fair.

Nothing's fair, she told herself. *Stop blaming and find a solution.*

Water. Her canteen was empty. She should find a way to fill it. At least that would give her something to put in her belly.

She followed a streak of slushy gravel up the creek bed to a bathtub-sized puddle of standing water. The surface was webbed with floating algae that piled up at the edges, making shirred lace on the granite. Young frogs darted around in the silt. Water bugs streaked through the ripples. It seemed strange that there could be so much life in the middle of winter. Surely it would freeze tonight. Could frogs live under ice?

Mallory knew she shouldn't drink from here. Amoebas, bacteria—shit like that could make her sick. Then she noticed the capillary of water trickling into the pond, feeding it. She followed it up into the rocks and found the spring, almost choked in moss, but there it was, bubbling right out of the ground—one of the cold springs the school was named after. Supposedly hundreds of these sprouted up all over the ranch, lacing together to form the river. But this was the first one Mallory had seen. Weird, that something so small could make a river.

She squatted down and the cramps tightened. Black spots danced behind her eyes. She wrapped her fingers around the GPS bracelet on her wrist, squeezed the metal band. But she wouldn't push that button. She wasn't going to give up. Not this time.

She steadied her breathing, looked for something to focus her eyes on. The ground here was littered with flint chips. Chert—worked stone, just like Leyland had told them to watch for. Several pieces had been chipped to a point—discarded Indian tools. She was kneeling at a two-thousand-year-old drinking fountain.

She cupped her hand into the water and took a drink. It tasted cold, earthy—what the heart of a tree would taste like, if you could drink it.

Her dizziness subsided. She filled her canteen.

Under her hand, the moss felt like a horse's muzzle, and she remembered the evening she'd stood with Olsen at the pasture, feeding apple slices to the filly.

She thought about Olsen's secret—her stepfather, her little sister.

Mallory didn't want to be anybody's substitute little sister. She'd played that part before, with Katherine.

But she also couldn't help being touched that Olsen had opened up.

She'd never had a girlfriend—like a real slumber-party

paint-your-nails kind of friend. Katherine had ruined that for her. Mallory got too close to another girl and she started thinking about the silver chain around her neck. She backed away, found a boy to hang out with, like Race.

She was sorry she hadn't told Olsen her own secret— about Katherine's last night, the figure on the Montroses' porch. But she felt relieved, too.

How could she be sure of a memory from when she was six? Her parents used to tell her things she did when she was small, until she started to believe she remembered them. The dream about the Montroses' porch could be the same kind of thing. A traumatic experience, combined with a new situation—you superimpose someone's face and start believing they were there.

She wondered how Olsen would react—whether she'd laugh it off, or take her seriously, or maybe even get angry. The hungrier Mallory got, and the more tired, the more reasonable her dream seemed. She'd heard Katherine—she'd called her friend *she.* Mallory was sure of that. But if Mallory said something, and she was wrong...

She decided to climb out of the creek bed, see where she was going.

She hiked up the hillside to an outcropping of boulders that looked like the head of a turkey.

From there, she had a view of the whole valley—the low hills, the dense carpet of live oaks turning chameleon gray under the clouds, a darker strip of green cypress trees that marked the river's course up ahead, and maybe, a little farther toward the horizon, a ribbon of brown—the access road.

Race had kidded her once, when she'd suggested they take a trip to the woods. She'd had this idea they'd hitchhike to La Honda, where the hippies used to experiment with LSD. They'd score some cheap wine and pot and spend the night in the redwoods. Race had laughed, a little nervous. *You in the woods? Man, the raccoons would eat you.*

Now, Mallory smiled. *Screw you very much, Race.*

She hadn't thought of him in days—not like she used to, anyway. It had only taken one night of sex to convince her they weren't in love. Weird how that had worked—like, now that it's too late, here's the emotional proof you just made a mistake. She didn't hate him. She didn't really believe he'd killed his mother. She just...wanted to avoid him. Their friendship had become dangerous, like the heroin. Most of the time, she no longer craved it, but if she got close...if she saw a bag of smack, she wasn't sure she'd be able to resist.

Maybe Race felt the same way. Finding his mother in all that blood—how could you share that experience with someone and not have the image burn in your mind, every time you looked at her? Mallory wondered where they would be now if Chadwick hadn't snatched her—if she and Race had taken that money and caught a bus out of town. They would've failed eventually, made each other miserable. She knew that now. Cold Springs had saved her. All she could do was hope Race would find something like that, too.

An icy wind was picking up, turning her cheeks and the end of her nose to sandpaper. She was about to rise, get moving again, when she heard a loud skittering noise—dislodged rocks rolling down the hillside in the woods behind her. Her fingers strayed to the hilt of her knife.

"Hello?" she called.

No response. Just the sound of a few last pebbles coming to rest. Mallory could see nothing that hadn't been there before—the trees, the cliffs, the afternoon growing steadily darker under dense gray clouds.

You won't meet any people, Leyland had promised. *This is all private land. Posted and patrolled. We're taking pains to make sure no one bothers you.*

Could she trust that?

Probably, if Hunter and Chadwick were on patrol. Chadwick had taken out that one sniper, Hunter had assured her, like it was nothing. And Mallory figured Hunter was just as tough. You could tell by looking at him—the guy was a predator.

Mallory tried to relax. Probably an animal had slipped. Do animals slip? Or maybe the rocks had come loose on their own.

But her heart still fluttered. Maybe it was just her hormones again, but she felt...anger in the silence, directed at her. She felt watched.

She found a dead mesquite branch, about four feet long, two inches thick. She broke the twigs off of it, hefted it. It would make a good walking stick. That's all. Just in case.

She made her way downhill.

She walked for another hour or so. The air turned colder and heavier, and it began to smell like snow. Mallory put on her jacket.

Her cramps flared up, rolling through her like lava lamp goo, and with them, the old withdrawal pains from the heroin. That didn't help her paranoia. Whenever she looked back, she could swear she saw flickers of movement in the trees. She heard the distant crack of twigs.

A counselor following her? No, a counselor would hang back. This was something pressing in—a presence on her back, as threatening as the cold front.

Another snap in the woods behind her—maybe fifty yards away. Mallory started jogging.

By the time she saw the river in the distance, she was shivering, her face drenched in sweat.

The river was narrower here than it was at camp—maybe thirty yards across—but the water roared in a swollen stretch of rapids. The banks were cut steep into the mud, the exposed roots of cypresses making basket nets along either side. It was too far to jump, too icy to swim. And it was in Mallory's way.

The daylight was fading, but she had to cross. She wasn't going to stay on this side all night—not with those sounds, the thing that was stalking her.

She picked her way downstream until she came to what she needed—a fallen tree, the trunk making a bridge across to the other side.

She didn't wait to get up her nerve. She could be across in three big steps.

But she'd underestimated how slick the bark was, how much it would bend and shift under her weight. She was halfway when she slipped, threw her walking stick into the air, and pitched into the water.

Her arm struck something hard. Water surged into her nostrils. Her clothes weighed her down; the current spun her and rushed her backwards downstream. She tried to stand, only to be swept back in. Finally, she clawed herself to the bank, pulling herself up by a tree root, and collapsed in the mud, gasping and nauseated.

Stupid. Race would laugh in your damn face.

She had no idea how far she'd been carried. She couldn't see the tree trunk she'd tried to cross. Her whole body trembled, and she wasn't sure whether it was from the cold or the shock, but she realized it didn't matter. She needed to move. She needed to get warm immediately.

And then she noticed her backpack was gone.

She walked downstream for a long way, but there was no sign of the pack. It had been ripped off her back and carried away.

Now, for the first time, Mallory felt truly alone. She looked at the GPS bracelet—that small green eye glowing at her, daring her to give up. She was in deep trouble. She could die out here. Just her goddamn luck, to freeze to death in Texas.

No, she told herself. *You can do this.*

But the darkening sky and the river and the trees seemed to be telling her otherwise.

She tried to remember what Leyland had told her to do in an emergency.

S.O.S. Survey. Organize. Strategize.

Okay, the survey was easy. Night was falling. She was wet and cold—her clothes soaked through, her backpack and med kit and thermal sleeping bag gone. Her limbs felt numb.

Mallory organized her supplies. She stripped off her jacket. She checked her leg sheath to make sure the knife was still there. The metal match they'd shown her how to use was still in her pocket. That was it. That's all she had.

Strategize? She needed warmth, right away. She needed to make a fire.

The only good thing that had come from her river ride was that she seemed to have lost whoever or whatever was following her. She couldn't hear it anymore—didn't feel its anger. Fire light might attract it to her again, but she had no choice. She had to have warmth.

After a fire, she'd create a shelter. She'd have to spend the night here, move on in the morning. Thirdly—only thirdly—she'd need to satisfy the gnawing hunger in her stomach.

She'd done lots of fires in base camp. It had been one of the prerequisites for the solo trip. Nevertheless, she had to remember the steps, mentally walking herself through.

She found an enormous tree that was hollow inside and decided that would be her shelter. She'd build her fire next to it. She used the hard dirt as her platform, put down a wrist-sized branch for the brace, piled the tinder on this. It took her three strikes to spark a flame to the tinder, and by that time her fingers were losing feeling. In a few minutes, though, she'd started a curl of fire and began to add the kindling. She got to the fuel stage, began adding larger twigs, then small logs.

She stood as close to the blaze as she could, feeling like something that had been pulled prematurely from the microwave—boiling on one side, frozen on the other.

A dot of ice melted on her cheek. She looked up. Snowflakes were falling, a scatter of oversized dust motes evaporating in the halo of her fire.

Great. Just great.

When her hands felt warm enough to work, she began cleaning out the tree trunk. Grubs and worms and beetles squirmed out of the dark, and these she threw onto the tarp of her jacket by the fire. Just in case, she told herself. Just in case.

By the time dusk was truly setting in, she had made her shelter. The snow had begun to stick to the ground like a crust of salt. Mallory backed into her hollow tree, now lined with moss and grass, and kept the fire blazing. She drank spring water from her canteen, but she avoided the grubs for now.

She couldn't seem to control her shivering. She wondered if hypothermia could set in so quickly.

She imagined she was back on the ropes course above the

river, suspended in the dark, her harness tearing. She was ready to make a deal with God, to get her the hell out of here.

Her last visit to her father's, just before she'd run away to the East Bay, she had walked into his bedroom and found him on his knees, his back to her, hunched over his bed in his business suit, praying. She couldn't have been more embarrassed if she'd found him in his underwear. Her dad, who'd never been to church in his life, who'd told her when she was a kid that God was a fairy tale, like Cinderella—her dad was *praying*. He didn't notice her. His fingers were laced, his lips almost kissing them as he spoke.

She'd stayed just long enough to hear him pleading quietly, promising God he would give anything. Please.

Then she'd left, easing the door closed behind her.

She understood finally what he'd been praying for . . . Her.

She'd blown up at him, cursed him, called him a monster because he didn't like Race, because he'd hit her mother once, years ago.

She had hurt him, just like Pérez said, and all he wanted was for her to be safe.

He'd sent Pérez to get her. That was a way of telling her he loved her. A twisted way, maybe. But he had tried.

She started crying—knowing that the tears were some damn chemical imbalance, her period making everything seem worse than it was.

Her dad was gone. She wanted to think she'd feel a hole in her heart if he were dead, but she wasn't sure.

This was her mother's fault—her mother and Chadwick. They had started everything going wrong, just because they wanted to fuck each other. They'd ruined two families. Her father's disappearance was on their heads.

Maybe Chadwick had treated her okay. Maybe he was even serious about helping her. Maybe, for a while, when she was scared in Fredericksburg, she'd even thought about confiding in him. But in the end, Mallory knew the main reason she hadn't told her dream about Katherine to anyone wasn't that she didn't believe the dream. She wanted to see what would happen if her worst suspicions were right. She wanted to see Chadwick punished.

She huddled into her hollow tree, facing the flames, her knife at her side. Her empty stomach seemed to be ripping itself out of her body. And as the night grew dark, her only company was the river and the fire and the sound of the hills moaning as they contracted under a hard freeze.

33

Race was crazy to be at the café. He knew that.

But he needed time to think. He had a decision to make. And he was running out of places to go.

He sat down at the sidewalk table where a month ago Mallory had been taken from him. He stared at a half-empty coffee glass, a chess game the last customers had left unfinished.

He couldn't go back to Nana's apartment. The visit from Chadwick and Jones had unhinged the old lady, made her start drinking and having conversations with Samuel and Talia in the middle of the night, and Race couldn't handle that shit.

His mother's house was sold—some family with a U-Haul already moved in. Race had stood down the block, watching as a boy lugged his wagon of toys up the front steps, a little girl kicked a soccer ball around the stumps of the palm trees like relay race cones.

Last night, he had stayed in the abandoned apartment building behind the café—up at the top of the stairwell where he and Mallory had made love. The BART trains rattled the windows, and a couple of derelicts in the gutted apartment below him had kept him awake, squabbling about laundry money. Race had kept his .22 semiautomatic in his improvised ankle-strap, close enough where he could reach it, just in case they came up the stairs. He didn't sleep until dawn, when the homeless guys wandered out to find their morning booze.

He couldn't handle being in the stairwell another night. Not because of the derelicts, but because the old carpet still smelled of Mallory. Her scent reminded him of their final night together—being pressed against her, how she would pinch his ears, letting him know when he was being too rough. The whole thing had been wrong—as wrong as finding her the heroin she wanted, feeding the death wish that made her want to turn into Katherine. But Race had followed her lead. He always did. And now he was trying hard not to think about her.

During the afternoon, he'd stolen a bike and made the long ride up into the hills—to the condo above the Caldecott Tunnel. He'd been hoping to find some money, but the place had been cleaned out, as if for good. That made Race nervous, made him wonder what was going on. He thought about staying there overnight, but the idea made his throat go dry. The place had worse ghosts than his mother's house; evil breathed into the air like corpse odor from the five or six years it had been occupied—radios and televisions playing in every room, twenty-four hours a day, to drown out the hatred.

Now it was night again, and he was back at his and Mallory's favorite café, where he had failed so miserably to help her.

He shivered, pulled his camouflage coat around himself. It stank. He stank. He had five twenty-dollar bills left— enough to eat for a few days, but this was a miserable time of year to sleep on the street.

He had to make a choice.

Race took out Chadwick's card, fingered the worn edge. He'd looked at this card every day. He'd memorized the damn number. He'd even called it once, but he'd gotten a machine, and hung up.

He could call again. He could even go to the city, to Norma Reyes' house. He would tell her first. Then she would help him. She would make the call for him, protect him from the consequences. He had known for years—ever since the day she defended him against that idiot who called him a monkey in fourth grade—that Miss Reyes was somebody he could trust. It had something to do with the sadness in her eyes, the loneliness that reminded him of his mom, those few times she was between men, when she wasn't high or drunk, and she paid attention to him. He could go to Norma Reyes.

Or he could do what he'd been told. He could wait and be silent.

He thought about Samuel—his dead big brother, whose memory had been resurrected to serve as a monster's skin.

She had promised no one else would die. She had promised to come back for Race and give him a fresh start, a new school, an easy life with plenty of money.

But she had also promised he would graduate from Laurel Heights. She said he could go to college, study history, get a Ph.D. if he wanted to. He could rewrite African-American history and turn the fucking world on its head.

She'd broken her promise.

For a while, his future had been part of her revenge—a thorn in the Zedmans' sides that served her purpose. Now, he was just a loose end.

Race hadn't seen her for days, but he had no illusions. She could find him at a moment's notice. She had almost killed him for saying as much as he had—for leaving the apartment, trying to warn Ms. Reyes.

It would be stupid to cross her twice.

He stared at the chipped chess pieces on the table, thought of Mallory teaching him the game, years ago, in third grade. She'd always told him he was smarter than she was, but in chess, like everything else, she always outmaneuvered him.

Inside the café, the evening crowd was settling in with herbal tea and baguette sandwiches. White families, white college students glanced at him apprehensively. When he caught their eye, they stared past him, pretending to be looking somewhere else.

He knew what they were thinking. He was a transient, taking up a table. He would bother them for spare change. Or mug them. Why didn't the café management tell him to move?

Race understood the hate that had driven the knife into his mother thirty-two times. He understood Samuel.

Race's take on it— Being black, you were never far away from a split identity. You always wrestled with a secret desire, a guilty wish that you could be someone else—just slip into a different skin for a while, be invisible, not the object of suspicion and resentment and fear. For him, for a Montrose, it was only a small step from that to schizophrenia, or homicide, or both.

He remembered the first time—when he was a little boy, after he'd told her what he saw, after the body had been found, washed up in a rotting piece of canvas on the shores of Hayward. She had grabbed his arm with such desperation that her fingertips left bruises. "That wasn't him. You understand? Samuel will take care of you. Samuel's your protection." And the light in her eyes had been just like Nana's—the refracted shimmer of a crystal with a crack in its heart. Whenever Race looked in a mirror, he feared he would start having that same look in his eyes. Since the night of Samuel's murder, Race feared that his whole life had been the product of a fracture— that *she* was his imagination, too.

He couldn't turn himself in. He couldn't betray her. Even now, after all she'd done, she was still his protection. She was still Samuel. He would have to find a sidewalk to curl up on tonight, a church basement to hide in. He would have to argue with the derelicts about laundry money.

He stared at Chadwick's card, pecking at the edge with his greasy fingernail.

A man's voice said, "Hi, Race."

The fear started in Race's fingers and worked its way up to his neck.

The guy in front of him had close-cropped blond hair, hazel eyes, a face like a baby who'd just gotten through screaming. He wore a black sailor's coat over black denim, a newspaper pinched in his left hand, his right hand in his jacket pocket, closed around something bulky that Race thought was a gun.

"Oh, come on," the man said. "Not even a hello?"

"Kraft," he said. "You're that David guy." Race had never seen the guy without a jacket and tie, never seen him looking so street.

David Kraft smiled. "Funny. Like you didn't know me."

Race's mind was going fast, running possibilities, angles. He was trying to figure what the hell this guy was doing here, what he wanted.

"I live down the street," Kraft told him. "I'm a neighbor, practically. You don't remember me from the old days? Didn't know I was an East Bay boy?"

Race could run for it. He knew the alleys. It was dark. But if that was a gun in Kraft's pocket, only three feet from his chest, Race didn't like his chances.

"Empty your pockets," Kraft said. "Very, very slowly."

Race pulled out his twenties, half a buck in change, the key to Nana's apartment tangled in pocket thread. Chadwick's card. A paperback copy of *The Bluest Eye* from his jacket. A spent bullet casing he'd picked up from Samuel's bedroom. A number two pencil.

Kraft said, "Unarmed?"

"Yeah."

Race made a conscious effort not to move his feet, not to tip off the ankle-strap in any way.

David Kraft tossed the newspaper onto the table. "Look."

It was folded to a story with a photo of the man's face, but it took Race a second to register who he was looking at.

Mallory's dad.

Fear started rolling around his stomach like a marble. He lifted the paper off the table.

He read about it for the first time—John Zedman reported missing three days ago, bloodstains found at his house. His body had been found today in an unoccupied townhouse in the Mission, discovered by one of the property owners, Norma Reyes. Ann Zedman, the deceased's ex-wife, recently suspended from her headmistress job at Laurel Heights on suspicion of embezzlement, was wanted for questioning in the murder, but was believed to have left town.

"Nice job," Kraft told him. "Hauling the body all that way, just for the effect. I mean, that was overtime pay, right there."

Race stared at the picture. *She* had done this. She'd promised no one would get hurt. "I didn't know. I didn't—"

"Oh, of course not," Kraft said. "Never. Right? And the name Katherine Chadwick—that doesn't mean anything to you either."

With his free hand, Kraft pulled out his keys and threw them on the table. The keys were attached to a metal figurine of Mickey Mouse, about two inches tall. It struck Race as a weird thing for a guy to have on his key chain.

"What you're going to do," Kraft said, "is drive. You got your learner's permit, Race?"

"No."

"That's bullshit. I've got access to your student files. I know your age, your mom's and grandma's addresses, your blood type and your fucking birthday. You know how to drive. You're going to drive me to a place where we can talk."

Race didn't move.

"Or you could scream for help," David Kraft added. "Call the cops. I guess you could always do that."

Kraft smiled, waiting.

Race picked up the keys.

"Good boy," Kraft said. "And Race—yes, it's really a gun in my pocket. In case you were wondering."

David Kraft's car was a blue SUV, parked at the hydrant half a block up Ocean View. What he must've done—he'd seen Race at the sidewalk. Kraft had circled the block, parked on the side street, walked up behind Race. But the gun—Kraft couldn't carry that all the time. The guy was like a junior business advisor or something. Straight out of college. He must've been watching for Race—watching a long time, waiting.

"No accidents," Kraft warned. "My dad's insurance won't cover you."

Kraft brought out his gun, a blue-steel H&K, and pressed it into Race's thigh. Race put the key into the ignition and tried to keep his heart from climbing up his throat. The Mickey Mouse bumped against his knee as he turned the wheel.

Kraft directed him south on Broadway, then into West Oakland on side streets Race had never seen before. Section Eight housing and junkie motels gave way to warehouses, which gave way to miles of razor-wire lots stacked with shipping containers. A few more deserted streets, then the flat-lands dissolved into asphalt and sea grass and crumbled right into the Bay.

Kraft directed him up to the shore, where a twenty-foot pier jutted into choppy black water.

To the south, the Port of Oakland's white cranes towered like dinosaur skeletons. To the north, the Bay Bridge glowed and hummed with traffic—thousands of commuters roaring by overhead.

A million people behind them in Oakland, another million across the Bay in San Francisco, and Race and David Kraft were totally alone.

"Get out," Kraft told him.

"I didn't know about Mallory's dad."

The gun pressed deeper into his thigh. "Take the keys out of the ignition, and get out of the car. It's a beautiful night."

Race did what he was told.

He stood on the uneven shore while David Kraft came around the side of the SUV, the sights of the H&K never leaving Race's chest.

Race found himself rubbing the little Mickey Mouse—trying to calm himself with the slick metal under his thumb.

He had to get away.

She had lied to him about not hurting anyone. She had killed Zedman. That meant she would lie about other things, too. Mallory was in trouble.

The .22 was still in his ankle holster, but he'd never get it out in time. Even if he did, Race sucked at shooting. He'd never killed anybody, never even fired the damn thing except in the air on New Year's Eve. He hadn't tried the gun since Chadwick made him drop it five stories off the fire escape. Maybe it didn't even work anymore.

David Kraft prodded him toward the water, then out onto the little pier. "About halfway. That's good. Now face me."

The wind smelled of car exhaust and rotting fish.

In the dim light from the Bay Bridge, David Kraft's face looked like metal, as if it had been hammered from the hood of his own car.

"Katherine Chadwick," Kraft told him. "Nine years ago last summer, I took a girl to a party. She was feeling down. I wanted to give her a thrill, show her I could pick up drugs, slum on the bad side of town, you know? So I took her to this house—this little fucking piss-yellow house in West Oakland, and Samuel Montrose stole her from me. Ruined her, got her so hooked on smack that she thought a gangster piece-of-shit like him could actually love somebody. She died, Race. Her parents failed her. The school failed her. I failed her. But most of all, she died because of Samuel. A piece of shit named Samuel Montrose. You look just like him, you know. Just like him."

Race was imagining that he could levitate straight up from this spot. He could see every important place in his life: his mother's house on Jefferson, Laurel Heights, Nana's apartment, Rockridge, Telegraph Hill. He had never traveled farther than he could see right now, from this spot, and he wondered if this was the geographic center of his life—the point where all the distances averaged out.

He couldn't die. He had to make someone believe him—Norma Reyes. If he could just talk to her again, look straight in her eyes and make her listen.

"The funny thing is," David Kraft said, "I came back to Laurel Heights thinking I would make peace with the place. I wanted to help the capital campaign. I wanted to forgive them for failing Katherine. For failing me. And what's the first thing I find out? You. Ann Zedman had accepted you as a student, let her own daughter be friends with you. And I understood from day one what your family was doing, Race. Fuckin' A. They were pissing on Laurel Heights, shoving you in everybody's faces. For months, I thought about killing you, but I'm not an animal. So I planted the gun in your locker. I made sure you got kicked out. But you're a tenacious little prick. You and your family—I don't know how you managed it, but you got the capital campaign funds and pinned it on Mrs. Zedman. You killed John Zedman, made it look like Chadwick did it. You set that all up beautifully. And I started figuring, well what the hell? Let's see how far the little prick can take it. So I called the media for you. I did every fucking thing to fan the fire, make sure Laurel Heights went down in flames. But the thing is, Race—you've done about as much for me now as you can. You're part of the problem, too. Your family can't just walk away. So tell me the truth now—who's got the money?"

Race thought about it—the answer least likely to get him shot. "Samuel."

"I'd like that. I'd like to believe he's alive. But see, I heard the hesitation there. I think Samuel's dead—a guy with an attitude problem like his couldn't live to be an adult. So who's got the money, Race? You might even live, you can tell me that."

"I don't have any money."

"One . . ."

Race imagined he was back on the fire escape, the metal rail peeling into oblivion, and Chadwick catching his arm—giving Race the chance to kill him, shoot him right in the face, but it would mean falling, bike-pedaling through five stories of air, and Race knew that was no choice at all. He had to live. He had to let Chadwick live. Even then, he couldn't fire a gun. How could he fire it now?

"Two . . ."

"There's nobody else," Race said. "It's just me. Just me."

"Three. Turn your back to me, Race. Kneel down."

"You'll never get the money."

"The money is secondary, Race. Very, very secondary. Now do what I said."

Race turned, sank to his knees. His hands grabbed his ankles, and he felt the .22 in its holster.

"You know what I got in the car, Race? I got lead weights. Big, bowling-ball-sized things. They hold down plastic tarps in windstorms. I'm going to rope them around your ankles. You'll go down in fifteen feet of water right here—standing up. At low tide, the sunlight will just touch your fingertips. And you will rot there. Nobody comes here, Race. Nobody except me. This place is mine. Now I'm going to share it with you."

And Race looked out over the dark stretch of shoreline—

rocks and wind and the stench of dead fish, an acre of desolation with a view of two cities.

He felt the boards bow under David Kraft's weight. Race's fingers worked their way into his pants leg, around the grip of the .22.

"Don't forget your Mickey Mouse," he told Kraft. "It's in my pocket."

"Katherine's," he corrected. And he patted Race's head, affectionately. "She gave it to me the week before she died. I'll remember, Race. Now why don't you pray or something? Do people still do that?"

And Race did pray, as he slipped the .22 out of its holster, trying not to move a single unnecessary muscle. He imagined his soul rising out of his body, the way his mother had always told him souls did, and choosing between trains—a BART train riding west, into the city, toward Norma Reyes, who was standing in her bathrobe on her porch. Or a fiery train east, toward Mallory and Texas, toward the Caldecott Tunnel where Samuel's condominium smelled like death, and Race would be another voice, another wisp of evil for the radio to drown out.

"This is for Katherine," David Kraft said.

He gently pushed Race's head down, to expose his neck, but Race fell sideways, turning, bringing his gun up to David Kraft's wide eyes so that two blasts sounded at once—a single bright snap that echoed over miles of empty water and dissipated in the roar of the evening commute.

34

Mallory woke with a start. There were snuffling noises in the darkness, something scuttling through branches.

The fire was dangerously low, and she was still shivering. Her clothes felt like plaster of Paris, melted against her skin, and snow had frosted her shoes where they stuck out of the hollow tree.

At the edge of the red arc of firelight Mallory saw something rustling in the brush. She thought about the thing that had followed her yesterday. She moved her arm slowly, wrapped her fingers around an icy rock the size of a grapefruit. A month ago, she wouldn't have had the strength to lift it. Now, she hurled it at the dark shape—hoping she pegged it.

There was a sick crunch, and then a flurry of scuffling, which died down but did not go away.

Drawing her knife, Mallory advanced and found that her rock had landed squarely on the head of a football-sized... something. A giant roly-poly bug with hair. A thrill of terror shot up Mallory's spine, until she realized what it was—a stupid armadillo.

Its armor hadn't helped the poor thing. Its snout was crushed, and it was lying on its side, one glazed eye red in the firelight, a bubble of blood coming out of its nostril. Its claws scraped weakly at the air.

Mallory's fear turned to shame. She hadn't even managed to kill it, just torture it.

She was too numb to think. Some other part of her took over, and she approached the thing with her knife. She stuck at its head. The first stab missed, but the second hit home. It was still not quick, but the thing died.

It was the first time Mallory had killed, and she didn't like it.

She sat there trembling. The armadillo's smell was horrible—some defense mechanism, Mallory guessed—but she couldn't move away. She knew she should stoke the fire. She would probably die if she didn't.

In the end, the cold wasn't what got her moving. It was hunger. Mallory was disgusted with herself, but she realized the knot in her stomach wasn't revulsion, but the desire to eat.

She had killed her first animal. She felt like she owed the poor thing something—to make something good come out of its pain.

I can't eat that, she told herself.

But the answer came immediately, Of course she could. Hadn't she seen them hanging dead in shop windows in Chinatown?

They have leprosy or something, Mallory remembered. The thing is disgusting. It's probably crawling with parasites.

So are you, came the answer. *You have a day to walk. You'll never make it without food.*

In a daze, Mallory went into the woods and got more wood. She heard more rustling sounds in the darkness, wondered if the presence that had followed her the day before was still out there.

Let it come, she thought. *I'm tired of being scared.*

She stoked the fire to a blaze. Then she went back to the armadillo.

She touched its shell, which felt like a warm patchwork of toenails. She turned the animal over and looked at its furry underbelly, its claws. She counted to herself—one, two, three—then made the first cut, splitting the body from neck to anus.

She was no hunter, no country girl. The best she could think of to give herself courage were science class dissections—she and Race freaking out over the fetal pig they'd named Wilbur—but the dissections hadn't been in the dark, with no gloves, and with the intent of eating the subject.

Mallory turned aside from the smell and the gore several times and tried to retch, but there was nothing in her stomach, and her hands were sticky with blood. She couldn't turn away from the work. She was covered in it.

She worked as if she were under a shell—as if she were the armadillo, and most of her upper brain functions had retreated into a safe, hardened place, leaving her body to its butchery.

At last, the armadillo was gutted, and Mallory had four slimy strips of flesh spit on a branch like a bloody shish kebab. She let the meat cook over the flames, watching the tiny slivers hiss and sizzle and burn at the edges, and her revulsion turned to fascination, and then to ravenous hunger. The smell was cooking meat, and her stomach approved.

She carried her prize down to the river and washed her hands, which seemed like an absurd civility once she'd done it. Then she went back to the fire and ate the meat, so hot it burned her tongue. It was tough and fine-grained, and tasted like pork chop. Mallory finished it all.

As she ate, she thought she could feel her eyes clearing, but then she realized there was a faint gray glow on everything. The dawn was coming. In the distance, she could hear a sound like sirens, but she knew it must be something else— some kind of bird waking up, or some forlorn animal.

She would walk again today, and she would get herself out of the woods.

A new energy wound up inside her like a motor. She looked at her hands, wondered how much of the red was fire and how much was blood.

Her old fears seemed absurd to her now. They belonged to a little kid two thousand miles away. Mallory could handle herself. She could damn well handle Samuel.

She made herself a promise that she would tell the truth when she got out of the woods.

Mallory sat, becoming comfortable with the idea, steeling her courage. The cold didn't seem so bitter now, and she sat by the fire until the sun came up, a murky yellow stain on the thick gray clouds.

35

Chadwick dreamed the snow was turning to rain, drizzling against the doors of the porch. He dreamed of police sirens, and his own breath turning into the soft vibrations of a silenced cell phone.

His eyes opened. His cell phone was rattling on the nightstand. There was a warm empty furrow in the sheets where Ann had been, and the rain he'd imagined was the shower in the bathroom. Somewhere in the distance, emergency vehicles keened like coyotes as they moved through the hills.

The morning sky was dismal gray. Chadwick had a moment of disorientation, wondering why the windows were on the wrong side of the room, why his bed was against the wrong wall. Then he remembered, halfway through the night, Ann had moved down the hall to her guest room. She had insisted, in case somebody knocked on Chadwick's door in the morning. She didn't want to embarrass him. But he had followed her, and the next few hours had infused his limbs with a pleasant weariness he was reluctant to shake off.

His phone vibrated again. He picked it up. The LCD read: *7:06 A.M. Caller: Cold Springs*.

He didn't recognize the speaker at first—a woman's voice, asking what the hell he had done.

Chadwick processed the question. "Kindra?"

"The FBI," she told him. "Get the hell out now."

"What?"

"That guy Laramie, a couple of other feds, maybe half a

dozen county deputies. They just left here for the Hill Country Sheraton."

He knew the police were scheduled to visit Cold Springs this morning. He was prepared for that. But seven in the morning?

He was about to tell Kindra he wasn't at the Sheraton. He was right upstairs, probably not fifty feet from her. But the sirens kept wailing, fainter and fainter, and some instinct told him to keep his location to himself.

"What happened?" he asked. "They found Pérez?"

"Yeah, they found him."

"He making trouble for us?"

"The biggest kind, Chadwick. He's been murdered."

Each granule in the texture of the ceiling abruptly came into sharper focus. He sat up in bed. "Where?"

"You don't have time, Chad. Those cops—"

"Tell me."

A beep—a waiting call on Chadwick's end of the line— cut off part of Kindra's profanity.

"A farmer found the body," she told him. "Pérez was laying face up on the side of a dirt road, tangled in a fence. According to Laramie, he was hit by a car, then took a bullet in the head. Satisfied?"

"We left Pérez alive."

"Yeah. And then what happened?"

"I didn't kill him."

"Shit." Jones almost sounded disappointed. "That lady at the convenience store—she called us in, gave the police our description. African-American woman, six-foot-eight white guy, psycho runaway girl—how many trios like us in Fredericksburg? I don't know how Laramie knew to question your little friend Joey, but he did that, too. They had me answering some pretty uncomfortable questions. The things they were saying about you . . . I'm sorry, Chadwick. I had to tell them about the Sheraton. Best I could do is warn you."

In the bathroom, the shower drizzled. Ann's voice hummed a soft tune that sounded like a lament.

Chadwick reached under the bed to retrieve his gun box,

then remembered he wasn't in his room. "Kindra, listen—any cops still at the school?"

"Three or four. Plus the sheriff. Why?"

"What are they doing?"

"Pissing off Hunter, mostly. They had a search warrant for your room. Hunter wouldn't let them search the rest of the lodge, so now they're waiting to get a new warrant faxed over. That guy from Oakland, the homicide sergeant—"

"Damarodas is there?"

"Yeah, the FBI dudes and he didn't get along too great. They left him here while they went after you. Damarodas wasn't too happy about that."

"What about Mallory?"

"I'm supposed to pick her up from the woods right now. Damarodas has a court order to see her. Hunter was going to fight it, but after the news from San Francisco . . ." She hesitated, as if waiting for him to finish her sentence.

"What news?"

"Don't yank my chain." Kindra's voice sounded brittle. "Did you do it, or not?"

"Should I pick an offense, or are you going to tell me?"

"John Zedman's body was found yesterday, in a town-house in the Mission. *Your* townhouse."

Chadwick stared at the clouds. He thought if he could just get to the window, crack it open and let the cold air sting him awake, he'd be okay. He'd realize Kindra's voice was just another sound he had misinterpreted in a dream.

"Zedman was shot dead," she said. "He was wrapped in a plastic shower curtain, driven into the city, hauled up a flight of stairs by somebody pretty strong, then stuffed in a small storage closet, doused in cologne to hide the smell. Sick shit, Chadwick. Killer could've just dumped the body in the ocean off Highway 1, but he wanted Zedman to rot in your old house, where your daughter died. Damarodas said the placement of the gunshot wounds was a lot like what happened to that kid nine years ago—Samuel Montrose. They figure the murder happened about the time you were in town, the night you and I separated."

Chadwick's mind fought the image, rejecting it like a splinter under the skin. He tried to remember John in his linen shirt and pajama bottoms, standing on his porch in Marin, the sunset at his back. John drunk on champagne, a $7,000 kindergarten quilt draped over his shoulders as he goaded Chadwick to show him karate moves. John clasping his shoulder, his breath stinking with gin, telling Chadwick that everything would be okay—they could tackle any problem. They had daughters to think about.

"Chadwick?" Kindra asked.

John could not be dead. Chadwick could not have spent the night with Ann—finally given up his guilt, tucked it under his bed for a few hours with his gun box—only to receive this news.

"Listen, Chadwick." Kindra's voice caught on his name. "Get off the phone, all right? Move. I don't care what you did, just get out of town. They catch you . . . Shit— I got to go."

The line went dead.

Bathroom faucets squeaked off. Pipes shuddered. The roar in Chadwick's ears didn't subside.

He stared at the LCD on his phone: *You have missed one call.*

He didn't want to retrieve the number. He figured the FBI wouldn't leave a message anyway. But he checked it, saw the San Francisco area code, the little envelope icon indicating voice mail. He replayed it.

Norma's voice: *"Pick up, Chadwick, you sorry pendejo. Race Montrose is here with me. Listen to him."*

The boy's voice came on the phone.

Chadwick listened, and for the first time he understood the trap closing around him. He saw everything he cared about destroyed, himself left alive to take the blame. And the last person to die would be the one Chadwick's conscience could least bear to lose.

He can describe her day, John had said. *He can tell me what she had for breakfast and where she slept and every punishment you put her through.*

Chadwick buttoned his shirt, tugged on his boots. He

thought of Mallory alone in the woods, her GPS bracelet blinking, betraying her exact position.

Ann came out of the bathroom wearing a White Level standard-issue towel, water beading on her shoulders. Her smile died when she saw his expression. "What is it?"

"Get dressed." He tossed her a blue dress from her suitcase. "The police are here. They think we're in San Antonio, only reason they haven't busted down the door yet."

"Bust down the door? Why?"

He told her the news—Pérez dead, John dead. He told her about the phone call from Norma and Race.

Her face, already flushed from the shower, turned redder. She crumpled the dress in her hands, threw it at his face. It expanded between them, the shell of a woman, then melted to the floor.

"You—did—this." Her words punctured the air like an ice pick. *"You* brought me here. You brought this on my daughter."

"Ann—"

"I should have insisted on seeing her, taking her home. But I stayed with you. I chose you over my family again. You pulled me off course, yanked me into some goddamn fantasy. Norma was right, Chadwick. She was right about you."

His chest hurt from her words, but he concentrated on Mallory—on the steady green blink of her GPS bracelet, the morning hike that would be taking her closer and closer to the dirt road that wended through the center of Cold Springs.

"Ann, listen. We're closer than anyone thinks—that's our only advantage. I know the pickup area. I can get to Mallory. But we're losing time."

"The police are here. You said so. Tell them."

"The sheriff won't believe us, even if we had time to persuade him. We have to get to Mallory *now.* Ourselves."

A knock on the door—hard, insistent.

Chadwick held Ann's eyes. If she opened that door, if she trusted the police, Mallory died. And yet, he knew there was no winning for him. Even if Ann trusted him, he felt certain he would leave this room having lost her—having finally awakened her to the fact that he was as good for her as a cold knife across her neck.

A muffled male voice told Ann to open up. The voice called her by name, announced himself as a police officer.

A screen rolled shut over Ann's face—the intimacy of last night, the tenuous happiness of five minutes before completely locked away.

"Go," she whispered. "I'll stall them. Go out the window."

"But—"

"My daughter," she said, her eyes hard. "Save her if you can, Chadwick, but I won't trust you with that alone. I'm talking to the police. I'll open the door whether you're here or not. Now get the hell out."

And then he was on the porch, and over the railing.

From his own balcony, Chadwick would've landed in the snow—a short, gentle slope, only a few feet from the concealment of the woods.

From Ann's balcony, he realized where he would land only mid-fall, after gravity made second thoughts impossible. He dropped straight onto the back deck of Hunter's office, crashing on top of a county deputy. The deputy's temple connected hard with the icy wooden railing on the way down. Hunter and Sergeant Damarodas stood three feet away, frozen in mid-conversation. In that second, Chadwick might've escaped—over the edge of the deck and into the trees—but by the time he recovered his own equilibrium, Damarodas had a pistol in his hand.

"Mr. Chadwick," he said. "You're working on your entrances."

"Stow it. Mallory Zedman is in danger."

Hunter and Damarodas traded looks, as if this continued a topic they'd just been discussing. Chadwick sensed a kind of reluctant alliance between them, and he registered what an odd pair they made—Asa in his brown Armani suit, his hundred-dollar silk tie, the outfit he reserved for courtrooms and television appearances; Damarodas looking like a fast-food restaurant manager in his polyester blends and his blue tie that might've been a child's clip-on. Only their expressions made them soul mates. They were soldiers pinned down in the same trench—men who had been forced to swallow a sour solution to a mutual problem.

"We got to stay right here, amigo," Hunter told him. "My lawyers are on the way. Until then, I'm afraid you've already given Laramie and Kreech enough rope."

"Asa, give me the GPS locator. Otherwise Mallory's going to die."

The tendons in Hunter's neck strained to burst his collar. "Jones is on the way to pick her up. Olsen is following her in the woods. She'll be all right."

"You're wrong." Then Chadwick told them about the call from Race Montrose. At Chadwick's feet, the crumpled deputy groaned, curling tighter into fetal position.

"The sheriff will never believe this shit," Damarodas said, but Chadwick could see his mind working furiously, fitting the pieces into place. "We leave this lodge, especially with an injured deputy lying there—we're going to bust open a legal shit-spout a mile high. Special Agent Laramie's gonna get a hell of a promotion."

"Damn," Hunter said. "God damn it—nobody fucks with my trust that way."

He reached in his coat pocket and threw Chadwick the GPS locator—a green bar of plastic the size of a deck of cards. "You'll never make it on the roads. Police got the gates blocked."

"Straight overland," Chadwick said. "Faster, impossible to follow. Gray levels should have the stables open by now."

"You're certifiable," Hunter told him. "Damarodas, give him your gun."

"What?"

"He overpowered you," Hunter said. "Remember?"

From somewhere inside the lodge, Sheriff Kreech's voice called out, "Mr. Hunter! Where the hell'd you go?"

Chadwick locked eyes with the sergeant.

Damarodas raised his gun. Then he dropped it, raised his

hands in surrender. "Shit-spout a mile high. I'm going to fuck-ing hate myself in the morning."

Chadwick scooped up his gun and hit the railing—tum-bling toward the woods and the river, where islands of snow were spinning downstream.

36

After her gory breakfast, Mallory cleaned up at the river as best she could. Her whole body was sore, her abdomen taut with menstrual cramps. She had no pads, no tissue, nothing except her clothes, but at least her flow wasn't as heavy as it had been the day before, and her uniform was black and already filthy.

She warmed herself by the fire until the wet sleeves of her jacket turned stiff and hot.

She wanted to bury the gutted shell of the armadillo. She owed the animal that much. But the ground was too hard to dig, even with her knife. Finally, she decided on cremation. She dropped the remains in the hot coals, and watched the tiny hairs curl to ash.

She adjusted the knife strap on her leg. She tugged at the GPS bracelet, still blinking on her wrist. She made sure her fire was out, the scorched armadillo shell covered in the ashes.

Mallory took one last look at her campsite—the hollow cypress tree where she'd spent the night, the bed of moss, the lean-to of snow-covered, woven branches. Not bad work, for cold hands in the dark.

A redtail hawk circled above. Mockingbirds rustled through the juniper branches, shaking off patches of snow as they pecked at the dusty blue berries.

She didn't want to leave the clearing. She felt connected with it, the same way she felt connected to that ratty stairwell where she and Race had made love. She would remember this place for a long time. It would hurt to remember. But she knew now that the important places almost always hurt.

The sky was overcast. She had nothing to guide her except a vague sense of where the sun had risen, so she struck out in that direction, hoping her course was easterly.

After a few miles of walking, she started hearing things behind her. Twigs snapped. Frozen leaves crackled. The skin on her neck prickled, and she felt the presence stalking her again.

She stopped to look back, but nothing was there. She was seized by the same irrational panic she used to have when she was young, taking swimming lessons at the Jewish Community Center, when she'd convinced herself there was a shark in the pool. She knew it was fantasy, but the terror made her claw up the wading steps all the same.

It was late morning when Mallory heard another sound directly ahead—a distant rumble that wasn't the river. It took her a moment to remember the sound of a car on a dirt road. The strange thing was, her impulse to turn away from it was as strong as her impulse to run toward it.

The presence behind her decided matters. She walked until she saw an opening through the trees.

The road was barely wide enough for one car, bulldozed shoulders piled high with frozen mud clods and clumps of cactus salted with frost.

She had a moment of doubt, wondering if this were the right road. If it was, where was the car she'd heard? Why hadn't it stopped? Perhaps she'd come out of the woods at the wrong place, maybe even on someone else's property.

What would she do if someone came along who wasn't from Cold Springs? She would look like a wild girl—an escaped killer with blood on her hands and her clothes. For a moment, she felt dizzy. Why had Hunter let her do this? What would keep her from hitching a ride again, escaping? She could bust off the GPS bracelet, be gone before anyone realized.

Then she realized how stupid that was. Where would she think of going?

Home was Cold Springs. No one else would understand what she'd gone through. Her team might. Olsen might. She wasn't going to leave until she found out what had happened to the others, until she was sure they all made it through the solo trip safely.

She reviewed her promise that she would talk to Olsen. It seemed scarier in the light of day, with the road in front of her. But she steeled herself. She would come clean. First opportunity. She owed it to her father. And to herself.

There had been no clear instructions about what to do once she found the road, so she decided to walk down it for a while, see what happened. Olsen had said they'd meet her this morning. Mallory didn't know if she was late, or how far into the morning Olsen had meant.

She walked toward what she assumed was north, thinking that this would be the way back to the main lodge. She imagined Dr. Hunter's face, all the counselors' faces, if she were to appear back at camp on foot, voluntarily returning. The idea made her smile.

Then she heard rustling, louder than before, the bushes right next to her parting. Before she even had time to grab her knife, Olsen appeared from the underbrush. "Well, kiddo, I had my doubts."

She wore a camouflage jacket over black fatigues. She was spattered with ice and mud, and grass stuck out of her short blond hair, but she grinned at Mallory with an enthusiasm Mallory found hard to decipher. It had been a long time since anyone beamed at her with pride.

Mallory relaxed a little, but she still felt invaded, watched. "You were tracking me?"

Olsen held up her gear—binoculars, a receiver for the GPS unit, an extra med kit. "You didn't make it easy, kiddo. But yes, I followed you. Good job."

Mallory's first opportunity to speak, just like she'd promised herself. But she couldn't get over her shock.

She understood Olsen being here. It made sense Hunter would have someone tracking her, just in case she got in serious trouble, but it seemed wrong that Olsen would reveal herself now, ruining the illusion that Mallory had been alone. It somehow undercut what Mallory had done. And the presence behind her in the woods had seemed evil, hateful, which didn't jibe with Olsen's smile. But Mallory had probably just imagined an evil intent, the way she imagined the shark.

Stick to your plan, she told herself. *Trust her. Tell her.*

Mallory was trying to get up the nerve to start when she saw the Cold Springs transport backing up toward them—a big blue van, reverse lights flaring white.

It stopped ten feet away. Kindra Jones got out of the driver's side and came around the front. She could've been stepping straight off of Haight Street—patent leather boots, corduroy slacks, flannel jacket and horn-rims, gold nose stud and rust hair pulled back in cornrows. Clean and showered— no blood or mud stains anywhere. An ambassador from the real world.

Just looking at her made Mallory's legs wobbly.

"Welcome back, girls," Jones said. "Sorry I overshot. Ain't used to this GPS stuff."

Mallory looked at the van, saw no one inside. "Where are the others?"

Jones hesitated, and Mallory knew something was wrong. "Leyland took them back to the lodge. Dr. Hunter asked me to come out and get you."

"Why separate vans?" Olsen asked.

Jones peered over her horn-rims. "Weren't you supposed to hike back alone, Miss Olsen? Isn't that normal procedure?"

"Mallory's Survival Week hasn't been exactly normal. I wanted to stick with her."

Mallory could feel the tension crackle between the two women, a quiet animosity that singed the air.

"Get in," Jones said. "It's too damn cold out here."

Olsen climbed in the shotgun seat. Mallory got in the back, disoriented by the smoothness of the upholstery, the pine air freshener, the heater going full blast. The doors rolled shut and the van headed away from the wilderness.

Mallory watched the live oaks go past, the cactus, white-tail deer raising their heads in the clearings as the van drove by. Morrison and Bridges would be waiting back at the lodge. There would be time to talk about their adventures. New privileges. All of Gray Level ahead of them. She didn't want to jeopardize that. She didn't want to tell her secret.

After a mile of slushy mud road, Jones said, "You tired of that bracelet?"

"A little," Mallory admitted.

"I got a key I can sell you."

In the rearview mirror, Jones' smile reminded her of Race's, on those rare moments he allowed himself to smile. She tossed Mallory a little metal rod that slipped into the bracelet's joint.

Olsen shot Jones a disapproving look. "Shouldn't you wait until we get back?"

"We're not following normal procedure, remember? She won't run. Will you, Mal?"

Mallory's hands trembled. She clicked the bracelet open, set it on the drink holder between the front seats. She rubbed at the pale skin of her wrist. She'd only worn the bracelet twenty-four hours, but taking it off made her feel exposed, the way she'd felt when she'd lost Katherine's necklace.

"I need to say something," she told the two women. "Something important."

Jones raised her eyebrows. "Doesn't bother me. Bother you, Miss Olsen?"

Olsen glared at her wristwatch, as if trying to contain her anger with Kindra Jones, the way she'd told Mallory to do on Thanksgiving, so long ago. *Ten minutes without an outburst. Starting now.*

Then she turned, tucked her left foot under her, forcing her attention back on Mallory with an insincere smile. "Go ahead, kiddo. What's on your mind?"

Mallory wanted to back out. She wanted to wait until Olsen wasn't angry, until Kindra wasn't around. The timing was bad. It would be easier to do nothing.

But that was the danger. It was always safer to do nothing—to curl up in the black leather chair, sit paralyzed with fear, stare at the doorway and hope no one died. If she waited until the lodge, she would get caught up in Gray Level. She would lose her courage to speak. Part of her would curl up in that chair and be six years old forever. She drew a shaky breath.

"The night Katherine Chadwick committed suicide, I saw a girl on the porch of the Montrose house. She talked to Katherine, handed her a brown bag, then went inside. It was only for a second, but I saw her. It was you, Ms. Jones."

For a moment, neither woman reacted. Then Jones laughed.

"Me? You think I dealt drugs for Chadwick's daughter?"

"You're Race's sister."

Olsen was watching them as if they'd just pulled some elaborate magic stunt. "What is she talking about? Jones?"

Jones said nothing.

They had reached the end of the mud road, the far edge of Hunter's kingdom, where a paved farm to market T'ed to the left and right, fields of corn and sorghum spreading out before them. Jones yanked the wheel hard to the left, throwing Mallory into the arm of the passenger's seat.

"What the hell are you doing?" Olsen snapped.

Jones cracked her window, threw out the GPS bracelet. "Relax, counselor."

"That was a three-hundred-dollar piece of equipment. The school's the other way."

"We're making a little detour."

Olsen looked back at Mallory, asking a silent question.

In the rearview mirror, Jones' expression was hardening—making her look very much like Race, but not Race... like some other enraged teenage boy.

Mallory thought of the river somewhere behind them, her lost backpack floating down toward the sea, or maybe stuck to some frozen branch, water breaking around it in a velvety arc. She wished she could trade places with the backpack right now, take her chances with the rapids.

"You're the older sister," she said. "I thought... when Race talked about his sister getting protected by Samuel, being sent away to live with her real dad, I thought he meant his pregnant sister in L.A., Doreen. But Doreen would've been a baby back then. He meant you. Talia's first husband—the guy's name was Johnny Jay. J for Jones."

"That were true, Ms. Detective, what the hell am I doing here?"

"Keeping an eye on me, using me as leverage against my dad. You were blackmailing him. You forced him to steal the school's money for you. He did it because he knew you'd kill me if he didn't cooperate."

"Man, I'm devious."

"Is she right?" Olsen asked.

Jones spun the car onto another side road. A quarter mile down, she pulled over with the driver's side wedged against a wall of corn, hit the unlock button for the doors. "Everybody out."

There was nothing outside—just icy road and cornfields. The van had a sliding door on the left side, behind the driver's seat, pressed up against the corn. Mallory's fingers wrapped around the handle.

"Jones," Olsen said, "start the car."

"We need to get out and talk." Jones' hand reached into her coat by her hip, as if she were unfastening her seatbelt. "The girl is partly right. I'm Race's sister."

"You're *what?*"

"I'm here because of Chadwick." Kindra looked back at Mallory, her eyes burning with intensity—Race's eyes, the moment he'd seen his mother dead. "Chadwick's the one you should be worried about, Mallory. He's a fucking monster. He killed Emilio Pérez the night after we talked to him. He killed my brother Samuel. And I'll tell you something else Olsen doesn't want you to know—Chadwick killed your dad."

"No." Olsen was shaking her head. "Mallory, he did no such thing."

"She doesn't want you to hear it. Your dad was found last night. Dead in Chadwick's old house. Shot three times, stuffed in a closet. Chadwick did that. And you'd better ask yourself why Olsen isn't surprised by the news, even though she was out in the woods with you all night."

Mallory's heart was unraveling into veins and arteries. This couldn't be true. None of it.

"You're the monster," Olsen told Kindra. "Mallory—don't listen to her. Chadwick would never do that. My backpack is behind you. Get the phone out. Do it now."

"Okay," Jones conceded placidly. "You don't want to get out of the car? That's fine. Messier, but fine."

The gunshot jerked Olsen back in her seat like an electric shock. She gripped her abdomen with both hands, gaped at Jones in disbelief, blood oozing through her fingers.

Mallory couldn't breathe, couldn't make her limbs obey.

Olsen opened her mouth, as if to protest, and a second gunshot blew a hole just above her kneecap, red mist erupting from the wound like a comet tail.

Mallory's brain managed one blunt command to her body: *Move.*

She shoved open her door and dove into the corn. The gun fired again. Glass shattered—the window where her head had been a moment before.

Mallory clattered away through the corn, her ears ringing. She couldn't see, could only feel the corn cutting into her, slashing at her sleeves.

"Come on, Mallory," Jones yelled, somewhere behind her. "You're running from the wrong person."

Mallory kept running. The gun fired again, a bullet hissing through a corn stalk inches from her ear.

Stupid, she scolded herself. *Jones can see the corn moving.*

She dove down, pressed herself into the snow.

She heard Jones picking her way across the field, slowly coming toward her.

"Mallory, I don't have a problem with you. But Chadwick is a killer. Katherine's death really messed him up. You got to see that."

Mallory knew the words were a lie. Jones had brought her to this field to die.

But her father . . . she pictured him huddled in the cabinet at Katherine's house, in the secret space where she'd played hide-and-seek among the broken clock parts. She imagined a gunshot wound opening in her father's chest, his hand clutching at the blood, his eyes wide with dismay. She wanted to cry. She wanted someone to blame.

"Olsen was helping him." Kindra Jones was rustling through the corn, getting closer to her. "They had the whole thing planned. You see that, don't you? Chadwick hates your parents. He hates you. You survived and his precious daughter didn't. Katherine was my friend, Mallory—she told me what her father was like. She killed herself because of *him,* because she knew what he was like and she couldn't live with the truth anymore. I'm here to stop him. I can't rely on the police to do that. I'm here to protect you and Race. That's Samuel's job, honey. That's what a big brother does."

"No," Mallory protested, realizing too late that she'd spoken aloud.

The rustling stopped.

Mallory heard a sound in the distance like horse's hooves, but it was only in her mind—her own heart hammering.

Survival rules. Survey. Organize. Strategize.

What was there to survey? Jones was strong. She was armed, and intended to kill her. Mallory was going to die.

No. Not without a fight.

She felt around her, found a peach-sized stone, smooth and heavy.

The rustling started again, then Mallory saw a patch of green, Jones' flannel jacket, and threw her stone as high and as far away as possible.

Somewhere off to the north, the rock splashed in the corn. Jones stopped, then her green flannel receded. She'd taken the bait. Now her back would be to Mallory.

Mallory slid her knife from its sheath, rose to a crouch.

"I'm going to leave here today, Mallory," Jones was calling. "El Salvador, buy me a house on the beach."

Keep talking, Mallory thought. *Give me a target.*

"No extradition, Mal. Nobody asking questions as long as you got money. You can come with me. You and Race both. New house, a new life. You ever been to the beaches in Central America, honey? I hear . . ."

Kindra's voice trailed off, and Mallory realized the clumping sound she'd heard before had become louder—a heartbeat against the earth.

The rhythm slowed to a patter, and she heard a man's voice, followed by Olsen's broken murmur.

Mallory's ears had to be deceiving her.

She glimpsed the patch of green again, directly ahead—Kindra's jacket. Mallory was considering a knife throw—remembering her four-in-ten average back in camp, Leyland telling her that was damn good for a novice. Four-in-ten, life and death, against a moving target. She was weighing those piss-poor odds when Chadwick's voice shouted her name.

There he was, rising above the corn on the back of the bay filly from Cold Springs—riding a goddamn horse, like goddamn George Washington. All her life she'd heard that's who he looked like, but she'd never seen the resemblance until now.

The bay's coat was glossy with sweat. Chadwick's clothes were torn and water-stained as if he'd ridden through a million tree branches to get here.

Their eyes met. Mallory couldn't say anything. She couldn't warn him; she couldn't even decide if she wanted to. She thought of when she was small—how she'd believed Katherine was so lucky having Chadwick as a father, a silent, gentle giant who would always protect her. And now here he was, riding to her rescue. Mallory wanted to cry. She wanted to break down and yell at him to watch out. But she couldn't do it. She resented him. He was a false hope, a hallucination—a chemical glitch of adrenaline and hormones and heroin withdrawal. Chadwick couldn't have ridden all this way in one morning. He would've had to start at dawn, before he even knew she was in trouble.

Chadwick's eyes were trying to communicate a thousand things. Then his attention turned—he must've seen Kindra Jones. He raised an old-fashioned revolver, but Jones had had plenty of time to aim. A shot thundered, the horse whinnied in pain and toppled, taking Chadwick with it. There was a sickening crunch, then the sound of the horse huffing, thrashing through the stalks.

When the commotion died down, Mallory heard Jones say, "Well, lookee here. My partner."

"Mallory." Chadwick's voice was tight with pain. "Run. Get out of here."

Mallory edged closer, knowing it was crazy. She could see through the screen of corn plants—Kindra standing over Chadwick, his leg bent at an unnatural angle. Chadwick's gun was gone. The horse was nowhere in sight. Blood painted a trail of crushed corn plants where the wounded animal must've gotten back on its hooves and run away.

Kindra paced around Chadwick, keeping the gun barrel trained on his head. "Samuel says hello, Chad. He says you should've stayed with your lady friend this morning."

"You've got the money from Laurel Heights. Twenty-seven million dollars."

"Not bad for an Oakland girl with a teaching degree. You find teaching rewarding, Chadwick? Shit, I do."

"You have what you want. Walk away."

Kindra's smile seemed sleepy, her eyes half lidded behind her glasses. "Katherine tells me you're right. She says to go on—catch my plane. She was hoping you'd stay at the hotel this morning, get caught by the FBI. I could live with that, Chadwick, knowing you'd spend the rest of your life in a fucking prison. But, see, here you are."

Mallory heard sirens in the distance.

Kindra kept pacing, ignoring the sound. "I don't know how you got here so fast. Calls for some flexibility, but I'm flexible. Hell, ten fucking years I've lived Samuel's life as well as mine—I'm damn flexible. All those years leading up to this. Right here, with you."

"You killed your own mother, John Zedman, Pérez. The police know about you, Kindra. Race came forward with the whole story. The police are on their way."

She laughed, but the sound was brittle. "Race, huh? Race did that." She yelled, "You hear him, Mallory? This killer, he blames me. He talks about the police, like he really wants to meet them. Come on out, honey. I want you to see this. Be good for you—closure, what your counselor would say. A real live abuser doll about to get crushed."

"Forget the girl," Chadwick said. "Let her go."

"You shouldn't have given my little brother your card, Chadwick. Not after what you've done to my family. You shouldn't have tried to protect me from those rednecks at that truck stop. There's only one protector in my family. Only one person who can do what needs to be done. Kill that bastard Ali. Take care of Race. Take care of Kindra. Katherine's talking to me now, Chadwick. She's pleading with me to spare your sorry-ass life. But I'm finally going to get her voice out of my head. I'm going to listen to Samuel on this one."

And Mallory suddenly understood her anger. She suddenly understood Jones. She remembered the rage that had made her take a hammer to her mother's apartment, let out nine years of hate, blaming her parents for what she'd become—for the path she'd started the night Katherine died.

The sirens kept wailing, closer now.

Mallory could run—get away clean, nothing but the dry snap of a gun discharge behind her. Nothing on her conscience. Justice served.

But she imagined Olsen's voice—Olsen, whose last words had been about trusting Chadwick. Olsen saying, *Some connections, you can't break.* Olsen, who was dead in a welter of blood in the front seat of the van.

"Mallory." Chadwick spoke her name in a tone she hadn't heard for a long time—since nine years ago, when he used to talk to Katherine. "Your father loved you. He was doing everything he could to protect you. If he were here, he would tell you he's sorry. He did the wrong things for the right reasons. Please believe me, that's what he would say."

Kindra raised her gun.

Mallory's heart shifted like a gyroscope.

She rose to her feet and rushed Jones like she was the obstacle course wall—closing five yards, the gun turning in her direction, the snap of a bullet ripping past her ear, but nothing mattered except clearing the obstacle. Mallory's shoulder slammed into Jones' chest so hard she felt ribs crack. Jones staggered backwards, collapsing into the frozen cornstalks, and Mallory gripped the knife in her hand, putting herself between Jones and Chadwick.

"Don't protect me," Chadwick groaned. "Run."

But Mallory had finally outgrown Chadwick's advice.

Wincing, Jones rose to a crouch, a dozen feet away. She looked dazed, but pleasantly surprised that Mallory had shown herself. "Katherine loves you, too, honey. Believe me, that's what she's saying."

The gun was still in Jones' hand. Her eyes were amber, just like her brother's.

She raised the gun toward Mallory, and with every ounce of strength, as if with willpower alone could drive steel through the trunk of a tree, Mallory threw the knife.

37

The next week was Christmas at Cold Springs, and a front blew up from the Rio Grande, bringing dry Mexican air that smelled of sage and brush fires. Sunshine soaked the hills until rattlesnakes came out to warm themselves on the granite and the deer became nocturnal.

Chadwick spent his days proctoring White Level study halls on the main deck, learning to walk with a boot cast, and coming to terms with the fact that he'd been yanked back from the edge of the precipice. He tried to convince himself that the danger had passed, that there was nothing else he needed to do.

On Christmas Eve, Olsen was released from the hospital in San Antonio. She arrived at the lodge to find most of the staff waiting for her, holding a welcome banner the tan levels had made in art therapy class. She insisted on getting out of her wheelchair and walking the twenty feet from the parking space to the door, Asa Hunter holding her arm. She smiled as the counselors applauded, but her face was clammy white, slick with sweat from the effort.

The doctors had told her how lucky she was. The shot to the leg had missed both artery and bone. The shot meant for her gut had instead drilled a hole through the muscles of her flank, narrowly missing her intestines. The surgeon speculated that the bulkiness of Olsen's winter jacket had saved her life, obscuring her form so that Jones' shot had been off-center.

Chadwick had a different theory. Jones wanted pain. She wanted Olsen's death to be as slow as possible, so she could return when she was done with her bloody work in the corn-fields and sit next to the dying counselor, memorize Olsen's voice, add it to the chorus raging inside her head.

Chadwick skipped the staff Christmas party. He stayed in his apartment that night, listening to Nat King Cole drifting up from downstairs. He lay on his bed and held Katherine's pic-ture in his hands—the little girl in the morning glories.

In a few weeks, Mallory Zedman would turn sixteen, Katherine's age. But her eyes, as she turned to him in the corn-field, her face speckled with blood, told him Mallory had grown older than Katherine ever was.

His sheets still smelled faintly of Ann. He thought of the afternoon he'd told her goodbye, Ann struggling for compre-hension as Dr. Hunter broke the news that her daughter—who'd just killed a woman in self-defense, had also splinted Chadwick's broken leg and stopped the bleeding in Olsen's thigh, all with the numb, mechanical efficiency of a sleep-walker—couldn't face the idea of seeing her mother.

Ann could've raised hell, could've insisted. It would've been the only bright point in Sheriff Kreech's day to help her battle the school, after he'd been deprived the pleasure of ar-resting anyone. Even Chadwick's assault on the officer had been explained away as accidental, thanks to Damarodas, and after the media got involved, making Chadwick into a hero on horseback, Kreech arresting him over a little thing like flattening a deputy would've looked downright trivial. But Ann hadn't asked for Kreech's help. She had complied with Mallory's wishes, hiding her hurt behind resentful silence, and one of the instructors, a stranger, had driven her to the airport.

Chadwick set Katherine's picture on the nightstand, trac-ing the arc of blue flowers around her head. He drifted to sleep, thinking about Mallory's hard new eyes, the sound of "Adeste Fidelis" coming from the Christmas party below.

Christmas Day dawned no different than any other. White levels assembled on the deck to work on their SATs. Tan levels cleaned the lodge fireplace and swept the floors. From the cafeteria, Chadwick could hear trainers' whistles and yelling down at Clearing One—a new team of black levels being broken in, drilled into the program.

After breakfast, he met Hunter and Olsen outside, and together they walked down the long dirt road toward the stables. Chadwick's broken calf-bone ached, despite the boot cast and enough Tylenol coursing through his system to kill a warthog. He didn't complain though, because Olsen didn't complain. She would grab his shoulder every few feet to steady herself, her other hand clamped on Hunter's forearm. She wore her old escort clothes—the denim jacket concealing the bulky bandages on her side. Her forehead was beaded with sweat. She walked with the slow determination of a nursing home patient.

"Probably look like those patriot guys," she managed. "Marching all banged up. Need a fife and drum."

"I ain't wearing no damn sash on my head," Hunter said.

"We can stop," Chadwick offered. "Bring her to the lodge."

"No," Olsen said. "She's been pulled around enough. The least I can do is go to her."

Hunter's mouth tightened with concern, but he winked at Chadwick, a little flare of pride in his eyes, gratification for Olsen's toughness.

Hunter seemed changed in recent days—more paternal toward the staff, especially toward Olsen. Chadwick knew Kindra's treachery had cut him deeply, made him angrier than he'd been in a long time. But rather than throw a knife into a tree, or chuck Special Agent Laramie off the top of a ropes course platform, Hunter had chosen to channel all his anger into making sure his people were okay. He spent more time at the staff parties, worked less in his darkened office, staring at the security monitors. He'd started dressing in gray fatigues, as if he were the one who had advanced a level. He even attended his first-ever county Chamber of Commerce luncheon, trying to make amends with the community.

They followed the road past the cattle workers, where the newest recruit, Mallory's old team member Bridges, was staring with apprehension at the school's training herd, ten head of Charolais. One of the ranch hands was giving him his first lesson in bovine logic—the nature of cow paths. "They always walk in a straight line, Bridges. They follow the leader. Take a lesson from that."

The girl Morrison had chosen carpentry. She was out in the field with the veteran gray levels, raising an A-frame for a new barn.

A hundred yards farther down, Mallory Zedman stood inside the split-rail fence of the pasture. She stroked her bristle brush over the bay mare's coat the way Joey Allbritton showed her, careful to avoid the gunshot wound in the withers that had felled the animal seven days ago in the cornfield.

Hunter motioned for Joey to come over.

Hunter told Chadwick, "I'll leave you all to it. Joey and I need to talk some horse-trading."

Hunter circled an arm around Joey's shoulders and led him out of earshot, down toward the granite cliffs overlooking the river.

Chadwick and Olsen approached Mallory, who had stopped her work and was standing at attention. She had that determined, dogged look that characterized Gray Level—the look of a small child tying a shoe, or a grown-up putting together an "easy-to-assemble" bookshelf. Gray Level was all about motion, working with one's hands. They didn't like standing at attention. Their byword was competence, and they quickly learned that everything was a skill to be remastered—not just their new ranch work, but eating, talking, thinking. Gray levels were constantly busy, sorting through the pieces of their old frustrations and failures, learning how to reassemble them, putting tab A into slot B.

"At ease," Chadwick told her. "How's your equine friend doing?"

"The veterinarian says the muscles will mend in a few weeks, sir. She won't be saddle-ready for a while, though."

The bay filly gave Chadwick a wide yellow eye, maybe remembering what had happened the last time he'd taken her out riding. She snorted—horse language for *Get the hell away from me.* Mallory took her reins to keep her from shying off.

Then, as if the sun were in her eyes, Mallory took a reluctant glance at Olsen. "How are you?"

"I'll live, kiddo. Thanks to you."

Mallory blushed. She ran her bristle brush over the horse's glossy hide, which twitched as if anticipating another gunshot.

By Hunter's order, no one was allowed to talk about the incident that made Mallory a hero, no one was allowed to make her feel different than any other gray level, but they all did anyway. Even new black levels had heard about Mallory Zedman, how she had stopped a killer with her hunting knife, saved her counselor's life. Her heroism had impressed the locals, had played briefly on national news at the culmination of what the media liked to call the Laurel Heights Affair. In one of those bizarre twists of fate that had built Hunter's empire, a potential PR nightmare had turned into a huge boon for business. AM radio talk shows touted Mallory as the product of a successful program—from a drug-addicted rebel who attacked her own mother to a self-reliant young woman who defended herself and saved two lives. Admissions calls were up fifteen percent. Offers to Dr. Hunter for television appearances and how-to-parent book contracts were rolling in. Even Chadwick found it rather frightening.

"I came to tell you goodbye," Olsen told Mallory.

Mallory picked a horse hair out of her brush. "Yeah. I figured."

"I'm going back to escorting. It's best you have a counselor who's not . . . involved in what happened. You understand?"

"You got what you needed from me. Now you're moving on."

"It isn't like that. You're my friend. I'll never move on. It's just . . . we're a little too close to each other, Mallory. You've got to step away from the mirror a little if you want to see anything."

Olsen held out her hand. Mallory hesitated, then took it.

When she released her grip, Olsen looked at Chadwick, ready to go.

If he was going to say something, now was the time. He had gone over the possibilities for days, rehearsing what he might say. But now, with Mallory in front of him, the words evaporated.

"I hear you're a natural with horses," he tried. "Star pupil."

"I'm doing my best, sir."

"Your father would be proud."

A shadow crossed over her face. "You blame me for not seeing my mom?"

"No. You have time for that. Your mother does, too."

Mallory stared at the horse, and Chadwick realized, with uncomfortable certainty, that Mallory didn't need anything else from him. She wanted him to leave. He was complicating matters, making her uncomfortable.

"I'll be going to see her next week," Chadwick said. "Laurel Heights is having the ground-breaking ceremony. In case you want me to tell her something."

"Yes, sir. Tell her that gun in Race's locker? It wasn't his. It was mine. He was protecting me. He didn't know a thing about it."

She wouldn't meet his eyes.

He knew she was lying about the gun. She hadn't put it in that locker. But he also knew why she was doing it—taking the heat for her friend, giving the school someone else to blame.

"You sure you want me to tell your mother that?" he asked.

She nodded. "I'm the one she needed to expel. Not Race. Tell her that."

"Anything else?"

"No. But, Miss Olsen?"

"Yes?"

"Apples are bad for them."

"What?"

"Apples. For horses. They like them, but there's too much sugar, traces of cyanide in the seeds. They eat too much, they'll get poisoned. In case you wanted to know, for next time."

Mallory went back to combing her wounded horse, as if Olsen and Chadwick were spectators who had seen the whole show, and now—surely—they must have reassembly work to get back to, like everybody else.

Chadwick wanted more—closure, closeness, that time he'd never gotten with his daughter. But Mallory was farther away from him now than she'd been a month ago, at the Rockridge café.

Teens defined themselves by separating from adults. Chadwick knew that. But he'd fought the process with Katherine, and the battle had never been resolved. Now Mallory was done with him, the same way she'd accused Olsen of being done with her. He had ridden to her rescue, but he'd failed to save her. And maybe, he realized—that was the whole point. Maybe his failure had given her exactly what she needed.

Hunter shook hands with Joey Allbritton, then came to rejoin them.

They walked back to the lodge in silence, Olsen's hand tight on Chadwick's shoulder, Hunter's bald scalp reflecting the winter sun like candlelight in chocolate.

"You get better fast," he told them. "We got a lot of business coming in. A lot of pickups."

"The price of notoriety," Chadwick said.

When they got to the door, Hunter put his arm out to block Chadwick's entry. "You're gonna take care of this girl, I hope. 'Cause if you lose her again, I'm gonna start assigning you only the jobs that come from New Jersey."

"I'll consider myself terrified."

Olsen gave him a wan smile. "Hunter's driving me into Fredericksburg this morning for physical therapy. You want to come along?"

"On Christmas Day?"

"I have an atheist boss and a Jewish physical therapist. Come on. We can find someplace open for lunch afterward, go over the case files for next week."

"Sure," Hunter griped. "Make it a business lunch, so I have to pay for it."

Chadwick felt a lump in his throat—grateful that he had friends, grateful that Olsen had given escorting—and him—a second chance. But he also knew his facade was about to crumble, the intricate patchwork of shock and adrenaline and false composure he'd relied on the last few weeks—hell, the last nine years. Now that he was out of danger, now that Mallory was safe, he felt that shell breaking up at last, and he wasn't quite sure what was underneath.

"You go ahead," he told them. "I'd better elevate my foot, maybe catch up on my reading."

Chadwick went inside, focusing his eyes on the cactus petal wreath that hung over the lodge fireplace, telling himself he could make it a few more steps, just to the stairs that led to his apartment.

Olsen and Hunter stood in the entry hall, watching Chadwick walk away. He moved up the stairs as if the pain he was worried about was in his chest rather than his leg.

"It's still hard for him," Hunter told her. "All that guilt over Katherine, stirred up again. I hope to hell that'll pass now."

"I wish I understood him," Olsen said.

"I've been working on that thirty years. It's a good hobby, but don't quit your day job."

Hunter held the door for her, let in a gust of Christmas morning air that smelled of wood smoke.

Olsen stepped outside, thinking about her own family— her little sister, her mother, her former stepfather in prison. She was ready to trust Chadwick. She had put aside her fear of leaving Mallory, her fear of believing a man could actually be a good and caring person, even if he did remind her of the father figure who had betrayed her. She was willing to believe, for the first time in her life, that there might be good men in the world, and she had stumbled across two of them in Hunter and Chadwick.

"I don't understand why he kept sabotaging himself," she told Hunter. "Even at the end, he couldn't fire on Kindra."

"Easy for us to replay it, with hindsight, say what he should've done."

"I almost think part of him wanted to get killed. Punished. I'm not sure why—whether that's about Katherine, or what happened in Thailand."

Hunter gave her a strange look. "What makes you say that?"

"Before I changed to counseling, I asked him about the day Race Montrose drew a gun on him, why he froze up... Chadwick told me about that Thai boy—the one you and he had to shoot in the Air Force, on guard duty. He told me that story."

Hunter stared off into the distance. "Did he?"

"He said that's why he hates using a gun."

She could see Hunter pulling the blinds over his thoughts, shutting himself off, backtracking from the new closeness they'd been developing all week. "Chadwick tells you something, he must have his reasons," Hunter said.

And before he got his expression completely under control, she saw the discomfort in his eyes, his intense desire to close ranks to protect a friend, even if he didn't understand the nature of the threat.

Truth sank into her like a stone, leaving slow heavy ripples.

She gripped the railing of the deck, the pain from the gunshot wound in her side suddenly making her dizzy.

38

The next Saturday at Laurel Heights, decorations from the canceled auction were finally put to use. Satin ribbons fluttered from the chain link fence. Loops of yellow and pink crepe paper coiled down the staircase railing. Classroom chairs were set outside in rows, with helium balloons tied to the legs, so the basketball court looked like a lollipop orchard.

Chadwick and Olsen left the seats for the paying customers—parents still arriving with kids in tow, bringing baskets of homemade sugar cookies and bundt cakes and coolers of lemonade for the reception.

The major construction would not start until the summer, but Ann had insisted on having the ground-breaking ceremony now, to mark the new year, and the restoration of a dream.

She had convinced the construction company to pour wet cement for a new sidewalk in the little yard behind the building, so the children could put their names on the project from the beginning. Already, most of the younger kids were running around with sticky white hands, their parents scrubbing the cement off with cocktail napkins, wincing as some got smeared on pleated slacks and taffeta skirts. Finally, the teachers cordoned off the yard, deciding that their overzealous headmistress's cement maybe wasn't such a good idea after all.

Middle- and upper-schoolers, much too cool to get their hands dirty, hung out on the back deck, shoving each other, talking too loud, showing off their new hair dyes—fuchsia and green and indigo.

At the edge of the group sat Race Montrose, the only

high-schooler who'd heeded the dress code for the event and worn a jacket and tie. His clothes underscored what was already obvious from the body language of the other teens—Race could sit with them, but he would never be one of them.

Chadwick's mouth tasted like metal. He wished he could force the kids to be nicer, but he knew the parent gossip network at Laurel Heights had been hard at work, disseminating the lurid details of the damaged life of Race's sister. They made sure everyone understood that Kindra Jones had murdered at least three people, including her own mother. She had targeted Laurel Heights and the Zedman family for destruction. And as evidenced by her grandmother, schizophrenia ran in the Montrose family.

The media had painted Race as the victim, living in fear for years, used as a pawn for his sister's malicious revenge. In the end, he had cooperated with the police. He had helped save Mallory's life, helped recover the stolen Laurel Heights funds by leading the police to Kindra's condominium, where the new account numbers were found. Even the gun in his locker, which had gotten him expelled in the first place, had been claimed by Mallory.

Still, the parents didn't want him back. The kids didn't want to deal with him. Chadwick could see it in their eyes, their raised shoulders, their stiffened necks. They ignored Race the way drivers ignore a flower-seller at a busy intersection. It would have been much more convenient, much easier, for all of them if Race Montrose just went away.

But Ann wouldn't let it happen.

The school board, smelling a wrongful termination lawsuit, had fallen over themselves reversing course on their treatment of Ann. She had agreed to resume her duties with no hard feelings and no legal action, as long as Race was part of the general amnesty.

Race was reinstated at Laurel Heights with a formal apology and no mark on his record. A family of alumni had even agreed to be his temporary foster family while the courts decided who would get custody.

Ann lost families over her defense of Race. Many came

back after the money scandal cleared, but others had not—not if their children had to go to school with *that* boy. Ann stuck by her guns. Race Montrose would not be punished for what his sister had done.

When she told Chadwick this over the phone, he wanted to slug the parents who disagreed with her. He wanted to break his nine-year edict of never, ever criticizing another parent, and ask what the hell they thought they were teaching their kids. He almost wanted to reconsider the offer Ann had made him during that phone conversation. Almost.

Even now, watching her step up to the PA system, he was tempted.

She called for everyone's attention with an old brass bell that had been sitting on her desk for years. Chadwick had never heard it ring. As the kindergarteners scampered into place and the last parents took their seats, Ann wrapped her hands around the corners of the podium.

"We made it," she announced, with all the certainty, all the absolute conviction of Asa Hunter on the drill line. "After a long hard fight and a few bad moments—"

She paused for nervous laughter.

"—we realized our goal. I'd like to thank Mark Jasper, our board chairman, for steering us through the crisis and soliciting the last three million dollars . . ."

Healthy applause. The man with the graying ponytail and the denim clothes waved, his eye twitching as Ann looked back at him—and Chadwick could tell he was a man who had lost a battle.

"And Norma Reyes," Ann continued, "for all her hard work."

More applause, a few appreciative whoops, a shout of *Ay, qué pico!* from one of the Latino parents. Norma waved the praise off with a grin.

"And David Kraft," Ann continued, "who couldn't be with us today, but who worked very hard to see this moment."

Halfhearted applause. Probably no one at the school had known David that well, any more than they had known him a decade ago, when he was a student.

According to Sergeant Damarodas, who had taken to giving Chadwick regular phone calls as a form of lingering punishment, David had disappeared shortly after the school scandal broke. His blue SUV had been found at the West Oakland BART station, no keys in the ignition, no signs of foul play. Missing Persons and Homicide had been notified, but David's parents told them that he'd packed his clothes before disappearing. They said David had been talking for some time about moving away, starting over, and they seemed relieved that he'd finally done it. Chadwick wasn't surprised. He wished the young man well. He thought it would be sad if the police treated him like a runaway child, rather than an adult who had the right to disappear. He hoped David finally found a place where he fit in.

Ann closed with a few comments about the construction, the new Laurel Heights they all would create together. She gestured to the corner of the court, where a small patch of asphalt had been jackhammered open, revealing soil that had not seen daylight in eighty years. This, she said, would be where the first foundation pylon was planted. She asked Norma Reyes to help her overturn the first spadeful of earth.

The elementary children craned their necks to see. They'd been sitting impatiently in front until now, but this was interesting. Digging in dirt, like writing in cement—this they could understand.

The ground was officially broken. Chadwick and Olsen applauded along with everyone else.

The crowd dispersed, adults and older kids to assault the food tables, children to scramble over their beloved jungle gym that would soon be demolished. Ann worked the crowd—inserting herself into groups of gossipy parents, seeking out the ones who were trying to avoid her and engaging them in conversation.

Norma Reyes stood by the broken ground at the far end of the basketball court, her hand resting on the shovel handle. Chadwick met her eyes, briefly, and his heart twisted. He knew she was thinking about another plot of ground, another ritual when she'd turned a spadeful of earth.

"You excuse me?" he asked Olsen.

"I'll grab a brownie," she said. "Just remember—you know, our pickup . . ."

There it was again—the tiny hesitation after her last word, as if she were about to say something else. He'd heard that in her voice all week, and had begun to wonder if it was the residual trauma of their morning in the cornfield. Perhaps, after almost dying, she was reluctant to put a period on the end of any statement.

Chadwick waited, but she said nothing else, just squeezed his forearm and headed for the dessert table.

He crossed the basketball court to where Norma stood.

She studied his face, his beige overcoat, his sand-colored clothes. Her eyes lingered on the boot cast.

"How much longer?" she asked.

"Six weeks. Old bones knit slowly."

"It hurt?"

"I've had worse. You should see the bruises from my ex-wife."

"The least that could've happened," Norma said, "is they break your jaw and wire your mouth shut. But no."

"You thought about my offer?"

She looked down at the chunks of shattered asphalt, the tree roots and dirt clods and stones—a small, carefully planned upheaval, a single-serving earthquake.

"Yeah." She propped the shovel handle against the fence. "Yeah, I thought about it. I finally learn how to hate you, and you pull something like that."

"I'm selling, regardless. If you'd rather, you can buy me out, keep the house . . ."

Her eyes burned with a small dark horror—the afterimage, Chadwick supposed, of the moment she'd opened the cupboard in the Mission house, let loose a spill of plastic and black hair and pale flesh that had resolved itself into the face of a friend. She said, "John used to say you only find one home in your lifetime—one true home."

"John also said never trust a Realtor."

"Send me the papers. I'll arrange the sale."

"And the college scholarship fund?"

"I'll be the trustee," she agreed. "Race will be the first recipient. The other Laurel Heights parents won't like that much, with me applying to be his legal guardian."

Chadwick heard the nervousness in her voice. He knew Norma faced an uphill battle in the courts, even if she could provide Race a home that was better than his grandmother's, much better than a foster home. She might lose her bid for custody, but she was trying. She had put herself on the line, opened herself up for hurt, because she wanted to help the boy. That in itself was a victory.

"The other parents," Chadwick told her, "can kiss my boot cast."

Norma wiped at the corners of her eyes. "Shit. I'm going to hope John was wrong about only getting one home, okay? I'm going to hope that for both of us."

She stood on her tiptoes, kissed him roughly on the cheek, then pushed him away. "Now get the hell out of here, will you? *Hijo,* you're worse than a broken mirror for luck."

He knew it would be the last time he'd ever see her, and she left his life just as she'd arrived—dismissing him, heading off to the party with the same determination as when she'd grabbed his wrist in a Los Angeles beer joint, twenty-eight years before, and dragged him out on the dance floor.

He stood alone at the lip of the broken asphalt, feeling warmer than he should have in the January chill. He didn't notice Ann until she walked back to the speaker's podium and turned off the microphone.

"Closure?" she asked him.

"As much as I can hope for."

She slipped a tape into the cassette player of the PA system, turned up the volume. The ethereal guitar work of Pat Metheny—as desolate and expansive as the Texas plains—drifted across the courtyard. Jazz drums set children bouncing on the play structure's clatter bridge.

"She'll do it, you know," Ann told him. "Norma will get custody of Race. They'll take care of each other. He'll graduate at the top of his class."

Chadwick listened for jealousy, or resentment. Ann would've been entitled. She'd been shunned by her own daughter, forced to officially expel her from Laurel Heights, thanks to the incident with the gun. Now she would pay the bulk of her salary for months, possibly for the rest of Mallory's high school career, to get Mallory through a program where Ann had no part, where her daughter would become someone she did not know, while Race Montrose finished his high school career in the program Ann had built.

But there was no bitterness in her voice. Nothing except that new sense of authority—clean and hard and hollow like the bore of a cannon.

"Mallory will make it, too," Chadwick said. "Maybe not the way you envisioned, but she'll make it."

Ann was conscious of her audience—the whole school community on the yard, the gossipers watching. Still, her eyes betrayed a touch of strain, of need.

"You belong in the classroom," she told him. "There's no reason for you to stay away from San Francisco now. You could teach here again. This is your home."

He watched children playing in the yard, three young girls turning the tire swing so fast they were a blur of ponytails and skirts. He tried to imagine these girls older, in trouble, on drugs, being picked up in the middle of the night by a stone-faced escort—someone like him. He couldn't imagine it. That was the problem—you never could, until it happened.

"This used to be my home," he said. "Not anymore."

"And me?"

The Pat Metheny song kept playing.

Chadwick said, "You're the most important person in the world to me."

"But you're leaving."

"Yes."

"Because I didn't trust you—the morning you went after Mallory?"

"No. Because you wanted to trust me. Because I want to trust you, too. I've looked up to you for most of my life. No relationship could hold up under that much pressure."

"I love you," she said.

He didn't meet her eyes. He didn't want to admit how close he was to caving in, his willpower whittled so thin it bent like a willow branch. It wasn't fair to choose between Laurel Heights and Cold Springs—between what he wanted, and what was good for him.

"I remember a seventeen-year-old girl," he said, "who would've scolded you for saying that."

"The girl grew up. But not in the way I envisioned."

Chadwick thought he heard relief in her voice. There was nothing else for her now, nothing between her and her school. Chadwick had snipped the last possible tether.

He held out his hand, and Ann grasped it. He could've been a visiting parent, or a reporter, or anyone who had come to the school for official business, and was now on his way out.

Mark Jasper came up, wanting to introduce Ann to someone, and Chadwick moved back toward the building, taking his time on his wounded leg. He climbed halfway up the stairs, where Olsen sat eating a sugar cookie.

"Well?" she asked.

"Two women—neither one slapped me."

"A record."

Over on the deck, the upperclassmen were clowning around, slipping pieces of ice down each other's shirts. Race Montrose stood to one side—not getting teased, not participating, just standing there in his church clothes, staring into his lemonade.

"You said hello to him?" Olsen asked.

"Not yet."

"You need to."

He met her eyes, and the truth clicked, like the gears in one of his father's clocks. He knew he hadn't been imagining her hesitation all week. He knew what she'd been struggling to say, and it was the same thing he'd been struggling to say for years. She was giving him a chance to go first.

"I lied to you," he said. His voice seemed to be coming out of someone else's mouth.

Olsen brushed a crumb from the edge of her mouth. "I know."

"When?"

"A few days ago. Bits and pieces have been falling into place for a month—talking to you, talking to Mallory, seeing you from two different angles."

"If you knew, why did you agree to be my partner again?"

She turned her face toward the upper windows of the school, where the long winter sun was streaking the glass the color of coins.

"You remind me of my stepdad," she said. "I think I'm supposed to make it work with you. I'm supposed to be your partner, because to do that, I have to drop some serious emotional ballast. I have to be honest with myself about my past, forgive myself. Maybe it's time you did the same."

The tire swing spun—right where John Zedman had stood wearing his kindergarten quilt, laughing and drinking champagne like there was every reason to celebrate, like guilt was not a predator that could follow a scent.

"You want the truth to come out," Olsen said. "You tried to tell me, through that story about Thailand. There was no boy in Thailand. Hunter and you never killed anyone on guard duty. You wouldn't have let yourself get set up and framed, you wouldn't have pursued the blackmailer in the first place, if you didn't know in your heart you wanted to be discovered."

For years, Chadwick had known the hook was embedded in his mouth—waiting for him to betray the slightest tremor, the least resistance on the line. But now that the truth was tugging at him, he was surprised to feel no fear. He was being reeled out of the pressure of the river bottom, back toward the surface, out of the darkness.

"Katherine thought she loved Samuel Montrose," he said. "He was mean-spirited—evil. He used my daughter, got her hooked on heroin. He was taking her apart, just for the fun of doing it."

"And you found this out *before* she died, not after."

Chadwick closed his eyes. He remembered the car ride

from Oakland, Katherine telling him so much to hurt him, so much he didn't want to hear.

"A week before," he replied. "I didn't know what to do. I could feel her just slipping away."

"You didn't do nothing, like your wife thought. You talked to John Zedman."

"John said we could take care of it. John's style was to confront people, make them back off. He and I went to Oakland. We tracked down Samuel, found him in the building where he dealt drugs, the same place his grandmother still lives. He was more than we'd bargained for. We argued with him. I just wanted him to leave Katherine alone. I wanted him out of her life. He pulled a gun."

"And so did you."

"I did, but I didn't have time to use it. John . . . he took out a .22. I didn't even know he'd brought it. He shot Samuel in the gut. Samuel kept coming. But he didn't fire. John fired twice more, hit the kid in the chest. I remember Samuel turning from the force, turning toward me, like he wanted me to see what had happened to him. And after he fell, I watched while John pointed the gun at Samuel's head. Only afterward, we realized the gun Samuel pulled wasn't even loaded. He'd been bluffing."

Chadwick couldn't read Olsen's face. Like a good counselor, she kept her expression nonjudgmental, calm in the face of atrocity. "You covered for Zedman. You became an accomplice to murder."

"John was terrified. He panicked when I suggested calling the police. He kept talking about his reputation, his family. He kept reminding me that he'd done it for me. We both knew the police would never buy self-defense. It would look like we'd hunted Samuel down and executed him. So we wrapped the body—we got it into the car. We dumped it in the Bay."

"But Katherine knew."

"She suspected. I couldn't hide the guilt in my face. I didn't admit to anything. Katherine didn't exactly confront me, but . . . she knew. I went to Texas to try to decide what to do. I was planning on telling Norma when I got back, taking prison time if I had to. I half expected Katherine to call the police herself. But when I got home, before I could send her to Cold Springs, she killed herself. Nine years, people have been telling me her death wasn't my fault. But it was."

The fog drifted through the eucalyptus branches across the street. Beyond the green expanse of the Presidio, the orange spires of the Golden Gate Bridge marched off toward Marin.

Olsen broke off another piece of her sugar cookie, took a bite. "That night Katherine visited the Montrose house, to tell Kindra her suspicions. Katherine wouldn't have OD'ed if Kindra hadn't supplied her pure heroin."

"It's still my fault."

"Kindra didn't trust her chances at justice against Zedman and you. She opted for her own kind of revenge. She became Samuel—she began torturing John Zedman. And you."

"Call Sergeant Damarodas. Or the press. Your decision."

Olsen sighed. "No. Not mine."

She pointed toward the little yard. Race Montrose was climbing over the ribbon, slipping into the shadows while his peers kept up their joking and jostling, cutting glances at Race only now that he had given up trying to be among them.

In a trance, Chadwick followed him.

The yard was canopied by a huge oak tree, wedged between a high wooden fence and the building, so it was always the darkest, coolest spot at school. The air smelled of wet sand and mulch and mud from class projects and butterfly gardens. Along the wall of the second-grade classroom, where a gravel path used to be, the newly poured sidewalk glistened gray as catfish skin, its wet surface already scarred with a hundred tiny handprints and childish signatures.

Race Montrose had hauled himself up on a sand table and was sitting cross-legged, bending a frayed pink plastic shovel in his hands.

Chadwick waited for the boy to see him.

Race looked up. His features were so much like his brother's, and his sister's—the angular jaw, the street toughness in his mouth, the fire in his eyes that said *Back off*. But there was something else, too—a look of expectation, of belief, like a child staring out the window on a cold night in a hot state, waiting for that seven-year snow—not caring that it might not happen, that it had never snowed in his lifetime. Still having faith it would tonight. Samuel and Kindra never had that look. Chadwick wanted to believe it was a capacity Race had inherited, alone among all his siblings, from his mother.

He imagined the determination it must've taken her, marching into Ann's office: *I want an application for my boy.*

"You were there that night," Chadwick told Race, "nine years ago, when we shot your brother. You hid; you watched as we rolled his body in a sheet and carried him out. You've lived with that ever since."

Race's eyes teared up—the eyes of a six-year-old child. "What are you going to do about it?"

"Apologize. But that seems pretty damn insufficient."

Race bent the pink shovel. The handle was broken, so it looked like the link in a chain. "That day on the fire escape? I almost shot you."

"Why didn't you?"

"Samuel used to hit me." Race said it softly. "He used to make me carry his drugs for him, figuring nobody would arrest a little kid. Kindra was always telling me he was this great guy. He protected us. But he didn't. He scared me worse than anybody. That night you and Mallory's dad showed up . . . you were talking about how Samuel was destroying her, playing with her mind, making her think he loved her. But I didn't know who you meant. I was too young to get that it was your daughter. I thought you were talking about Kindra. You could've been."

The breeze shook a leaf off the oak tree. It fluttered down to the new sidewalk, stuck in the wet cement like a tiny boat.

"Is that why you never told anybody?" Chadwick asked.

"I did tell someone. I told Kindra. You saw what happened."

"I'm sorry. That isn't enough, but I'm sorry. I was trying to protect my daughter. I never meant to kill anyone."

Race studied him fearfully, though fearful of what, Chadwick wasn't sure.

"What was it like," the boy asked him, "knowing you killed somebody and got away with it?"

No one had ever asked Chadwick that. He had never talked to anyone about the murder—not even John. The question drew something out of him like a lightning rod, siphoning off emotions he didn't even know he'd been accumulating.

"I should lie to you," Chadwick decided. "I should tell you I couldn't live with it. Or I should say the only reason it didn't bother me was that John Zedman pulled the trigger. The truth is, all I cared about was Katherine. Then and now. If I could have her alive again, I would change history, stop her from taking those drugs. But Samuel's death? I stood by while Samuel was murdered. I helped conceal a crime. And God help me, if Katherine hadn't died, I think I could've learned to live with it."

Race set down the plastic shovel. He traced a figure in the sand with his finger—a picture or a word, it was hard to tell which. "What Kindra would say? You deserve to die. She would say if I didn't have the guts to kill you, I should at least tell on you."

"Kindra could be persuasive."

Race shook his head. "Who would it help—me? Ms. Reyes? Kindra turned into Samuel. She *was* Samuel. It scares me that I might wake up someday and hear voices, forget who I am. I'm not going to let it happen. I'm not going to do what she would've done."

"So what will you do?"

Race glared at him, as if he'd just thrown down a gauntlet. "I'm going to finish Laurel Heights. I'm going to college. What's the best degree you got?"

"A bachelor's in history."

"Then I'm going to get better than that. A Ph.D. And you're going to pay the cost."

Despite himself, Chadwick felt a smile tugging at his lips. "All right, Dr. Montrose."

"Now get the hell away from me," the boy said. "This is

my school. Those clowns out in the yard don't know it yet, but they're going to find out."

Chadwick was gratified to realize it sounded very much like something Norma Reyes would've said.

He left Race Montrose on his sand table, small oak leaves fluttering down around him, some of them sticking in the sidewalk, making a permanent impression.

Race sat alone in the little yard, thinking about the day he and Mallory had first become friends in the second grade, right here at this sand table.

He hoped she knew what she'd done for him, how much he envied her courage. He hoped she'd find what she needed in Texas.

He got up, brushed the sand off his dress slacks. He took the key chain out of his pocket—a silver Mickey Mouse, a house key, a key to a Toyota SUV. There was a spot on the corner of the sidewalk, where the two boards met, that was as cold as a refrigerator, the cement unmarked, still almost liquid. Race knelt down and pushed the keys into the goop, then smeared the surface smooth. He pressed his hand over the spot, hoping his print would harden there—remain for years, for all time. He wrote his name with a stick—RACE MONTROSE, CLASS OF 2006.

Then he got up. He didn't care what the kids said about his jacket and tie, or the cement on his hand, or anything else. He had things to do. He had a future ahead of him. And God help him—he was going to learn to live with it.

"Well?" Olsen asked.

"I'm done."

She stared at him, as if weighing the truth of the statement. Then she took one last look at Laurel Heights—the old building with its ivy-covered chimney, potato prints hanging in the windows.

"It's a good place," she decided. "But for most kids? This isn't reality. Come on—let's make our pickup."

She took the stairs quickly, and when she looked back up at him, a small challenge in her eyes, he realized that she had already forgiven him his sins. The young always forgave quickly, always came back eventually, because what other choice was there?—even for the most wayward child, even for the most flawed parent.

"You've got two bullet holes in you," he reminded her. "Don't you dare run faster than me."

In front of the school, azaleas were exploding in full spring color. Premature, but then again—this was San Francisco, his old hometown. There was no seasonal compass. Maybe the flowers had been blooming all winter.

Maybe Chadwick had only noticed when it was time to notice.

ABOUT THE AUTHOR

RICK RIORDAN is the author of four previous novels featuring private investigator Tres Navarre. His work has won the Anthony, Shamus, and Edgar Awards. A middle school teacher by day, he lives with his wife and two sons in San Antonio, where he is at work on his next Tres Navarre thriller.

SOUTH TOWN

A NOVEL OF SUSPENSE

RICK RIORDAN

If you enjoyed
Rick Riordan's *COLD SPRINGS,*
you won't want to miss any of his
electrifying, award-winning mysteries!
Look for them at your favorite bookseller.

And read on for a tantalizing early look
at Rick's next Tres Navarre mystery,
SOUTHTOWN, coming soon in hardcover
from Bantam Books.

SOUTHTOWN

by

Rick Riordan

SOUTHTOWN
by
Rick Riordan

On sale in hardcover May 2004

Fourth of July morning, Will Stirman woke up with blood on his hands.

He'd been dreaming about the men who killed his wife. He'd been strangling them, one with each hand. His fingernails had cut half-moons into his palms.

Sunlight filtered through the barred window, refracted by lead glass and chicken wire. In the berth above, his cell mate, Zeke, was humming "Amazing Grace."

"Up yet, boss?" Zeke called, excitement in his voice.

Today was the day.

A few more hours. Then one way or the other, Will would never have to have that dream again.

He wiped his palms on the sheets. He shifted over to his workspace—a metal desk with a toadstool seat welded to the floor. Stuck on the walls with Juicy Fruit gum were eight years' worth of Will's sketches, fluttering in the breeze of a little green plastic fan. Adam and Eve. Abraham and Isaac. Moses and Pharaoh.

He opened his Bible and took out what he'd done last night—a map instead of a Bible scene.

Behind him, Zeke slipped down from the bunk. He started doing waist twists, his elbows cutting the air above Will's head. "Freedom sound good, boss?"

"Watch what you say, Zeke."

"Hell, just Independence Day." Zeke grinned. "I didn't mean nothing."

Zeke had a gap-toothed smile, vacant green eyes, a wide

forehead dotted with acne. He was in Floresville State for raping elderly ladies in a nursing home, which didn't make him the worst sort Will had met. Been abused as a kid, is all. Had some funny ideas about love. Will worried how the boy would do when he got back to the real world.

Will looked over his map of Kingsville, hoping the police would take the bait. He'd labeled most of the major streets, his old warehouse property, the two biggest banks in town, the home of the attorney who'd defended him unsuccessfully in court.

He had a bad feeling about today—a taste like dirty coins in his mouth. He'd had that feeling before, the night he lost Soledad.

Exactly at eight, the cell door buzzed open.

"Come on, boss!" Zeke hustled outside, his shirt still unbuttoned, his shoes in his hands.

Will felt the urge to hurry, too—to respond to the buzzer like a racetrack dog, burst out of his kennel on time. But he forced himself to wait. He looked up to make sure Zeke was really gone. Then he slipped Soledad's picture out from under his mattress.

It wasn't a very good sketch. He'd gotten her long dark hair right, maybe, the intensity of her eyes, the soft curve of her face that made her look so young. But it was hard to get her smile, that look of challenge she'd always given him.

Still, it was all he had.

He kissed the portrait, folded it, and tucked it into his shirt.

Something would go wrong with the plan. He could feel it. He knew if he walked out that door, somebody was going to die.

But he'd made a promise.

He put the Kingsville map in the Bible, and set it on the desk where the guards were sure to find it. Then he went to join Zeke on the walkway.

After chow time, Pablo and his cousin Luis were hanging out in the rec yard, trying to avoid Hermandad Pistoleros Latinos.

The HPL didn't like Pablo and Luis getting all religious when they could've been dealing for the homeboys.

Luis tried to joke about it, but he still had bruises across his rib cage from the last time the *carnales* had cornered him. Pablo figured if they didn't get out of Floresville soon, they'd both end up in cardboard coffins.

Out past the guard towers and the double line of razor wire fence, the hills hummed with cicadas. Lightning pulsed in the clouds.

Every morning, Pablo tried to imagine Floresville State Pen was a motel. He came out of Pod C and told himself he could check out anytime, get on the road, drive home to El Paso, where his wife would be waiting. She'd hug him tight, tell him she still loved him—she'd read his letters and forgiven the one horrible mistake that had put him in jail.

After twelve long months inside, the dream was getting hard to hold on to.

That would change today.

He and Luis stood at the fence, chatting with their favorite guard, a Latina named Gonzales, who had breasts like mortar shells, gold-rimmed glasses, and a wispy mustache that reminded Pablo of his grandmother.

"You want to see fireworks tonight, miss?" Luis grinned.

Gonzales tapped the fence with her flashlight, reminding him to keep his feet behind the line. "Why—you got plans?"

"Picnic," Luis told her. "Few beers. Patriotic stuff, miss. Come on."

Pablo should have told him to shut up, but it was harmless talk. You looked at Luis—that pudgy face, boyish smile—and you knew he had to be joking.

Back home in El Paso, Luis had always been the favorite at family barbecues. He held the *piñata* for the kids, flirted with the women, got his cheeks pinched by the *abuelitas*. He was *Tío* Luis. The fun one. The nice one. Wouldn't hurt a fly.

That's why Luis had to shoot someone whenever he robbed an appliance store. Otherwise, the clerks didn't take him seriously.

"No picnic for me," Officer Gonzales said. "Got a promotion. Won't see you *vatos* anymore."

"Aw, miss," Luis said. "Where you going?"

"Never mind. My last day, today."

"You gonna miss the fireworks," Luis coaxed. "And the beer—"

A hand came down on the scruff of Luis' neck.

Will Stirman was standing there with his cell mate, Zeke.

Stirman wasn't a big man, but he had a kind of wiry strength that made other cons nervous. One reason he'd gotten his nickname "the Ghost" was because of the way he fought— fast, slippery and vicious. He'd disappear, hit you from an angle you weren't expecting, disappear again before your fists got anywhere close. Pablo knew this firsthand.

Another reason for Stirman's nickname was his skin. No matter how much time Stirman spent in the sun, he stayed pale as a corpse. His shaved hair made a faint black triangle on his scalp, an arrow pointing forward.

"Compadres," Stirman said. "You 'bout ready for chapel?"

Luis' shoulders stiffened under the gringo's touch. "Yeah, Brother Stirman."

Stirman met Pablo's eyes. Pablo felt the air crackle.

They were the two alpha wolves in the gospel ministry. They could never meet without one of them backing down, and Pablo was getting tired of being the loser. He hated that he and Luis had put their trust in this man—this gringo of all gringos.

He felt the weight of the shank—a sharpened cafeteria spoon—taped to his thigh, and he thought how he might change today's plans. *His* plans, until Stirman had joined the ministry and taken over.

He calmed himself with thoughts of seeing his wife again. He looked away, let Stirman think he was still the one in charge.

Stirman tipped an imaginary hat to the guard. "Ma'am."

He walked off toward the basketball court, Zeke in tow.

"What's *he* in for?" Gonzales asked. She tried to sound cool, but Pablo knew Stirman unnerved her.

Pablo's face burned. He didn't like that women were allowed to be guards, and they weren't even told what the inmates were doing time for. Gonzales could be five feet away from a guy like Stirman and not know what he was, how thin a fence separated her from a monster.

"Good luck with your new assignment, miss," Pablo said.

He hoped Gonzales was moving to some office job where she would never again see people like himself or Will Stirman.

He hooked Luis' arm and headed toward the chapel, the rough edge of the shank chafing against his thigh.

"Like to get a piece of that," Zeke said.

It took Will a few steps to realize Zeke was talking about the Latina guard back at the fence. "You supposed to be saved, son."

Zeke gave him an easy grin. "Hell, I don't mean nothing."

Will gritted his teeth.

Boy doesn't know any better, he reminded himself.

More and more, Zeke's comments reminded him of the men who'd killed Soledad and put him in jail. If Will didn't get out of Floresville soon, he was afraid what he'd do with his anger.

He was relieved to see Pastor Riggs' SUV parked out front of the chapel. The black Ford Explorer had tinted windows and yellow stenciling on the side: *Texas Prison Ministry—Redemption Through Christ.*

The guards only let Riggs park inside the gates when he was hauling stuff—like prison garden produce to the local orphanage, or delivering books to the prison library. The fact the SUV was here today meant Riggs had brought the extra sheet glass Will had asked for.

Maybe things would work out after all.

Inside the old Quonset hut, Elroy and C.C. were hunched over the worktable, arguing about glass color as they cut out pieces of Jesus Christ.

Will let his shadow fall over their handiwork. "Gonna be ready on time?"

Elroy scowled up at him, his glass cutter pressed against an opaque lemony sheet. "You make me mess up this halo."

"Should be white," C.C. complained. "Halo ain't no fucking yellow."

"It's yellow," Elroy insisted.

"Make Jesus look like he's got a piss ring around him," C.C. said. "Fucking toilet seat."

They both looked at Will, because the picture was Will's design, based on one of his sketches.

"C.C.'s right," he said. "Can't have the Savior looking less than pure. Might disappoint those kids today."

Elroy studied him.

He could've snapped Will in half if he wanted to.

He was a former wildcatter with arms like bridge cables, serving forty years for second degree murder. His foreman had called him a nigger one too many times and Elroy had punched the guy's nose through his brain. The left side of Elroy's face was still webbed with scars from the white policemen in Lubbock who'd convinced him to give a full confession.

"You done shown me the light, Brother Stirman," Elroy said, real sober-like. "Can't disappoint those children."

C.C. tapped the stained glass until it split in a perfect curve along the crack. "You both full of shit. You know that?"

Elroy and Zeke laughed.

C.C. was a nappy-haired little runt with skin like terracotta. He could talk trash and get away with it partly because Elroy backed him up, partly because he was so scrawny and ugly his bad-ass routine came off as funny. He also worked in the maintenance shop, which made him indispensable to Will. At least for today.

At ten o'clock, the buzzer sounded, signaling all trustees to their jobs, the rest of the inmates back to their cells. Pablo and Luis arrived a minute late, completing the flock.

Pastor Riggs came out of his vestry. They all joined hands for prayer.

Afterward, the Reverend went back into the vestry to write his sermon. The trustees settled back to their work, getting ready for the juvies' visit at one o'clock.

Will wrote notes for his testimonial. Luis and Pablo got out their guitars and practiced gospel songs in that god-awful Freddy Fender style they had going. Elroy, C.C. and Zeke worked on the stained glass.

The panel would show Jesus in chains before Pontius

Pilate. It was supposed to be finished by the time the juvenile hall kids got there from San Antonio, so they could hang it behind the preacher's podium, but the trustees knew it wouldn't be ready. Pastor Riggs had agreed they could work through lunch anyway. He'd seemed pleased by their enthusiasm.

Two civilian supervisors showed up late and plopped folding chairs by the door. One was a retired leatherneck named Grier. The other Will had never seen—a rookie, some laid-off farmhand from Floresville probably, picking up a few extra dollars.

Grier was a mean son-of-a-bitch. Last week, he'd talked trash to Luis the whole time, describing different ways HPL was planning to kill him. He said the guards had a betting pool going.

Today, Grier decided to pick a new target.

"So, C.C.," Grier called lazily, palming the sweat off his forehead. "How'd you get two Cadillac jobs, anyway? Gospel *and* Maintenance? What'd you do, lube up your nappy ass for the warden?"

C.C. said nothing. Will kept his attention on his testimonial notes and hoped C.C. could keep his cool.

Grier grinned at the younger supervisor.

Reverend Riggs was still in his vestry. The door was open, but Grier wasn't talking loud enough for Riggs to overhear.

"Good Christian boy now, huh?" Grier asked C.C. "Turn the other cheek. Bet you've had a lot of practice turning your cheeks for the boys."

He went on like that for a while, but C.C. kept it together.

Around eleven, the smell of barbecue started wafting in—brisket, ribs, chicken. Fourth of July picnic for the staff. The supervisors started squirming.

About fifteen minutes to noon, Supervisor Grier growled, "Hey, y'all finish up."

"We talked to the Reverend about working through lunch," Will said, nice and easy. No confrontation. "We got these kids coming this afternoon."

Grier scowled. Continents of sweat were soaking through his shirt.

He lumbered over to the pastor's doorway. "Um, Reverend?"

Riggs looked up, waved his hand in a benediction. "Y'all go on, Mr. Grier. I don't need to leave for half an hour. Get you some brisket and come back. I'll keep an eye on the boys."

"You sure?" But Grier didn't need convincing.

Soon both supervisors were gone, leaving six trustees and the pastor.

Will locked eyes with Pablo and Luis. The Mexicans reached in their guitar cases, took out the extra sets of strings the pastor had bought them. At the worktable, Elroy pulled a sweat-soaked bandana off his neck. C.C. handed him a half-moon of white glass, a feather for an angel's wing. Elroy wrapped the bandana around one end of it. Zeke unplugged his soldering iron.

Will got up, went to the Reverend's door.

For a moment, he admired Pastor Riggs sitting there, pouring his soul into his sermon.

The Reverend was powerfully built for a man in his sixties. His hands were callused and scarred from his early years working in a textile factory. He had sky-blue eyes and hair like carded cotton. He was the only hundred percent good man Will Stirman had ever known.

This was supposed to be a showcase day for Riggs. His prison ministry would turn a dozen juvenile delinquents away from crime and toward Christ. The press would run a favorable story. Riggs would attract some big private donors. He'd shared these dreams with Will, because Will was his proudest achievement—living proof that God's mercy was infinite.

Will summoned up his most honest smile. "Pastor, you come look at the stained glass now? I think we're almost done."

The old preacher went down harder than Pablo had hoped.

Riggs should have understood the point of the glass knife against his jugular. He should've let himself be tied up quietly.

But Riggs acted outraged. He said he couldn't believe everything he'd worked for was a lie—that all of them, for months, had been using him. He tried to reason with them, shame them, and in the end, he fought like a cornered *chupacabra*. Elroy, Pablo and Stirman had to wrestle him down.

Zeke got too excited. He smashed the old man's head with the soldering iron until C.C. grabbed his wrists and snarled, "Damn, man! That's his skull showing!"

Pablo took a nasty bite on his finger trying to cover the preacher's mouth. Elroy had blood splattered on his pants. They were all sure Riggs' yelling and screaming had ruined the plan. Any second the guards would come running.

But they got Riggs tied up with guitar string and taped his mouth and shoved him, moaning and half-conscious, into the corner of the vestry. Still nobody came.

Elroy stood behind the worktable so anybody coming in wouldn't see the bloodstains on his pants. C.C. and Zeke huddled around him, staring at the stained glass as if they gave a damn about finishing it. Zeke suppressed a schoolboy giggle.

"Shut up, freak," Luis said.

"*You* shut up, spic."

Luis started to go for him, but Pablo grabbed his shirt collar.

"*Both* of you," Stirman said, "cool it."

"We got Riggs' car keys," Elroy murmured. "Don't see why—"

"No," Stirman said. "We do it right. Patience."

Pablo didn't like it, but he got a D-string ready. He curled the ends around his hands, moved to one side of the door. Luis took the other side.

Stirman sat down in his chair, in plain sight of the entrance. He crossed his legs and read through his testimonial notes. The son-of-a-bitch was cool. Pablo had to give him that.

Pablo's finger throbbed where the pastor had bit it. The copper guitar string stung his broken skin.

Finally he heard footsteps on gravel. The rookie supervisor appeared with a heaping plate of ribs.

Stirman smiled apologetically. "Pastor Riggs wants to talk to you. Prison major came by."

"Hell," said the supervisor.

He started toward the vestry and Pablo garroted him, barbecue and baked beans flying everywhere. The supervisor's fingers raked at the elusive string around his neck as Pablo dragged him into the corner.

The rookie had just gone limp when Grier came in.

Luis tried to get him around the neck, but the old marine was too wily. He sidestepped, saw Zeke's soldering iron coming in time to catch the blow on his arm, managed one good yell before Elroy came over the table on top of him, crumpling him to the floor, Grier's head connecting hard with the cement.

Elroy got up. He was holding a broken piece of white glass and a mess of red tags. The rest of the glass was impaled just below Grier's sternum.

Grier's eyes rolled back in his head. His fingers clutched his gut.

C.C. slapped Elroy's arm. "What the hell you do that for?"

"Just happened."

They stood there, frozen, as Grier's muscles relaxed. His mouth opened and stayed that way.

Five minutes later, they had his body and the garroted rookie stripped to their underwear. The rookie was only unconscious, so they tied him up, taped his mouth, crammed him and Grier's corpse into the tiny vestry with the comatose Reverend.

Elroy and Luis got into the supervisors' clothes. Grier's had blood on them, but not that much. Most of Grier's bleeding must've been inside him. Elroy figured he could cover the stains with a clipboard. Luis' clothes had barbecue sauce splattered down the front. Neither uniform fit exactly right, but Pablo thought they might pass. They didn't have to fool anybody very long.

Elroy and Luis put the supervisors' IDs around their necks. They tucked the laminated photos in their shirt pockets like they didn't want them banging against their chests.

C.C., still in prison whites, made a call from Pastor Riggs' desk phone, pretending he was the maintenance department foreman. He told the back gate to expect a crew in five minutes to fix their surveillance camera.

He hung up, smiled at Stirman. "They can't wait to see us. Damn camera's been broke for a month. We'll call you from the sally port."

"Don't screw up," Stirman told him.

"Who, me?"

With one last look, Pablo tried to warn Luis to be careful.

He couldn't shake the image of his cousin getting shot at the gate, his disguise seen through in a second, but Luis just grinned at him. No better than the stupid gringo Zeke—he was having a grand time. Luis threw Pablo the keys to the Reverend's SUV.

Once they were gone, Stirman picked up the phone.

"What you doing?" Pablo asked.

Stirman placed an outside call—Pablo could tell from the string of numbers. He got an answer. He said, "Go."

Then he hung up.

"What?" Pablo demanded.

Stirman looked at him with those unsettling eyes—close-set, dark as oil, with a softness that might've been mistaken for sorrow or even sympathy, except for the hunger behind them. They were the eyes of a slave ship navigator, or a doctor in a Nazi death camp.

"Safe passage," Stirman told him. "Don't worry about it."

Pablo imagined some Mexican mother hearing those words as the boxcar door closed on her and her family, locking them in the hot unventilated darkness, with a promise that they'd all see *los etados unidos* in the morning.

Pablo needed to kill Stirman.

He should take out his shank and do it. But he couldn't with Zeke there—stupid loyal Zeke with his stupid soldering iron.

Thunder broke, rolling across the tin roof of the chapel.

"Big storm coming," Stirman said. "That's good for us."

"It won't rain," Pablo said in Spanish. He felt like being stubborn, forcing Stirman to use *his* language. "That's dry thunder."

Stirman gave him an indulgent look. "Hundred-year flood, son. Wait and see."

Pablo wanted to argue, but his voice wouldn't work.

Stirman took the car keys out of his hand and went in the other room, jingling the brass cross on the Reverend's chain.

Pablo stared at the phone.

Luis, Elroy and C.C. should've reached the back gate by now. They should've called.

Or else they'd failed, and the guards were coming.

In the corner, wedged between the unconscious supervisor and Grier's body, Pastor Riggs stared at him—dazed blue eyes, his head wound glistening like a volcanic crater in his gray hair.

Out in the chapel, Zeke was pacing with his soldering iron. He'd done an imperfect job wiping up Grier's blood, so his footprints made faint red prints back and forth across the cement.

Stirman pretended to work on the stained glass. He had his back to the vestry as if Pablo posed no threat at all.

Pablo could walk out there, drive the shank into Stirman's back before he knew what was happening.

He was considering the possibility when Zeke stopped, looking at something outside. Maybe the lightning.

Whatever it was, his attention was diverted. The timing wouldn't get any better.

Pablo gripped the shank.

He'd gone three steps toward Stirman when the guard came in.

It was Officer Gonzales.

She scanned the room, marking the trustees' positions like land mines. Stirman and Zeke stood perfectly still.

Gonzales' hand strayed toward her belt, but of course she wasn't armed. Guards never were, inside the fence.

"Where are your supervisors?" she asked.

She must've been scared, but she kept an edge of anger in her voice—trying to control the situation, trying to avoid any hint she was vulnerable.

Stirman pointed to the vestry. "Right in there, ma'am."

Gonzales frowned. She took a step toward the vestry. Then her eyes locked on something—Pablo's hand. He had completely forgotten the shank.

She stepped back, too late.

Zeke crushed her windpipe with the soldering iron as she tried to scream. He grabbed the front of her shirt, pulled her down, Gonzales gagging, digging in her heels, clawing at Zeke's wrists.

Stirman got hold of her ankles. They dragged her into the

corner, where they taped her mouth, bound her hands. Zeke slapped her in the head when she tried to struggle.

Pablo just watched.

He was a statue. He couldn't do a damn thing.

Stirman rose, breathing heavy.

"Bind her feet," he told Zeke.

"In a minute," Zeke murmured.

He tugged at Gonzales' belt. He started pulling off her pants.

"Zeke," Stirman said.

"What?"

"What are you doing?"

"Fucking her."

Gonzales groaned—dazed but still conscious.

Zeke got her pants around her thighs. Her panties were blue.

The phone in the vestry rang.

"Zeke." Stirman's voice tightened.

Officer Gonzales tried to fight, huffing against the tape on her mouth.

Pablo wanted to help her. He imagined himself driving the shank into Stirman's back, coming up behind Zeke, taking him, too.

He imagined the back gates opening, himself at the wheel of the Reverend's SUV, the plains of South Texas unfolding before him, Zeke's and Will Stirman's crumpled bodies far behind in his wake. He just wanted to get back to his wife.

The vestry phone rang again.

"Zeke," Stirman said. "Get off her."

"Only take a minute." He was untying the drawstring of his prison pants. His hands, arms and neck were pale sweaty animal muscle.

Pablo took a step forward.

Stirman's kidneys, he told himself. *Then Zeke's carotid artery.*

Stirman turned. He saw the shank, locked eyes with Pablo.

"Give me that," Stirman ordered.

Pablo looked for his courage. "I was just . . ."

Stirman held out his hand, lifted his eyebrows.

Pablo handed over the shank.

Stirman walked behind Zeke, who was now in his underwear, straddling Gonzales' huge bare thighs.

Stirman grabbed his cell mate by the hair, yanked his chin up, and brought down the shank in one efficient thrust.

It should have ended there, but something inside Stirman seemed to snap. He stabbed again, spitting cuss words, then again, cursing the names of people Pablo didn't know, swearing that he had tried, he had fucking tried to forget.

Afterward, Gonzales lay with her clothes half off, her gold-rimmed glasses freckled with blood. Zeke's body trembled, waiting for a climax that was never going to happen.

"Get the phone," Stirman said.

Pablo started. The vestry phone was still ringing.

He stumbled into the pastor's office, picked up the receiver.

"Damn, man." C.C.'s voice. "Where you been?"

C.C. said the way was clear. They'd taken down two more guards—one at the gate, one in the watchtower. The keys to the armory had yielded five 9mm handguns, a 12-gauge shotgun, and several hundred rounds of ammunition. Elroy and Luis were manning the sally port, waiting for the SUV.

Pablo put down the receiver. His hands were cold and sweaty. Some of Zeke's blood had speckled his sleeves. He took one last look at the bound supervisor, Pastor Riggs, Grier's body slumped at their feet.

No other choice, he told himself.

He went into the chapel.

Stirman was kneeling next to Officer Gonzales, dabbing the blood from her glasses with a rag. Zeke's dead arm was draped across her waist. Gonzales was shivering as Stirman told her it was okay. Nobody was going to hurt her.

Stirman rose when he saw Pablo. He pointed the shank at Pablo's chin, let it glitter there like Christmas ornament glass. "I *own* you, amigo. You are my new right-hand man. You understand? You are mine."

No, Pablo thought.

As soon as they got through those gates, Pablo and Luis would take off by themselves. They would head west to El Paso, as far from Will Stirman as they could get.

But Stirman's eyes held him. Pablo had blown his chance. He'd frozen. Stirman had acted. Stirman had saved Gonzales. Pablo had done nothing.

Pablo clawed at the fact, looking for leverage. He said, "Who are Barrow and Barrera?"

Stirman's jaw tightened. "What?"

"You were saying those names when you . . ." Pablo gestured to Zeke's corpse.

Stirman looked down at the body, then the terrified face of Officer Gonzales. "Couple of private investigators, amigo, ought to be worried today. Now get the SUV."

Eleven minutes later, right on schedule, Pastor Riggs' black Ford Explorer rolled out the back gate of the Floresville State Penitentiary, straight into a summer storm that was starting to pour down rain.